CAROLYNE AARSEN

Love Is Patient

A Heart's Refuge

Steeple
Hill®

Published by Steeple Hill Books™

STEEPLE HILL BOOKS

Steeple
Hill®

Recycling programs
for this product may
not exist in your area.

ISBN-13: 978-0-373-65136-8

LOVE IS PATIENT AND A HEART'S REFUGE

LOVE IS PATIENT
Copyright © 2004 by Carolyne Aarsen

A HEART'S REFUGE
Copyright © 2004 by Carolyne Aarsen

www.SteepleHill.com

Printed in U.S.A.

CONTENTS

Books by Carolyne Aarsen

Love Inspired

Homecoming
Ever Faithful
A Bride at Last
The Cowboy's Bride
*A Family-Style Christmas
*A Mother at Heart
*A Family at Last
A Hero for Kelsey
Twin Blessings
Toward Home
Love Is Patient
A Heart's Refuge
Brought Together by Baby
A Silence in the Heart
Any Man of Mine
Yuletide Homecoming
Finally a Family
A Family for Luke
The Matchmaking Pact
Close to Home

*Stealing Home

CAROLYNE AARSEN

and her husband, Richard, live on a small ranch in Northern Alberta, where they have raised four children and numerous foster children and are still raising cattle. Carolyne crafts her stories in her office with a large west-facing window through which she can watch the changing seasons while struggling to make her words obey.

LOVE IS PATIENT

How priceless is Your unfailing love. Both high
and low find refuge in the shadow of Your wings.
—*Psalms* 36:7

This book is for all my readers, young and old.
Thanks for taking time to let my stories into your
lives. I'd also like to thank Rik Hal for his sailing
help. Hope I got it right.
Thanks also to Laurie Hanchard for helping me
with accounting information.

Chapter One

She hadn't thought he'd be this young. Or this tall.

And if Dylan Matheson knew the real reason she was applying for the job he advertised, Lisa Sterling suspected his gray-blue eyes could become as cold as arctic ice.

Lisa followed Dylan into his office. Another man stood as they entered. He looked older than Dylan and a little thicker around the middle.

"Lisa, this is Perry Hatcher. Perry, Lisa. He'll be sitting in on the interview, as well." Dylan performed the introduction as he strode around his large desk to his leather chair.

Lisa shook Perry's hand, feeling more comfortable with him than she had with her potential boss.

"Sit down, please," Dylan said, indicating the chair in front of the desk. The floor-to-ceiling windows behind him put him in shadow, giving her a tactical disadvantage.

He sat and hitched his chair forward in one smooth motion. Controlled and in charge. "So, Lisa Sterling.

Tell me why you want to work for Matheson Telecom," Dylan said.

Lisa had memorized her spiel and practiced it in front of the mirror. It was positive. Confident.

But laying her reasons out in front of this very self-possessed man on his territory was a different proposition. She had expected an older man, not someone with thick brown hair that waved over his forehead, softening the harsh planes of his face.

Help me out here, Lord. I absolutely have to get this job. I promise…I'll go to church if I get it.

The prayer was automatic, and harkened back to when she and her stepbrother, Gabe, had their parents and they were a family that attended church regularly. The bargaining, however, was a new touch her stepfather would have disapproved of.

She overrode her second thoughts, took a deep breath and started.

"I know that you're a nationally known company that's expanding rapidly and that you have vision for the future direction of telecommunications." She kept her smile in place, held the cool gray-blue of his eyes and kept her hands held loosely in her lap to remind her to relax. "Your head office is in Vancouver, and was started by your father, and you started this branch office only a few years ago, but it's already growing." She glanced sidelong at Perry to include him in the conversation, but mostly to slow herself down.

Don't talk too much. Don't let Dylan Matheson guess your information comes from inside. "This company is going places. I'd like to be a part of that."

But mostly I want to find out why your company fired my stepbrother after falsely accusing him of theft.

Wisely she kept the previous thought unvoiced.

Dylan Matheson nodded, apparently satisfied with her explanation. He handed Perry a copy of her résumé, then Dylan leaned back in his chair, his thumb stroking his chin as he read.

Lisa concentrated on slowing her racing heart, willing herself to be quiet.

When Matheson Telecom had first hired him, Gabe Haskell had spoken in glowing terms about the company and how pleased he was to get an accounting job with them right out of college. Lisa never had any hint that he was unhappy with his work or that they were unhappy with him.

This job was her best opportunity to find out what had really happened.

"When would you be free to begin?" Dylan asked, his voice quiet. Even. Controlled.

Lisa stifled the swift surge of hope. "I can start next week." She would need to give notice, but Tony knew she was looking for another job and he knew why.

"This job might require some travel," Dylan continued, folding his hands on the desk. "Would you be able to accompany me on business trips? Or is there a boyfriend who might object?"

"No boyfriend."

Though she had learned valuable lessons in the wrong kind of men from her mother's life, Lisa still managed to make her own mistakes in the boyfriend department.

Single life was less complicated, and practically heartbreak-free.

"Why do you want to leave your current job?" Dylan continued, glancing at her résumé. "Legal secretary at Mercurio, Donnelly and Abrams. Quite a reputable firm."

Lisa's heart flipped over.

This would be the trickiest part of the interview. She would have preferred not to use Tony as a reference. Explaining a gap of three years in a résumé, however, was harder than edging around the real reason she wanted to quit.

"I need a challenge and a change," she said, choosing her words with care. "I feel I've gone as far up professionally as I can reasonably hope."

And my married boss keeps coming on to me.

Dylan's gaze zeroed in on hers as if questioning her reply, but she didn't look away. Tony was the one at fault, not her.

"I was wondering if I might ask a few questions myself, Mr. Matheson, Mr. Hatcher?" Lisa asked, moving the interview onto territory she could control.

Dylan leaned back, rocking lightly. For a moment Lisa thought he was going to object.

"Go ahead, Miss Sterling," Dylan replied. Perry just nodded.

Lisa glanced down at the paper she'd brought to help keep her on track. "Why did your current secretary leave?"

"She was going on maternity leave and then decided she wanted to stay home with her new baby instead of coming back to work."

That sounded reassuring. "You talked about trips. How often would you expect me to accompany you?"

"As long as I'm around, once a month to our Vancouver office. There might even be a couple of times Perry will need you to accompany him on overseas trips."

In spite of her initial hesitation at taking the job, she felt a frisson of excitement. Once a month to Vancouver? She could arrange to meet Gabe and talk to him face-to-face, rather than over the telephone. Try to talk some sense into him before his growing anger with Matheson Telecom pushed him to do something rash.

"Am I going to be working for both you and Mr. Hatcher?"

Dylan glanced at Perry as if seeking confirmation. "You would be working for me for about a month. After that, Mr. Hatcher will be taking over from me."

Lisa's mind raced, trying to fit in this new piece of information. She had figured on working for Dylan. Dylan's brother had been the one to fire Gabe—she had counted on using Dylan to find out what she needed. She couldn't accomplish that working for Perry.

Could she do that in the month Dylan was still here?

"Do you have any other questions?" Dylan asked.

"No. Just those few."

Dylan stopped swiveling. "Then, Miss Sterling, you're hired. It will become official after we've checked your references."

Lisa didn't even know how tense she'd been until she relaxed back against the chair. "Thank you very much," she said quietly, hoping her relief and her nervousness didn't show.

A month as Dylan's secretary might not be enough. But if she didn't take this job, she had no way of helping Gabe at all.

"Do you have any other questions for either myself or Perry?"

"Maybe you can give me a rough idea of what you expect from me?"

"That sounds like a good plan." Dylan smiled fully now, and Lisa was surprised at how it relaxed his features. Softened the hooded look of his eyes.

And for the span of a heartbeat she felt an unprofessional tug of attraction.

Don't even start, she warned herself, flipping open her notebook. He's your new boss. You're the secretary.

And he's the enemy.

Lisa pushed the drawer of the file cabinet shut with her fingertips, as if minimizing her contact with it. This was the second morning in a week she had come to the office early hoping to do some investigating without Dylan, Perry or the other office workers seeing her. She knew she couldn't expect to uncover anything major so soon. But she'd hoped to find more than she had. Which was nothing.

Dara, Dylan's sister-in-law, had called yesterday, wanting—no, demanding—to talk to Dylan, but he'd been away. When Lisa hung up, guilt had her heart thudding in her chest. Gabe had worked under Dara before he was fired.

Heavy footsteps in the hallway sent her scurrying to her desk. She sat at her computer—which was already on—looking busy with the file on her desk.

When Dylan came into the office she looked up with a careful smile. "Good morning, Mr. Matheson."

"Good morning, Lisa. You're here early."

Very early, she thought, stifling a yawn. To beat Dylan to the office she had to show up at least an hour and a half before the office opened. Tony was a hard worker, but not the workaholic Dylan seemed to be. "I had some work to catch up on, Mr. Matheson."

He stopped in front of her desk, angling her a quizzical grin. "Please call me Dylan."

In her mind she heard the echo of her previous boss. Please call me Tony. And she had. Bad move.

So she just nodded politely. As long as she was working for him he'd stay Mr. Matheson.

"Anything come up yesterday?"

"Your sister-in-law, Dara, called. She seemed to think I was putting her off when I told her you weren't available."

Dylan shrugged. "She can be quite insistent." He gave her another smile, one that softened the angles of his face.

Lisa couldn't help acknowledging his appeal. And that was why she'd never call him Dylan.

"I'm in all day today, though," he continued. "You won't have to put her off if she does call."

"Good enough." She glanced at the file folder on her desk, making it look more urgent than it was. Dylan waited a moment, then left.

* * *

"Your mother is on line two, Mr. Matheson."

Dylan shook his head at the official address. Since Lisa had started he'd been trying to get her to call him Dylan. Once in a while she'd slip, but for two weeks he'd been Mr. Matheson to her. Made him feel like his father.

He hit the intercom button. "Thanks, Lisa."

Then he sucked in a long, slow breath and picked up the phone.

"Hello, Mother."

"Dylan, darling. Your sister Chelsea tells me you won't be coming until Thursday evening. You'll miss the luncheon her future in-laws are having on Wednesday."

Trust his mother to dispense with the niceties and dive right in. "You mean we're not eating enough at the rehearsal party and at Chelsea and Jordan's wedding?"

Stephanie Matheson was silent a moment, as if trying to figure out what he'd said. "It's just a chance to get to know each other," she said finally, a sigh of displeasure sifting through her voice. "Just a small affair. Why can't you come?"

"I've already booked the flight, Mother." Dylan leaned back in his chair, massaging his forehead with his fingertips. The faint pressure was starting already. "I won't come any sooner."

"And you'll be staying at the house until the anniversary?"

"Of course." Not his choice, but staying in a hotel was not worth the gentle insurrection that would be staged by the combined forces of his sisters and his mother. He would have preferred a little more distance from his father. He would also have preferred to leave after the wedding. He had a ton of work to do before he left the company. He had an important meeting with his new partners the day of his return flight, but his parents' thirty-fifth anniversary was important and he knew he had to attend. Besides, it was sort of a swan song—the last time he would see his father as a partner in Matheson Telecom. When he came back, he would jump right into his new job.

So for the ten days they were going to be together, he and his father, Alex, would have to at least pretend to get along.

"That's wonderful. And of course you'll be bringing an escort to the wedding and our anniversary?"

Dread dropped on his shoulders.

When Chelsea had phoned to get his tuxedo size for the wedding she'd told him he had better bring his current girlfriend or she and his mother would find someone for him. However, since the phone call and the present moment, he and Felicia had broken up.

If he let his mother know he was coming alone now, she would be on the phone before it was cold in her hands, arranging, plotting and planning with her sisters and all the mothers of eligible daughters who were "so wonderful, Dylan."

A light knock at the door granted him a momentary respite.

"Just a moment, Mother," Dylan said, then laid his hand on the mouthpiece. "Come in."

Lisa entered, holding a sheaf of papers for him to sign. When she saw him on the phone she half turned as if to leave again, but he waved her in. "I'll just be a moment," he said quietly.

He tucked the phone under his chin and uncapped his pen.

"Amber and Erika wanted to have a welcome-home party after the wedding," his mother continued. "As if I have time. Honestly, those girls seem to think putting together a party is as easy as ordering coffee." Stephanie laughed lightly as Dylan's signature on the letters grew larger, bolder. His sisters organizing a party. Now, there was a scary proposition. Giggly girl-friends and heavy hints.

"Anyhow, they were wondering if your girlfriend was going to be coming with you. What's her name again?"

Dylan's pen dug into the page. "Felicia won't be coming." His ex-girlfriend's deceit still stung. That she had been seeing someone else had been bad enough. That it had been one of his employees made it worse.

Ex-employee, he amended.

"I told the girls you would probably come alone."

Dylan could practically feel his mother's spine stiff-ening. It wasn't enough that one sister had dutifully married young and provided his mother with grand-children, that his brother was also married and that a second sister was going to make the trip down the aisle. Stephanie wanted to see Dylan settled, as well.

Trouble was, he had never found anyone who capti-vated him enough to take the chance. His mother was always telling him he looked in the wrong places. He wondered where the right ones were.

"I wouldn't worry about coming alone, son," his mother continued, her words coming out in a rush. "The girls invited some of their friends to the wedding. We've arranged for you to take one as an escort. Do you remember Kerry? Lovely girl. Goes to church. Just a sweet little thing."

The chill in his blood got colder.

Lisa removed the top letter so he could sign the one below.

"Mother, that's not necessary."

"I know you, Dylan. You'll come alone like you always do."

The slight edge in his mother's voice told him how serious she was about this. And what was in store for him if he didn't show up with someone. Anyone.

Dylan had sat through tough negotiations with rival companies, bluffed his way through contract negotiations with suppliers, all without losing his self-control. But his mother's desire to see him wed was an immovable force against which he had bumped time after time.

His headache grew with each passing moment. Showing up without somebody, *anybody,* to create a buffer between his mother, his sisters and his sisters' friends would create a nightmare.

Lisa took the signed letters from him.

"Excuse me a moment, Mother," he said. He looked up at his secretary. "Just wait, Lisa. I need to go over a few things with you."

"Oh, my goodness," he heard his mother say over the phone. "I'm sorry, Dylan. I didn't realize you were busy."

Dylan smiled at Lisa in apology for taking up her time. And gave her a second look. Her curly blond hair was tamed today, pulled back from her face in an intricate arrangement of pins. Funky without looking too offbeat. Her soft brown eyes were framed by thick lashes. Her high cheekbones were softened by the dimples lurking at the corners of her mouth. She smiled back, releasing the dimples.

And he felt a faint stirring of attraction.

Was he crazy? Hadn't he learned his lesson from Felicia?

"Well, then, we'll be seeing you Thursday evening?" his mother was asking.

Dylan pulled himself back to the reality of his mother and the conversation they were having.

"Of course," he said, leaning back in his chair.

"And your father really needs to talk to you about the business."

"I thought the problem with that accountant was dealt with."

"Not completely, I guess."

Lisa suddenly bent to gather the papers on his desk, then pointed over her shoulder at her office. He nodded. He could talk to her later. No telling how long his mother wanted to chat.

Then, as Lisa straightened, her eyes caught his, her gaze intent. And once again a frisson of awareness tingled through him.

Lisa usually avoided his gaze. Made minimal eye

contact. As the door closed behind her, he wondered what had caused the change.

"Come as soon as you can, Dylan. Your father really needs to have you around." Stephanie paused, as if hoping Dylan would fill the momentary silence. But he wouldn't bite. If his father wanted him around, Alex could phone and say so himself. But he never did. "You take care of yourself, son," his mother was saying. "Love you."

Dylan echoed his mother's reply, then said goodbye. As he hung up, his eyes fell on the desk calendar his mother had given him. It was a pad with a Bible verse for every day. He hadn't looked at it for a month.

Yet he was looking at today's date. And today's verse. Maybe Lisa had kept it current.

Idly he turned the calendar toward him to read it better. "As a father has compassion on his children, so the Lord has compassion on those who fear Him" was the verse for the day. And that was just the trouble, wasn't it? His father's continuing compassion for one child in particular. Ted.

Charming, exuberant, unreliable Ted.

When Alex Matheson had approached Dylan five years ago to quit his successful job with a marketing firm and join Matheson Telecom, it was with the tantalizing promise that Dylan would be taking over the head office in Vancouver.

But when the time had come, his brother, Ted, had been given the reins of the company instead, with no explanation on his father's part. Dylan, angry with his father's betrayal of trust, had left to take over the

Toronto branch of Matheson Telecom. He'd lost himself in his work, determined to prove his worth.

Since then the two of them spoke only when necessary.

The Toronto branch had done well, but Dylan chafed at the restraints put on him by his brother and father in the head office. When Dylan saw his father wasn't going to change anything, he started making his own plans and grooming Perry Hatcher to take over.

Dylan pushed away from his desk and strode to the window looking out over the Toronto harbor. He used to have a sailboat docked there, just a small sloop, but setting up this branch of the company took up all his extra time. That it was now more successful than the Vancouver branch was bittersweet proof to his father that Alex Matheson had made a mistake.

Now his father wanted him to come back and clean up behind Ted. And his mother wanted him to come with an escort. If he didn't, he would have to spend the entire visit home avoiding his sisters and their friends.

This wasn't going to be much of a holiday after all, he thought with a light sigh.

Lisa closed the door behind her and slowly blew out a shaky breath.

When Dylan had mentioned "accountant," her heart had plunged. She was sure he was talking about Gabe. And she was also sure from the way he'd looked at her that guilt had been written all over her face. What if he found out about her connection to Gabe?

She didn't know how he could. She and Gabe had

different last names. When she had filled in the paperwork for employment she hadn't marked the box asking if any family members worked for Matheson Telecom. Gabe had already been fired, so technically he wasn't working for the company anymore.

She was too jumpy, that was all. If she wanted to help Gabe, she'd have to perfect her innocent look.

Trouble was, Gabe's phone calls were starting to frighten her. He had called again just last night, angry and frustrated.

She had tried to reason with him not to quit his current job as a salesclerk. But he was feeling depressed and wondering why he should bother doing honest work when his employer didn't believe him.

Thankfully he had settled down when she'd told him that she was working for Matheson Telecom. That she would get to the bottom of what had happened. Gabe just needed to be patient.

Patience wasn't Gabe's strength. Ever since they'd been put into foster care after their parents died Lisa had watched out for Gabe. When she'd graduated from high school she got a job and an apartment and applied to have Gabe move in with her. Thankfully, Social Services had agreed.

In high school Gabe had started hanging out with a bad crowd. After a close brush with the law, Lisa had pulled him away from this rowdy group of boys, scared that Social Services might separate them. She had put her own life on hold to take care of him. To give him a chance. His graduation from college with a degree in accounting had been a celebration for

Lisa and a validation of all the sacrifices she had made for him.

Now he sounded as if he was going to throw away everything she had done for him unless Lisa could find a way to clear his name. She had to find a way to get to Vancouver, she thought. Had to find a way to help him. He was the only family she had now.

Settling down in front of her computer, she opened the most recent file and began typing, her fingers still trembling from the close call a few moments earlier. The routine of the work slowly eased her jitters, so that when Dylan emerged from his office at the end of the day she was fully in control.

He stopped in front of her desk, dominating the space with his presence. His tie was loosened, the sleeves of his shirt rolled up, giving him a casually vulnerable air. "I wanted to ask you if you've got that spreadsheet done."

Lisa looked up at him, her secretary smile in place. "Almost, Mr. Matheson. So if you want to wait a moment, I can show you the sales figures."

"Please, just Dylan." He scratched his forehead with an index finger, looking hesitant. "It's past five o'clock. Why are you still here?"

Because she was hoping to look through some more files when he was gone. She had so little time with Dylan still around. She was starting to feel a little panicky. In less than a month he would be gone, and she still hadn't found anything substantial.

"Just like to get done."

"Very dedicated." He crossed his arms over his chest, his head tilted to one side as he looked at her.

"Is there something else you wanted?" she asked, her heart kicking up shards of guilt. She just wanted him to go.

He sat down in the chair across from her desk, as if he was settling in for a chat. "Yes. I want to stay here and avoid my sister's wedding and my parents' anniversary."

"Why would you want to do that?" Lisa was surprised at his sudden disclosure. In the past week he had been polite, but a bit distant. Just the way she liked it.

"Because if I go, my mother is going to play matchmaker and I'm going to end up trying to avoid yet another sweet but boring young lady." Dylan sighed, rubbing his hand over his face.

"Why don't you find someone yourself?"

"I should," Dylan said heavily. "But I'm going to be so busy with company business while I'm there that anyone I take would be sitting around while I dealt with that."

An impulse jumped into her mind. She needed to get to Vancouver. In less than a month Dylan, and her one solid connection to the Matheson company, was going to be gone. It was the perfect opportunity, and before she could even think about it, she spoke. "I could go with you. Help you with your father's problem. Pose as your girlfriend. Could cover two things in one easy solution."

Dylan's head snapped up. He stared at her a moment, then nodded, a grin crawling along his lips. "You know, that would be a great idea. I think it could work just perfectly."

Lisa beat down a flurry of nerves.

Vancouver. Already.

She didn't want to think about the implications of attending the wedding as Dylan's escort. She'd deal with that as it came. For now, she'd have an opportunity to meet his family. And maybe, just maybe, his work would involve the conversation he'd had with his mother in his office this morning. Things were starting to come together quite nicely.

"I'll have to phone my mom and tell her," Dylan said, pushing himself to his feet.

Lisa frowned. "Tell her what?"

"To make up an extra bedroom. I usually stay at my parents' place."

Sleeping with the enemy. Lisa pulled in a steadying breath. "Okay. I'll let you arrange that, then." Lisa turned back to her computer, quelling a sudden rush of nerves. This was a good thing, she reminded herself. Staying at the Matheson house would bring her closer to the family and any potential source of information.

"One more thing, Lisa."

She turned to him, her smile cautious.

"Pack something dressy for the wedding and the anniversary party." Dylan gave her a crooked smile, then left.

Second thoughts swirled through her mind as Dylan closed the door behind him. With each request he made she felt pushed into an ever-shrinking corner.

What had she done? Bad enough that she was working for him under false pretenses. Now she was going to Vancouver burdened with even more.

Don't think about it. You're doing this all because of Gabe.

And staying that close to Dylan?

That thought crept into the part of her mind that couldn't help acknowledging Dylan's appeal. His good looks.

She quashed the idea ruthlessly. Dylan was her boss. And part of the company that had falsely accused her brother.

And if she didn't want a repeat of Tony, she would do well to keep her professional distance.

Chapter Two

The runway flew past her window. Lisa's exhilaration built with the speed of the plane. Then she was pressed back against the seat as the front of the plane lifted off the ground, the city of Toronto dropping away from them.

Point of no return.

Anxiety trembled through Lisa. No time for second thoughts. She was on her way.

Lisa glanced at her seatmate. Dylan casually thumbed through a magazine as if he was sitting in his living room rather than within a thousand tons of steel hurtling through the air.

When Lisa had phoned Gabe to tell him she was coming to Vancouver, his skepticism had fed her nervousness and planted the seeds of second thoughts.

She shook them off. If she was careful, there was no reason the Mathesons or Dylan should discover her plan. And if she was right, her actions would be vindicated.

And how do you fit this with the promise you made in Dylan's office? To go to church if you got this job?

Whatever your lips utter you must be sure to do. The thought slipped into her mind, ringing with clarity. Gabe's father used to laughingly quote this passage from the Old Testament laws whenever Lisa made one of her many extravagant promises.

Lisa and her mother didn't go to church until Trish met and married Gabe's father. Rick Haskell introduced Lisa and Trish to church. And God. They went regularly and Lisa attended Bible classes, eagerly absorbing the teachings.

But after the accident that killed Lisa's mother and Gabe's father, Lisa's faith took a blow. She didn't trust God, and neither she nor Gabe had attended church since.

Dylan glanced up and caught her gaze. "How are you doing?"

"Good." She looked away, out the window at the patchwork of fields and roads spread out below her, pushing her doubts and her guilt aside. "This is quite a rush. Flying."

"You don't fly often?"

Lisa quelled her embarrassment. "Actually, this is my maiden flight."

Dylan was silent, and she couldn't help looking over to check his reaction.

His gray-blue eyes held hers, his mouth pulled up in a half smile. "You've never flown before?"

"I know it's an anomaly in this peripatetic age, but no, I've never flown before."

"Well then, we're even." His half smile was full-blown now, crinkling the corners of his eyes, softening the austerity of his features.

Lisa frowned. "How do you figure that?"

"I've never heard words like *anomaly* and *peripatetic* used in the same sentence."

She laughed. "Sorry. That's a holdover from a game I used to play with my stepfather and…" Just in time she caught herself from saying Gabe's name. "And he used to challenge me to find unusual words," she amended, stifling her beating heart. "Then use them as often as possible in one day."

"Where is your stepfather now?"

"He died ten years ago."

"And your mother?"

"She died at the same time." The flicker of sorrow caught her by surprise. It had been a long time since anyone had asked about her parents. A long time since anyone had cared.

"I'm sorry to hear that. You must have been about fifteen when that happened. Where did you go then?"

"Foster home." She looked down at her hands, twined tightly on her lap. Each question of Dylan's probed places in her life that still felt painfully tender, even after all the years. And they created a discomfort she wanted to deflect. Well offense was the best defense. "What about your family? What are they like? Busy? Happy? I guess I should know, if I'm supposed to be attending as your escort."

Dylan held her gaze, his expression intent. As if he knew she was avoiding his questions. But thankfully he simply smiled and rubbed his chin. "My parents' names are Stephanie and Alex Matheson. Married thirty-five years."

"Hold on a minute." Lisa pulled a pad of paper and a pen out of her briefcase. "I think I might need to write this down."

"Always the secretary," murmured Dylan.

"That is my job, Mr. Matheson," she said, scribbling down his parents' names.

A strong finger pressed down on her pad of paper, catching her attention.

"Since you're also my escort slash girlfriend, it would look better if you called me Dylan." He smiled again, his eyes holding hers.

Lisa couldn't look away. She could lose herself in those eyes. More gray now, soft and inviting.

She blinked, breaking the insidious spell he seemed to be weaving.

"Okay." She tossed him a smile, then looked back down at the pad of paper. "You mentioned your parents. Tell me about the rest of your family."

"They're just family. You'll meet them one at a time."

"And I'll forget them the same way. A computer I'm not."

Dylan shrugged, and Lisa sensed in him the same reticence she had just displayed. For a moment she thought he wasn't going to say anything.

"My mother's name is Stephanie, as I said, and she doesn't stand on formality, either. My father is Alex. Tiffany is younger than me and looks the most like me," he said. "She's married to Arnold. They have two children, Justin and Tammy. Chelsea is twenty-five, pretty, but then I'm prejudiced. It's her wedding we'll be attending. After her come twin sisters, Erika and Amber, unmarried, with more single girlfriends than Solomon had wives. Sometimes they live at home, sometimes they rent an apartment downtown. I'm not sure what it is this month."

"Sounds like you're a very lucky man." Lisa couldn't keep the light note of envy from her voice. "All those sisters."

"I also have a brother. Ted."

Lisa looked up from her scribbling, her heart skipping at the sound of his brother's name. The man who had fired Gabe. "And where is he?"

"Ted is married to Dara. He is a partner with my father in the company." His hands, clutching the armrests of his seat, betrayed the emotion his voice and expression held back. Then he glanced at her, loosening his tie and unbuttoning the top button of his shirt. "And that's my family."

Lisa put the pad of paper away and looked out the window, sensing they weren't going to be talking much anymore. It seemed they both had their secrets.

"I called my mother, and she's expecting us for supper," Dylan said, slipping his cell phone into his briefcase.

"Supper?" Lisa's heart did a slow flip in her chest. "Already?"

"I guess they're anxious to meet you," he said with a sardonic lift of his mouth.

Lisa stifled another attack of nerves as they walked

to the gleaming row of rental cars, their footsteps echoing hollowly in the concrete car park. "Wow, meeting parents," she said lightly as Dylan unlocked the trunk of the car. "Something else to add to my 'things I've never done before' file."

"No boyfriends you dated that wanted you to meet Mom and Dad?" Dylan asked, dropping their suitcases into the back.

"No parents to reciprocate."

Dylan held her gaze, his expression growing serious. "I'm sorry. That was unforgivable. I had forgotten."

"It's okay. With your family you probably can't imagine someone going it alone in the world." She didn't want to sound whiney and hoped her flippant tone would put him at ease.

"So how long has it been since you've been back home?" Lisa asked when they were settled in the car.

"About half a year." Dylan glanced over his shoulder as he reversed the car out of the parking lot. "I usually go home more. My sisters and my mother have come to visit me a few times in Toronto."

"So what's been keeping you away this time?"

Dylan's only response was a shrug. Another mystery.

He switched lanes, sped up and switched again, the traffic becoming more congested and busier as they entered the canyon of buildings in the downtown core.

Then buildings fell away, trees loomed ahead and within seconds they were speeding through silent, dark woods.

"Is this Stanley Park?" she asked, twisting in her seat to get a closer look at the decades-old trees forming a lush canopy above and beyond. "Right in the middle of the city like this?"

"One of Vancouver's true beauties," Dylan said. "You could spend a couple of days just walking around this park."

"I might have to try that someday," Lisa said, trying to take in the size of the trees, the depth of the forest. It looked cool, inviting. Secretive.

A young couple walked along one of the paths, pushing a stroller, a younger child in shorts and a T-shirt bouncing ahead of them. Sunlight filtered through the trees, dappling their figures. A family.

Lisa watched them, turning her head as they fell behind, envy surprising her. Then Dylan rounded a curve and they were hidden from view.

She turned, watching the approaching bridge, the two lions guarding the entrance. Suspension wires swept gracefully between two pillars. The bridge went on, higher and longer. Far below them she saw large ships and barges pulled by squat tugboats. Sailboats fluttered amongst them like ballet dancers weaving through a pack of wrestlers.

She craned her neck to see better, watching as the boats slipped through the water. "What a beautiful sight."

"Ever sail before?" Dylan asked.

Lisa shook her head. "Never."

"I'll have to take you in the family's boat if we have time."

"Your family has its own sailboat?"

Dylan threw her a puzzled frown. "Yes."

The tone in his voice implied an "of course." As if it

was the most natural thing in the world for a family to own something as luxurious as their own boat. Lisa had never even owned her own car until she had paid off Gabe's and her student loans. And that car was a fourth- or maybe even fifth-hand beater.

Sailboats, in her mind, were equated with the very upper class. A group of people who moved in a world far beyond her everyday reality.

She swallowed down a flutter of nerves.

Dylan followed the freeway, bordered, as well, by trees. He swung off onto an exit and soon they were climbing another hill, the road twisting back on itself. The higher they went, the more expansive the view behind them and the larger the homes.

When Dylan finally turned into a curved driveway bordered by a stone fence, Lisa couldn't help but stare at the sight that greeted her. The house soared three stories above her, all glass and lines and cantilevered levels. A glassed-in balcony swept along the front, following the curve of the huge bow window that broke the austere lines of the house. The same balcony was echoed one floor below, but smaller. The entire building was a stark white against the deep green of the cedar trees surrounding it on two sides, dark and mysterious.

"Ugly, isn't it?" Dylan said dryly as he parked in front of one of the doors of a four-car garage. "The house, I mean. Mom has always dreamed of designing and building her own home. So my father bought this lot, and found a contractor willing to work with Mom. Together they created this monstrosity."

"It's very impressive," she said cautiously.

"Mom paid for impressive. You'll have to tell her so."

"If it's something she designed herself, then it's amazing."

Dylan looked down at her, his expression softening. A faint smile crawled across his lips, deepening the line that ran from his nose to one corner of his mouth. "Tell her that and she'll fall in love with you," he said.

Lisa couldn't look away and he didn't. Love? From a mother? That had been a while, she thought with a twinge of sorrow. *And what would your mother say about the deception you're playing now?*

She pushed the thought resolutely aside and was about to get out of the car when Dylan laid his hand on her arm. She pulled back.

"If we're supposed to be together, you might want to avoid avoiding me like that," Dylan said with a faint smile.

"Sorry." Lisa felt silly. It was just a casual touch, yet it had sent a tingle up her arm.

"I feel I should warn you about a few things before we go in. I have never brought any of my girlfriends home to meet my parents yet. The fact that I'm bringing you here will make them suspicious. And when my sisters and mother get suspicious, they get nosy. I hope to head them off when possible, but don't be surprised if they ask you a bunch of questions."

"Like how we met?"

"We'll tell them we met at work."

He sighed lightly, drumming his fingers on the steering wheel.

"I'm guessing there's more?" Lisa said, prompting him.

"Yes. Every time I've mentioned a girl to them they always ask me if she's a Christian." He waved his hand as if dismissing their concerns. "Don't be surprised if that comes up somewhere in the conversation. I know we're technically not 'together,' but they don't know that."

"Don't worry. I think I can handle myself."

"That's what I was hoping. I'll get the suitcases."

Lisa gave him a bright smile, which faded as she got out of the car. Deeper and deeper, she thought with a flash of panic.

It's just a game, she reminded herself. Just a game.

She took a deep breath and followed Dylan up the stone walkway to the main entrance of the house.

The double oak doors at the top burst open and two young women launched themselves at Dylan. He dropped the suitcases just as they grabbed him.

"Dylan, you came."

"We've been waiting and waiting."

"Chelsea thought you wouldn't show."

"How was your flight? How are you? It's been ages."

The words fluttered around them as the girls clutched Dylan's arms, bracketing him like matching bookends.

The twin sisters, Lisa guessed as she watched the exuberant reunion. Their short caps of dark brown hair were the same shade as Dylan's. Where he was tall, they were of slight build, coming only to his shoulder. They wore matching hip hugging blue jeans, artfully faded. One topped them with a bell-sleeved shirt in peach, the other a fitted T-shirt and a wooden beaded necklace.

One of the girls stood on tiptoe to kiss Dylan soundly on the cheek. "We've missed you, big brother."

"I missed you, too, Erika."

Dylan turned to Lisa, beckoning for her to come forward.

She steeled herself for the all-too-familiar tightening of her stomach. How many times had she endured these "first meetings" in the many families she'd been brought to? The acknowledgments, the reserve that always greeted her. The moment of awkwardness, the hard work that accompanied all these initial moments.

It's just a game, she reminded herself again, angry with her nervousness. You don't need their approval. She took a slow breath and smiled.

"Erika. Amber. I'd like you to meet Lisa Sterling," Dylan said, turning toward her. "My…girlfriend."

Dylan's use of the term reminded her of the role she was playing.

Years of experience made Lisa lift her chin and take a few more steps up the stairs to come to Erika and Amber's level. She met their quizzical gazes head-on.

Then, to her utter surprise, she felt Dylan slip his arm around her waist. Pull her close to him.

He was almost as much of a stranger as his sisters were, yet she felt a curious sense of being protected. Cared for.

Don't be silly, she reminded herself with a jolt. It's just part of the show. But she didn't pull away.

"Lisa, I'd like you to meet my sisters, Amber and Erika. The easiest way to tell them apart is to remember that Erika is the more talkative one."

"Thanks a lot, Dylan. Perfect introduction for us. I hate to think what you told her on the trip up. She's going to think we're a couple of airheads. Which we're not." The twin in the peach angora sweater pouted at her brother, then turned back to Lisa. "I'm Erika."

Lisa caught Dylan's knowing smirk and tried not to smile.

"Welcome to our home, Lisa," Amber said, shaking Lisa's hand, as well. "Mom told us you're Dylan's secretary. I hope he doesn't make you work too hard while you're here."

"Come on, you make me sound like an ogre," Dylan said with a laugh, pulling his sister to his side.

"Kerry is coming over later," Erika said, giving her brother a gentle punch. "She's looking forward to seeing you. And Ted and Dara wanted to come by, too."

"Isn't that nice." Dylan dropped a light kiss on his sister's head, his smile forced.

Then to Lisa's relief he let go of her. She followed the girls into the house, Dylan behind her.

White and light and angles was her first impression. A boldly colorful print dominated the wall above the sweeping staircase. A single metal sculpture glinted at her from an alcove below the stairs.

It wasn't just a house, she realized, her footsteps echoing in the wide-open foyer. It was a showcase.

"Cozy, isn't it?" Dylan's sardonic voice broke in to her thoughts.

"It has its own beauty," Lisa said, awed by the space captured by just the entrance.

"Dylan hates this house," Amber said with a laugh. "He's still complaining that Mom and Dad sold our other place."

"That house had personality. I feel like I should be under anesthetic when I come here," Dylan groused.

As Lisa followed Dylan's sisters down the spacious hallway, she caught a glimpse of what must be a living room with tall windows, gray furniture and ocher accents. A set of French doors to her right showed her a room done up in darker tones. Den? Library? She didn't have time to take it in. Erika and Amber kept walking, going past another set of doors to yet another room and finally turning a corner into a large open kitchen area.

Light poured into the room from windows two floors high. A white table, already set with yellow place mats and gleaming white-and-blue china, was tucked into one corner of the room. Plants softened the brightness here, adding a warmth absent in the rest of the house.

Through a large expanse of glass Lisa saw another view of the landscaped gardens, and beyond that a breathtaking vista of Burrard Inlet bisected by the bridge they had gone over and edged by the hazy skyline of downtown Vancouver.

Money, was the first word that slipped into her mind. Money enough to pay for all this.

Lisa pushed down a flurry of panic. In what dream world had she hatched her silly scheme to try to bring justice for her stepbrother against this family? A family with enough money to build a home whose cost she couldn't even begin to calculate.

"Dylan, how are you?"

Lisa took a calming breath and turned to see an elegantly clad woman step around the counter, her arms out to Dylan.

"Hello, Mother."

Lisa was surprised at the warmth in Dylan's voice and the note of yearning in his mother's. She found she couldn't look away, a bittersweet pain clenching her heart as she watched Dylan enfolded in a warm embrace, his arms encircling his mother's shoulders.

"I missed you, son," Dylan's mother said, her hands stroking his thick hair, her eyes taking in his features as if she was seeing him for the first time.

This was Stephanie Matheson, Lisa reminded herself, as if remembering a school lesson.

Dylan gave his mother another hug, then turned to Lisa, gesturing for her to come near. She was surprised at the clench of nerves tightening her stomach. Being a guest in this amazing home brought to a head what she had gotten herself into. Suddenly it was not only Dylan she was trying to fool. Now it was sisters, parents. Family.

The plan that had seemed so straightforward back in Toronto now took on an ominous note.

"Lisa, this is my mother, Stephanie Matheson."

Lisa held out her hand, keeping her smile intact as she met eyes the same piercing gray-blue as Dylan's.

"Welcome to our house, Lisa. I'm so glad you don't mind staying here." As Stephanie took Lisa's hand, she tipped her head to one side, as if conducting her own interview.

Lisa took Stephanie's hand in hers and shook it firmly, holding her gaze measure for measure. Think of Gabe, she thought. You're here because of Gabe.

But when she let go of Stephanie's hand, she chanced

a quick glance at Dylan, surprised to see him studying her with a faint smile on his face.

She looked away. She couldn't afford to get distracted. So Dylan had a family. That shouldn't matter.

She was here to take care of her own family.

Chapter Three

Dylan pushed the sleeves of his sweater up his arms and gave himself a quick inspection in the mirror. Could use a haircut. He ran his hand over the shadow on his jaw. Probably should have shaved. He was looking a little scruffy.

And why did he care? He certainly never worried about how he looked in front of his family. He was sure Lisa wouldn't notice.

He stepped out of the bedroom and walked down the hall. The door to Lisa's room was open. He heard her voice.

His sisters were being surprisingly friendly, he thought, knocking lightly on the door. He pushed it open farther, but Lisa sat with her back to him, talking on a cell phone.

Feeling foolish, he was about to leave when she glanced over her shoulder. Her eyes grew wide and she quickly snapped the phone shut.

"Sorry," Dylan said. "I thought you were talking to one of my sisters."

Lisa shook her head, dropped the phone into her open briefcase on the bed, then clicked the case shut. "No, I was just…just checking…my messages."

She didn't look up at him, which puzzled Dylan even more. Why was she looking so guilty about checking her phone messages?

"Is everything okay?" he asked. "With the room?"

She got up, flashing him a quick smile. "It's lovely. Much nicer and much larger than a hotel room."

"I thought I should let you know that we should head down for dinner."

"Should I have changed?" Lisa glanced down at the narrow skirt she had worn on the airplane.

"You look fine." He didn't know of too many women who could come off a four-hour flight and look so fresh. Her skirt was barely wrinkled and her shirt looked as crisp as when they'd boarded. "I just changed because I get tired of wearing a suit."

"Okay. I suppose we should go, then." But as she passed him he heard the muffled ringing of her cell phone.

"Do you want to get that?" he asked as she spun around.

"No. No." Lisa waved her hand as if dismissing the call. "He can leave a message." She flashed him a quick smile, then left the room, leaving Dylan no choice but to follow her. And wonder how she knew it was a "he" that was calling.

And why she didn't answer it.

* * *

The wave of laughter that rolled down the hallway from the kitchen was a stark contrast to the panic clenching Lisa's stomach.

That had been too close. She had been so anxious to connect with Gabe that she hadn't thought to shut the bedroom door. When she'd heard the phone ringing again, she'd known it was him calling her back, which had sent her heart up into her throat.

"Lisa. Wait a minute."

She swallowed and turned to face Dylan, praying the guilt she felt wasn't written all over her face.

"You're losing a hairpin." As he reached up to catch it, his warm fingers brushed her neck. She jerked her head back, feeling immediately foolish.

"I'm sorry," she said, biting her lip as she took the pin from him. "I'm not usually this jumpy." The phone call was a lesson to her. If she had to connect with Gabe, better do it away from this home. Being in the very home of the people she wanted to investigate put her at a disadvantage.

As she slipped the pin into her hair, she felt the urge to pray. To ask for help as she floundered through this uncomfortable situation.

"It's okay. My family can seem intimidating, but they're not." Dylan tipped his head, as if studying her. "Just be yourself, only yourself as my date. I think they'll like you."

His faint smile should have smoothed away her disquiet. Instead it created more anxiety. She wasn't supposed to have any relationship with this family.

"There you are." Stephanie paused in the doorway of the kitchen, holding a steaming dish, an apron covering her skirt. "Why don't you two stop chitchatting and join us?"

Stephanie's comment made it sound as if she had caught them lingering. And again Lisa felt a warm flush rise up her neck.

"Well, I suppose we should get going, then," Dylan said with a smile. "I'll lead the way."

The first person Lisa saw was an older version of Dylan leaning back against the counter, flipping through a magazine. Alex Matheson, Lisa presumed.

But where Dylan's hair was dark, Alex's was sprinkled with gray. And where Dylan's eyes were a hard gray-blue, his father's were a softer shade of hazel.

He glanced up as they came closer, a broad smile brightening his face.

Dylan acknowledged his father's presence with a curt nod in greeting, then turned away as if a necessary but tiresome obligation had been dealt with. But as he did, Lisa caught a flash of pain in his father's eyes.

Dylan walked over to a young woman sitting at the table looking intently at a bridal magazine. "Kind of late to be changing your mind, Chels."

The woman looked up, then jumped off her chair, nearly upsetting it. "You made it. You came." She threw her arms around his neck, squeezing him tight.

"You can let go of me, or you're going to be out one groomsman." Dylan pulled back from his sister's exuberant embrace, but kept his arm around her waist.

Dylan turned to Lisa. "Chelsea, I'd like you to meet Lisa."

Lisa held out her hand, feeling more like a fraud with each family member she met.

Chelsea took her hand, giving Lisa a quick nod and a welcoming smile, then gave her brother a little dig in the ribs. "You know, you're the first…woman associated with Dylan that this family has ever met."

"I'm sure Lisa needs to know that," Dylan said with a shake of his head. "And this is my father, Alex." Dylan's voice lost the note of loving warmth when he introduced his father, and again Lisa wondered at the rift between them.

"Nice to meet you, Lisa," Alex said, taking her hand in both of his and squeezing it tight. "Welcome to our family."

To Lisa's surprise, she felt a lump forming in her throat at his greeting and the warm and welcoming smile he bestowed on her. They didn't know her at all, yet she felt as if she was being accepted like a fellow family member.

"Thank you," she said, suddenly short of words.

"And with the twins is their friend Kerry." Lisa turned to face a smiling young woman bracketed by the twins. But Kerry had eyes only for Dylan. "Hello, Dylan," Kerry said, her voice low. And sweet.

Lisa got an inkling of Dylan's dilemma and felt a flash of pity.

"We're not late, are we?" Another female voice behind them made Dylan's head snap up, his eyes narrowing as a chorus of hellos greeted this new arrival.

Curious, Lisa turned around. A tall, willowy brunette wearing an eye-catching red shift entered the room. Following her was a man of about the same height, wearing a suit and tie.

"Hello, everyone." The brunette paused at Alex's side, leaning sideways to brush a kiss near his cheek. "How are you, Dad?" She didn't wait for a reply, but turned to Dylan. "So the prodigal son has returned." She reached Dylan, but he didn't echo her greeting. Nor did he raise his arms to her as she did to him.

"I didn't know you and Ted were coming."

Lisa's heart plunged.

Would Dara recognize her as Gabe's stepsister? Her mind raced backward, wondering if she had ever sent Gabe a picture of herself. The man beside her must be Ted. Dylan's brother.

Lisa felt suddenly exposed and panicky. She tried not to shift behind Dylan. To hide.

But so far Dara had eyes only for Dylan, and Ted was ignoring them both. "Your mother told me you were going to be here, so I thought I would surprise you." Dara laid her hand on Dylan's shoulder, giving him a light shake. "So, surprise."

But Dylan didn't look surprised. Nor did he look as pleased as Dara sounded.

Dylan shifted away from her, looking toward Lisa. "Dara, Ted, I'd like you to meet Lisa Sterling, my date." Lisa felt her heart jump at the last two words. It sounded so final.

Dara's hand slid down from Dylan's shoulder as she slowly turned around. Her brown eyes narrowed, zeroing in on Lisa.

Here it comes, thought Lisa, her heart jumping like a kangaroo. She tried to smile. Tried to look casual.

But before Dara could speak, Ted reached past his wife and shook Lisa's hand, his smile far more welcoming than Dara's.

"This is a first for us," Ted said with a light laugh. "Nice to finally meet one of Dylan's girlfriends."

"Supper's ready," Stephanie Matheson announced, bringing a large casserole dish to the table. "Dylan, you can sit on the far corner of the table. Lisa, I've put you beside Dylan." Stephanie's smile held the same warmth that Alex's had. And as Lisa sat at the table, second and third and even fourth thoughts assailed her.

She should have taken Dylan's offer of a hotel. It would have been better for her and Gabe if she had maintained a distance from this family.

She hadn't expected to meet Dara and Ted this soon. Nor had she expected to like this family. It created a confusion she couldn't dismiss.

"You should sit on the end, Kerry." Amber moved over from her place kitty-corner from Dylan. Amber flashed Lisa an apologetic look. "Kerry's left-handed."

Lisa returned Amber's smile, but couldn't help notice the way Kerry eyed Dylan.

The bustle died down as everyone sat at the table. Stephanie took her husband's hand and gave it a light shake. "Will you pray, Alex?"

Alex shook his head.

Lisa could see a faint line crease Stephanie's forehead. It disappeared as she glanced around the table with a light smile, then everyone bowed their heads. At the last moment Lisa realized what was happening and dropped her head, as well.

She closed her eyes as Dylan's mother began praying.

"We come to You, Lord, in humbleness of heart and praise You for the lives you have given us. Thank You, Lord, for safety in travels. For the food we can eat and enjoy together. Thank You too, for Lisa and Dylan's visit…"

Lisa felt a slow melancholy wrap itself around her heart. How long had it been since she had heard the sincere prayer of a believer? How long had it been since she'd heard anyone pray for her?

Stephanie's prayer was a reminder of what she had pushed out of her life in bitterness. A knot caught in her throat.

Then, thankfully, the prayer was over. Around her Dylan's family broke into a flurry of conversation. Lisa kept her head bowed a moment, shoring up her scatter-shot emotions.

"Sorry about that." Dylan's quiet voice beside her made her look up. He was looking down at her, a bemused expression on his face. "I hope you weren't too uncomfortable?"

Lisa shook her head. "It's been a while since I've prayed before meals."

"You used to?"

"Yes, when…" She stopped talking. Nothing personal, she reminded herself, turning to the salad in front of her.

"And what are you two plotting?" Dara asked, leaning forward to catch their attention, but it was Dylan who had her eye. "Takeover schemes? How to rescue the company?"

Again Lisa felt her face flush at Dara's implication.

"I'm sorry," Dylan said smoothly. "I didn't mean to look like we had secrets." And thankfully he said no more than that.

"So, Lisa, how did you meet Dylan?" Amber asked, her voice full of innocent inquiry.

"In the office." Lisa decided to play this as straight-forward as she could.

"Convenient," Dara said.

"Yes, it is," Lisa returned, determined not to let this woman bulldoze her. "I guess I got a little more than I bargained for when I applied for the job."

Dylan's sidelong grin and wink was one of cocon-spirator, and the connection created a quiver of aware-ness.

"I thought you made it a rule never to get involved with your office staff," Amber said with a touch of petulance. She seemed to sense that Kerry was out of the running.

"And I hear you've been spending time with a certain hockey player, Amber," Dylan added. "Something I remember hearing you say you'd never do."

The blush on Amber's face evoked a wave of laughter.

Though Dylan had neatly parried Amber's obvious schemes, Erika didn't seem ready to give up their cham-pioning of Kerry as potential partner for Dylan. "Did we tell you, Dylan? Kerry works for that company that manufactures the newest in e-books. Kerry, tell Dylan about the new one you're working on."

Kerry's face lit up. She scooped her streaked blond hair behind her ear, her blue eyes fairly sparkling. Though she liked to dress well, Lisa was seldom self-conscious of her appearance. But being confronted with Kerry's beauty-queen good looks, she felt like a frump.

"E-books have been vastly underrated," Kerry said, leaning forward, her shining lips parted in a smile wide enough to show her perfectly aligned teeth. "But we've come up with a platform that makes the possibilities for our e-book wider than most of the limited-use, dedicated devices that have come up in the past." Kerry kept her eyes on Dylan, her smile coy as she absently toyed with her long hair.

"How does this relate to Matheson Telecom?"

"It could make a good addition to our product line," Dara put in, her smile competing with Kerry's.

"I think we've spread ourselves far enough," Dylan said, stabbing his salad with his fork.

"Dara might be right," Ted put in. "A company that doesn't move ahead goes behind."

"From the looks of things, we're doing that already," Dylan said, tension entering his voice.

"I don't think we need to talk business at the supper table," Stephanie said with a tight smile. "Chelsea, have you gotten hold of the caterers to finalize details?"

The conversation turned back to the wedding, leaving Lisa wondering again at the tension that existed between Dylan, his father and his brother.

The rest of the meal was a sparring match of words

and jokes, half-finished sentences. Laughter was the dominant emotion. And questions. But after Stephanie's quiet warning, no business was spoken.

As she tried to eat, Lisa couldn't keep up with half the conversations, but she didn't mind. Far easier to be simply a silent bystander.

She noticed that in spite of the general air of togetherness around the table, Dylan and his father exchanged no more than a few sentences. Though Dylan hardly looked at his father, Alex's eyes were constantly on his son as if hoping for some connection.

"Have we met before, Lisa?" Dara asked suddenly. "The more I see you, the more familiar you seem."

Lisa kept her smile in place even as icy fingers tickled her spine. "My mother always told me my face was a dime a dozen. Maybe that's why."

Dara laughed lightly. "Maybe." But Lisa could tell Dara wasn't satisfied with the reply.

Lisa folded her napkin and laid it on her plate. She felt suddenly ill and wanted to leave. But she didn't want to be the first away from the table.

She looked up to see Alex watching her, a light frown on his face. Surely he didn't recognize her, as well?

Lisa steeled herself for another round of questions.

"I think we should finish this meal, Stephanie," Alex said, much to her relief. "We can have dessert in the living room."

He pulled a large worn book from a shelf behind him that was part of the kitchen cabinets. Lisa recognized a Bible. A well-read Bible.

He handed it to Stephanie.

"Why don't you read, dear?" she said softly.

He shook his head. With a slight nod of acquiescence, Stephanie took the book and paged through it. As she did, arms were crossed, faces turned toward her as a feeling of waiting permeated the room. This was normal routine, Lisa realized, sitting back in her chair.

"We always have devotions after our meal," Stephanie said, smiling at Lisa. "If you're uncomfortable with that, you are welcome to leave."

"No, this is fine." She glanced around the table, underlining her lack of objection. "Please, go ahead."

"Instead of reading through our usual devotions, I thought I would simply read a psalm." Stephanie glanced up at Lisa as she slipped her reading glasses on. "So that Lisa doesn't feel completely out of the loop."

Lisa felt that way already, but she simply smiled her thanks.

"Psalm thirty-three." Stephanie brushed a strand of hair back from her face and began to read. "'Sing joyfully to the Lord, you righteous; it is fitting for the upright to praise him….'"

The cadences and rhythms of the psalm washed over Lisa. Familiar enough that she could almost hear Rick Haskell's voice reading the words. A light pain settled in her chest, an echo of the one she'd felt in the airplane. Just like this family, Rick used to read the Bible after supper. Sometimes in the evening, as well. Unbidden, her thoughts returned to the angry place she revisited each time she thought of their deaths.

"'From heaven the Lord looks down and sees all mankind; from His dwelling place He watches all who live on earth, He who forms the hearts of all, who considers everything they do.'"

If God could truly see everyone, why had He taken Rick and her mother away from her and Gabe? What had they done to deserve such a loss?

"'We wait in hope for the Lord; He is our help and our shield. In Him our hearts rejoice, for we trust His holy name. May Your unfailing love rest upon us, O Lord, even as we put our hope in You.'"

As Stephanie read the last words of the psalm, Lisa lowered her head. How could she put her hope in God? In the past few years the one thing she had discovered was that if she didn't take care of herself, no one else would.

Stephanie closed the Bible, and Lisa once again caught the appeal in her glance as she looked to her husband. But again he shook his head. Was this his job? Lisa wondered.

Stephanie glanced around the table, then lowered her head and began to pray. And against her will Lisa felt a gentle urging, a faint voice calling her.

Whatever your lips utter you must be sure to do.

She bit her lip, thinking of her silly bargain with God. But she was a person of her word, and she would find a chance to go to church.

But first she needed to get out of this house. It was too risky staying here.

And it was too hard being in the middle of this obviously happy and close family.

Dylan paused in front of Lisa's door. It was slightly ajar and the light shone through the opening into the hallway. He should just keep going, but he wanted to make sure she was okay. She'd seemed a little jumpy at suppertime.

He knocked lightly on the door.

"Who is it?"

"Me. Dylan."

He heard a rustling sound and then she was at the door. She had changed into sweatpants and a hooded sweatshirt, her hair now hanging loose over her shoulders. The casual dress made her look vulnerable. More approachable than the immaculately dressed secretary he saw more often.

"What can I do for you, Mr. Matheson?" she asked, holding the door like a shield. "Sorry. Dylan."

So much for approachable. "Just wondering how you were feeling. You seemed a little tense downstairs."

"I'm sorry. I felt a little out of place." She looked up at him. "Look. This wasn't a good idea. I should be staying at a hotel like you suggested. I feel like I'm putting your family out."

"You're not at all." Dylan dropped a shoulder against the doorjamb. "Besides, Dara told me that she's bringing some files here tomorrow. Figured it would be easier if we looked at them here, rather than in the office."

Lisa bit her lip, as if considering.

"Look, if it's a problem, we can rent a hotel room. Work out of that."

Lisa shook her head. "No. That's not convenient at all." She glanced up at him. "And for some reason that seems even more compromising than staying here with your parents in the house."

Dylan held her eyes as the faint implications of what she was saying hung between them.

"My dad's at the office and my mother will be running around for the wedding," he said with a light smile.

A spark of awareness arced between them. He let it play out a moment, wondering where it came from. What he was going to do about it.

Lisa lowered her eyes and drew back into the room. "Okay, then. I guess I'll be seeing you tomorrow. What time do you want to start?"

"Eight o'clock okay for you?"

She nodded. "I'll see you then," she said softly, and closed the door.

But Dylan waited, as if trying to analyze that elusive moment.

He would do well to remember Felicia.

And that Lisa was just his secretary.

Chapter Four

Lisa closed the file and rolled the kink out of her neck, easing the tension that had been building the past hour. The stress that pinched her upper shoulders didn't come from her surroundings, however.

Outside the large glass doors behind her, light played through the trees, dancing over the table as classical music played softly through speakers discreetly mounted in the ceiling. The book-lined walls and the two leather couches flanking a fireplace were a temptation she had been ignoring for the past four hours.

Instead the stress came from spending the morning bent over files or staring at a computer screen matching vendors with invoices and getting nowhere close to any thread connected to her brother.

Lisa glanced at Dylan sitting across the table from her. His sleeves were rolled up to just below his elbow, his tie knot hung below his opened collar and his hand was buried in his thick hair. He looked as frustrated as she felt.

As if feeling her scrutiny, he looked up, his disheveled air softening his features. "All done with those?"

"For now. Haven't found anything suspicious, though I'm no accountant."

"You don't need to be an accountant to do what we're doing." Dylan pushed himself away from the table they had set up in the library. " My father just wants us to back up what Dara found about Gabe."

The mention of her brother's name coupled with the irritated tone of Dylan's voice gave Lisa a start.

Lisa took a calming breath. "Why didn't she press charges?"

"My father wouldn't let her. Said he wanted to wait and see how bad the damage really was." Dylan shrugged. "He's a lot more generous than I would have been."

Lisa unconsciously clenched her fists. She said nothing, sure that if she even parted her lips a heated defense of her brother would spill out.

"And now it's time for lunch." Dylan stood. "We'll eat in the kitchen."

Lisa got up and followed him out the door, protesting. "I thought we'd go to a restaurant for lunch." Where she could pay for her own meal and not feel even more indebted to him and his family.

"Why would I want to do that, when all my favorite foods are right here?" Dylan said, and kept walking.

Dylan pulled two plates wrapped in plastic out of the refrigerator and with a flourish set them on the marble countertop. "Madam, lunch is served."

Each plate held a croissant layered with sprouts, cucumber, tomato and cuts of meat. Tucked beside it was a salad made with multicolored leaves garnished with swirls of carrot and fresh peppers.

"How did you do that?" she asked with mock surprise as he rummaged through a cutlery drawer.

"Secret recipe. A little bit of salt, a sprinkle of cilantro and a whole dose of pleading. My mom made them before she left this morning." Dylan unwrapped the plates and set one on the eating bar in front of her. "Pull up a stool and we'll eat," he said as he tucked the napkin and silverware beside her plate.

Lisa held back. Lunch with just the two of them in the house created an awkward intimacy that wouldn't have happened had they eaten at a restaurant.

"Stop hovering. No one is around. We don't have to pretend right now." Dylan sounded slightly peevish.

Lisa tucked her head down as she pulled up the stool. Were her feelings so transparent? "Sorry, I just feel a little out of place here."

"I gathered that."

She glanced sidelong at Dylan as she unfolded her napkin, taking her cue from him.

He caught her glance and tilted her a half smile. "Don't worry, I'm not the praying type."

"But your family certainly seems to be." Lisa thought back to the supper yesterday. There'd been no awkwardness in the after-supper routine. Everyone had seemed at home with it, even Kerry, Ted and Dara, the guests.

"I used to be." He gave a light shrug as if brushing away his past.

"So what happened?"

"Neglect more than anything." He angled his chin toward her. "What about you? You ever go to church?"

She nodded. "When my parents were alive. Yes."

"What made you stop?"

"Their deaths."

Suddenly, to her surprise, she felt Dylan's hand on her arm. But he didn't say anything, and his silence combined with the comforting heaviness of his hand created a surprising bond. His touch was one of solace.

"You still miss them."

"I don't have anyone else." The lie splintered the fragile connection and she pulled away. To cover up, she went on the defensive. "Does your alienation from church have anything to do with your father?"

Dylan sliced through his croissant with one quick movement. "Partly."

"What happened?" Lisa knew she was overstepping the boundary between secretary and boss, but she had eaten with his family, was staying in their home. The boundaries were growing blurrier each minute.

Dylan drew in a long, deep breath, then shook his head. "I'm not going to bother you with the details. I was foolish enough to trust that my own father would keep his word." He was smiling, but the sharp edge in his voice gave lie to the casual face he was putting on the situation. "And let's just say Ted has been proving my misgivings correct ever since."

His ambiguous words made Lisa even more curious. In the short time she'd worked for Dylan she'd sensed he had a steady, solid nature. The kind of man her mother had sought until she found Gabe's father. Dylan's bitterness jarred. Like an off-key note in a harmonious song.

"Is that why you're going to quit?"

"Mostly. I've been waiting too long. It's time I took my life in my own direction." He angled his chin at her lunch. "Now, eat up. We've got a lot of work ahead of us yet before we head out again tonight."

Lisa caught a flash of yellow through the trees and ran out the door to meet the cab, relief sluicing through her.

Though she had told Dylan she would help him out by being his escort at the wedding, she drew the line at accompanying him to the rehearsal and the rehearsal dinner the family was attending this evening. She desperately wanted to connect with Gabe.

She hopped inside the cab, giving the cabbie Gabe's address, and half an hour after they left Dylan's place, they pulled up in front of a dingy apartment building. Lisa's heart sank. Squat, dark apartment blocks flanked her brother's, and beyond that she saw what looked like the industrial section of Vancouver.

For this she had denied herself countless little luxuries, worked overtime and prayed? So that her brother could end up here?

She pressed the button beside her brother's name, and when she heard his heavy voice answering, she knew he had been sleeping.

As she walked up the stained linoleum of the stairs, she heard the sounds of fighting, a stereo thumping out a deadening bass rhythm.

Home sweet home, she thought, knocking on her brother's door. But in spite of the surroundings, her heart rose with the anticipation of seeing Gabe.

The door opened and Lisa stifled a cry of dismay. Gabe's brown hair lay flat on one side of his head and stuck up on the other. He hadn't shaved. His wrinkled T-shirt and jogging pants looked as if he'd slept in them.

"Hey, Lise," he said, running his fingers through his hair, smiling at her. "Great to see you."

He'd known she was coming, she thought as disappointment flared within her. Surely he could have made some attempt at getting ready?

Then he stepped forward and her arms came up and she was holding her little brother close.

"I missed you, sis," he said giving her a bone-crushing hug.

"I missed you, too." Lisa pulled back, running the palm of her hand over his hair as if to neaten it, love and affection warring with her ever-present desire to improve, to make him better than he was.

"Sorry I look like this. I came off a long shift at work yesterday. Slept most of today." His mouth stretched in a yawn, underscoring his comment. "Come on in. I made you some coffee. Just the way you like it."

Lisa couldn't help scanning the living room as they walked through it, thankful to see that the apartment was reasonably tidy.

"I even have cream," Gabe said, holding aloft a small cardboard container.

"Place looks pretty good, Gabe," Lisa said with forced cheer. She pushed aside a stack of newspapers from the table and sat on the kitchen chair, watching her brother working in the kitchen.

"It's not as nice as my other place was, but hey, we know why I can't afford that anymore. I was lucky enough to find a roommate on such short notice." He handed her a cup of coffee and sat down across the table from her. He smoothed his hair and stifled another yawn. "I can't believe you're actually here in Vancouver."

"I certainly didn't think I'd ever be here this soon." She smiled at Gabe, warmth and love enveloping her. "How's your job?"

Gabe shrugged, stretching his arms out. "It's work and it pays the rent."

"Have you been looking…"

"That's why the stack of newspapers," Gabe said abruptly. "But I can't get a job without a reference and I can hardly use Matheson Telecom. So for now I'm stuck selling telephones and trying to pay bills out of minimum wage." His words spilled out in an angry flow. "I know what you did to help me get this degree. The lousy jobs and the lousy bosses." He shoved his hands through his hair in a gesture of frustration. "Sorry. I'm just running out of patience."

"It's okay, Gabe. I've got a good job now."

Gabe drew in a deep breath. "And how is it working for Dylan Matheson? Never met the guy, but from the way Dara talks, he was just a cape away from being a superhero."

Lisa had to smile at Gabe's description. "He's an ordinary guy." More ordinary than her first impression of him. "The job is interesting," Lisa said carefully. "I haven't discovered anything helpful. I did meet Dara and Ted."

"Ted kind of stays in the background. Dara's the real power." Gabe leaned back in his chair, balancing it on two legs. Lisa stifled an automatic reprimand. It was his chair. His apartment. "She's a piece of work, isn't she?"

"What do you mean?"

"The whole time I was working for her I got to hear how she wanted to take care of me. She took me out for supper a bunch of times to ask me how I liked my job." He shook his head in disgust. "Things started looking a little shaky and just like that—" he snapped his fingers "—Gabe Haskell is gone and there's no way I can get a reference."

Lisa fingered the handle of the mug. "Did you ever talk to Alex Matheson?"

"Dara wouldn't let me. Told me he wasn't interested." Gabe rocked his chair a moment, pursing his lips.

"Didn't you suspect something was going on?"

"Why do you think I got fired?" Gabe dropped his chair down.

"Are you saying it was a setup?"

Gabe looked at her as if to say, *you silly girl,* and for a moment Lisa felt like the younger of the two, not the other way around.

"If you knew you were right, why didn't you challenge her?" she asked. "Why didn't you go talk to Ted? To Alex?"

"She wouldn't let me. Told me it would make things

worse." Gabe pushed himself up from the table and turned away from Lisa, his hands on his hips.

"Gabe, what's going on? What happened there?"

"It's a mess, Lisa. And I don't know how to untangle it." He spun around, caught her by the hands. "You've got to prove me innocent. Without a reference to explain my departure I'll never get a job as an accountant again. Especially in this day and age." He squeezed her hands tighter and tighter as his anger built. "Makes me wonder why I should stay honest."

"Don't you even think about it," Lisa warned, squeezing back. "You've seen what happened to your friends in high school. You've got to do things the right way."

"Much good it's done me so far," he snapped.

"Gabe, please listen to me." Lisa caught his face in her hands, his stubble scratching her palms, and unconsciously she sent up another quick prayer for help. "If you're innocent and Ted or Dara have been the ones fooling with the books, it will come out. I'm working on it now. Me and Dylan. He's smart. He'll find out the truth." Her own defense of Dylan surprised her. And as she held Gabe's gaze, she could feel the tension flowing out of him.

Thank You, Lord.

The words came from her past, but in spite of a long mistrust of God, she experienced a moment of thankfulness.

"It will come together. I promise."

Gabe's slow smile seemed to seal her declaration. "You're the best sister I could have asked for, you know?" He returned to his chair and sighed lightly. "I haven't prayed for a long time, but I catch myself wondering if I should. Maybe it will help."

"I don't suppose it can hurt."

"Do you still pray, Lisa?"

Lisa thought of her promise to attend church. "Not like I used to."

"I miss it sometimes. But then I think of my dad. Your mom. Us." He shook his head. "It's just you and me, Lisa. You and me against the world."

She nodded at the words they used to encourage each other when it seemed things were conspiring against them. Teachers, social workers, bosses. How many times had she come home from work, dejected and tired, and Gabe had encouraged her and given her the boost she needed? And how often had she done the same for him?

"You and me, buddy. Always and always."

Dylan ran up the walk to the house, whistling a soft tune. The rehearsal and supper had gone better than expected. Though Lisa hadn't attended, her presence in their home, at the supper last night, had all seemed to serve notice to his family that he was, for the moment, taken.

He unlocked the front door of the house and ran up the stairs. But Lisa wasn't in her room. Nor was she in the study or the TV room, or by the swimming pool in the backyard.

She'd said she was going for a walk. Surely she should have been back by now. Had she gotten lost in the woods behind the property?

He was at the back of the house when he heard a vehicle. By the time he walked around past the front Lisa was unlocking the side door. She wore her hair loose this evening, a bounce of curls on her shoulders. The pink shirt and the faded jeans made her look like a cute teenager.

"Hey, there," he said softly so as not to frighten her.

She whirled around, dropping the key. "Where did you come from? I didn't think you'd be back yet." Her words tumbled out in a welter of confusion.

"I ducked out early," he said, puzzled at her reaction. "I thought you would have been back by now."

As Lisa bent to pick up the key, Dylan could see her hand was trembling.

"Are you okay?" he asked.

"Yah. Sure. I'm fine." She laughed lightly. "Just went out for a little while." She handed him the key. "Here."

"Keep it," he said. "You never know when you'll need it again." He looked at her more carefully. Her cheeks were flushed and she wouldn't look him in the eye. Why was she acting so strangely?

"So the rehearsal went okay?" she asked, zipping her purse shut. "No major disasters?"

"We decided to save those for tomorrow," he said with a grin, hoping to put her at ease. He reached past her and opened the door. "Did you want something to drink?"

She shook her head. "I think I'm going to go to bed."

Dylan stifled a beat of disappointment. He had hoped to spend some casual time with her, away from files and computers and his family.

"I imagine you'll want an early start tomorrow?" she asked as they walked toward the stairs.

"I may be a workaholic, but I'm not that bad. Tomorrow this house is going to be a zoo," he said, inwardly shuddering. "Between my sisters, the hairdressers and the photographers, I don't think we'll find a room to work in, let alone some peace and quiet." He stopped at the bottom of the stairs, his hand resting on the metal newel post.

Lisa took one step up, then half turned. "Does that mean my boss is going to let me sleep in?" she asked with a quick grin.

"Go ahead and try. Chelsea is so wound up, she'll be pacing the halls at first light."

"I can imagine she'd be nervous. That's quite a step she's taking."

Dylan held her gaze, wondering. "You ever come close to that?"

"Getting married?" She laughed. "Not a chance. I've found out the hard way that my stepfather was a rare man. Committed and caring and, even more important, willing to change." She grew quiet, her eyes taking on an inward look.

Dylan couldn't let her comment lie, wondering what she meant by it. "You don't think most men are willing to change?"

Lisa gave him a quick sideways look. "No. I think a lot of men are stubborn and proud."

"I know a lot of women who fit that description, as well."

Lisa shrugged his comment off. "I'm sure. But

somehow in a man the two emotions seem to be more intense." She angled him a quick smile. "And now that you've received your Lisa lecture, I'm really going to bed."

As Dylan watched her sprint up the stairs, disquiet nudged away the pleasure he had felt just moments ago. And he couldn't help but wonder if she was alluding to the situation between him and his father.

He gave the cold metal of the post a quick tap, as if beating down his thoughts. He doubted she gave his family even a second thought.

Chapter Five

Lisa blotted her lips and tried once more to apply her lipstick. She felt like a stuffed doll, dressed up, fluffed up, perfumed and powdered.

The tangerine-hued dress she had chosen had fit the bill perfectly in the surroundings of the upscale clothing store. Reflected back at her from the mirror of the church's bathroom, it looked flamboyant and overly provocative.

Too late to change it now.

Sucking in her breath, Lisa tossed the matching gauzy scarf over her bare shoulders, smoothed down an errant curl and left the bathroom.

As she entered the foyer the first person who caught her eye was a man in a tuxedo. His broad shoulders were emphasized by the dark cut of the jacket. The white shirt set off the dark color of his hair. He looked stunning.

Lisa's heart flipped once slowly as she recognized Dylan, now transformed.

He wasn't smiling as he came walking toward her, and Lisa's second thoughts about the suitability of her dress crowded back.

"You look amazing," he said softly.

Lisa couldn't think of anything to say in return. Nor could she look away.

"I'm supposed to escort you to your seat," he said, taking her hand.

"I thought that was the usher's job," Lisa said, momentarily bereft of coherent thought.

"Orders of the high command. I'm supposed to make you feel as comfortable as possible." His smile eased some of the tension as he drew her hand through the crook of his arm. The practical part of her told her to pull away, keep her distance. But a small corner of her mind, the empty part that she usually kept a lid on, slowly opened and released a gentle yearning for the closeness he offered.

So she let her hand rest on the stiff material of his coat, let her mind acknowledge the warmth of his arm.

He stopped a moment in the vestibule of the church and Lisa felt her heart flutter again.

The front of the church was a mass of pink Asian lilies and white roses, accented with draped netting. Candles flickered from holders flanking the arrangement. The end of each pew was decorated with swags of chiffon and lilies. Accenting all this splendor was a string quartet, their quiet strains of classical music adding an understated sophistication.

Elegantly expensive.

"I'm guessing I'm supposed to put you on the bride's

side of the church," Dylan said, scratching the side of
his head in mock puzzlement, unaffected by the display
in front of him.

"Seeing as how I know her name and not the groom's,
that would be the logical choice." Lisa found her voice
and grabbed at her sense of humor to keep her fear at
bay. The Matheson home should have been enough to
show her how much money they had compared to her
and Gabe. This "simple" wedding underscored it.

Dylan led her to an empty spot a few pews back
from the front of the church. As she sat down, he leaned
over her, a hand on the pew in front of her and beside
her. She felt sheltered by his hovering presence.

"Are you going to be okay by yourself?" His gentle
half smile nudged her heartbeat up a notch.

To cover up her reaction she flashed him a bright
smile and nodded. He waited a moment, as if he was
going to say something further. Then he pushed himself
away and left.

Lisa forced down a knot of panic, fiddling with the
clasp on her purse.

You and me against the world. Gabe's words came
back to her, and panic fluttered in her chest once again
as she looked around at the perfection that surrounded
her. The world she and Gabe were against.

What if Gabe was wrong about these people? What
if he *had* stolen the money and she was lying to Dylan's
family for nothing?

She had to believe her brother, she thought, clutching the purse with damp hands. Gabe had no reason to
lie to her.

Except he had done it before.

Lisa's mouth felt suddenly dry as doubts piled on questions.

Gabe wasn't perfect. Neither was she. And Gabe was all she had. She had to fight for him. For now that meant she had to believe him and she had to stay focused on her plans.

In time the pew beside her filled with other people she didn't know, the women's perfumes blending with the scent of the abundance of flowers in the front of the church.

After a while the music changed, a photographer hustled to the front of the church and a rustling through the gathering signaled the beginning of the ceremony.

One of the ushers led the groom's parents down the aisle and sat them down on the other side. After that, Dylan made another entrance, escorting his mother. He sat Stephanie down, his hand resting on her shoulder. He leaned over, talking to her. Stephanie looked up at him, covered his hand with hers and smiled up at her son, her pride evident on her face.

As Dylan turned back, he glanced at Lisa and gave her a quick wink.

It wasn't supposed to mean anything, but combined with the obvious love he had for his mother and his consideration a few moments ago, it created a surge of confusion.

A few moments later a side door near the front of the church opened and the groom, Jordan Strachan, and his attendants filed in, standing in a precise row at the front. Lisa wasn't going to look at Dylan, but it was as if her eyes had their own will and were drawn to his tall figure.

To her consternation, he was looking back at her.

Then the tempo of the music changed again, the congregation shifted and from many of the pews camera bulbs flashed as Amber, the first of the five attendants, came walking down the aisle, wearing a plain navy blue sheath. Silver and cream ribbons were wound around her neck, fluttering far down her back. Simple, thought Lisa, yet formal, setting off to perfection the bouquets of pale pink lilies.

Then, after the last of the attendants were assembled at the front, a hushed murmur flowed through the church, the music swelled and the congregation rose.

Lisa turned to watch Chelsea, now transformed from the bubbly young woman she had met to the classic, blushing bride. Her eyes shone with a happiness that Lisa knew she had never felt. For a moment she felt a clutch of jealousy.

Jordan came forward to take Chelsea from her father, and they exchanged a look that radiated absolute love.

Lisa swallowed down a sudden swelling in her throat, caught up in the purity of their emotions. When she saw Alex kiss his daughter and take his place by his wife she bit her lip to stop its trembling. A storm of odd feelings swirled through her. Even if one were to take away all the exterior trappings of this wedding, Lisa instinctively knew that the happiness and joy she saw now would be as strong in twenty-five years.

Thankfully the minister came to the front and gently

put the nervous couple at ease, moving easily from slightly jocular to more serious as he opened his Bible.

"Jordan and Chelsea have chosen Ecclesiastes 4, the second half of verse 12. 'A cord of three strands is not quickly broken.' Knowing Jordan and Chelsea, I find this verse especially appropriate. The two of them have asked to stand before God and His people to be married. Their marriage is not just Jordan and Chelsea, but Jordan, Chelsea and their Lord, whom they love and serve. A powerful cord of three strands."

As the minister spoke he elaborated on the strength they would receive, as well, from their family. From their community of believers.

The words created a subtle attraction. Gabe's father, Rick, and Lisa's mother, Trish, had enjoyed such a relationship. Their faith had been the cord that bound their family together.

So why had God taken them from her? If God was such a loving God, how did He allow the threefold cord to break?

The memory of her loss jolted her back to reality. She forced herself to think of why she was here. To figure out how she was supposed to exonerate her brother. Lisa turned back to the minister as he wound up his address to the couple, inviting them to speak their vows.

Chelsea's shining eyes, her future husband's stirring words, as he spoke vows they had made up themselves, came across as so authentic and heartfelt.

Though she hardly knew them, Lisa found herself wanting to believe this couple would find their happy ever after. And why not? Lisa thought. Chelsea had a good example in her parents.

Stephanie and Alex had held hands the entire service. Stephanie had brushed away a few tears, and to Lisa's surprise, so had Dylan's father.

Lisa's eyes strayed once more to Dylan. He stood one level below the bridal couple, his hands clasped in front of him, his expression serious as he watched his younger sister pledge her life to her husband.

Dylan was just her boss and a means to an end. But the more she watched him from the safety of the church pew, the more attractive he became. The way he tilted his head down and to the side as he listened. The indentation his mouth created when he smiled his now-familiar half smile. How the light seemed lost in the dark of his hair. He looked even more handsome than the groom, and Lisa couldn't help a stirring of pride in her escort.

At precisely that moment Dylan shifted, caught her eye. Once again their gazes meshed and held, and Lisa felt a faint longing.

"So what God has joined together, let not man put asunder." The preacher's voice boomed out, authority and conviction ringing in the words, echoing in the vastness of the church building. The minister's words yanked Lisa out of the dangerous zone she had slipped into.

Dylan was temporary, she reminded herself, quickly averting her gaze. He needed her and she needed him. Strictly business.

The rest of the service went by in a blur. Lisa could

hardly wait until it was over. She couldn't control the ebb and flow of her emotions. From yearning to loss to anger to yearning once again. It was tiring and it had to stop.

Finally the organ started up its joyful celebration music and Chelsea caught the hand of her new husband. With happy smiles and a few waves at people in the audience, they started down the aisle.

And once again Lisa couldn't keep her eyes off Dylan. The crisp white shirt and dark coat were perfect foils for his dark hair and startling gray-blue eyes. He looked like a movie star, she thought as he walked down the aisle. Then he turned, caught her eye, smiled and was gone.

As the family filed out, Lisa was pulled into the wake, Tiffany's husband alongside her. While they walked out, he pointed out various members of the family he seemed to think Dylan's escort should know.

She was part of the family and yet not.

Stop this right now. Lisa clenched her fists, as if squeezing the falsely beguiling thoughts away. She wasn't a part of this and would never be. Especially not if they found out who she really was—the sister of "that accountant."

Thankfully there was no receiving line, and as she walked out of the church into the warm summer air, she saw Dylan waiting for her.

His smile widened as he caught sight of her.

"There you are," he said softly as he came to her side. "We have to go get pictures taken at the studio. Come with me."

His voice was pitched low, his last three words sounding like an intimate invitation. Lisa didn't want to read more into them than mere convenience, but the peculiar feeling that had gripped her in church would not be dispelled.

"Surely I don't need to come?"

Dylan shrugged, shook his head, his eyes holding hers. "It would just make things easier. After that we go straight to the reception, so you may as well come with me."

Lisa nodded, forcing herself to look away from his mesmerizing gaze. It was the startling contrast of those gray-blue eyes and dark eyebrows and hair that always caught her attention. Like a puzzling surprise that needed further investigation to figure out.

Not because she was falling for him. Not at all.

The twins had found a ride with a friend, so Dylan and Lisa rode by themselves to the photography studio. Lisa kept thinking of the ceremony she had just witnessed. Dylan was quietly whistling one of the songs from the service.

Being Dylan's escort had seemed so simple back in Toronto. It had been easier to think of this all in the abstract rather than the concrete. In her life she had much experience with coming and going into other families, so she'd thought this would be much the same.

Until she'd seen Dylan greeted with a hug from his mother. Until she'd sat through a church wedding that was more than just a tradition, more than an idle gesture. Sincere prayers had been spoken, heartfelt songs had been sung. In spite of Dylan's distance from his father, she saw a love for God that spanned generations. Grandparents from both sides of each family were there. Aunts, uncles and cousins.

This was a family with a history of togetherness and faith.

"You're pretty quiet," Dylan said finally as they followed the limousine into the parking lot of the photography studio.

"Tired, I think," she said, unable to look at him. She felt as if she had put herself out on a limb, first taking on the job, then meeting his family. Each move, each event pushed her further and further out to a world she had to negotiate with care. If they knew about Gabe…

And she had a whole week to get through yet.

It's just a game, she thought. Just play it through till the end.

She was about to get out of the car when Dylan caught her arm.

"Lisa, just a minute," he said, his voice quiet.

With a frown she turned to him, wondering what he might want to say.

"I want to thank you for doing this for me. You really have no idea what you've saved me from." He smiled, and Lisa felt again that unwelcome nudge of attraction.

"Not a problem, Dylan." She glanced at him, affecting a breezy air. "I got a taste of what you were in for the other night at suppertime."

Dylan angled his head to one side, as if studying her. "I also want to thank you for all the extra time you've put in."

"I'm not phoning the labor relations board yet."

Dylan laughed. "I wish I had your ability to turn things into a joke." He leaned back against his window, as if settling in for a heart-to-heart chat.

Something Lisa didn't have the defenses for now. "You know the saying 'Laugh and the world laughs with you. Cry and you'll end up on an afternoon talk show.'" She winked at him, hoping she could keep this up.

"You've got this tough exterior," he said. "Yet I get a feeling that's due to hurt layered beneath."

Lisa's heart wanted to believe that what she would say mattered to him. Her yearnings for family had often included someone exactly like Dylan. But she knew the reality of the situation. She needed him to find out the truth about her brother. She couldn't afford to let him into her life. Couldn't open the tiniest crack to him.

Yet, yet…

"Everyone has some hurt in their life," she conceded quietly, giving him the few crumbs she dared. Then she dared a little more. "I know you have."

Dylan rubbed the bridge of his nose and sighed. "What do you mean?"

Lisa had gotten too far to quit now. "Your father. You. Ted. Today I saw a family that has solidity. Harmony. Except for a few harsh notes."

He turned back to her and gave her a careful smile. "And you care because…?" He angled his head to one side.

"Because I don't have a family," she said quietly, her defenses worn down by the ceremony she had just witnessed. By Dylan's nearness. "Because I would give all I have for even a small part of what you have in your family."

"That's important to you?"

"What is rare becomes precious." Lisa stopped the words flowing out of the lonely place.

"I think people in your life have let you down, too." He caught her hand, tugging on it.

She couldn't allow this to happen, she warned herself. She couldn't start allowing him in. Because what would she have when they went their separate ways? What she had before. Only Gabe.

"Actually, there have been a lot of people in my life. A superb and varied cast." She pulled away from him with a light laugh. "Too bad I haven't quite figured out the plot." With a twist of her wrist she had the door open and she was outside. Two quick breaths and equilibrium was restored.

She closed her eyes, pressed her lips together as she pulled into herself and the secret place she retreated to when her life was being taken apart by psychiatrists and social workers.

Take care of yourself. Take care of Gabe, she repeated as she mentally wrapped her layers of protection around herself.

You and me against the world.

The photographs took longer than the hour Dylan had promised and Lisa had to endure the subtle torment of seeing Dylan under selected lighting posing with his family, his sister. With each flash of the photographer's bulb, each new pose, she found herself watching him more and more.

It's just the tuxedo, she thought. It gave him a distinguished air that showed her a man who was at ease with himself no matter the circumstances. A man who could smile away the teasing of his family, who could give as good as he got without any rancor or anger.

Finally the last pose was held, the last photo snapped. Lisa slipped on her sandals and stood, brushing her dress down in anticipation of leaving.

"Wait a minute." Chelsea motioned to Lisa and her heart sank. Surely Chelsea didn't want her in the family picture? "I think Dylan and Lisa should get their picture taken. We've never had one of Dylan and a girlfriend." Chelsea caught Dylan by the arm, bringing him to the center of the studio with a swish of her taffeta dress. "C'mon, Lisa."

Lisa held back, her eyes darting to Dylan, pleading with him silently. They couldn't do this. It was a farce.

Dylan tried to talk his way out of it, but soon the other sisters joined the chorus. He turned to Lisa and with a shrug held out his hand to her.

She had no choice but to join him.

"That looks great," the photographer enthused. "The colors of that dress with the tux. Superb." He walked over to them and pushed them closer together. "Put your hand on her shoulder, the other on her waist." Dylan obliged and Lisa fought the urge to push it off. She felt exposed, standing here with him in the circle of light, surrounded by his family.

"Okay…Lisa, is it?"

Lisa felt Dylan's hand squeeze her shoulder and she looked up, realizing she hadn't paid attention.

"Lisa, put your opposite hand on Dylan's hand at your waist. Now lean back, just a bit. Dylan, you come forward."

Lisa could feel Dylan's breath teasing the hair at her temple, could feel the heaviness of his hands on her shoulder and waist.

"Smile for the camera, Lisa," Dylan whispered in her ear.

"This is silly," she whispered back.

"Just play along," he replied, the hand at her waist squeezing her lightly. "We don't need to keep the pictures." He caught her fingers through his and pulled her ever so gently closer.

"That's great," the photographer said. "Just great."

Lights flashed and Lisa started.

"Just a couple more." More flashes.

They were posed again, this time face-to-face.

"Look at each other with a big smile," they were encouraged.

Lisa didn't want to look up into his eyes again. Didn't want to feel herself slowly being drawn into his personality, himself.

Love at first sight was only for fairy tales and people who couldn't think for themselves.

Everything is just a game, she reminded herself as she lifted her chin. And you know the rules. She had to act like a loving escort. Had to treat him as if he was special. He was technically her boss, after all.

But as Dylan looked down at her, she found herself wondering how she was going to manage to treat this whole thing like a game for six more days.

* * *

Dylan took a quick gulp of punch, looking around at the hall where the reception was being held. Fountains and gorgeous tall centerpieces, flowers and netting decorated the elegant room. All around him people laughed and joked. In the middle of the dance floor couples moved to the rhythm of the music.

He'd done his duty dance with the bridesmaid, his sisters, his mother and a few aunts. He'd caught up with some uncles and a few cousins who had waylaid him a couple of times.

And thanks to his duties, he still hadn't had a chance to dance with Lisa. She was supposed to be with him, yet it seemed that she had danced with everyone but him.

As Dylan watched, the young man she was dancing with caught her hand and pulled her close to tell her something. Lisa listened, then pulled back, laughing.

Dylan knew he had nothing to be jealous of. Lisa was just here for his convenience. He would be foolish to deny Lisa a good time, but he didn't think she needed to be having that much fun.

Especially when he didn't feel as if he was. Her words in the car about his family had found a home. He knew he had to fix what was wrong in his relationships, but how could he when his misgivings about Ted had been proven beyond a doubt? The fact that he was here trying to untangle the mess created under Ted's leadership should prove to his father conclusively that he had made a mistake.

Yet Alex said nothing. Did nothing.

And spending this much time with his family un-

derscored the distance between him and his father. He
was surrounded by family and friends, yet he felt completely alone.

He didn't have to be. Amber and Erika had been won-
derfully prudent, though they had each taken along a
couple of friends. Not once in the course of the evening,
however, had they approached him or introduced him to
any of their girlfriends. Not once had he been forced to
dance with a giddy young girl whose breathless conversation was sprinkled with *like*s and *you know*s.

Lisa's presence was doing exactly what he had hoped
it would. The wedding he had been dreading was
turning out just fine. So why wasn't he feeling happier?

"Hey, Dylan." His father's brother, Anton
Matheson, caught him by the arm, turning him around.
"How are you, boy?"

Dylan grinned at his uncle and allowed himself to be
drawn into a hearty hug. Anton was shorter than Dylan
by a head, but he exuded a force of will that made him
seem a foot taller. Anton pulled away, his dark eyes
piercing Dylan's. "So how are you really?"

The shift in his uncle's tone moved the conversation from a casual give-and-take to the shakier territory of emotions.

"It was a lovely ceremony."

Anton nodded, the overhead lights glinting off his shiny
forehead. "I heard you're quitting. Leaving the company?"

"It's time to move on. I'm not going anywhere."

Anton's slow smile disappeared into the wiry brush
of his mustache. "I'm sorry to hear that. I'm sure your
father is even more so."

Annoyance twitched through him. "Truthfully, Uncle Anton, I think this makes things a whole lot easier for my father. He can keep Ted in charge without any guilt."

"I think your father is struggling with his own regrets."

Dylan tugged at his tie, feeling suddenly restricted by it. "I wouldn't know. I haven't heard much from him."

Anton nodded, brushing his index finger over his mustache. "Pride is a strong Matheson trait. You might have to make the first move."

"I have." Dylan tossed down the last of his punch, stifling his annoyance. His uncle didn't need to be treated to a display of family disunity.

Anton caught Dylan's angry gaze, a soft smile playing around his lips. "Your father does care about you."

Dylan put his cup down and leaned forward. "Uncle Anton, I really appreciate that you're trying to do this, but I've given all I can as far as my father is concerned. I've come to help the company. Not him. And if my father is really concerned about our relationship, then I would say it's up to him to do something about it."

Dylan felt the anger leave him as he spoke.

Anton nodded. "I know what you're saying, Dylan. And you're right. Now let's talk about something pleasant. Maybe that lovely young woman you're with. Tell me some more about her."

Dylan glanced at the dance floor where Lisa was laughing at something her partner was saying.

"Her name is Lisa."

Anton nodded, and Dylan could almost hear his smirk. "She's beautiful."

Dylan didn't have to echo that remark. But it made him uncomfortable to talk to his dear uncle about a relationship that was strictly for convenience.

It made him feel guilty. As if he was using Lisa.

Lisa and the man on the dance floor made another twirl, and thankfully the music came to an end.

"Well, here's my chance to dance with her, Uncle Anton. I'll catch you later."

Anton waved him off. "Go. Enjoy yourself."

Couples drifted off the dance floor as Dylan walked toward Lisa. With a surge of relief Dylan watched as Lisa shook her head, obviously declining another dance. Then, turning, she walked straight to him.

"Did you have a good time?"

"I've had more fun at the dentist," she muttered, keeping her smile intact.

Dylan couldn't help but laugh, surprised at the relief he felt at her annoyance. "He couldn't have been that bad—you danced two dances with him."

"He didn't understand the meaning of the word *no.*" Lisa shook her head. "Maybe he's dyslexic."

"He's my cousin."

Lisa stopped, looked away and then back at him with a shrug. "Sorry. I didn't know."

"Can't pick your relatives."

"Oh, the joys of splashing in the gene pool."

Dylan laughed out loud as pleasure spiraled up in him, replacing his earlier melancholy.

The music changed tempo, the lights dimmed and

Dylan glanced at the dance floor. Couples were moving closer together. In the middle he saw his sister Chelsea with her new husband, her arms clasped around his neck. He saw his parents, Tiffany and her husband.

Everyone paired up. Belonging to someone.

"Can I have this dance?" he asked, looking back at Lisa.

"I'm not very good at slow dances," she said with a light laugh.

"It's not hard. Just follow my lead."

"I'm not much good at doing that, either."

"Try," Dylan urged. He caught her hand and took a step toward the dance floor, smiling encouragement at Lisa.

With a laugh she finally gave in. Then they were on the floor, facing each other.

"Do we have to pretend to be a devoted couple?" Lisa asked with a touch of irony in her voice.

"No, but you can pretend you're having a good time." Dylan pushed down his disappointment at her response. He caught her hand in his, slipped his arm around her waist.

"I don't know if I can rise to the occasion," she said, flashing him a teasing grin. "But I can slide over to it."

"Then you'd be dancing," he replied, laughing, thankful once again for the equilibrium her sense of humor created.

However, when he pulled her closer, Dylan drew in a slow breath, feeling a release from the tension of the past few hours.

It was like coming home, he thought, turning slowly in time to the music. As if everything crazy in his life suddenly made sense with Lisa in his arms.

It was ridiculous to think that a girl he had just met could mean anything to him. And, even more, she was his employee. He blamed his feelings on the corny sentiments that single people often felt at weddings.

But the litany of practical phrases couldn't explain the absolute rightness of having her in his arms.

He held her, beguiled by her touch, the faint scent of the shampoo in her hair. She wore no perfume, no other fragrance, yet he caught the fragile scent that he now recognized as peculiar to Lisa.

All too soon the dance was over, the lights came up and the moment drifted away with the last haunting notes of the music. Lisa didn't look up at him as she slowly straightened. Her fingers trailed down the lapels of his coat. Had she felt it, too?

Dylan wanted to say something, to deepen the connection they had just experienced.

Then, finally, she glanced up at him, her eyes sparkling with mischief. "Don't look so somber, Dylan. Life is too serious to be taken seriously." She tapped her fingers on his chest, then pulled away. Dylan scowled at her, disappointment spiraling tightly through him. How could she so casually dismiss what had just happened? Hadn't she felt it, as well?

"I'm going to freshen up my lipstick," she said, taking a step back. "Thanks for the dance."

As she turned and walked away, annoyance twisted through him. Lately little satisfied him anymore.

Chapter Six

A sliver of light played across Lisa's eyelids, pulling her out of the half-sleeping state she had drifted in and out of for the past hour.

She glanced at the clock beside her bed. Six-thirty.

She wouldn't be able to sleep anymore, even though fatigue still pressed down on her. The party last night hadn't wound down until three-thirty. Then she had stayed with the rest of the family, cleaning up what they could and loading up the presents in the van hired for the purpose.

She was still tired, but hoped to spend some time this morning without Dylan around. Hoped to ease the jangling in her nerves that had started last night when Dylan had held her in his arms. She had tried to rationalize her reaction, but couldn't get past the part of her that had responded to him.

Thankfully the bathroom was unoccupied, so she had a quick shower. She slipped on a pair of loose-fitting pants and topped it with a T-shirt. Dylan had declared that they would take the morning off, but she hoped to get in a few undisturbed hours of work in spite of that. It would remind her why she was here.

She crept down the carpeted stairs, pausing a moment outside the study. The lonely echo of a dripping kitchen tap was the only sound to break the utter stillness of a house asleep. She felt like a burglar.

Suppressing a shiver of guilt, Lisa let herself into the study. In a matter of moments she had the computer booted up and the files she needed laid out on the table. She glanced at her careful notes to get herself up to speed and started the methodical work she had begun before the wedding.

In spite of the emotional investment she had tied up in this work, she found a peculiar serenity in the tediousness of the matching process, and soon her agitated spirits were soothed.

The muted bonging of the grandfather clock in the corner marked off the hour. Startled, Lisa looked up at the time. Eight o'clock and still no sounds drifted down from the bedrooms upstairs.

Lisa rolled her shoulders, and as she looked around the room she gave in to the lure of the bookshelves crammed full. Just a moment, she promised herself. A break.

But as her fingers trailed along the spines of the novels, she felt the pull of familiar titles—classics and modern novels that had at one time granted her solace either from the tedium of a boring job or the stress of the responsibility of raising Gabe.

She moved along and was confronted by a section

of nonfiction books. And from the sounds of the titles, all of them Christian books.

Books by theologians jostled modern books promising help and guidance for life's various circumstances.

A Bible lay on its side on one of the shelves and Lisa picked it up. To put it away, she told herself. But she couldn't find an empty space for it.

So she held it, her fingers lightly tracing the embossing on the cover. She flipped it open and glanced down the pages, the familiar words drawing up memories from another period in her life.

Lisa ran her finger down the pages as if touching the words made them more real. She knew the patterns and rhythms. Once they had been a part of her life; once they had given her comfort. She started reading.

"'How lovely is Your dwelling place….'" She whispered the words of Psalm eighty-four, the phrases part of a life left behind when she and Gabe had walked away from the graveyard as orphans.

But the words created a yearning she had long suppressed. "'Better is one day in Your courts than a thousand elsewhere.'" The language was dated, but it dived deep into her heart. And she remembered the promise she had made when she'd prayed her foolish prayer in Dylan's office. To attend church.

"Excuse me."

The voice at the door scattered the emotions of the moment and she slapped the Bible shut, laying it on the shelf in front of her.

She turned to face Dylan's father as he entered the

study, her heart fluttering with guilt. "I'm sorry. I didn't mean to intrude."

"Don't apologize." Alex smiled carefully at her and lowered himself into one of the leather chairs flanking the fireplace. "Our home is yours as long as you are here." He indicated the sofa diagonally across from him. "Sit down a moment." Alex let his head drop against the back of the chair, but kept his eyes on Lisa. "Are you enjoying your stay here?"

She nodded as she sank into the soft leather of the couch, once again aware of the kindly warmth this man exuded.

"You and Dylan…" He paused, then smiled at her. "How long have you been dating?"

Lisa held Alex's gaze, her emotions in turmoil. Though this man had been involved in what had happened with her brother, she remembered his warm welcome. The connection she felt with him that she couldn't simply pass off. She was surprised no one had asked the question sooner. But the ruse she and Dylan were playing was Dylan's secret to keep and to divulge.

"Our relationship has been somewhat ephemeral," she said, the vagueness of her words making her wince inwardly. Nerves always brought out the long words.

"I see." Alex nodded, a smile playing around lips identical in shape to those of his son's. "In spite of that, Dylan seemed quite attentive to you when you were dancing."

Lisa couldn't stop the flush that warmed her cheeks. She chose silence as her answer. Anything she said would either accuse her or make her look as if she was making excuses.

"You'll have to excuse my bluntness," Alex said, his fingers doing a light dance on the armrest of his chair. "Though we've just met, I have a good feeling about you. You're the first girlfriend of Dylan's that the family has ever met."

Lisa felt even more of a fraud.

"I guess what I'm trying in my clumsy way to say is, I still hope he'll find someone good," he continued. "That one of my boys will make good choices." His voice seemed tinged with regret.

Lisa assumed he referred to Ted and wondered what his vague comment meant.

"I've only known Dylan a few weeks, but I think you can trust him to do that," she said quietly.

Alex raised his head at her defense of his son, his eyes lighting up. "Dylan is a man of principle and values. I haven't always been fair with him."

Lisa thought of how Dylan's voice grew harsh whenever he talked about Alex. She shouldn't care what happened between them.

But as she looked at Alex she couldn't help but remember how he and his wife had held hands during their daughter's wedding. How he had glanced at his wife a few times with such obvious love in his eyes.

"But you are a good father," she said softly. "And Dylan can be thankful for such good parents."

"I understand your parents are dead. I'm sorry to hear that."

"They died a while ago. I was fifteen."

"So young. How did you manage?"

"I was always kind of independent." In spite of her

casual words, she felt a warm glow at his concern. What she wouldn't have given for even a scrap of what Dylan had with his family.

"I sensed you were a woman of strength. But I want you to know that as long as you and Dylan are together, this family is yours, too."

Lisa held his gaze, and to her surprise she felt her eyes tear up. Alex had given her more than a scrap. He had given her everything he had.

She looked away, unable to speak.

As if sensing her discomfort Alex pushed himself away from the chair and walked over to the table. "Have you and Dylan made any headway on this problem?"

His tact gave her a chance to quickly wipe away the moisture from her eyes. "It's too early yet," she said, thankful that she sounded more composed than she felt. "All we've been doing is matching invoices to vendors…." Her voice trailed off as she hesitated over her next suggestion. "What I really think you need to do is hire an external auditor to take care of this."

Alex waved off her suggestion, then picked up a file and thumbed through it. "Maybe later. But right now I prefer to keep this internal until we find out for sure what that accountant has done."

"That accountant" happened to be her brother. The words were a chilling reminder of where she secretly stood in this family.

On the opposite side.

A sudden edginess propelled her off the couch. "If you'll excuse me, I'm going to go back to my room," she said.

Alex glanced up at her, smiling again as if he hadn't heard the tight tone of her voice. "Breakfast is very casual this morning. Our housekeeper put a few things out on the buffet in the dining room, so please help yourself."

"Thank you."

"I should let you know, as well, that most of the family will be leaving for church at about ten-thirty. Just so you don't think we're deserting you."

Lisa felt a jolt of disappointment that he automatically assumed she would be staying behind. At one time she would have gone. Her eyes slid past him to the Bible on the shelf.

Whatever your lips utter you must be sure to do.

"I was wondering…" She drew in a shaky breath, then plunged ahead. "I was wondering if it would be possible to come along?"

Alex's head snapped up. Then with a half smile reminiscent of Dylan's he nodded. "That would be wonderful. We'll let you know half an hour before we leave."

She returned his smile, then walked out of the study. But a sudden restlessness made her turn toward the dining room instead of up to her bedroom.

As promised, the buffet along the wall held a glass-covered plate of assorted muffins, a carafe of coffee, plates of fruit. She was still alone, so Lisa took her plate of food out onto the deck. Wicker chairs were pulled up to a glass table; Lisa sat down in one of them.

A soft breeze sifted up the hill, swishing through the fir trees bordering the property. Below her, softened by the early-morning haze, lay the inlet and the city of

Vancouver. Lisa couldn't help a wry smile as she buttered her muffin. You fraud, she thought, taking a bite. Acting as if this is so natural.

Only a week ago she had been sitting on a completely different balcony, staring directly at the apartment block only a few meters across the alley from hers, also eating a muffin. Only, hers was plain bran, picked up from the day-old bakery section of the convenience store close to her apartment.

This one had a hint of mango and spices she couldn't identify. Gourmet muffin, she thought, taking another pleasurable bite, eaten on the balcony of a gourmet home.

"So, here's where you're hiding."

Lisa spun around, almost upsetting the plate on her lap.

Dylan stood behind her, shoulders hunched, his hands in the pockets of his blue jeans. His shirt was unbuttoned, revealing a T-shirt underneath. His feet were bare.

Lisa felt her heart do a slow flip, his casual dress affecting her just as much as his formal dress of yesterday had.

"You've finally decided to get up?" she asked, covering her reaction to him by turning back to her breakfast.

"Finally? I've only gotten about five hours' sleep." He pushed himself away from the wall and walked over to the table. "How's the food?"

"Superlative."

"Most people would just say good," he said with a grin. He dropped into the chair across from her, propping his ankle on his knee as he massaged his neck. His hair was still damp from his shower. "What are your plans?"

Lisa wiped her mouth, wondering what his reaction would be. "I'm going to church with your family."

Dylan did a double take. "Church? Why?"

Lisa felt suddenly self-conscious. "I used to when I was younger."

"Do you feel you need to confess something?" Dylan asked, slanting her a playful grin.

He's just joking, Lisa reminded herself, pushing down the flare of shame his words kindled in her. "I just feel like attending church," she said, setting her knife across her plate. She couldn't eat any more.

"That would leave me on my own." Dylan almost pouted. "I guess I'll have to come along."

"Surely you don't have to keep up this devoted couple thing?" Lisa protested. Spending every waking moment with him was making it too hard to maintain her professional distance.

Dylan shrugged and picked up an uneaten strawberry from her plate. "Maybe I want to go, too?" he said, popping the strawberry into his mouth.

"I can hardly stop you." She stood up, brushing the few wayward crumbs from her pants, and picked up her plate.

"Wait a minute." He caught her lightly by the wrist and took the other strawberry from her plate.

"Why don't you get your own?" she said with a nervous laugh. His fingers were warm. If it hadn't been for the plate she held so precariously, she would have pulled her hand back.

"Not that hungry," he said, licking his fingers. He looked up at her, his hand still shackling her wrist. "Did you have a good time last night?"

She nodded and gently reclaimed her arm. "You have a wonderful family." It was easier to talk about his family than the dance they'd shared. Or how for the rest of the night whenever they were apart her eyes had found and followed him. "I had a nice chat with your father in the study this morning."

"Did you, now." Dylan squinted up at her, rocking lightly in his chair.

Lisa thought of the pain she saw on Alex's face each time Dylan turned away from him. "I like your father, Dylan."

Dylan's laugh was without humor. "And I think he likes you. Too bad you're just my secretary."

It was the truth and it shouldn't have hurt. But it did.

"I better get ready," she said softly, turning away. To her dismay, however, Dylan followed her.

One of the twins sat at the table, hunched over a section of the newspaper, eating a bagel. She was wrapped in a fuzzy bathrobe, her wet hair slicked back from her face.

"Hey, Amber," Dylan said, tousling her hair. "Get all the hair spray out?"

Amber tilted her head backward to look up at her brother. "Barely. What about you?"

Dylan gave her hair a light tug. "I don't use that girly stuff."

"Really? Then why is most of Erika's pomade gone?" She turned around, grinning at him. "She said you borrowed it."

Dylan just shrugged off her comment and pulled up a chair. Amber glanced at Lisa, her smile growing. "Not only that, he used my blow-dryer. I think he was just trying to impress you, Lisa. Dylan hardly ever fusses with his hair."

Lisa didn't think the comment required a response, and Dylan was paging through the newspaper, patently ignoring his little sister.

"I'm going to get ready," Lisa said.

Amber frowned up at Lisa. "Ready for what?"

"I'm coming to church with you and your family. If that's okay."

Amber scratched her cheek with her forefinger, looking disheartened. "Yeah. I guess."

"If it's a problem…"

"No, that's not it. It was just that Erika and I…" She flipped her hand Lisa's way. "Never mind."

"It's just you had plans?" Dylan asked without looking up. "Inviting someone to come along, perhaps?"

Amber's blush verified Dylan's comment, and Lisa stifled a laugh. A person had to give the girls marks for persistence.

"I'll be ready in a while, Dylan," Lisa said, her hand brushing his shoulder in a subtle proprietary motion. A silent signal to Amber.

Now Dylan looked up. Then he smiled as he realized what she was doing. "I'll be waiting," he said, catching her hand. He squeezed it, and when Lisa tried to pull it back he held it for just a split second longer, then let her go.

Lisa felt her cheeks grow warm, and she regretted her

impulse. But by the time she was back in her room, her heartbeat had returned to normal.

She pulled out a cheerfully embroidered peasant blouse and a denim skirt, hoping they were suitable for church. Neither her mother nor Rick had fussed much about clothes when they'd attended, but had emphasized respect and modesty in their choice of clothing.

As Lisa styled her hair, she thought of those Sunday mornings. Remembered the gentle chaos of getting four people to one place at the same time, neatly dressed and clean. Then the church service and the feeling of reverence and awe blended with the presence of God's love that came from worshiping with fellow believers.

It was a wonderful time of her life. Something she wanted for herself and her children.

Something that Dylan's family had.

Cued by the minister, Dylan and the rest of the congregation sat down. As Dylan sat, he took another quick glance at Lisa, who was still clutching the hymnal they had just sung from. Her head was bent and her hair, worn loose this morning, hid her face. She seemed to be intently reading from the hymnal.

When she had told him this morning that she wanted to go to church, he couldn't have been more surprised than if she had asked to go to a bar. Granted, he didn't know her that well, but he'd assumed that church and faith were not important to her.

They weren't important to him, either. As he had told Lisa, it wasn't anything big and dramatic that had caused his slide away from faith and church. Moving to Toronto, away from his family, had been the first step. Working six days a week to prove himself had been the second. Sunday had been his only day off, and he'd started resenting getting up early to go to church. He'd begun to date girls who had nothing to do with church and zero interest in matters of faith. And slowly his church attendance had eased off to nothing.

He used to feel guilty on the Sunday mornings he was up early for the occasional meeting or a flight out of town, but that had passed, as well.

It was sad how easy it had been to drift away, he thought. Now that he was here, he was sorry he had cut out this part of his life.

Dylan pulled the Bible out of the rack and turned to the passage announced by the minister.

"'How lovely is Your dwelling place, O Lord almighty. Better is one day in Your courts than a thousand elsewhere.'"

To his surprise, Dylan felt a throb of guilt, edged with sorrow. He had missed all this, he thought, following the words with his index finger as the minister read them. The words drew back old memories—of happier times when he and his brother were friends, not enemies. When they were both unaware of the words *favoritism, injustice.* When they weren't in competition for their father's affection.

Dylan read on, allowing the words to gently dislodge memories of better times.

And how could they go back to that?

He was quitting the company to strike out on his own. Under Ted's guidance the company that his father had started and was hoping to ease away from was starting to unravel.

And he and his father and his brother spoke to each other only when necessary.

He closed the Bible before the minister finished reading and slipped it back in the holder with a hollow *thunk*. He didn't want to read about family unity and respect anymore. Right now he didn't have a lot of respect for his father and his lack of backbone. And his frustration with his brother hardly promoted family unity.

He was actually thankful to his father right now for asking him to come and help figure out what had happened to the company. Up until now he'd been still having second thoughts about leaving Matheson Telecom.

He didn't anymore.

But even as resentment sifted through him, he couldn't help but listen to the minister's words. He spoke of the yearning God had to be closer to His people. How God wanted us to be yearning for Him. In spite of his resistance, Dylan felt the words push against the walls of anger and bitterness he had erected against his father and brother. He felt as if he hardly dared let God's love breach that. Because then what reason would he have to keep going down the road he had taken?

When the minister announced the song after the sermon, he was still thinking, wondering.

Lisa pulled the hymnal out of the rack and opened it up. As the organ played a short introduction to the song, she lowered her head. He saw her swipe at her cheek, heard a faint sniff.

She dug in her purse and pulled out a tissue. As she wiped her nose, she angled her head. Dylan was shocked to see the glistening track of tears on her cheeks. But before he could say or do anything, she was looking down again.

· He glanced down at the hymnal on her lap, reading the first few lines of the song.

"The tender love a father has for all his children dear…"

The words drew out a mixture of emotions. Dylan had a father who preferred one son over the other.

Lisa had no father at all.

For a moment sorrow replaced Dylan's anger, and it was that shared sorrow that made him slip his arm around her shoulders. Draw her to his side.

Her slight resistance was followed by a gentle drifting toward him, and he pulled her closer. And once again he felt that same connection that had sparked between them last night.

That it had happened in church seemed to add a blessing to the moment.

Pull yourself together, Lisa commanded herself, bending over the sink of her bedroom's en suite. She splashed cold water on her puffy eyes, wiped her running mascara and drew in a deep breath.

She didn't have to feel guilty anymore. Her obligation had been fulfilled. She had gone to church just as she had promised.

So why did she feel as if her carefully constructed life was unraveling piece by piece?

The moment in church when she had so clearly felt the call of God to come to Him and let Him be a father to her still brought tears to her eyes. And she hardly ever cried.

Almost as precious was the memory of Dylan putting his arm around her. A pang of yearning sang through her, agitating a flurry of emotions she never thought she'd feel again.

Dylan is leaving and you are living a lie.

That cold reality sobered her more than the water had.

She left the sanctuary of her bedroom to join the family outside.

And of course the first person she saw when she stepped through the large glass doors to the deck was Dylan. He stood in profile to her, talking with his mother. As he smiled she felt the advent of her previous feelings and she quickly looked away, frustrated at how quickly they had returned.

"Lisa, can I get you anything to drink?" Alex was beside her, smiling down at her.

"No. Thanks."

"And how did you enjoy church?" he asked, drawing her aside.

Lisa glanced up at him, at the features so like his son's, except softened by age. "I'm glad I went," she said, glad she could be honest about something. "It was a real blessing."

Alex's smile blossomed. "I'm so glad to hear that."

"Dad, here's your iced tea." Ted joined them then,

handing his father a tall frosted glass. "Well, hello, Lisa. Where have you been hiding? I stopped by an hour ago, but neither you nor my brother were home."

"Dylan and Lisa came to church with us," Alex said quietly, a faint edge to his voice.

Ted's eyebrows shot up and he quirked her a wry grin. "Dylan? In church? You are a surprising influence on my brother, Lisa. I guess there's hope for him after all."

"Well, false hope is better than no hope at all," Lisa quipped.

"So have you and Dylan been able to corroborate what Dara has discovered?" Ted asked her. "I know she's been quite upset about the whole problem. Quite disturbing."

Lisa nodded, wishing she'd taken Alex up on his offer of something to drink. She might have missed talking to Ted. There was a hollow heartiness about him that rang false. As if he was trying too hard to be who he was. She never felt comfortable around him.

"Nothing that's jumped out at us yet." She angled him a quick glance. "Maybe he didn't do it."

Ted laughed. "Oh, he did it, all right." Ted turned to his father. "I still don't know why you're bothering with this. It's over. We found out who did it. Let's carry on."

Alex swirled his iced tea in his glass and shook his head. "It's not over yet, Ted. I want to be sure beyond any reasonable doubt that we have done the right thing."

Ted bit his lip and jerked his head to one side, as if holding back some retort.

"What's not over yet?" Dylan asked, coming to stand beside Lisa.

She kept her eyes on Alex, but every fiber of her being was aware of Dylan behind her. She caught the faint scent of his aftershave, then almost started when he laid a light hand on her shoulder. Part of the act, she reminded herself, suppressing another shiver.

"Your make-work project," Ted said with a sigh. He gave his brother a quick glance. "The job Dad dragged you back here to do in the hopes that he could talk you into staying with Matheson Telecom."

Lisa felt Dylan's fingers tighten on her shoulder, but his voice betrayed no emotion at all. "That won't happen, Ted. But I'm glad to help out while I'm here."

"Trust me, Dylan. It's a setup. There's nothing to do here." Then he turned and left them.

Dylan released the pressure on Lisa's shoulder, but didn't remove his hand. "Is that true, Dad? Was my coming here just a ruse?"

Alex's gaze was steadfast, his smile tinged with regret. But he shook his head. "No, Dylan. I truly need your help in this matter."

"You know my abilities are limited. So are my resources. If you are serious about this, you'll hire an outside auditor."

"Trust me on this son. Not yet."

"Trust." The word exploded above her head, and Lisa almost flinched at the anger in it. "May I remind you that it was trusting you that got us into this mess, Dad."

Alex winced, then nodded. "You're right, son."

Lisa chanced a quick glance up at Dylan. His jaw was set, his eyes narrowed.

She felt caught up in a storm of feelings, yet felt as if they were on the verge of something big. Important.

The moment stretched between them, then Alex turned away.

Dylan's hand slipped off her shoulder and he drew it over his face. "I need to get out of here," he said, glancing down at her. "You want to come for a drive?"

She looked back over her shoulder at Alex, who now stood beside his wife. She wanted to run after him. Pull him back. Make him face his son's anger and deal with it.

For Dylan's sake and his own.

But Dylan was supposed to be her boyfriend, and until he told her different, she was to keep up the pretense. "Sure. Let's go."

He slipped his arm over her shoulders and together they left. Lisa knew the act was for his family's sake, but for a small, exultant moment she pretended he had done it because he wanted to.

Chapter Seven

"Lisa, breakfast is on."

Dylan's voice on the other side of her bedroom door gave Lisa a start. She'd been standing in front of the mirror in her bathroom for the past ten minutes, trying to tame her unruly curls.

"Be right there," she called out, pulling a face at the tangle she'd managed to create.

Not that it mattered what she looked like, she thought, wrinkling her nose at her reflection. She wasn't trying to impress anyone.

Or was she?

Two days ago, before the wedding and before the church service, Dylan had simply been an overly attractive single boss.

Now, forty-eight hours later, Lisa felt as if all the barriers she thought she had put in place against his charm had been breached by his attentiveness. By seeing him with his family. By pretending to be a part of it by being his girlfriend.

She thought of the church service yesterday. For so many years she'd blamed God for her parents' death. But yesterday she had felt as if God was waiting. As if the breach between them was of no matter to Him. All she had to do was trust Him.

Could she?

"You coming?" Another knock on the door pulled her back from her reverie.

"I'm coming." Lisa turned away from the girl in the mirror and her very serious thoughts and joined Dylan in the hallway.

"Did you sleep well?" he asked, his smile warm, welcoming.

She nodded, suddenly shy around him.

The shrill ring of a cell phone from her room shot straight to her heart. It could only be Gabe. She had promised him she would call him last night and give him a update. She had forgotten.

"You going to get that?" Dylan asked.

"I'll meet you downstairs." She gave him a quick smile and walked into her bedroom, shutting the door firmly behind her.

"What have you found out?" Gabe's voice rang through the cell phone. Lisa glanced over her shoulder, hoping Dylan was gone.

"Nothing yet." She kept her voice low as she walked into the half bath, feeling like a criminal.

"What has Dara given you?"

"Just the invoices and purchase orders for the past six months."

"You won't find anything there. She's decoying you. You need to get into the office."

"How do you know?" And once again Lisa's suspicions flared.

"You sound like you doubt me." Gabe's voice rose a notch.

"I don't, Gabe. You know that."

"I don't know that anymore. You haven't been to see me in two days."

"Gabe, I've been kind of tied up."

He was silent a moment. "With Dylan? At Stanley Park?"

His words sent her heart into her stomach. "How did you know?"

"I phoned the house to ask for you. Someone told me you were at the Park. So I took the bus down there. I saw you with him."

Lisa closed her eyes, pressing the cell phone against her ear. "Gabe you can't phone here for me. If these people find out that you're my brother…"

"You and Dylan won't be so cozy anymore, will you?"

"Stop it, Gabe," she snapped, suddenly impatient with her brother. "I'm doing what I can and I'm doing it all for you." She took a slow breath, trying to calm her beating heart. Time to move on to another topic. "How is work going?"

Silence.

"Gabe, what's wrong?"

"I'm thinking of quitting."

Lisa's heart started right up again, memories of other disappointments crowding in on her devotion to her brother. "Don't do that, Gabe. Please."

"Lisa, it's a dead-end job. The pay sucks and the work is boring. I've met up with some guy who runs a shipping company. He needs a part-time accountant."

In his overly optimistic voice Lisa heard echoes of other opportunities that had sounded too good to be true. "I thought you said you couldn't get another accounting job without a reference."

"Well, this guy doesn't need a reference."

"Shouldn't that tell you something?" Lisa closed her eyes. And prayed. "Gabe, I'll come see you as soon as possible. Maybe tonight. Please. Don't quit yet. Something will happen here. I know it."

His silence pressed heavily down on her.

But Lisa knew how Gabe's thoughts went and how impatient he could be. "Hang in there," she said, struggling to sound positive. "I'll come see you tonight."

He sighed. "Okay," he said, reluctance edging his voice.

Lisa closed her cell phone and sighed lightly. *Dear Lord,* she prayed, *I don't deserve to talk to You, but please take care of Gabe. Please don't let him do anything silly.*

It was such a short prayer. And uttered so spontaneously. Yet Lisa felt a gentle peace surround her.

Dylan was already hunched over his desk, fruit and a bagel on a plate at his elbow. He looked up when she came in. "I thought I would get started." He held her gaze a moment, a soft smile curving his lips. Thankfully he didn't ask her about the phone call.

Lisa put a plate of food together and joined Dylan in the study. She sat down at the computer and worked at finishing the job she'd started on Friday.

Though her attention was on her work, she couldn't help the occasional glance Dylan's way. One time he was looking at her, but as soon as their eyes met, he looked away.

Lisa didn't want to read anything into it. Couldn't.

She was finished and walked over to Dylan's table and pulled another file. A piece of paper, stuck to one of the files, fell to the floor.

Dylan picked it up, wrinkling his nose. "This thing's a mess." It was crumpled and stained with rings from a coffee cup. "Does it look like anything?"

Lisa took the folded-over piece of paper from him. "Looks to me like messy bookkeeping. It was just stuck to one of the files," she replied. She tried to peel the folds apart. "I could try steaming them."

"I can do it."

"I don't mind. I need the break."

"The kettle is in the pots-and-pans cupboard beside the stove," Dylan said.

The kitchen was empty, and Lisa easily found the kettle, surprised that Dylan would know. When she and Gabe had lived together, the only pan he'd been able to find was the frying pan, and that was because it was always in the sink or on the stove.

While the water was boiling she tried one more time to pry apart the folds of paper with a knife, but succeeded only in ripping it a bit more.

The steam was pouring out of the kettle now and she held the paper above it, careful to avoid burning her hand. The paper slowly crinkled away until she could unfold it.

It was an invoice. Inside was another paper, a memo to Dara. In Gabe's handwriting.

"Don't know if I can keep doing this," Lisa read. "Ted needs to know."

Her heart skittered, and deep inside she felt as if something had been yanked out, torn up by the roots. The words shouted at her.

Keep doing this? Doing what? And what did Ted need to know?

Lisa lowered the memo, her hands shaking. Her first reaction was to crumple up the paper and throw it in the garbage. Her second was to grab it and run across town to her brother to ask what it meant.

She glanced quickly around the kitchen, then folded the paper and slipped it into the back pocket of her pants. She couldn't let anyone see this until she had talked to Gabe about it.

She doubted Dylan could have seen the memo. It was smaller than the invoice and tucked right inside, no edges showing.

She smoothed out the invoice, her fingers trembling. Pulling in a long, steadying breath, she walked back to the study, hoping, praying her face didn't reveal any of her doubts and fears.

Dylan glanced up when she came back. "Anything important?"

"Just another invoice." The lie didn't come easily to her, but Dylan didn't seem to notice her discomfort.

"I was hoping it would be something more exciting than that," Dylan said with a light laugh.

"Me, too." Lisa spun away, pretending to be engrossed in the paper, the crinkle in her back pocket sounding as loud as gunshots in the quiet of the study.

She sat down and laid the innocent invoice on her desk. She glanced at the name of the customer and on a sticky note jotted down the customer name.

"I just need to run upstairs a moment," she said, glancing at Dylan, wishing her cheeks weren't so flushed.

Dylan looked up. Smiled at her. "Sure."

Lisa walked out of the room, then ran up the stairs. As she slipped into her bedroom she felt more and more like a criminal. Was she stealing? Was she as bad as her brother?

As she hid the memo in her suitcase, she stifled a surge of guilt. She would show Dylan once she had talked to Gabe. Once she found out what had really happened.

Three hours later Dylan pushed himself away from the table he was working at and came to stand beside Lisa.

"Well, I'm done here. How are you making out?"

Lisa jumped, then glanced up at him. Look casual.

"I've married all the invoices to the purchase orders," she said. "And from what I've seen everything fits."

"So nothing there."

"Not in this file." She took a breath and took a chance. "I think we need to get into the office files and computers. It would be faster for one thing, and easier for Dara," she said, hoping her voice sounded more casual than she felt. What if he asked her why? What would she say?

Dylan tapped his pen on the desk. "I think you're right." He slipped his hand through his hair and leaned back against the desk. He glanced down at Lisa, his teeth catching one side of his lip. "Do you get the feeling this is a waste of time?"

"Ted seemed to agree with you."

"I get the feeling Ted wants nothing more than for me to get myself out of here and back to Toronto." Dylan sighed and pushed himself away from the desk. "Which makes me want to go see what we can find at the office."

Thirty-five minutes later they were escorted into an office adjoining a large warehouse. The reception area was spacious and light, furnished in much the same fashion as the Matheson home. Large impressionist paintings hung on the wall. The sparse furniture had a European look.

"Can you tell that Mom redid this place, as well?" Dylan murmured to Lisa as he opened the large smoked-glass door for her. "Same down-home country atmosphere."

Lisa stifled a quick laugh. "Your mother has exquisite taste," she said quietly. "Maybe you should get her to come and do something with your office in Toronto."

"Even if I was staying with Matheson Telecom, I wouldn't. It's not my style."

They approached the receptionist half-hidden behind a waist-high sweep of metal and glass. She glanced up, her eyes flicking over Lisa, then coming to rest on Dylan. Her smile changed as she reached up and smoothed her hair. "Hello, Mr. Matheson. Your father is in," she said, leaning slightly forward. Her shining eyes and breathy voice exuded a welcome Lisa was sure she didn't extend to just anyone who walked in the door. The secretary smiled again, and Lisa felt a surprising pinch of jealousy.

"Lisa and I will just go straight in." Dylan glanced her way and smiled at her. A spark of previous emotions flashed through her. When Dylan had danced with her.

Lisa wrenched her gaze away, reaching for control.

She was almost there when they walked past Alex's secretary into Alex's office and saw Alex at his desk.

And Dylan dropped his arm over her shoulder.

It's just an act, she reminded herself even as she felt the gentle flush of connection at the warmth of his arm.

"Dylan. Lisa. So nice to see you here." Alex got up, the delight in his voice showing Lisa even more than his beaming smile how pleased he was to see them together. "Are you two touring around?"

Dylan's fingers tightened on her shoulder, but he didn't take up his father's invitation. "We don't have time, Dad. We're here to check out some files in the office."

Alex tapped his fingers lightly on the desk. "I'll have to talk to Dara about it."

When Alex left, Lisa edged away from Dylan. Thankfully he got the hint and lowered his arm. Which, to Lisa's dismay, didn't make her feel any more comfortable than before.

She walked over to a set of chairs flanked by tables. Brochures lay on the table advertising the various products handled by Matheson Telecom and Lisa picked one up, pretending interest in it.

Gabe's phone call this morning had left her jittery and out of sorts. The memo only added to it.

But as she glanced at Dylan, who still stood in the center of the room watching her, she knew there was another cause.

The tentative advance and retreat happening between her and Dylan was more than the show they were putting on for the sake of his family. Last night no one had been around and she had felt the pull of attraction, gently irresistible and seemingly innocent.

At the same time she didn't dare give in. Her secret hung between them like a menacing shadow. Sooner or later it would come out, and anything they had shared to that point would be swept away.

Later, later.

"I can't seem to find Dara." Alex came back, looking apologetic. "I was so sure she was here today."

"All we need to do is look at the most recent files, Dad," Dylan said, his voice edged with anger. "Surely Dara doesn't need to be around for that."

Alex glanced at Lisa, then at Dylan, raising his hands palm up in a gesture of surrender. "I'm sorry, Dylan. If you had called before you came, you might have caught her. She knows where they are."

"What about Ted? Surely he can help us."

"Ted was never that involved in the bookkeeping."

"Which was part of the problem," Dylan said.

"Dylan, please…" Alex held his hand up in a placating gesture. "This will all get solved sooner or later. We just need time."

Dylan clenched one hand into a fist and tapped it against his side. Lisa echoed his frustration both with Dara and Alex. Why was he being so evasive? Was he protecting Dara, as well?

And in that moment Lisa understood Dylan's discontent with his father's relationship to him.

Yet threaded through that was her conversation with Alex only yesterday morning. His wish that one of his sons would make wise and good choices.

Something else was going on. She couldn't figure out what, but somehow it hinged on Alex. And what kind of choices he was going to make.

"So we're just supposed to sit around and twiddle our thumbs while we wait for Dara to decide whether or not she's going to give us access to her office?" Dylan's question was surprisingly quiet, but Lisa felt his exasperation.

Alex smiled a sad smile. "No. You're supposed to be on holiday."

Dylan blew out his breath in an exasperated sigh. "Dad, you asked me to come and help you figure this problem out. I'm trying to do that, but not getting a lot of cooperation from either you or Dara. And Ted doesn't have a clue what's going on. I hope this isn't an elaborate waste of Lisa's and my time."

"You have to believe me when I say it is making a difference, Dylan. But today you won't be able to do anything. Why don't you take a break for now." He smiled at Lisa. "Take Lisa out on the boat. The work will keep for an afternoon. Trust me, it will all come together. Hopefully soon."

Dylan shook his head, his shoulders sagging lightly as if in defeat. "I guess that's the crux of the matter, isn't it, Dad? Trust. You should give some serious thought to how you want us to proceed."

Alex almost winced. "Can we carry on this conversation some other time?" he asked quietly.

"I've nothing more to say. For now." Dylan glanced at Lisa and held his hand out to her. "I guess we have the afternoon free."

What could she do but take it?

As his fingers wrapped around hers, his eyes held her gaze. "So, what do you think of going sailing?"

Lisa swallowed down the sudden uplifting rush of pleasure. She was supposed to be helping Gabe. But as Alex had said, they couldn't right now.

But could she afford to spend the afternoon with Dylan? And what would Gabe say when he found out?

"Go ahead, Lisa," Alex urged. "Dylan's an excellent sailor. You can trust him."

Dylan threw his father a puzzled glance, then with a shrug turned back to Lisa. "What do you say?" he asked, his voice pitched low.

Lisa felt the intimacy of his tone, was drawn into the intensity of his gaze and against her better judgment said yes.

"So which one is your dad's boat?" Lisa asked, staring through the forest of masts bobbing up and down in the marina. The sun flashed off pristine hulls, gleaming chrome and brass overwhelming the tiny flashes shot off by the water.

"It's the sloop on slip E over there. I doubt you'd be able to see it, though."

Lisa stood on tiptoe, scanning the various boats, then nodded. "Oh, yes. There it is."

Dylan jerked his head around, frowning his puzzlement. "How do you…" Then he caught the joke. "Very smart. And what do you think of the ketch beside it?"

Unable to stop the mischief that had caught hold of her, Lisa rolled her eyes in mock disgust. It was as if getting away from his family and from his work had allowed them to choose their relationship. And she was tired of intensity and seriousness.

"Like I don't know my boats. Look at its mast. That's no ketch."

"And it is a…" Dylan prompted, picking up on her mood.

"If you don't know, I'm not going to enlighten you," she said with an airy wave of her hand.

Dylan tugged on the brim of her hat, pulling it lower over her eyes. "We'll see how cocky you are once you're out on the water," he said with a grin.

As she followed him along the dock she felt the tensions of the morning drift away with the light breeze that teased her hair.

She breathed in the peculiar scent of the harbor—water, the faint scent of diesel and the underlying smell of fish. Gulls wheeled above, taunting them with their strident cries. Below them, water gurgled against the pilings, slapped the hulls of the boats.

It was going to be a glorious day.

"This one, right?" Dylan said, stopping in front of a midsize boat. It looked to be about thirty feet long, its mast stretching far above them.

She glanced at the prow of the boat and saw *The*

Stephanie written in flowing cursive. "You're more percipient than you look," she said with a grin.

"And percipient enough not to use that word instead of perceptive, which is what it really means."

"I rest my case," Lisa said with a grin. "So this is the vessel."

"It's not a big boat, but it handles like a dream," Dylan said. He untied a line and climbed up into the boat. "Hand me the gear and then I'll help you on."

Lisa gave him the thermos and cooler holding food that the housekeeper deemed necessary for a trip out on the boat. Then Dylan held out his hand.

Lisa's hesitation was minute.

"You don't have to be afraid," he said, smiling his encouragement. "The boat won't tip. I promise."

She took his hand, but was disappointed by how quickly he let go of her hand. As he unlocked what looked like a small door broken into three parts, Lisa glanced upward. The tiny flag at the top of the mast seemed impossibly high.

Her stomach lurched and she grabbed the nearest rope to steady herself.

"What's wrong?" Dylan asked.

"How are you going to get that sail all the way up that mast by yourself?"

"I'll use the halyard on the main and the furlings on the jib."

"Furling. Is that like a small furlong?" she joked, trying to cover up her nervousness and her lack of knowledge. She had never been on a boat before. And now she was going to allow Dylan to take her out onto the ocean?

Dylan laughed, sliding the boards up and setting them aside. "Come down below a moment. We can put the food away and I can give you the grand tour."

Lisa rubbed her damp palms against her pant legs and followed Dylan through the narrow entrance and down the ladder to a small room belowdecks. A family picture hung on a short wall above a small couch built into the side of the boat. The kitchen had a small stove with an oven, a sink and counter and cupboards directly above them. Everything a person needed for a long trip.

"Okay, landlubber," Dylan said, glancing around. "A few lessons. The front of the boat is the bow, the back is the stern. If you're hungry, you can make something in the galley. Behind you is the head, self-explanatory if you take a look, and to get back up to the cockpit you clamber up the companionway."

Lisa blinked, trying to absorb the information Dylan seemed to take delight in deluging her with.

"Since this is belowdecks, I'm assuming a whole other vocabulary awaits me once we go up the—" she gestured to the ladder behind Dylan "—companionway."

"We haven't even started on mainsails, jibs, lines and sheets."

Lisa grinned. "Just tell me when I'm supposed to say, 'Avast, me hearties' and I'll try to keep up," she said, looking around the snug interior of the boat. "This is cozy," she added.

Dylan tapped a pole leading up from the floor of the interior, looking around, as well. "I've spent a lot of happy hours on this boat."

Lisa didn't think she imagined the wistful tone in his voice. "Did you go with your family?"

"Mostly just me and my dad," he said quietly, looking past her as if seeing other memories.

Lisa stopped the questions that almost spilled out. It wasn't any of her business. She didn't need to tangle herself any deeper in the affairs of this family.

Yet a gentle sorrow seeped through her for the hurt she heard in his voice. An echo of the regret in his father's voice when he spoke of Dylan.

"I have to check the engine room," Dylan said. "You can go above deck and enjoy the weather."

As he moved to pass her, their eyes met. He slowed, she didn't move and awareness sparked between them. In the close quarters it was almost palpable.

Stop this now.

Lisa pulled her gaze away, turned and escaped up the companionway into the sunshine above. As she sat down on the bench beside the wheel, she took a long slow breath.

Dylan's movements below set the boat rocking lightly.

She shouldn't have come here. Shouldn't be spending this personal time with Dylan. She was trespassing over the boundaries she had set herself, moving into a place that would be too hard to escape.

A gull's cry pulled her attention away from her disquiet, and the slight rocking motion of the boat soothed her anxiety.

It was just a short sailing trip. When would she ever have a chance to experience that?

The day was going to be just fine, she assured herself, the tension easing from her shoulders. What was happening between her and Dylan was simply a product of spending more time together than she had with any man for a long time.

As long as she was aware of that, she could handle it.

Chapter Eight

Dylan turned on the fuel, opened the sea cock and ran through the usual presailing check. His movements were sure, practiced, old habits slipping back as easily as putting on worn shoes.

The routine alleviated the moment of tension created by the allure of Lisa.

The vessel that had once seemed roomy enough with four people aboard now seemed cramped and crowded. He and Lisa would constantly be bumping into each other, and from her reaction a moment ago he sensed she would be the one constantly pulling away.

He wrote the barometer reading and closed the log book with a light laugh at his own whimsy. Her reaction shouldn't concern him. It was just a day away from work, that was all.

It was the thought of taking the boat out, not being with Lisa, that quickened his heart, he reassured himself.

It had been a long time since he had gone sailing. In

Toronto all his time was spent at Matheson Telecom, to the detriment of many relationships and his leisure time.

And now he was moving to another company where he would have to prove his worth.

Dylan pushed the thought aside as he switched on the radio and listened. Shipping traffic sounded light. He quickly checked the weather. All the pieces were in place for a perfect day. Enjoy the moment, he thought as he clambered up the companionway.

He started the engine. The motor turned over immediately with a muted growl.

"Lisa, do me a favor," he said, checking the gauges. "Look over the stern and see if water is coming out of the exhaust."

The boat rocked slightly as Lisa moved and leaned over. "I see water pouring out from something."

"Good. Thanks."

"Water coming out of a boat is a good thing?"

Dylan glanced up at the worry in her voice. Smiled at her comical expression. "Water comes in from the sea and goes into the cooling part of the engine, then out the exhaust. Like air flowing past the radiator of a car."

"Landlubber question coming up," she said, sitting down again. "If this is a sailboat, why do you have an engine in it?"

"It's much easier to maneuver out of the marina with a motor than a sail. And quicker." He pulled out a life jacket. "Here. Put this on."

Lisa held up the lime-green personal flotation device and pulled her lower lip between her teeth. "You realize, of course, this color is going to totally wash out my complexion."

Dylan laughed, thankful once again for Lisa's easy humor, always ready at hand. "Better your complexion than having you washed overboard."

"Just how far are you planning to go? Tokyo?"

"I guess we'll see where the day takes us." He jumped off the boat and untied the spring lines, then the bow and stern line and got back on. He put away the lines and took his place behind the wheel of the boat.

As they motored out of the marina, Dylan could feel the tensions of the past week ease away, soothed by the movement of the boat, the light breeze on his face. The promise of a beautiful day of sailing ahead canceled out the puzzle of his father's actions.

"This is the most I've seen you smile since I've met you," Lisa said, angling him a grin.

"I've missed this," he said quietly, navigating his way through the throngs of boats.

"Toronto is on the water. Didn't you ever go sailing there?"

"No time."

"Are you going to have time at your next job?"

Her casual comment hit a vulnerable spot. "I'll be busy." He would be going nuts, he amended. Starting over. Trying to prove himself.

Was he doing the right thing?

It was too late for second thoughts, but they hovered in his mind nonetheless.

"Mr. Upwardly Mobile," Lisa teased. "Ted doesn't seem to work as hard as you do."

"Ted is his own person," Dylan said, hoping his reply sounded more forgiving than he usually felt toward his older brother.

Lisa pushed her billed cap farther back on her head, as if to see Dylan better. "I get the feeling you're not filled with fraternal devotion to Ted."

"Fraternal," he said, flashing her a teasing glance. "Most people would say brotherly."

"It is related to brothers. From the Latin word *frater* meaning brother. Also connected to fraternity."

"You like fooling with words, don't you?"

Lisa smiled, lifting her face to the light wind. "Among other things."

She didn't elaborate and Dylan was content to leave her to her little secrets. He knew there were more. One being the person who had called her a couple of times on her cell phone, whom she never talked about. He was also fairly certain she had gone visiting the same person the evening of the rehearsal party he had attended alone.

She had told him at the interview that she was unattached. So who was this mystery person?

"So when do you hoist the mizzenmast?"

Dylan pulled his attention back to Lisa. "This is a sloop. Only has one mast. A boat with three masts has a mizzenmast, and you only hoist sails."

"Oh, that's right. I read that somewhere," she said, snapping her fingers. "Did you ever sail a boat with more than one mast?"

Dylan shook his head. "We had a larger boat than this at one time, but it still only had one mast. Dad traded it off on this smaller boat because the rest of the family seldom came along." He couldn't help but smile, remembering how relieved his sisters had been that they no longer had to be coerced into coming along. He could never understand their reluctance. To him, sailing had been the ultimate release. A place to get away from the stress and tension of school.

The one place he and his father were on equal footing.

"So you and your dad sailed a lot?"

"Almost every chance we could get." Dylan turned the boat into the wind and slowed the engine. "Come here. I need your help now."

Lisa pointed to herself. "Me. As in this landlubber?"

"This is easy. Just hold the wheel exactly where it is. I need to pull up the mainsail and unfurl the jib."

Lisa got up, suddenly looking nervous. He moved over so she could take the wheel.

"Don't look so tense," he joked.

"I'm not tense," she replied. "Just terribly and extremely alert."

"You don't have to white-knuckle it." Dylan let go as soon as she had the wheel. "Just hold it right where you have it. Nice and steady." He waited a moment. "You okay?"

"I'm fine. You just go unfurl some sails."

Her bottom lip was clamped between her teeth and a deep frown pulled her eyebrows together. He was about to make another comment, but kept it to himself. Once she saw that the boat wasn't going to take off, she'd be fine.

In a matter of moments he had the mainsail up. He untied the furling line and pulled the jib sheet.

The sails started undulating as they caught their first taste of the wind.

"Dylan. What's going on?" Lisa's voice had flown up an octave. "Those sails aren't supposed to flap like that, are they?"

"They're just filling up," he called back, unable to stop laughing. "Just steer to port."

"Office language, please."

"Your left."

As he worked his way back, the sails, seemingly satisfied with what was offered, filled with a snap. The tug pushed Dylan's heart against his chest, the familiar expectation of exhilaration sending his blood singing through his veins.

"This boat is tilting. Is it supposed to tilt like this?"

Dylan came up beside her and let her struggle along a moment. "You're doing great, Lisa. A natural."

"Well, it's been fun, but I have to scream now. Please take over."

"Here. Let me help you."

He stood behind her, placed his hands over hers and gently corrected their course.

She drew in a deep breath, but to his surprise didn't pull away. Of course, as tightly as her hands were wrapped around the wheel, he doubted she was able to move at all.

"It's not as hard as it looks," he said as her hair tickled his chin. She smelled as fresh as sea air, with a hint of feminine sweetness. "Just keep the boat pointed in this direction for now and we'll be fine."

The boat skimmed over the water, the pull of the

sail singing through the lines. Dylan's spirits responded, thrilling to the faint groan of the boat, the tautness of the sail.

Lisa hadn't moved since he had come up behind her, but her hands no longer held the wheel in a death grip. He couldn't see her face, but could feel her slowly relaxing.

"It goes pretty fast," she murmured, still holding on to the wheel.

"The wind isn't even that strong today. Sometimes this boat just flies." Dylan shifted his weight, his arms brushing hers. "You didn't put on your life jacket."

"I'm a good swimmer."

Dylan didn't push the point. Once they got farther out, he would have to insist she put it on. But for now he didn't want her to move. Wanted to enjoy the feeling of protecting her. Sheltering her.

And so far she didn't seem to mind him standing right behind her.

They sped away from the harbor and swooped under Lions Gate Bridge.

"This is a very different vantage point than when I first came here," she said, her head tilting up to look at the bridge as they sailed under it. "You promised you'd take me sailing when we drove over that bridge. And here I am."

Dylan looked down at her upturned face. A dimple danced beside her mouth and her eyes shimmered, turning a soft hazel in the sunlight. When her head bumped his shoulder, her eyes swung around to his and a mixture of emotions tumbled across her face. He caught a glimpse of yearning that called to his own loneliness.

Without stopping to think or analyze the right or wrong, he caught her chin with one hand, turning her face a fraction toward his.

She shifted her body ever so slightly toward him. Rested her head back against his shoulder.

When Dylan lowered his mouth to hers, she didn't move or resist.

The boat straightened. Lisa pulled away. "What's happening?"

"Got distracted," Dylan murmured, catching the wheel and turning it back to starboard. As the sails filled again, Dylan glanced down at Lisa.

She hadn't moved away from him. Dylan took a chance and placed his hands over hers and rested his chin lightly on her head.

Just as when they'd danced at Chelsea's wedding he couldn't banish the sense of rightness he felt. As if every silly thing in the world would make more sense if only they could stay this way. Together.

He brushed his chin over her head, unable to suppress his good humor. He had never had feelings like this for any woman he had ever been with.

Yet he knew less about her than he did about any of the other women he had dated.

The unwelcome thought lurked on the edges of his mind and he suppressed it. Pushed aside his second thoughts.

He had a beautiful woman in his arms. He had favorable winds, a warm sun and open water ahead of him.

It was as close to perfection as he could expect.

* * *

Lisa didn't want to move. In fact, if she could have her way, time would stop, would remain in this moment while she savored every nuance, every image.

The fresh smell of the water breaking away from the boat, the faint groaning of the lines holding the sail, the warmth of the sun.

Dylan's arms around her creating a haven of safety. They didn't have an audience now, so there was no need to pretend.

And what about your own pretense?

Lisa bit her lip as guilt crowded out the peace of the moment. Things were starting to overlap, feelings seeping out around loyalty.

She was standing in the arms of the kind of man she had dreamed of since she was a young girl. A man who had the kind of family she had always wanted.

And if they found out who she was, it would all disappear as quickly as fog when the sun came out.

Dear Lord, what have I started? How can I fix all this?

Her prayer was born of a desperation to find a way to satisfy her own conscience, newly aroused by the church service the other day. She needed to help her brother. She wanted to be a part of Dylan's life.

But she couldn't do both.

"Thanks for the lesson," she murmured, ducking under Dylan's arm. She felt suddenly chilled and slipped her sweater on. And then her life jacket.

She didn't look at Dylan. Instead she concentrated on the water, squinting against the light dancing on the waves.

Another sailboat surged past them, the laughter of the occupants following in its wake. Lisa pretended to be intent on its progress, envying the people their light spirits.

How had her life gotten so complicated? Her plan had seemed so easy before she went for the interview. Find information. Help her brother. Foolish of her to think that she could take this all on herself.

She blinked against a surprising onslaught of tears.

I've been foolish, Lord. I've been stubborn and I've been proud, she prayed. *Please forgive me. Help me get through this. Show me what I should do.* Her prayer was a muddle of questions, a confusion of thoughts. Yet, as before, she felt a gentle peace cover her. Nothing had been solved, but she no longer felt alone.

"Are you okay?" Dylan's voice broke into her thoughts and she turned to face him, her smile genuine now.

"I think so."

He frowned at her cryptic response, but thankfully didn't press her.

Lisa drew on old coping skills honed with each move she and Gabe had made to a new foster home. New situations and emotions.

This was where she was at the moment. She didn't need to think back or ahead. She had to control the things she was directly involved in right now.

She turned her face up to the sky, soaking in the warmth of the sun and allowing herself pleasure in the feel of the movement of the boat dancing over the water. The jagged mountains edging the harbor set a romantic counterpoint, clearly underlining the uniqueness of this time and place.

She chanced another look at Dylan. He stood on the deck, feet slightly apart, his hands resting lightly on the wheel. He looked more relaxed than he had since she had met him.

"So if we're heading away from Vancouver with the wind at our back, how do we get back?" she asked, trying to lighten the tone of the afternoon.

Dylan angled her a smile. "Maybe we won't. What would you think of that?"

The teasing comment tantalized her, bringing back all the emotions of the kiss they had shared. A kiss she shouldn't have allowed to happen.

She thought of the two of them staying here, in this self-contained place—each surge of the boat pulling them farther away from Vancouver and the complications of their lives there.

It was too compelling a thought and she couldn't reply.

"What would you miss?" Dylan asked, carrying on the fantasy.

Lisa leaned over the side, watching the flow of water streaming past the boat.

She'd miss her brother, but she couldn't tell Dylan that. What else did she have to miss? "I'd probably miss my blow-dryer," she said with a grin. "Maybe my thesaurus. How about you?"

Dylan shrugged, looping his forearms over the wheel, looking straight ahead. "I don't use a blow-dryer."

"Just pomade, I understand. I bet you'd miss your family, though."

"Probably."

"Your mother, your father?" Lisa couldn't stop herself. Each time she saw Alex and Dylan the strain between them bothered her more and more.

"I suppose I'd miss him, too."

"You *suppose* you'd miss your father? That seems a strange way to say it."

Dylan rested his chin on his stacked hands, the faint breeze teasing his hair. He sighed deeply. "I love my dad. I just don't love what he does."

"And what does he do?"

Dylan didn't answer for a moment and Lisa kept silent, content to let the moment draw itself out.

"You know the story of the prodigal son?" he asked. "From the Bible?"

"My stepfather read it to me a couple of times," Lisa said. "Next to the story of Joseph it was one of my favorites."

"Did you ever feel sorry for the older brother?" Dylan tilted his head, held her gaze.

Lisa paused, pondering that thought. "Sometimes. A little bit."

"I always did. I could never figure out why Jesus had to make that poor guy out to be the bad example."

"Well, he was the ungrateful one." Lisa leaned forward, then sat up as her life jacket dug in to her knees and the back of her neck. "He wasn't happy to see his brother come back."

Dylan noticed her discomfort. "You can take your life jacket off it you want."

Lisa had donned the flotation device as a feeble protection after Dylan had kissed her. "That's okay. I feel safer with it on." She realized the double entendre too late. "So why do you sympathize with the older brother?"

"Because in many ways, I'm him," Dylan continued, looking back at the boat. "Birth order aside, of course."

"Ted being the wastrel, I take it."

Dylan laughed. Corrected his course. "I have lost track of how many times my father has given Ted second chances."

"Your father is a good man. I think he's fair and trustworthy. It's that quality that makes him do that."

"My father broke trust with me when he put Ted in charge of the company here in Vancouver."

The suppressed anger in his voice made her wince. "Ted is the older brother."

"That was my father's reason, as well." Dylan straightened. "Anyway, that doesn't concern me as much as it used to. Once I'm back on my own, the company can slide down the tubes the way it's going now."

"Surely the company isn't doing that badly."

Dylan shrugged. "Maybe not, but Ted has never been leadership material. The fact that money had gone missing for so long doesn't say much about his control of either his wife or the company."

Lisa felt a flare of hope. "What do you mean, control of his wife?"

"She's the one who hired that accountant. He worked under her so in a way I hold her responsible for his actions."

Don't know if I can keep doing this. Ted needs to know.

Lisa felt as if the words on Gabe's memo were burned on her forehead for Dylan and all the world to see. "So you don't know if Ted was in charge or if Dara was in charge."

"I don't know if Ted has ever been in charge of anything."

Lisa knew she did not imagine the tone of bitterness in Dylan's voice. "Surely Ted must have been able to do *something*. Why else would your father give him so much responsibility?"

"My father has always had a soft spot for Ted, and Ted has used that to his advantage. All my life I've tried to live up to Dad's expectations. But it hasn't done me any good." Dylan flashed Lisa a casual smile. "And now that's enough about my brother, my father and all the other things in my life that I can't control."

Dylan's comment reflected feelings so close to hers that Lisa felt a flash of connection. "That makes me think about what the minister was talking about on Sunday. About letting go."

"That's one thing about religion I've always had the hardest time with. Letting go. Letting God." Dylan spun the wheel of the boat. "I guess that's why I stopped going to church."

"I used to go to church," Lisa said softly, looking at the islands ahead of them. "Me and my family."

"Did you enjoy it?"

Lisa nodded. "My mother and I seldom went when I was growing up. When Rick and—" she stumbled, almost mentioning Gabe's name "—and my mother got married, he was a strong Christian, so we all started going." She bit back the flow of words—her nervousness making her chatty.

"So what made you want to go with my family?"

Lisa pulled her legs up, pressing her knees against the bulk of the life jacket. She cast about for the right way to articulate her reasons. "A promise I'd made." And that was all she was going to tell him.

"Yet you seemed sad in church."

Lisa only nodded. That day in church Dylan had given her his hankie to wipe her tears. He was probably wondering what that had been about. But she couldn't tell him. Couldn't share the sorrow she felt over her fractured life. Her parents dead. Gabe living in a dumpy apartment and all the while she was lying to one of the kindest families she had ever met.

"I missed my parents," she said simply, surprising herself at her confession. "I didn't think I had any more tears in me, honestly. It's been ten years since they died."

"It's okay to be sad. It shows you loved them."

"I enjoyed the service, too, though." Through it all she had heard God calling her. Drawing her back into a relationship with Him. The only one that mattered.

"What did you like about it?"

"It would be easier if I said it was nostalgia," she said. "The sort of thing happy families do. You know, the Norman Rockwell calendar pictures. But it was more than that. I realized I missed God."

He didn't respond to that. Their silence was broken only by the swish of water against the hull of the boat, the faint groaning of the mast and the line, holding the wind in the sails. A gull wheeled overhead, its piercing cry adding a melancholy note to the day.

After a while Lisa let her gaze wander around, over to Dylan. To her astonishment and discomfort, he was looking directly at her.

"You continually surprise me, Lisa Sterling," he said quietly. "Just when I think I know who you are, something else comes up."

"Better to be a surprise than a shock, I guess," Lisa said, her forced laugh pushing away the gentle intimacy of his remark.

"You might be that, too."

Foreboding slivered through her at his oblique comment. If he only knew....

She hugged her knees tighter, the plastic buckle of the life jacket digging in to her legs. A small penance for her evasions and secrets.

Enough, enough. She was doing what she had to do. Her first priority was Gabe.

"Tomorrow is my parents' anniversary party," Dylan said after a while. "You still up to going?"

She realized he was giving her a gracious out, and for a flicker of a heartbeat she was tempted to take it. "I promised to come to both events—the wedding and the anniversary," she said, resting her chin on her knees. "I like to keep my promises."

In her peripheral vision she saw Dylan nodding his head, the faint breeze teasing his hair around his face. "I sensed that about you. You are an honorable person, Lisa."

She didn't allow herself to follow that comment through. She shifted in her seat.

"You getting bored?" he asked.

She quirked a challenging grin at him. "What if I say yes?"

"Then I'll make you unbored." Dylan winked at her, spun the wheel and pulled in two lines. The boat listed and sped up. "Hang on and lean back. We're going for broke."

Lisa clamped one hand over her mouth, stifling a squeal as the boat lurched. Dylan laughed aloud, a spray of water flecking his hair.

But Lisa said nothing, her heart thrumming with a mixture of anxiety and exhilaration as she clung to the boat. They went faster, skimming over the water, the hull thumping over the waves, the sound getting louder.

Dylan flashed a grin at her, as if taunting her. On they raced, the boat tilting so far that all Lisa saw when she looked down from her perch was the deep gray water rushing past the boat.

Dylan looked like a pirate, his shirt billowing around him, his hair falling over his face as he held the wheel. Water sprayed as they flew over the water, and Lisa laughed out loud in sheer pleasure.

She didn't want him to stop. She wanted this mad rush of freedom to take them away from Vancouver and the complications of their lives back there. Just her and Dylan.

When Dylan finally eased the sheets and the boat slowed, Lisa felt a thrum of disappointment.

"I'm impressed, Lisa," Dylan said. "I thought for sure you were going to yell at me to stop."

"No. It was great." Lisa couldn't stop grinning. "What a rush."

Their eyes met. Held by the shared experience. And when Dylan held out one hand to her, Lisa didn't even stop to think. She slipped off her seat, took his hand and let him pull her to his side.

Then she let him kiss her again.

And this time she gave in to an impulse and lifted her hand to his head. Slipped her fingers through his thick, dark hair and let herself pretend that all this—the kiss, Dylan, this moment—was normal.

She didn't want to contemplate how this would end. For now she had this moment and she intended to treasure it. To savor it.

A memory for her to draw on when this was all over.

Chapter Nine

"Okay, Lisa, who is this man and what did you do with my brother?" Ted stood in the side doorway of his parents' house, barring Dylan's and Lisa's entrance. He grinned at his own joke, his hazel eyes flicking over them both in unwelcome speculation. "The Dylan Matheson I know would never play hooky and go sailing in the middle of a weekday no matter how pretty the girl. And he's been with enough."

The afternoon had been so wonderful, so entirely perfect, Ted's insinuations couldn't even get a rise out of Dylan.

"I thought maybe you were avoiding me and Dara," Ted said.

"I didn't know you were coming for supper. And I took Lisa sailing because she's never been before," Dylan said, waiting for his brother to let them by. He glanced at Lisa, her hair a tousled mass of curls framing her face. She had taken off her hat and her cheeks had been kissed by the sun. She looked adorable and he had to resist the urge to kiss her again.

"Mom was getting ready to call up the Coast Guard." Ted stood aside to let them by.

"She knew where I was," Dylan said easily.

Stephanie stood with her back to them, wiping the table, when they entered the kitchen, Dara was loading the dishwasher and Erika was leaning on the counter chatting on the phone.

Alex looked up from the newspaper he was reading at the table and smiled at Lisa, then Dylan.

Dylan held his glance a moment, his mind sifting back to what he and Lisa had talked about. He wished he could understand exactly what his father was doing. He wished he could simply, as Lisa suggested, trust his own father.

Stephanie, catching the direction of Alex's gaze, looked over her shoulder, then straightened, her hand on her chest. "There you two are. What happened?"

Dylan shrugged away her concern, though he couldn't ignore the guilt her worried face gave him. "Lost track of time," he said, bending to kiss her on the cheek.

"My Dylan? Losing track of time?" Stephanie held his shoulder with one hand and gave him a long, hard look. She looked over at Lisa as if for confirmation of what she had just heard.

"Our brother, transforming into a human being right in front of our eyes," Ted said, dropping into a chair beside his father.

"Hey, Dylan." Amber came up behind him, grabbed Dylan and spun him around. "Where were you? We were getting worried. You're never late."

"Lisa and I went sailing," he said, flicking his little sister under her chin.

Amber blinked. Threw a puzzled glance at Lisa. "In the middle of the day?"

Dylan shook his head at his family's unsubtle bewilderment. They made him sound positively neurotic.

"Did you two have supper? I've some left," Stephanie said, flipping her hand in the direction of the kitchen. "Ted and Dara were coming over, so I had lots."

"Thanks, Mom, but we grabbed a burger at a drive-through on the way home."

"Burgers? My goodness, you must have been hungry," Dara said.

"Some people like burgers," Ted said, glancing at his wife.

Dara turned away, her shoulders stiff. The tension between Dara and Ted was palpable, making Dylan thankful he and Lisa had missed supper.

"Hey, Dylan, Erika and I are going to a movie. We're leaving in half an hour," Amber said. "Do you wanna come?"

Thankful for the diversion, Dylan turned to Lisa. What better way to finish off a perfect day than by spending it in a darkened movie theater with Lisa? Even if he had to do it with his little sisters.

"What do you think, Lisa? Are you up to a movie?"

Her glance darted to Dara, then back to him. "I...I don't know. I, uh, was thinking I might go out on my own."

He frowned at her, puzzled at the change in her

demeanor. All the way home she had been a laughing, pleasant companion alternately serious and teasing, never at a loss for words. But since Ted had met them at the door she had said absolutely nothing.

"Sure. I could bring you wherever you want to go."

"No…no…it's okay. I'd like to go by myself."

Her hesitant speech was nothing like the laughing, confident girl he had spent the day with. What was going on? "Are you sure? I don't mind driving you."

"Goodness, Dylan. Let the girl be. I doubt she's spent more than a minute away from any Mathesons since she got here," Ted said with a forced laugh.

Dylan threw him a warning glance, peeved both with his brother's interference and Lisa's sudden change.

But Ted's words reminded him of the rehearsal party. Lisa had elected to stay home then, as well, and when he'd come back early, she'd appeared to be just coming back from somewhere. And had acted just as unsettled.

Lisa toyed with her hat, her eyes avoiding his. "I better get going," she said quietly.

Fifteen minutes later Dylan stood by the window of the study, watching Lisa get into a cab and leave. Dylan propped his shoulder against the window, pondering the puzzle of Lisa. Just before she left he'd overheard her talking to someone on her cell phone in her bedroom and she hadn't sounded happy.

The kisses they'd shared this afternoon had been surprising and had created a need to know more about her. So on the way home he had tried to draw more out of her. Her past life. What she did for fun. How she spent her time.

And while she was fun and witty and chatty, what he had found out could be written on a postage stamp.

Dylan pushed himself away from the window, his thoughts an unorganized chatter. He wanted their relationship to change. To deepen. This afternoon was a movement in that direction.

But where was it going?

He was leaving as soon as he was finished here. And when they got to Toronto, they would be going their separate ways.

They didn't have to.

He allowed the thought to settle. Played with it. He knew that compared to any other girl he had ever dated, she was by far the one he felt the closest to. The one who filled a need in him that others didn't.

But there were questions surrounding her that needed answering before they moved on. And she didn't seem willing to answer them.

With a light sigh he walked past her computer, glancing down as he did so. His eye caught the crumpled invoice lying beside it. When he had given it to her this morning he'd been quite sure there were two pieces of paper stuck together. But Lisa had said it was only a single invoice.

He picked it up, looking at it more closely. The invoice was white, but it had bits of yellow paper still clinging to it. He was right. There had been another paper.

He flipped through the file, but found no similarly stained memo. In fact, he found no yellow paper at all.

So where was it?

Dylan closed the file, impatiently tapping his fingers on the green folder. Why had she lied to him about it?

And where was she going right now?

Frustration battled with weariness. His father had asked Dylan to come and sort the business out but wasn't helping him. The woman he was growing more and more attracted to was becoming more and more of a mystery.

What was he doing here anyway?

"So what does this mean?" Lisa laid the memo carefully down on Gabe's table, her heartbeat pushing heavily against her ribs.

Gabe read the memo and clutched the back of his head with his hands. "Where did you get that?"

"It was stuck inside an invoice that was stuck to the outside of a file. I'm guessing Dylan and I weren't supposed to see it." Lisa leaned forward, resting her elbows on the table. "What couldn't you do anymore, Gabe? What did you neglect to tell me?"

"Did you show that to anyone?" He spoke without any of his previous bluster.

"No. I had to lie to Dylan about it. I hid it in my bedroom." Lisa cringed inwardly as she thought once again of the subterfuge she'd had to practice to get the memo to Gabe without Dylan's knowledge. It hurt to think of the puzzled look on his face this evening when she had said she wanted to go out.

She had never been very good at lying. And after the two kisses they'd shared, her duplicity bothered her even more.

Gabe leaned his head against the window, rolling his forehead back and forth. "Have you gotten into the files in the office?"

"No. Dylan and I spent the day sailing. Dara was gone and Alex didn't think we should go looking without her around."

Gabe hit the window with his fist and spun around. "I thought I threw that memo away."

"You didn't answer my question, Gabe. What does it mean?"

Gabe fell into the chair across from her, looking defeated. "You have to promise to just listen, okay?"

"Listen to what?" Her impatience made her short-tempered. "You haven't said anything worthwhile yet."

"Just listen." He held his hand up in warning. He tunneled his hands through his hair, clutching his skull. "Remember how when I first came to Vancouver, I had trouble finding a job? So I was running out of money and I met some guy."

Lisa sat back, clutching her midriff with her arms, an all too familiar tingle of dread beginning in her stomach. She bit back her anger and listened as Gabe had asked her to.

Gabe quietly related a story that echoed ones she had heard before. The wrong crowd. Questionable activities. A brush with the law.

"Lucky for me, they couldn't pin anything on me because I wasn't really involved. Just along for the ride. So I got off. No criminal record. Nothing. I made a deal with God that I would never do that stuff again. Then I met a girl. A nice girl. She worked for Matheson Telecom. Told me they were looking for an accountant. So I applied and got the job." Gabe stopped here, tapping his thumbs together. He gave Lisa a wavering smile. "Needless to say, I didn't make any mention of my little adventure. Things were going really well. Then one day I found a set of duplicate invoices. One was for less than the other. I wasn't supposed to see them both. I asked Dara and she sat me down and told me if I didn't keep my mouth shut I would get fired. She said she had asked around, had talked to that girl. She said she knew about my activities and that I had lied on my application about any involvement with the law." Gabe closed his eyes and rubbed his forehead with his forefinger. Just as he used to when he was a little boy. "And I had. But what could I do, Lisa? Nothing came of it. Nothing happened. Next thing I know she was getting me to do just the work on her father's company. They're customers of Matheson Telecom. It looked a little fishy to me and when I asked her about it, she said to mind my own business. Then there was talk around the office of missing money. I got scared, wrote the memo and got fired."

"Why didn't you tell me this right away?" The dread in Lisa's stomach grew with each word her brother uttered. "Why didn't you go to Alex?"

Gabe shook his head. "And tell him what? That I lied on my job application? Tell him that I thought his daughter-in-law was cheating him?"

Lisa thought of her own job application and her own evasions. She could hardly call Gabe out for that when she wasn't innocent, either.

"Did you do anything wrong, Gabe?"

He looked away. "I did what I was told until I realized it was stupid to be manipulated like that."

Dread clutched Lisa with chilly fingers. "Did you take any money, Gabe?"

Gabe's gaze flew to hers. "Not a penny. That's why you have to get into my computer. That will let you know if anything's been done on it. It's the only way she could have moved stuff around." Gabe held Lisa's gaze. "Didn't you go to the office this afternoon?"

Lisa pushed back a beat of guilt. "No, I told you—Dara wasn't in and Alex wouldn't let us access the files without her being around."

"I'll give you my password to get into my computer. If it's still there." He pulled out a piece of paper and wrote something down on it. "This is it. You don't have much time, you know."

Lisa knew that far too well. Each day she spent with Dylan brought them closer to the end of their time here. And each visit to Gabe created a combination of subterfuge and fear of being found out.

She glanced at her watch. She didn't dare stay away too much longer.

"I better go," Lisa said, getting up. She leaned over her brother and dropped a light kiss on his head. "You take care. I'm going to see if we can get into the office soon. Love you."

Gabe caught her by the hand. "I never tell you often enough, do I? How much you help me?"

Lisa smiled down at him, her heart overflowing with love. "I think I know," she said softly, absently brushing a strand of hair away from his forehead, just as she used to do when he was younger. "I have to help you. You're all I've got."

* * *

"Now Dylan's got himself a girl,
"And she's a pretty thing."

Erika and Amber stood on a stage at the front of the hall decorated with balloons and ribbons in honor of Alex and Stephanie's anniversary. Laughter swept over the large group of people seated at tables as the twins looked up from the crumpled paper they held between them.

"We hope that this one sticks around
"Long enough to get a..."

Erika paused, her grin mischievous.

"Raise," she said.

"That doesn't rhyme," someone called out from the crowd.

"Neither does stock option," Amber said, singling Dylan out with her smile. "And that was our only other choice."

Lisa glanced sidelong at Dylan, wondering how he took this bantering. But Dylan was sitting back in his chair, his tie loosened, his hands folded over his stomach, laughing as hard as anyone else.

Amber sent a wink in Lisa's direction. "Thanks, Lisa, for daring to show up to yet another Matheson family function, Mom and Dad's anniversary. You deserve a medal."

"She deserves our sympathy," Ted called out in an overloud voice from another corner of the hall.

Lisa couldn't stop the blush that reddened her cheeks at the implications in the comments. Nor could she stop the surge of guilt at the deception she and Dylan were playing out.

And the deception she herself was playing out on a family that had accepted her with open arms and an open heart.

She endured an instant of pain, intense and familiar, remembering the many times she and Gabe had stood in the hallway of a new home, wondering how they were going to fit in. The Mathesons had taken in Dylan's unknown girlfriend with grace and aplomb and love. Even the twins had accepted her and had offered clothing and makeup and little inside jokes and stories about Dylan that made him both more endearing and kind.

And now she was sitting through this evening watching skits and hearing poems that portrayed family life in the Matheson household. Listening to remembrances that showed what a close and loving family they were.

The twins' poem moved on to the other family members and they finished to a round of applause. They sketched a quick bow and winked at Lisa.

"Mom and Dad want to say a few words now, to end the evening." The twins gestured toward their parents, who got up from their seats at the head table and made their way to the stage, holding hands as they often did.

Alex tapped on the microphone and looked around the room with a huge smile.

"We are so thankful that all of you could come here. And we're especially thankful for all the work Erika, Amber, Ted, Dara and Tiffany did. We're thankful Dylan and Lisa could come from so far away."

Lisa tried not to squirm at the pairing of her name with Dylan's. Just as if they were a real couple.

"We're thankful Chelsea and Jordan were willing to accommodate our anniversary around their honeymoon."

Huge cheers went up for the newly married couple.

"This evening has been a blessing to Stephanie and me." Alex glanced sidelong at his wife and they shared a look of love so deep it made Lisa smile just to see it. "But with our thanks, we want to thank our Lord for His enduring love. His blessings through good and bad times. What we have on this earth is less important to us than who we are. And in everything we've done, Stephanie and I have hoped and prayed that we have shown our children that. Thank you all for coming. There's lots of food yet. The party's not over until the last Matheson is gone. Have a good evening yet."

Glasses were tinkled all around the hall signaling a request for a kiss, and Alex and Stephanie graciously responded. Their kiss was discreet but warm. Another cheer went up, and with a quick wave Alex and Stephanie returned to their seats.

A wave of voices rose around them. But Lisa couldn't look at Dylan. Couldn't talk to him. Instead, in an attempt to pretend busyness, she toyed with the silvery hearts sprinkled on the heavy damask tablecloth, while her heart grew heavier and heavier. Each day she and Dylan spent together brought them closer to the end of this time together. She felt an urgency that no longer was attached only to finding out what she could for Gabe. Now her urgency had as much or more to do with Dylan.

Sooner or later she had to tell Dylan who she really was. Which would mean she would not return to Toronto with him.

And that would be the end of the dream.

"Excuse me," she murmured to Dylan and the people sitting at their table. She got up and walked outside, feeling suddenly claustrophobic. Once outside, she took a deep breath of the blessedly cool air. She leaned her elbows on the railing of the balcony, watching how the gold lights of the downtown buildings of Vancouver spangled the water across the bay. Under other circumstances she would have been entranced. But tonight guilt weighed heavily on her heart.

Lord, what have I started? Lord, what do I do? How do I get myself out of this? I am starting to care for this man. And care for his family.

"Hey, are you okay?" Dylan came up behind her, resting his hand on her shoulder.

"Just wanted to get a breath of fresh air," Lisa said, staying where she was.

"It was getting a bit close in there, wasn't it?" Dylan's fingers lightly stroked her shoulder. "I hope you weren't too embarrassed with the girls' poem?"

Lisa spun around, holding his gaze. "I don't know what I felt." She wished she could be more articulate. More honest.

"I know what I did." Dylan's eyes glittered in the reflected light and his expression grew serious. He ran his finger along the side of her face. "Lisa, something is happening between us. I know you feel it, too."

Lisa wanted him to stop, but his words soothed the ache of yearning that had been growing since she met him. Just a few more moments, she thought, closing her eyes and her mind to the second thoughts that clamored for attention. Just a few more memories.

He held her shoulders and drew her close to him, his breath sighing through her hair. "Let's get away from here." He took her hand and led her along the balcony to a set of stone steps that led to a discreetly lit garden.

The grass was damp from the shower this afternoon, but Lisa didn't mind. She was glad to get away from the party and be where she wanted most to be right now.

Alone with Dylan.

They followed the edge of the manicured lawn, staying close to the flower gardens that sent out a heady mixture of scents. They followed a path to a gazebo, and Lisa's heart quickened when she saw it was empty.

Their footfalls echoed on the wooden floor, and when they were under the roof, Dylan turned to Lisa and drew her into his arms.

Lisa swallowed, sent up a prayer for strength, then leaned back.

"Dylan, I'm starting to feel so guilty about what we're doing to your family," she said, pressing her hands against his chest. "Every day I feel like more and more of a fraud. I don't know how long I can do this anymore. Your family is so great and they are acting like I really am your girlfriend." She stopped, the word catching in her throat. "And I really like them."

Dylan drew back, a light frown pulling his dark eyebrows together. "What are you saying?"

Lisa looked straight ahead, focusing on his loosened tie. "I think we should tell them the truth."

"And what is the truth?" Dylan lifted her face with

his finger, smiling down at her. "That we don't like each other? That what happened on the sailboat was just an act? That what is happening now is staged for the benefit of my family?" He cupped her chin with his hand, his eyes intent on hers. "I don't think that's the truth, either. Not anymore."

At her center unvoiced and uncertain feelings swirled as she grasped at the meaning of his words. Did she dare hope that they might have a future?

She drifted toward him, drawn by the emotion in his voice, by her own uncertain and changing emotions.

She laid her hand on his chest, as if forestalling the inevitable, trying to find some solid ground on which to make a stand.

Lisa swallowed as he lowered his head to hers. She stopped him, her emotions seesawing between her changing feelings for him and the precariousness of her situation.

She had to tell him.

She couldn't tell him. Because if she did, everything she had right now would be lost.

"But I'm not a girlfriend, am I?" She didn't want an answer, but she had to speak the words aloud.

Dylan shrugged, still holding her. "I think you are. I think I feel more for you than I've felt for any so-called girlfriend I've ever had."

His words wrapped themselves around her, teasing, alluring. And dangerous.

"You know what your problem is, Lisa?" Dylan asked, his hands clasped at her waist. "You think too much."

"First time I've ever been accused of that," Lisa said with a light laugh.

Dylan smiled back. "I think we have a future, Lisa. I really do."

Lisa closed her eyes as he lowered his head. His kiss was gentle, sweet.

And heartbreaking.

"Okay, I figured I'd find you two out here."

Like a clumsy hand sweeping away a spiderweb, Ted's slurred voice whisked away the beautiful and fragile moment. Lisa dropped her hand and sucked in a deep breath, willing her heart to quit pounding.

"You two look pretty cozy," Ted said, coming into the gazebo. He swayed a little, as if he'd been drinking. "I do b'lieve this is the first time I've ever seen you with your arm around a girl."

Ted turned to Lisa, his eyes glazed. "Did you know that your boyfriend schedules his dates on his handheld computer?" He nodded slowly. "Just marks them in along with business meetings and reminders to pick up his dry cleaning."

Lisa heard Dylan sigh and she glanced sidelong at him. He crossed his arms over his chest, looking slightly bored. "And why do you think Lisa would want to know that?"

Ted rocked a little, grinning. "So she knows what she's in for." Ted glanced over at Lisa. "Course, how many boyfriends make their girlfriends work on their holiday? Huh? But that's our Dylan. He's found the ultimate girlfriend. A secretary. That's my brother. Always efficient."

Lisa felt a pang of hurt that shouldn't have bothered

her. She *was* Dylan's secretary, in spite of the whispered promise she had heard only moments ago. In spite of feelings that were changing.

"Lisa is more than a secretary, and you know that, Ted," Dylan said, pulling Lisa even closer. Lisa clung to him, drawing from his strength.

"So why do you have her helping you? You come sweeping in here—" Ted waved a feeble hand in Lisa's direction "—with your secretary. Come to fix everything. Maybe even my job."

"You know I don't want your job, Ted. I'm quitting the company. The last thing I want to do is sweep in and take over."

"So why are you hanging around here, poking your nose into the books?"

"Because Dad asked me to."

"Did you find what you're looking for?"

Lisa watched Ted, listened to the bravado in his voice. And she wondered how much he knew about Gabe and Dara.

"If we could get into the office, I'm sure we would find more than what we've been finding by only looking through the files Dara has given us," Lisa blurted out.

She clamped her lips together as Ted's swivering gaze landed on her. What had made her blurt that out and draw attention to herself?

"Really? And how would you know what to look for, Miss secretary slash girlfriend?"

"I think you've said enough, Ted," Dylan said, annoyance edging his voice.

Ted shook his head slowly. Laughed a humorless

laugh. "Haven't said enough, really. Never say enough." He took a step closer to Lisa. She could smell the liquor on his breath. "Let me warn you, Lisa. My brother? Cold. No fun. Busy, busy, busy. Such a hard worker." He swayed a moment and Dylan grabbed him. "Dara didn't love him. Said she couldn't."

Dylan's eyes were narrowed, his lips thin. "You better go back, Ted. We didn't invite you here, and Lisa doesn't want to hear what you have to say."

"I think she does." Ted laid a hand on Lisa's shoulder. "Did you know your Dylan used to date my wife? But she didn't want a cold fish like him. She only wanted me. Just me."

Lisa felt a surprising flash of jealousy. But as she looked more closely at Ted, beyond the anger that clenched his jaw, she saw pain in his eyes. And she heard the uncertainty in his voice.

"Then it's a good thing she married you, isn't it?" Lisa said quietly, feeling suddenly sorry for him.

"Let go of her, Ted," Dylan warned, taking a step nearer his brother.

Lisa gently shook her head in warning at Dylan. She sensed that Ted wasn't a threat. "I'm sure she still cares for you."

Ted blinked, as if trying to absorb what she'd said. He let go of Lisa's shoulder and looked past her, his bluster and bravado slipping away like clothes off a hanger. "I don't know anymore." Ted sank onto a bench lining the gazebo, his hands holding his head. "I don't know if she loves me anymore." His words were slurred. Almost as if he was crying.

"Why shouldn't she, Ted?" Lisa asked.

"She doesn't talk to me anymore. Full of secrets." He rubbed his hands over his head again and again.

Lisa felt her heart quicken. Maybe Ted knew something after all. "What secrets, Ted?"

Ted looked up at her, his bleary eyes blinking as if trying to focus on her. "That's why they're secrets. I dunno about them."

"Lisa, don't bother trying to talk to him now. He's had too much to drink." Dylan tugged on Lisa's arm.

Lisa glanced back at Ted, feeling torn.

Ted needs to know.

Lisa wondered what he knew. And wondered, if Dylan talked to him, if Ted would let it out.

She didn't stop to examine her motives. Lisa ran to his side and caught Dylan by the arm, stopping him. "I think he needs to talk to you, Dylan," she whispered. "Listen to him."

Dylan clenched his jaw, staring at Ted, who still sat hunched over, then looked down at Lisa, his features softening. "Why should I talk to him now?"

"Because he's your brother." And because he might be able to help my brother.

"Ted has never needed anyone. He's only used people."

"Well, he needs you now." Lisa tugged lightly. "Please talk to him."

"Why does this matter so much to you?" Dylan touched Lisa's cheek lightly, smiling now.

A week ago it would have been solely because of Gabe. But now…

"Family is a gift from God," she said softly, her words sincere. "And I think this is a chance to fix a few things in yours."

Dylan's expression grew serious. "You really believe that, don't you?"

"I do. Don't waste this opportunity."

Dylan shook his head, but he let Lisa lead him back to Ted's side. He hunkered down beside his brother. "Ted, what's wrong?"

Ted ran his fingers through his neatly combed hair again and again, still looking down. "I don't think Dara loves me anymore."

"Why do you say that?" Dylan asked, his own voice quieter.

Ted looked up at Dylan. "She never talks to me anymore. She's always so busy. All she talks about is you and Lisa."

"What do you mean?"

Ted slowly shook his head. "She's tired of having to run files around for nothing. She doesn't have time. When she's home all she does is say how she wishes your dad would stop putting pressure on her to cooperate."

"What do you want me to do, Ted?"

"This is a waste of time," Ted said. "Tell Dad to stop pokin' around. It's all Dara can talk about. We found out who did it. Just let it go. Please. She's scared Dad's trying to find a way to get me out and put you in."

"Okay, Ted. I'll talk to Dad. We're not getting anywhere on it anyhow."

Lisa stifled a flare of panic at Dylan's assurances. Ted was supposed to confirm her suspicions. Help her clear Gabe. This was not what was supposed to happen. What had she done?

Dylan pushed himself to his feet and caught Ted by the hand. "Don't worry about this anymore. It will be over soon."

Lisa closed her eyes. *Dear Lord, this wasn't supposed to be the outcome.*

What was she going to do now?

Chapter Ten

She couldn't sleep anymore. What she had done last night flipped and spun through her mind, keeping her awake.

She should have shown Dylan the memo right away before her emotions for this family interfered with her plans. But if she gave Dylan the memo now, he would wonder why she had kept it from him.

With an exasperated sigh she tossed off the blankets, wrapped her robe around her. She pulled the offending piece of paper from a drawer in her room and left.

She drifted down the stairs, making her way to the study.

The door was half-open and she quietly slipped through it. The early-morning light was already creeping in. She hesitated a moment, glancing over her shoulder, then strode to Dylan's desk, opened the file folder on the top and laid the memo inside, letting part of it show above the file folder's edge.

As she closed the folder she felt a tick of relief. Maybe it would make the difference. And maybe it would incriminate her.

Either way, time was winding down. She couldn't help Gabe anymore. Her fantasy with Dylan was coming to an end in spite of his whispered promises.

Dylan would return to Toronto, and then he would leave Matheson Telecom for his new job.

Pain, hard and sharp, surged through her at the thought of him leaving. She couldn't stop it and she couldn't change it. And she couldn't go back to Toronto with him.

She looked around and saw the shelf that held the Bible. With a cry of sorrow she stumbled toward it like a lost person seeking home.

She snatched it off the shelf and held it close.

What do you hope to find here?

Panic clutched at her as the conversation she and Dylan had had with Ted spun up once more. Dylan was going to stop looking. Gabe was still seen as guilty. What was going to happen to him if she quit now? She knew from experience that if things didn't get resolved she didn't know what Gabe would do.

But how could she convince Dylan to keep digging without letting him know who she was?

She couldn't tell him. Not yet.

With a tired sigh she dropped into the large leather sofa facing the fireplace. She tucked her feet under her and snapped on the light, creating an intimate cone of luminance in the darkened study.

She paged through the Bible, her previous question

nagging at her. Did she want answers to her dilemma? A solution to the problems she had taken on?

Was she hoping to recapture the connection she'd felt so strongly in church?

She paged past the prophets to the New Testament, the Bible opening to the book of Peter. Her eyes skimmed the words, then stopped.

"God opposes the proud, but gives grace to the humble. Humble yourselves therefore under God's mighty hand that He may lift you up in due time. Cast all your anxiety on Him because He cares for you."

Lisa read the words again. And again. They pressed against her, exposing her even as they gave her comfort. She knew that she had to let go of her plans, yet if she did what would happen to Gabe? To her?

For the past few days she had allowed herself a fantasy. That Dylan really was her boyfriend and she was a part of this family. That together they would prove Gabe innocent.

But it wasn't going to happen once Dylan and his family heard the truth from her. And even if she didn't tell them, Dylan was leaving the company. Would she go back to Toronto and pursue the faint hope Dylan had held out to her in his whispered promises last night? Would those promises still hold once he found out she had lied to him?

Please, Lord. Just a little while longer, she prayed as the loneliness of the past few years and the sacrifices she had made for Gabe in her personal life nagged at her resolve. *Let me hold on to this dream just a little more?*

But even as the prayer formulated in her mind, she knew God wouldn't answer it. She knew what she had to do. She closed the Bible and set it aside. *Cast all your anxiety on Him because He cares for you.*

Lisa pressed her hands against her face, her emotions warring with truth. *Help me, Lord. Help me find the right time.*

The door to the study creaked open and Lisa whirled around, her hand on her chest.

It was Dylan. His hair was still tousled from sleep and whiskers darkened his cheeks. He wore a loose T-shirt and blue jeans. And he looked even better than he had last night in a suit and tie.

"Hey, there," he said, his voice still sleep roughened. "You couldn't sleep, either?"

Lisa shook her head, her heart throbbing in her chest in a confused combination of fear and anticipation.

Dylan walked into the study and stopped by the end table beside Lisa's chair. "When I saw the light under the door, I thought you were my mother. She sometimes comes in here early in the morning and has her devotions."

"I'm…I'm…sorry. I'll leave." Lisa struggled to untangle her feet from her long robe to stand, but Dylan caught her by the shoulder and eased her down.

"It's okay. She doesn't do it every morning." Dylan came around the couch and hunkered down in front of her. He caught her by the hands, toying gently with her fingers as he smiled up at her. "I was thinking about you this morning."

In spite of her resolve, a soft yearning grew within her at his touch, at the intimacy of his lowered voice. Giving in to an impulse, she reached out and feathered his hair back from his forehead, letting her fingers trail down the rough stubble of his cheek.

"I was thinking about you, too." The words slipped past her defenses. She fought back the reality of their situation, deferring the moment when she was going to tell him the truth.

"So why couldn't you sleep?" Dylan lifted her fingers to his lips and kissed them lightly, his eyes on hers.

His soft question coupled with the touch of his mouth roused an agitation of feelings within her.

Tell him. Tell him now.

No. Not yet. This is too precious.

Lisa held his eyes as she swallowed hard against the shame she could feel pushing its way up her throat.

You promised you would at the right moment.

But she couldn't. Not with Dylan so close. So dear.

She knew what was happening. Somehow, in the process of trying to save her brother, she had lost her heart. And when Dylan leaned closer and touched his lips to her cheek, she knew she was going to wait.

"I didn't think I'd ever find anyone like you," he said quietly, pushing her aside so he could sit beside her. "It sounds corny, but you make me feel whole."

He sighed, still holding her hand as he angled his chin toward the Bible. "Were you reading it?"

"I was. I feel like I need to connect. To find peace." Her words trailed off as the contradiction of what she had been reading and what she should do warred within her.

Dylan reached past her and pulled the Bible off the table. "What were you reading?"

"First Peter. 'Cast all your anxieties on him.'" Lisa

laughed lightly, trying to dispel the heaviness that had crept over them. "Easier to read about than do."

"Do you have a favorite passage?" Dylan leafed through the Bible, angling her a smile as he did so.

"First Corinthians 13."

"Ah. The love passage." Dylan flipped through the Bible and found it. "'If I speak in the tongues of men and of angels, but have not love, I am only a resounding gong or a clanging cymbal,'" he read, his voice growing quiet. Reverent. "'Love is patient, love is kind. It does not envy, it does not boast, it is not proud.'" Dylan paused there, his finger resting on the passage. "That covers quite a lot of territory, doesn't it?"

"It also makes love so much more than a simple word."

"Loving someone can be the hardest thing to do," Dylan said, setting the Bible aside. "It's not always a soft, mushy emotion."

Lisa leaned back against the buttery leather of the couch, her eyes on Dylan as a surprising peace drifted over her. She kept quiet as she thought about what he had read. About love.

God's love.

Her love.

She let the word slip through her mind, drifting, incomplete. She loved her brother. She loved her parents.

But what she felt for Dylan was something completely different. And she felt the stirring of a newer, even more frightening emotion. She glanced at Dylan quietly leafing through the Bible. He looked up at her.

Like ice water flowing through her veins the realization dawned. She loved him.

She couldn't. It was too soon. Too sudden.

Yet even as her thoughts negated it, her heart told her it was true. Dylan was exactly the kind of man she had been looking for.

Why had she found him now? And under these circumstances?

The door behind them swept open and light poured out of the ceiling fixture.

"Oh, I'm sorry," Stephanie said, standing in the doorway. "I didn't know you were here."

"I'm just leaving…right now," Lisa said softly. "I need to have a shower." She gave Dylan a sad smile, then left, wishing she could outrun what she had just discovered.

"Dylan, I'm sorry. Was I interrupting something?"

Dylan smiled. "Believe it or not, I was reading to her out of the Bible."

"The Bible?" Stephanie's voice betrayed her confusion. She tightened the sash on her red silk robe, glancing over her shoulder as if seeking confirmation.

"Yes. First Corinthians 13, if you must know."

"Dylan. That's…" Dylan felt his mother's hand on his shoulder. Heard the wonder in her voice. A wonder that echoed his own. "You don't know how I've prayed that you would find someone who would share…" She stopped again, emotion stopping her.

Dylan stood, turning to Stephanie, and saw the glisten of tears in her eyes. He gave his mother a gentle smile.

"She's a wonderful girl, Dylan. I sense that she's seeking the Lord."

Dylan looked past his mother at the open door of the

study. In spite of the tender moment they had shared, he still felt as if a part of Lisa was evading him. As if there were things about her he didn't know. "I wish I knew exactly what she was seeking."

Stephanie took him by the arm and pulled him onto the couch Lisa had just left so suddenly. "You just have to be patient, Dylan. Something you're not very good at as a rule."

"Thanks for the vote of confidence, Mom," Dylan said, suppressing a sigh.

"In all other respects you are an amazing, wonderful person and any girl would be lucky to have you." Stephanie gave his captured arm a shake as if to get his full attention.

"So why do I get the feeling I don't know her very well?"

"You've only been together a short while," Stephanie said quietly.

"Yet I really care about her," he reluctantly admitted, knowing what chain of events his confession would create. His mother would tell the girls and they would be all over him like a bad suit giving advice on dating and the best place to go looking for engagement rings.

"Dylan, I'm so happy. Your father and I have prayed so long that you would find someone to care about. Someone who could share your faith."

Dylan held his mother's longing gaze, his own doubts coming to the fore. "I don't know if we share that, Mother. A faith."

"She came to church with you. You were just reading out of the Bible together."

Dylan leaned back, sinking into the cool leather of the couch, feeling inadequate in the face of his mother's conviction. "Don't give me too much credit, Mom. I haven't done either for a long time."

"But you're doing it now." Stephanie stroked Dylan's hair back from his face much as she had when he was younger. "And God acknowledges each small step you make. 'A bruised reed He will not break, a smouldering wick He will not quench.'"

Dylan laid his head back, suddenly tired. "That's exactly how I feel. Like a bruised reed. Not enough life to stand, but not completely bent over yet."

"In your faith life?"

"And my personal life. And my professional life." Except with Lisa. With her he felt fully alive. Strong.

"You're still angry with your father about Ted, aren't you?" Stephanie's voice was quiet, but her pain and sorrow poured through her words. "I was hoping this week together would remove some of that. I was hoping you would change your mind about leaving and stay with the company."

"It's too late for that, Mom." Dylan sighed, pressing his forefinger to his temple. The holiday had appeared endless before they left, but it had flown on wings. Now, as the end neared, he wished for more time. "As for Dad, I'm not as angry as I was. Especially not after listening to poor Ted last night." Dylan tilted his head toward his mother, the couch sighing with the movement. "He's far unhappier with Dad's decision than I ever was, Mom."

"I know."

The simple admission caught him unawares.

"So does your father," Stephanie continued, slipping the silky ends of her robe's sash through her fingers.

Dylan glanced out the window of the study. From where he sat he could just see the early-morning sunlight glinting gold off the office buildings of downtown. Morning in the city.

He used to love coming early to his office and watching the sun come up, wondering what the new day was going to bring.

But for the past few years all that morning had brought was a sense that he was simply marking time. His work in Toronto didn't challenge him and didn't give him enough control to make any decisions that would take the company in dramatic new directions. Though he had done well in the branch office, the real authority still came from Vancouver.

"So why does he allow Ted to simply flounder on?" Dylan asked.

"You're not the only proud person in this family, Dylan. It's hard for your father to admit he's made a mistake. Just as it's hard for Ted to admit he can't do the job. Just as it's hard for you to simply tell your father that you should be in charge of the company, not Ted. And now that you're quitting the company…"

"I'm not going to wait anymore."

Stephanie swung around to face him, leaning close to him, her eyes flashing, her jaw set. "No. Instead you're going to run away. And you're wrong about your father. He's not as driven as you. And he's much softer.

I love him for it, but when it comes to the business, Matheson Telecom needs someone like you."

Her anger washed over him, surprising in its intensity. His mother was usually all softness and gentleness. He listened.

"Your father needs you to confront him and tell him that enough is enough. If you want to be in charge, then tell him that. If you do, you will give Alex and Ted an easy out. Like I said, in their own way they have pride, as well." Stephanie brushed a hand over her forehead, as if brushing away her anger. "You're the only one I can talk to right now, Dylan. Ted has his own problems, and your father has his own secrets...." Her voice faltered and as quickly as the movement of clouds across the sun, her anger faded away. "I don't know what's going on anymore. I only know that since that accountant Gabe was fired things have gone all haywire in this house. Right now you and Lisa and the twins are the only people in this house who don't have any secrets."

But Lisa did have her own secrets.

"I want this family whole again, Dylan. I want things the way they're supposed to be in a family that confesses to love the Lord."

"And I'm supposed to be the one to do it, Mom?" Dylan asked quietly. "What if I don't even know myself about my relationship with the Lord?"

"God never forgets you, Dylan. He never lets go. You have been a child of God since you were born and I cling to that promise every day." Stephanie caught his hand and held it between her own. "Every day your father and I pray for you and for all our children. We have prayed that you would find a relationship with God."

The words gave him comfort. Strength.

He turned his mother's hand over, tracing the raised veins in the backs of her hands as he used to as a child. "I haven't prayed for a while, Mom. I don't know how to start."

"Do you want to?" Stephanie's voice was a soft whisper, as if she hardly dared voice her request too loud.

Dylan nodded.

"Okay. You start with something simple and I'll pray it for you. We'll keep going like that."

Dylan bent his head, pushing aside the voices that had lured him away all these years. The voices that told him God was for women and weak men. The thoughts that fooled him into thinking that he could be strong on his own.

With his mother beside him, he dug down to the bedrock of his faith. To the God he had known as a child.

"Dear Lord," he prayed, "I don't know where to start. I only know that I want to know You more."

Stephanie responded, adding her own prayer. And as her voice lilted through familiar cadences, her sincerity pouring through in the touch of her hands on his, in the feeling in her voice, Dylan felt his unraveling ends slowly becoming whole.

And he let God into his life again.

Lisa sat at her computer desk, her mind a storm of thoughts and emotions.

Since her epiphany in this very same place this morning, she couldn't find a place in her mind that brought her serenity.

She knew only the truth would. But the truth was a double-edged sword. It would bring her peace, but it would also sever any hopes of a continuing relationship with Dylan.

She turned back to the crumpled invoice lying beside her computer. Dylan didn't want to look anymore, but she couldn't quit. Though she loved Dylan, she had made a promise to herself to help her brother. And she had to go through with that. No matter what the cost.

She had pulled the invoice out of the file and was looking at it again, sensing that it held more than just a hiding place for the memo.

She booted up her computer and punched in the date of the invoice. A list of other invoices came up, but not this one. Why had Dara not entered it?

An invoice with the same date for the same company came up. But for a different amount.

She frowned at the invoice, wondering what she was supposed to be seeing. She realized she had taken the wrong piece of paper to Gabe's. Instead of the memo, she should have taken this invoice.

"I didn't think I'd find you in here anymore."

Dylan's voice swept over Lisa's swirling thoughts, bringing love and helpless yearning in its wake.

She turned to him. How could she not?

He rested his hip against her desk, bringing him close enough that she could smell his aftershave. He had tidied up since she'd seen him last. "You seemed a little upset this morning. Are you okay now?"

His deep voice, coupled with his concern, rekindled her emotions. Created a faint hope she hardly dared nurture.

She looked away, quashing her feelings. "I'm okay." Which was a lie. She knew that no matter what happened to her in the future, she would not walk away without scars from this time spent with Dylan.

"Okay enough to come have breakfast with us?"

"There's a few things I want to finish up yet." Besides, she had spent too much time with his family already and she felt a need to get her relationship with Dylan back to where it should be. Back to where it was safe. If that could even happen.

"Don't you have the feeling we're missing something?" she asked, pushing aside her feelings. "Something that's right under our noses?"

Dylan waggled his hand, as if considering. "I don't know. Not that it matters. I told Ted we'd back off, and Dad doesn't seem to be too involved."

"If your father wasn't, why would he ask you to come here?" Lisa fought down her panic. Dylan had to keep going. If they didn't find out the truth, she was afraid of what would happen to her brother. "Ted is the one asking you to quit, not your father."

Dylan shrugged. "I wish I knew what he wanted. I need to sit down and have a heart-to-heart with him before we go."

"You don't have much time," Lisa said quietly, her concern shifting from her brother to Dylan. She got the feeling that Alex cared about the problems in the company, but that he also had his own agenda in dealing with them.

The sharp ring of the phone made Lisa jump. Dylan ignored it.

"Shouldn't you get that?" she said.

He shook his head as he ran his finger lightly over her cheek in an intimate gesture that made Lisa quiver inside.

Dylan smiled a crooked smile. "My mother thinks I should talk to my dad, as well. Are you two in cahoots?"

"No. But I like your parents. A lot."

"And she likes you. A lot." He grew still, his eyes holding hers.

He's going to kiss me, Lisa thought, her heart skipping in her chest. I want him to.

I can't let him.

"Dylan, Dara's on the phone for you." Amber stuck her head in the study. "Says she has something important to tell you."

Dylan blew out his breath and glanced back at his sister. "Thanks, Amber. I'll take it in here." He reached behind him and caught the phone off his desk, but didn't move from Lisa's side.

Lisa moved to get up, to give him privacy, but he gently laid his hand on her shoulder, forestalling her. As if negating Ted's comment about Dara and Dylan. Reassuring her he had nothing to hide.

"So, Dara. What can I do for you?" Dylan smiled down at Lisa, his fingers lingering on her shoulder. His smile held, then faded.

"I'm glad to hear that, Dara," Dylan said. He nodded as if listening to more that she had to say, then slowly pulled his hand away from Lisa, frowning. "How did you manage to do that?… No, I hadn't heard anything about it… Are you sure that's where the money came from?… Of course I'll tell Dad…. Ted already knows…. Well, I guess that ties it all up. Thanks, Dara. This makes things a lot easier for everybody. Congratulations." Dylan pressed a button ending the phone call, then turned to Lisa. "Dara managed to get into Gabe's computer. She found the money that's been missing. So that officially ends our part of the job."

Lisa stared at Dylan as his words slowly found their way to her mind. She tried to grab hold of them. Make them make sense. "So where's the money? How did she manage to find it? Is she sure it's his?"

"She said she found it in an account he'd set up under a numbered company." Dylan pushed himself away from her desk. "That makes the next step that much easier. We'll have to be pressing charges against that accountant now."

"What do you mean press charges?"

"If the missing money is in his account, he's guilty." Dylan frowned at her. "This isn't a problem, Lisa. This is a good thing. Now we can finally put this all behind us." He caught her by the hand and pulled her to her feet. "Now we can focus on the really important things," he said with a grin.

Lisa couldn't look at him. Couldn't think. Her mind was a whirl of thoughts and confusion. She had seen Gabe just a few days ago. He hadn't said anything about money. He wasn't living as if he had any extra. Where could it have come from?

It was as if her heart had frozen, sending ice through her arteries.

Was Gabe guilty after all?

Dylan gave Lisa's hands a little shake, as if trying to catch her attention. "Why so glum? It's over. No more digging into files. No more listening to evasions. We've only got one more day here. Let's spend it doing something fun."

Fun? Lisa tried to gather her thoughts. Tried to put them in some kind of order. Gabe was innocent. She knew it. She had to believe it.

"How did Dara manage to find the money now?" she asked, refusing to give up on her brother so quickly. "According to your father it's been missing for a while now. How come she didn't find it any sooner?"

"Dara said it took her a while to hack in to Gabe's computer. She found evidence of a numbered company and a bank account in that name. The money was in that bank account."

"I don't know, Dylan," Lisa said, pulling her hands away from his, needing the distance to focus on what she had to say. "I don't have a good feeling about this. Seems to me that finding this money is too convenient. Why didn't she find it sooner? Why didn't Dara let us come and work in the office? There are just too many questions."

"What do you care, Lisa? All that's come of this is more work for yourself."

"I knew this was going to be a working holiday," Lisa said, struggling to find the right words to explain herself without looking guilty. "And I'm still your secretary." She lifted her hands in a gesture of surrender. "I just have the feeling that Dara is hiding something."

Dylan shrugged. "What?"

Lisa drew in a long, slow breath, willing her racing heart to slow down. Much depended on how she handled this.

She held up the invoice that had been lying beside her computer. "Do you remember this? You found it stuck to the outside of a file."

Dylan nodded, his smile fading away.

Lisa swallowed a knot of nervous tension. She had put herself in this position, after all. "There was a memo tucked inside the invoice that I didn't think much of." She pulled it out from under the invoice and handed it to Dylan. "Until I read it."

He angled her a puzzled frown as he took it. Then he read it himself.

"What in the world…?" He looked over the paper at Lisa, his eyes now a stormy gray. "Why didn't you think it was important?"

"And this invoice doesn't show up anywhere," Lisa continued, forced by her own misconduct to avoid answering his question. Deflect and distract. "I have been checking and double-checking, but it hasn't been entered in any place I can find."

Dylan didn't reply right away, as if still waiting for an answer. Then he took the invoice from her and glanced at it.

"This is for Dara's father's company." He laid it down again. "We didn't get those files."

"Why not? Dara told us she gave us everything that had been handled in the past year." Lisa finally dared to meet his gaze. "This invoice is only three months old. Two months before the accountant was fired." Lisa could not say his name, afraid that even mentioning Gabe would shout out her guilt.

Dylan took another look at the invoice, then at the memo.

"Do you think these two are connected?"

"I didn't give the invoice much consideration until this morning." *Until the idea that you might be quitting made me desperate to do something. Anything. Including directing your annoyance toward me.* "I think it's pertinent."

Lisa kept her eyes on the computer screen in front of her and hit a key to deactivate the screen saver. And waited.

Dylan tapped his fingers against his thigh as if trying to make up his mind. "Part of me wants to laugh off what you're saying. I want to be finished with all of this." He angled her a puzzled glance. "Yet this memo and this invoice make me think twice, even with Dara finding the money." He slapped his hands against his legs as if making up his mind. "We'll go to the office today and see if we can get into Gabe's computer. Then we can look for ourselves."

The tension in Lisa's shoulders ebbed. She had bought Gabe a little more time and another opportunity.

At what cost?

"I'll just run upstairs and change. I'll meet you at the car." She needed the paper with Gabe's password on it.

She doubted Dara would give it to her. And if she had a chance, she had to risk one more call to Gabe.

Before Dylan could say anything Lisa turned and left.

Once in her room, Lisa pulled out the pants she had been wearing when she had visited Gabe last and shoved her hands into each of the pockets. Nothing.

Dylan is waiting. Hurry.

She opened her purse and riffled through it. Still nothing.

With trembling hands she grabbed her cell phone and punched Gabe's number in. No answer. Relax, relax, she told herself, and tried again. Still no answer.

She glanced around her room agitation building. Where could she have put it? She tried the pants again, then the shirt she had been wearing. As she threw it on the bed in disgust, a piece of paper fluttered to the carpet. Lisa pounced on it.

Thank You, Lord, she breathed, aware of the irony of her prayer as she glanced at Gabe's password.

I hope this works, she thought, remembering to change her clothes. She ran a quick brush through her hair and left it hanging to her shoulders. A quick glance in the mirror of the bathroom revealed pallid features dominated by wide oval eyes. *Help me through this, Lord, and I'll tell Dylan the truth. I will.*

On her way downstairs she ducked into the office, grabbed an empty computer disk and slipped it into her purse, just in case she needed a copy of whatever she might find. Continuing out the door, she went to the car where Dylan was waiting.

As they left, her heart fluttered in her chest with a

mixture of nerves and anticipation. She hoped what they discovered would prove Gabe's innocence and not his guilt. And that Dara hadn't changed Gabe's password.

Chapter Eleven

Dylan turned off the street and slowed the car over the speed bump straddling the entrance to Matheson Telecom's parking lot. He glanced sidelong at Lisa, who hadn't said anything during the entire trip over. A few times he'd thought of asking her about the memo.

He didn't want to know what she had to say. He preferred to think of the time they had spent in the study that morning. Holding her in his arms. Kissing her. And most important, reading the Bible with her.

Those things were real. And those things were part of Lisa, as well. He had to believe that. His questions about the memo could come later. Once they were in Toronto they would be away from all this. And they would have a chance to pursue their changing relationship.

Where it would lead, Dylan wasn't sure. But he knew that for now they shared a common faith, and that was the best place to begin any relationship.

He swung the car into an empty space beside his

father's parking stall. Alex's silver car gleamed as it always did. His father had always taken good care of the things he owned. Stewardship, he called it. Dylan wished Alex had spent the same time and care on his company the past few years as he had on his material possessions.

He couldn't help but wonder about his mother's advice. Was confronting his dad about Ted's appointment the way to solve the current dilemma?

And even more so, did he want to be in charge?

One thing at a time.

"So, you ready to go?" he asked Lisa as he shut off the engine.

She nodded, and as soon as he had his own door open, she was out of the car.

As he followed her into the office he wondered again at her intensity, her desire to get to the bottom of this whole matter. She was the only one who seemed to really care. Other than Dara.

They didn't even bother stopping at the receptionist. Instead they went straight to Dara's office.

She sat at her desk, ramrod straight in front of her computer. Her gray suit was crisp—not a wrinkle in sight. The white shirt peeking out from the vee of her suit coat was immaculate. She wore her hair down today, softening the sharp lines of her face, but her overall appearance was one of a woman in charge, giving her the same air of control he knew all too well from the brief time he had dated her.

Except lately he had seen a few fissures in her iron restraint.

Dylan knocked lightly on her open door to announce himself.

Dara looked up, and her eyes grew wide. "What are you doing here?" Her frown deepened. "And what is *she* doing here?" Dara angled her chin toward Lisa, not even bothering to use her name.

"Last I checked, my name is still on the Matheson Telecom letterhead," Dylan said lightly, surprised at her anger. "And Lisa is helping me with this little problem."

"But we don't need any help…" Dara sputtered. "It's over. I found the money. That's why I phoned you." She pushed herself away from her desk with an abrupt movement

"I guess I wouldn't mind seeing for myself," Dylan said easily, forcing himself to stay calm as Dara stormed around the desk.

"Everything…is…fine," she said, leaning toward him, enunciating each word with harsh emphasis.

"Then it won't matter if we go looking, will it?" Dylan asked. "Just to double-check. I hauled myself all the way here from Toronto at my father's request, no less. I don't think it would be so bad if I checked things out myself." He gave her a casual smile, but his interior radar was on full alert. He'd been going through the motions to appease his father. But Dara's behavior struck a warning chord he couldn't ignore.

Why the anger? Why was she so upset? If things were truly over, as she so emphatically stated, why should she care if he checked for himself?

He thought again of the memo. Wondered at her involvement in what had happened.

Dara's eyes flicked over Lisa, then narrowed. "And you need to take her along?"

"Lisa has been gracious enough to help me. In fact, she was the one who encouraged me to finish what I started."

"And why should she care?"

Dara's question fed Dylan's niggling suspicions.

"She probably cares because she's spent quite a few days helping me. She has a time investment to consider, as well."

"But she's been compensated for that." She gave Lisa a sly glance. "Quite adequately, I'm sure."

Dylan bristled at the unpleasant insinuation threaded through her comments.

"Dylan is a generous boss," Lisa cut in, her tone full of innocence. "As I'm sure you know for yourself."

Dylan suppressed a smile. Lisa could hold her own. He caught her eye and winked. Pleasure spiraled within him when she returned his smile.

Without another word Dara turned to her desk and pulled a key out of one of the drawers. "Here's what you'll need to get into his office. It's two doors down." She scribbled a notation on a pad of paper and handed it to Dylan, but her eyes were on Lisa. "And here's his password. No promises it works. I just lucked out when I figured it out, so I may have written it wrong. I was going to get a tech in tomorrow to clean the files off it—that's why I went through it once more to see if I could find anything else. Just drop the key off here when you're done."

"Thanks, Dara," Dylan said, taking the paper and handing it directly to Lisa. "You've been most cooperative."

She didn't say anything—just kept staring at Lisa. "You live in Toronto?" she asked all of a sudden.

Lisa gave a start, but nodded.

"East York?"

"Why do you ask?"

"Just curious" was her cryptic comment. She turned to Dylan. "Happy hunting," she said with a faint smile. "Just close the door on your way out."

Gabe's office had been emptied of everything but a desk and his computer, but it still held a faint musty smell of papers.

"We may as well get started," Dylan said, fidgeting while Lisa booted up the computer. He thought of the promise he had made his brother, then wondered why Ted was so anxious to have him back off.

"We'll start with that bank account," he said, pacing around the desk. "Try to see if you can find it somewhere."

He stopped behind her, then started pacing again.

"Dylan," Lisa said, glancing up at him, "why don't you get a coffee or something?"

Dylan held her gaze. Smiled at her. "You trying to get rid of me?"

"Your prowling is making me nervous."

"Do you want anything?"

She shook her head, looking back at the computer. She glanced at the paper Dara had given them and punched in the combination of letters and numbers, frowning in concentration.

"Okay. I'll leave you to it. Be back in a bit." He paused, waiting for some kind of sign that things were still the same between them, but she wasn't looking at him. As he walked down the hall to the coffee room he wondered again at her desire to get to the bottom of this.

Relief swept through Lisa when Dylan finally closed the door behind him. Now she could work in private.

Dara's password hadn't gotten her in. That was no surprise to Lisa.

She carefully slipped Gabe's password out of her pocket, then punched it in. The pattern seemed vaguely familiar, but she didn't have time to puzzle it out. She hit Enter.

And she was in. She put the paper back into her pocket.

She thought she'd start with the easy stuff. On a hunch she clicked the icon showing her the most recently used documents. And there they were. One labeled Wilson Engineering, Dara's father's company. The other was a number that she suspected was the company account.

Lisa highlighted the files she thought she needed, and while she copied them to the disk drive she flicked through the properties. From what she could see the files had been accessed just this morning. And the numbered account looked as if it had been created after Gabe left.

Exhilaration pumped through her. This information, combined with the memo, could be just what she needed to clear Gabe's name.

Seconds later the disk in the drive was whirring, saving the information she had found. She pulled the diskette out of the drive and slipped it into her purse just as she heard a light knock on the door.

She quickly restarted the computer. Thankfully the speakers weren't connected, so no little ditty gave her actions away.

"How's it coming?" Dara swept into the office and came to stand beside Lisa.

"I'm having some problems logging on," Lisa said, making a show of glancing at the paper Dara had given her. "I've tried this one a couple of times."

"I may have written it down wrong." Dara took the paper from Lisa, but she didn't look at it. Instead she looked at Lisa more closely. "You know, I've said this before, but you look very familiar."

Lisa shrugged the comment off, uncomfortable under Dara's relentless scrutiny. "I'm fairly unremarkable."

"That's not very complimentary to yourself, is it?"

"I know who I am."

"Do you? I wish I did. Know who you are."

Fear tingled up her neck, but Lisa held Dara's gaze, projecting innocence. "Why? I'm only around for a short while. Soon Dylan and I will be going back to Toronto."

"Yes. And Dylan will be leaving Matheson Telecom." Dara's smile held no warmth. "And it would only be fair if I added, 'and leaving you.' Dylan is like that, you see. Has never held on to a girl for longer than a few weeks." Dara scribbled something on the paper. "Try this one."

Lisa glanced at it and forced a polite smile. Another useless password. "Thanks for this." She looked back up at Dara. "And the advice."

Dara waved a careless hand at her. "Think nothing of it."

I'll try not to think of you at all. Lisa waited until Dara closed the door behind her, then folded up the piece of paper and slipped it into her pocket. She wasn't going to waste any more time playing Dara's games. She hoped she had what she had come for.

She turned Gabe's computer off, looking around his office.

What hopes had he brought to this job? she wondered, trailing her hand over his desk. He had been so excited when he phoned her to tell her about the job. All the hard work and sacrifices she had made had been worth every moment.

She slipped her purse over her shoulder and got up. Once she showed Dylan what she suspected, Gabe's name would be cleared.

And hers would be mud.

She thought of the wondrous moments with Dylan in the study. When he had read the Bible to her.

Love is patient. Love is kind.

Would he be patient with what she had to say when she finally dared tell him the truth? That afternoon on the sailboat he had spoken so strongly of how important trust was to him. How it had hurt when his father had broken trust with him.

Could he forgive her for what she had done to him? Would he understand?

She pressed her fingers to her aching forehead, praying, unsure what to ask for. What to say. Now that she had proof that her brother was innocent, she felt curiously deflated. She wanted to help her brother, but the cost had been too high.

Why had Dylan come into her life this way? Why couldn't they have simply met under normal circumstances? A man and a woman who were attracted to each other.

But it hadn't happened that way. She had sought him out. Had used him and his family.

How could she face them?

She drew in a deep breath. She had made her own decisions. She had made her own mistakes. She knew what God required of her and what she had to do. When she and Dylan got home she was going to show him what she had discovered. And then she was going to tell him the truth.

She strode out of the office, looking for Dylan. One more step and this would all be over.

There was no fresh coffee made in the coffee room. Dylan pulled a face at the dark brew sitting in the glass pot.

He should go back to Lisa, but was strangely reluctant to do so. He would have thought the moment they had shared in the study would have brought them closer together. And it had.

For a while.

And then she had retreated.

And he had read the memo that she had lied to him about.

The thought stuck in his mind, like a dirty stick that wouldn't be dislodged. Why hadn't she shown him right away? He didn't quite believe her excuse that she'd thought it unimportant. Lisa was thorough and diligent.

Restless again, he walked over to his father's office. His secretary was gone, but the door to Alex's office was open. To Dylan's surprise, his father was inside. Dylan knocked lightly on the door.

Alex stood by the window, his arms crossed. His suit coat hung crookedly on the back of his chair, and his tie was undone. Dylan was taken aback. At the office, his father always presented nothing less than a professional appearance.

Alex glanced back over his shoulder, and when he saw Dylan he gave him a tired smile. "This is a surprise, Dylan. What brings you here?"

"Dara phoned this morning," Dylan said. "She said she found the missing money in a bank account set up by Gabe."

"I heard that." Alex rubbed the back of his neck with a slow movement as if even that was too much effort for him, staring out the window again. "Is that why you came?"

Dylan carefully closed the door behind them, but didn't bother to sit down himself. He was here now. Might as well get straight to the point.

"The night of your anniversary Ted had a talk with me, Dad. He asked me to back off this investigation. Why would he do that?"

Alex slowly turned to face him, sorrow lining his face. "Ted and Dara have been under a lot of pressure the past few weeks. Actually the past few months. This whole business with the accountant has made things even more difficult for them. Ted feels threatened by your presence here, Dylan."

"Why should he, Dad? From what I understand he doesn't even want to be in charge of the company."

"I know."

Dylan thought of the conversation he'd had with his mother just that morning. Could she be right? Was his father waiting for some kind of direction? Some kind of leadership?

"At the risk of bringing up old history, it makes me wonder again why you gave him the job you promised me."

Alex sighed and dropped into his chair. "Please sit down, Dylan."

"I can't stay too long, Dad. Lisa is with me. She's busy in Gabe's office right now."

"Doing what?"

"Trying to find out whatever we can from his computer."

"Well, I won't keep you, then."

And for the first time since he had come home, Dylan got a sense of what his mother was saying. Alex looked beaten. Tired.

"I've got to go." But he stayed where he was, suddenly reluctant to leave. In two days he would be back in Toronto, and then in a few weeks finally free from Matheson Telecom.

What would happen to the company then? Ted didn't want the responsibilities he had, nor was he capable of carrying them out. His father looked as if he was carrying too much himself. He looked broken and weary.

Dylan thought of pride. His own. His father's. And he knew what he had to do.

"We'll talk again, Dad," he said softly. "I promise."

"I'd like that," Alex said, a faint smile pulling on his mouth.

And as Dylan walked back to Gabe's office he felt as if events were slowly falling more heavily on his shoulders, pushing him in different directions. He had thought he had his life all mapped out before he came here. The company he would be working for was up-and-coming. Not direct competition to Matheson Telecom, but it had the potential to be. He would be in on the ground floor—a fancy term for starting over.

And he would be working the same crazy long hours he had when he first started the Toronto branch, trying to prove to his father and himself that he was worthy.

Was it worth it?

A few days ago he had gone sailing with a woman who was slowly becoming special to him. He was actually building a relationship with someone he cared for.

Because he had taken the time for it.

What would happen to him and Lisa when he left Matheson Telecom? When he immersed himself in a new job? A new place where he had to prove himself all over again.

"Hey, Dylan."

Dylan spun around as Lisa walked out of his thoughts and into his line of sight. She was smiling. "I got what we came for. I want to have another look at it on the computer at home."

Dylan looked down at her, his own questions about

her spinning around his mind, melding with the ones about his father.

He didn't want to go to the computer at home. He didn't want to think about crooked accountants. Fathers who made mistakes.

Decisions he had to make.

He wanted them to be together as they had been on the boat. As they had been for that magical moment in the gazebo. When all he had to worry about was how often he thought he could get away with kissing her.

Lord, I don't know what to do. I'm too confused. Too mixed up about my father. My brother.

Lisa.

"Are you okay?" Lisa caught him by the arm and gave it a light shake.

Cast all your anxieties on him.

He certainly had enough to cast.

"Let's go home," he said, covering her hand with his.

She nodded and they left.

"Were you able to find anything?" Dylan asked as they got into the car. "You weren't in there very long."

"I only needed to copy the most recently used files, and I found those right away."

"You didn't want to look at them while you were there anyway?"

"Some of the programs I would need for that were taken off the computer."

"I'll be mighty glad when this is all over," he said, starting the car and pulling out of the parking lot. "I sure hope whatever you've got on that disk will finish this once and for all."

* * *

"I was so sure I copied the files properly," Lisa said, staring at the error message on her computer screen, her heart filling her throat. How could this have happened?

She hit a key, shut down the program and started over again, trying to keep the panic at bay.

Dylan stood beside her, his arms crossed. "Do you remember the names of the files? I could get Dara to e-mail them to us as an attachment."

"No. I don't think that would work." The last thing she wanted was for Dara to know that she had gotten into Gabe's computer. Especially when Dara had given them the wrong password in the first place. "I think part of the problem is the programs. I might not have the right one on this computer to open it." She opened up another window, trying to search for a program that might be able to read the file. Still nothing.

Dylan rocked lightly, then picked up the memo again. "You know what would make the most sense?" he said softly.

"What?" Lisa asked, turning to him.

He looked down at her, his mouth lifted in a smile.

Lisa felt the too-familiar push and pull of her longing for him and the reality of their situation.

"If my father would hire an auditor and stop trying to solve this thing internally." Dylan crouched beside her. "But that won't happen."

Lisa looked down at Dylan, resisting the urge to touch him. Her affection for him grew stronger every day. And alongside her changing feelings for him had come a renewal in her faith life. This morning he had read to her from the Bible, and for a brief and shining moment all was well in her world. She had felt close to him. Close to the Lord. The peace she had been seeking for so long, the love she had been waiting for was all there, surrounding her and holding her up.

But she knew that in the next day or so she had to choose. Obedience, or a relationship that had started with a lie.

"So, we can't pursue that," Dylan said, pushing himself up. "Let's get out of here. I've spent too much time here already."

He reached out to Lisa. She glanced once more at the blank computer screen, hope dying within her.

Tonight she had to find a way to contact Gabe and tell him that she had done all she could for him.

But for now she took Dylan's hand and let him pull her up into his arms. She allowed herself a moment to enjoy the warmth and strength of his embrace before she pulled away.

Dylan pulled Lisa a bit closer, brushing the top of her head with his chin. "You're awfully quiet tonight," he said.

"Most people don't like to chat when they're watching a movie," Lisa murmured, pulling away from him and drawing her sweater around her.

Dylan picked up the remote as the credits of the movie started rolling and turned the television off. "Well, the movie is done—you can chat now."

"Hard to do on demand." Lisa curled on her side of the couch, looking everywhere but at him.

During the movie she had been more than content to cuddle up against him. Now that it was over, she had withdrawn as she had this afternoon when they had come back from the office.

He wished they could go back to this morning. That precious moment of connection he had felt with her. Short of pulling out the Bible again, he wasn't quite sure how to re-create that.

Love is patient.

He knew what he had to do. Let go. Let God. Put everything in His hands. Even Lisa.

"Once we're back in Toronto, Lisa, nothing has to change between us. Just because you won't be my secretary anymore doesn't mean…" He let the awkward sentence lie heavily between them.

Very suave, he thought, repressing a frown. What was it about her that turned him inside out?

Lisa moved closer, pulling one of his hands into hers. She pressed it to her cheek, and hope bloomed in Dylan.

"I don't deserve this, you know," she said softly, still avoiding his gaze. "You are the most wonderful person I've ever met. This morning…" She paused, her voice catching on the words. She drew in a deep breath and continued. "This morning I felt closer to God than I have since my parents died. This morning I felt a touch of the peace that I knew God could give me." She looked up at him now. Dylan was shocked to see her eyes brimming with tears. "I want to thank you for that. And for so much more." She leaned closer to him and touched her lips to his cheek. "You are an amazing

person, Dylan Matheson." And as she drew away, three
faintly whispered words tantalized him.

I love you.

But before he could ask her if he'd heard right, she was
off the couch and running down the hallway to the stairs.

Chapter Twelve

"Lisa, please open the door. We need to talk."

Lisa hunched down on the floor, holding her arms over her head, praying Dylan would leave. She couldn't talk to him now.

Dylan tried the door, the rattle of the doorknob sending a chill down Lisa's back. He gave another knock, then stormed off.

Forgive me, Lord, she prayed. Forgive me, Dylan.

She waited a few more moments, then opened up her cell phone, its outline wavering in her vision. Tears slipped from her eyes as she punched in Gabe's number. As she clutched the phone to her ear she heard Dylan's car spinning down the driveway, the sound an angry counterpoint to the shrill ringing of Gabe's phone.

What had she done?

She had agreed to watch the movie with Dylan only because the girls were going to join them. Then one of the twins' friends called. Something better was going on somewhere else, and Amber and Erika were gone. Mr. and Mrs. Matheson had gone out for supper with some friends.

So it was just Dylan and Lisa alone in the house, which had proved to be too intimate. Too dangerous.

She hadn't meant to tell him she loved him. The words had come out, pushed past the walls she'd been slowly trying to rebuild against him.

Lisa palmed her tears away, sniffing as she willed Gabe to answer. She had to talk to him. Had to connect and remind herself of her main purpose.

"Hello?"

"Gabe, it's me. Lisa."

"I'm so glad you called. Did you find anything? What's the matter? Are you okay?"

"No. Well…yes." She sniffed.

Her phone beeped in her ear and Gabe's voice cut off.

"Gabe. Are you there?" Lisa pressed the phone closer.

Nothing. She glanced at the screen. Her battery was dead.

Lisa threw the phone down and pressed the heels of her hands against her eyes as if holding back the confusion of her thoughts. Now what? She needed to talk to Gabe. Tell him what was happening, then confess everything to Dylan.

Gabe. Dylan. Both bounced back and forth, each creating a mixture of emotions.

She loved Dylan.

She had lied to Dylan.

Gabe was innocent.

Lisa jumped off the bed and grabbed her coat. She had to talk to Gabe. This back and forth was wearing her down, confusing her more than anything she'd had to deal with before.

It wasn't right to keep deceiving Dylan and it was wrong to go against what she knew God wanted for her. But before she told Dylan what was happening, she had to tell Gabe what she was planning.

She slipped downstairs and quickly called a cab, praying one would come before anyone came home. As she opened the door, the shrill ring of the phone echoed through the empty house. Lisa's heart leaped into her throat.

She didn't dare answer and quickly stepped outside. The cool evening drizzle dampened her hair and she shivered into her coat. She didn't want to wait in the house.

Then twin cones of light swept up the drive and Lisa ducked back into the tall shrubs lining the driveway. As the vehicle turned around, relief made her legs weak. It was her cab.

She slipped into the vehicle and gave the driver directions to Gabe's place. Then she sat back and prayed as the cab drove down the hill, blending into the traffic heading across the inlet.

Vancouver was hard enough to navigate in the dark and the rain. Trying to follow a vehicle made it even harder.

Thankfully the light on top of the cab made it easier to spot.

Dylan knew he'd never make a spy or detective. After

almost losing the cab on Lions Gate Bridge, he opted for staying fairly close, hoping neither the driver nor Lisa would notice him following.

He felt heartsick and ashamed, but Dara's phone call to his cell phone just before he came home from his aimless drive had fed his own confusion. And when he saw the cab pull out of his parents' driveway just as he was returning, he knew he had to follow.

The cab finally pulled up in front of a dingy apartment building, and as Dylan drove slowly past the vehicle, he saw Lisa get out, pay the driver and walk over to the doorway. He kept going, pulled in to the nearest alley and turned off his car.

Now what? Follow her again? Try to talk to her again?

He locked up his car feeling more and more foolish, and strode down the wet sidewalk. What if this was all just an innocent mistake? What if the person Lisa was seeing was just an old friend? Maybe even a boyfriend.

I love you.

He was sure he hadn't imagined that. So why had she run away? Again?

Dylan stopped in front of the doorway Lisa had gone through and looked at the names beside the numbers. Most of them were faded, but one had a fresh name printed beside it. Haskell.

Dylan's heart dropped like a stone. Dara was right.

"I can prove that Dara put the money into that account, Gabe. I saw on the computer that the money was transferred after you left."

Gabe leaned back in his chair smiling a tired smile. "If you can't read the disk, you don't have proof."

"I was hoping you could have a look at it."

"On what?" Gabe waved his hand around the sparse furnishings of the apartment.

Lisa chewed her lower lip, trying to think. "Is there some kind of Internet café around here? They'd have computers."

"That's not going to work. I left Matheson Telecom in the morning. If it was set up after I left, and you can get on my computer to prove it, then you might have proof."

"I doubt I could get in again. If Dara knows I got in, all she would have to do is change the password."

"Or corrupt the files. I'm surprised she didn't do that anyway. And you said she's getting a tech in to clean off the computer tomorrow." Gabe sighed, leaning back in his chair. "May as well give up, Lisa. Things just aren't working our way."

Lisa sank into the chair across from Gabe. "So what do we do?"

"I guess I just take that other job."

Lisa shook her head and held her hands up. "No, Gabe. Don't do that."

Gabe banged his hand against the table, his sudden anger startling Lisa. "You're so full of advice on what I should and shouldn't do." He ground out the words. "You haven't done a thing for me. Nothing."

His words shot straight to her heart, plunging in like a knife. "How dare you say that, Gabe?" she asked, squeezing her hands together as if holding back her hurt. "Everything I've ever done has been for you," she said softly. "Getting the job. Coming out here. Pretending to be Dylan's girlfriend." Her voice caught on Dylan's name.

Silence dropped between them, broken only by the muffled sounds of traffic outside. Feet walking down the hall inside.

Lisa drew in a long slow breath, willing her own erratic emotions to soften. "I've put a lot on the line for you, Gabe. More than you can know."

She felt Gabe's hands on her shoulders and she reached up to cover one with her own.

"I'm sorry, Lisa. You're right," Gabe said.

A light knock at the door was her only warning.

"It's open," Gabe called.

And Dylan walked in.

Lisa dropped her hand and pulled away from Gabe, shock sending ice through her veins. Too late. Too late.

The words echoed mockingly through her head as she stood to face Dylan, her red cheeks condemning her more than anything she could say.

Dylan's eyes flicked from Lisa to Gabe and back again, the dim light of the apartment casting harsh shadows across his face.

"How long has this been going on?" His voice whipped through the air.

Lisa wet her lips, trying to find the right words, the right way to explain her subterfuge. "I'm sorry, Dylan. I should have told you."

He took a step back, as if trying to keep as much distance between them as possible. "Didn't your *boyfriend* mind all the time we spent together?"

"No. You've got this all wrong." Lisa held out her hand to him, entreating him, realizing how the scene Dylan had stumbled on must have looked to him.

"Lisa is my stepsister. She came here to help me," Gabe said, anger edging his voice.

Dylan's sharp laugh stripped away most of the hope Lisa still held on to. "Why don't I feel relieved about that?"

Lisa could say nothing in her defense. Nothing that would change the bitter reality of what he was saying. She felt Gabe's hand on her shoulder. A small comfort.

"Is this why you took the job?"

"I wanted to help my brother. Yes."

"Were you ever going to tell me?"

Lisa fought down the panic that threatened to choke her. She could feel her future crumbling beneath her feet, but even as she struggled to salvage the tiniest step, the anger and betrayal in Dylan's eyes showed her it was doomed. She said nothing.

"I'll bring your things tomorrow on my way to the airport."

The icy finality in his voice cooled any shred of hope she had clung to.

"If it's okay with you, I would like to come to the house to pick them up. I'll come after you leave."

"I don't want you to bother my family."

"She just wants to get her stuff, Dylan…" Gabe began.

Though thankful for his defense, Lisa shook her head. "I want to tell your parents and family myself what I did," she said to Dylan. "I believe I need to confess to them."

Dylan caught her pleading glance. Hesitated.

"Why did you lie to me, Lisa?"

He was still talking. A flicker of hope. "I had to do it to get the job. To get close to your father," she said, the truth sounding even more stark spoken aloud.

"All necessary for your role."

Lisa couldn't reply; her actions condemned her as much as Dylan's words did.

"So everything that happened, all the things we shared were fake? Just part of this role you were playing?"

"Those were real, Dylan," Lisa cried, her heart breaking at the angry hurt in his voice. "I meant everything I ever said to you."

Dylan lowered his hand, his eyes now cold. Sharp. "All the secret phone calls, the mysterious trips were about helping out someone who stole from the company—the company I'm a part of?"

"I didn't steal anything," Gabe snapped. "And if Lisa lied to you, it was because of me. I'm the one you should be angry with. Not her."

"I wanted to help Gabe," Lisa said, wishing he could understand at least a small part of her reasons.

Dylan's gaze stayed on Lisa, his anger directed solely toward her. "You know, I really thought we had something," he said. "For the first time…" He stopped there.

"I think we did, Dylan." Lisa fought down her panic at the words they were using. *Had. Did.* Past tense. "I care for you. And I was going to tell you about Gabe. But I had to take care of my brother first."

"Why?"

Lisa drew some small sliver of hope from even that one word. From the little she knew about Dylan, he didn't stay to talk when he was angry. He left.

"Gabe is all I have in the world. Everything I've ever done has been for him. So when I found out he was fired, I knew it couldn't be true. And I had to help him." She willed the right words to come. Prayed for the right thing to say. "Family takes care of family. We help and take care of each other. And make sacrifices." Lisa took a small step closer to Dylan, holding his eyes, praying he would understand, even though she knew she didn't deserve even that. "I've struggled more than you can know about what to do. I've prayed about this…."

"Prayed? Pardon me while I try to work my head around this. You prayed about how you were going to lie to all of us?"

Lisa pressed her hands to her chest, struggling to find the right words. *Please help me, Lord. I know I was wrong, but I'm trying to make this right.*

"When I first started working for you, my faith didn't mean much. So it was easy to deceive you. But going to church with your family, watching them and listening to them brought me back to the faith I used to have. I knew I was wrong, but didn't know when to tell you." She felt Gabe come up beside her and lay his hand on her shoulder as if to give her strength. She looked up, holding Dylan's angry gaze. "I found something precious with your family, Dylan. Their faith is an example to me. But more important, I found something precious with you. When we read the Bible together, for the first time in my life I felt something pure and true and right happening in my life. I'm not perfect, Dylan. My faith is weak. But I discovered something important in the time we spent together. Something I don't want to let go of."

"That seems convenient, Lisa."

Hurt, she pulled back, closer to Gabe. Her brother. "You know it's true, Dylan."

"What do you know about truth? You're no different than Dara. Actually you're better. At lying. You certainly had me fooled."

He spun around and left, the click of the apartment door sounding like a gunshot in the silence.

Dylan rested his hands on the steering wheel of the car, staring at his parents' house, rain pattering on the roof of the car. His anger had had a chance to cool, but his frustration and mistrust still simmered below the surface.

I trusted her, Lord. I believed in her.

As he trudged up the walk, rain slipping down his neck, he wondered what his next step should be.

Give it all up?

And leave Lisa behind when he left for Toronto tomorrow?

The thought spun through his mind, bringing sorrow and hurt in its wake. But what else was he going to do?

He shook his coat off and hung it in one of the massive cupboards just off the foyer. The house was eerily silent. A thin sliver of light slipped out from under the door of the study and Dylan walked toward it. He didn't want to be alone.

His father sat in one of the chairs, the light beside him creating an intimate atmosphere.

As Dylan came in, Alex looked up from the book he was reading. "I thought you and Lisa had decided to stay home."

Dylan sank onto a couch and massaged the back of his neck. "We did. Then we had a disagreement."

"Do you want to talk about it?"

"I don't know what to say." He laughed shortly. "I don't know what to think."

Alex thankfully didn't acknowledge the vague comment but put his book down, his attention focused completely on his son. "Do you want to tell me what is wrong, Dylan?"

Dylan blew his breath out and looked over at his father. Saw again the lines that bracketed his mouth. The weariness he'd noticed this afternoon. The same weariness he felt himself.

"I just found out that Lisa is Gabe Haskell's sister." As he spoke the words aloud Dylan felt again the twist of betrayal.

"How do you know that?"

"Dara phoned me this evening. Told me that she suspected there was a connection between Lisa and Gabe. So I followed Lisa this evening and found her at Gabe Haskell's apartment." Dylan pushed himself off the couch. He paced around the room, his agitation and frustration needing an outlet. "She never told me who she was when she applied for the job. Never said anything about her brother. And all she could say now was that family takes care of family. Like it's some kind of creed she lives by."

"It's not a bad one."

"And that takes precedence over truth and what is right?" Dylan stopped behind a chair, grasping the back of it with his hands. "He stole from us, Dad. He took money that didn't belong to him. And his sister spent time with us as a family pretending to be someone she wasn't. She didn't just lie to me. She lied to all of you. So don't stand up for her."

"I'm not so sure Gabe stole from us."

His softly spoken words caught Dylan's full attention. "What?"

"I never truly believed he did. And if he did, he didn't do it alone."

Don't know if I can keep doing this. Ted needs to know.

The words of the memo sifted back into his memory. The memo that Lisa had hidden from him. The memo that had been attached to an invoice they couldn't trace.

Dylan pulled his hands over his face, wishing he had a few moments to think. To figure out what was really going on. "Can you please explain what you're talking about?" he asked tiredly.

"Sit down, Dylan. We need to have that talk we were supposed to have this afternoon. And you're leaving tomorrow. So now is the only time we have."

Dylan lowered himself onto the couch again and laid his head back. "First tell me—if you think Gabe didn't do it, why did you ask me to come here?"

Alex leaned forward, his hands clasped. "I wasn't sure enough about Gabe's guilt or innocence. But I couldn't allow him to stay with the company as long as there was any shadow hanging over his name." Alex sighed lightly. "I had suspected for a while that if Gabe had done it, Dara was involved. And if Dara was involved, I suspected Ted was, as well."

"What do you mean?" Dylan frowned, trying to grasp this new information. "How did you come to that conclusion?"

"I didn't allow Ted complete free rein over the company when I let him take over." Alex tilted Dylan a wry smile. "In spite of what you think, I wasn't entirely sure of Ted's abilities, either."

"Which makes me wonder again and again why you put him in charge."

"I know that's a sore point with you, Dylan. And I know I did wrong by you." Alex got up slowly. Walked over to the window and stared out, as if trying to find answers there. "Like I told you this afternoon, I am well aware of Ted's failings. I am also well aware of your abilities. I guess I was hoping, in some foolish way, that the older brother would take on some of the characteristics of his younger brother given the right circumstances."

"You told me it was because he was married."

"That was a very important reason. Ted had extra responsibilities when he and Dara married."

"Married very quickly, I might add," Dylan said.

Alex turned to Dylan. "I doubt Dara ever told you why she broke up with you and married Ted so quickly?"

Dylan shook his head. What he had just lost seemed infinitely more precious than the shallow relationship he and Dara had had those many years ago. It no longer mattered.

"Dara told us she was expecting Ted's child. Her father insisted they get married. Ted felt the same way. He loved Dara. So they got married." Alex opened his hands in a gesture of surrender. "I could have given Ted the Toronto job instead of you, but I wanted him closer to home where we could give them some guidance and direction."

Dylan stared at his father as his words swirled around, a chaos of ideas and sounds. "But they don't have…" His voice trailed off.

"It turned out that Dara wasn't pregnant after all," Alex said softly.

Dylan lost his breath as the conversation shifted into unknown territory. Anger followed close behind.

"Why didn't anyone tell me?" he cried, hurt pushing the words out as he faced down his father. "Ted is my brother. I care what happens to him."

Alex smiled a gentle smile. "I'm sorry, Dylan. We wanted to tell you, but Ted was adamant that we keep it quiet. Especially from you."

"Why?" Dylan could only stare at his father, trying to comprehend what his brother had gone through.

"Because of your history with Dara. And, I suspect, because he thought that Dara had come to him on the rebound from you."

"But I'm his brother. This is my family. Surely I had a right to know."

"In hindsight, yes, we should have told you. I wanted to a number of times, but I think Ted felt a mixture of guilt and shame over what had happened."

Dylan's perceptions shifted as he tried to keep up. All

his previous knowledge of his brother took on a different hue. One idea pushed to the surface, startling in its clarity.

They weren't so different after all.

Ted had been duped by his girlfriend, too.

"I wish I had known." Dylan pulled his hands over his face. "I would have been here for him." He closed his eyes as he thought of Ted, caught in events that pulled him along to places he didn't want to go. Thought of himself and Lisa.

"We thought that Dara and Ted loved each other. But I'm worried about their relationship now."

"Was Dara involved with the accountant? With Gabe?"

"I don't think so."

"I keep coming back to the question—why did you want me to come? Why didn't you hire an outside auditor?"

"Because Ted had gone through enough with Dara. I was hoping that if you came, if Dara knew that you would be looking around, she would cave in and let me know what was really going on. And if Ted was involved, I wanted to find out from him."

"I don't think he was, or is. Lisa showed me a memo that Gabe had written to Dara. In it he said he didn't know if he could keep doing this and that Ted needed to know. To me it implicates Gabe and, at the same time, Dara."

"Do you have a copy of this memo?"

Dylan nodded, feeling again the sting of humiliation when he thought of Lisa and what she had done to him.

"I want to show it to Dara. To see what she will say."

"I think you've given Dara enough chances, Dad. I think it's time you do what I've been asking you to do for a while now. Bring in an outside auditor."

"I will, but not right away. I am still hoping that if Dara knows what we know, she'll come clean. It would save your brother further humiliation."

Dylan acknowledged this small concession with a curt nod. His father's defense of Ted made more sense, but he still didn't like it.

"I sense you're not happy with that." Alex sat on the coffee table across from Dylan, leaning toward him, his elbows resting on his knees. "I'm not, either. But it would be freeing for Dara to have a chance to confess. To realize that in spite of what we know we are still giving her a chance. God gives us many, many chances, too, Dylan. I think it would be unwise and uncaring of me not to do the same for Dara."

Dylan remembered his mother's comment about secrets. "Does Mom know about all this?"

"She knows about Ted and Dara, of course. But I haven't told her about my suspicions about Dara. I didn't want to worry her. She's had enough on her mind about them as it is."

"I think you should tell her what's happening. Sometimes the things we dream up can be worse than the reality."

Alex looked up and held Dylan's gaze. "I'm hoping the same can be said for you."

"What do you mean?"

"I have something to ask of you, Dylan. I didn't do what I promised and I know it's caused a lot of bitterness for you. My only feeble excuse is that I felt trapped and caught by my concern for Ted. It wasn't that I loved him more. It was just that I knew he needed me more. I want to ask your forgiveness for not giving you the job I promised. For not being the father to you that I should have. I don't deserve it, but I have to ask."

Dylan looked up at his father. Saw again the shadow of sorrow in his father's eyes. Thought of the burden he had been carrying all this time. Thought of the sorrow that could have been averted if only Alex had told him everything.

But would he have listened?

"I think you need to know that I love you, Dylan," Alex continued quietly. "And that I want to make things right between us. My pride has caused problems. Pride in my family. In my company. But I think God has brought me to a place where I've learned to let go of that." He pushed himself to his feet and walked away. "I'm sorry, Dylan," he said, standing by the window again. "Sorry for wasting your time this past week and sorry for wasting those years of your life."

"But my years weren't wasted, Dad," Dylan said, the truth coming to him in a flash of insight. "I learned to work on my own. To stop seeking your approval and to appreciate my strengths. And as for the past week…" He stopped there.

"This past week," his father prompted, "you had time to spend with your girlfriend. A girl, I must say, we have been very pleased with in spite of what you've just told me about her."

His father's approval of Lisa was bittersweet.

And suddenly truth washed over Dylan. He wasn't innocent, either.

"I also have a confession to make, Dad," he said softly, cringing at his own pride. His own duplicity. "When we first came here Lisa and I weren't really dating. Yes, she's my secretary, but I asked her to pretend to be my girlfriend. To keep Mom and the girls off my back."

"I don't blame you," Alex said with a smile.

In spite of the intensity of the moment, Dylan had to laugh.

"And what is your relationship now?" Alex asked.

Dylan sighed. "It changed, grew. But now I don't know what to think about her anymore."

"Do you love her?"

"I've never felt this way before."

"Sounds to me pretty close to love."

"So what do I do?"

"Give her a chance. Like I was willing to give Dara a chance. Like God gives us a chance every minute of every day."

"But how can I carry on a relationship that was built on deceit?"

Alex laid his hand on Dylan's shoulder. "Yours or hers?"

That was it. Dylan knew he had no right to be angry with Lisa.

"Lisa has been on her own for years," Alex continued. "Gabe is her only family member. Give her credit for taking care of him in the only way she knew how. God works in mysterious ways, Dylan. Maybe everything came together for a purpose."

Chapter Thirteen

The early-morning breeze brushed over Dylan as he hunched over the Bible he had taken out on the deck. He had hardly slept all night, reliving again and again the words he had thrown at Lisa in anger.

Love is patient, love is kind. It does not envy, it does not boast, it is not proud.

Dylan read and reread the passage he and Lisa had shared just yesterday. Remembered what she had told him. Family takes care of family. As his father had taken care of Ted.

He continued. *Love does not delight in evil, but rejoices in truth.*

The reality he had to face was that he had no more right to get angry with Lisa over her deception than his family did over his.

But their relationship that had started with deception had become truth. She had become special to him. He loved her.

The words settled quietly into his mind and stayed. He loved her.

He had never been able to say that about anyone else before, but he knew for a certainty that this was real.

Dylan closed the Bible and looked out over the bay, past the office buildings. Somewhere out there was the dingy apartment block where Lisa had spent the night.

He shouldn't have walked out on her, he thought with a pang of shame. But the hurt and pride had been too great. But how could he go back?

What do I do, Lord? How can I fix this?

He thought of what his father had told him last night, heard once again the faintly whispered words Lisa had spoken last night, just before she had gone upstairs. Before she left for Gabe's. *I love you.*

Help me, Lord, to overcome my own pride. Love is not proud.

"Good morning, Dylan."

He glanced up to see Amber standing in the doorway, her hair artfully arranged in a style reminiscent of Lisa's funky hairdos.

"Hey, there. How come you're all dressed up?"

Amber frowned at him. "How come you're not? You were going to drop me off downtown on your way to the airport this morning."

His flight to Toronto. His important meeting with his future business partners. He had forgotten about both.

"What time is it?"

"Seven o'clock. I need to be downtown at eight, and your flight leaves at nine-thirty."

Panic tightened his midsection. How could he have forgotten?

But he had to talk to Lisa before he left. Try to salvage something from yesterday's mess.

If he rushed, he might be able to squeeze a few more minutes out of his schedule. It wasn't enough time to fix what had gone wrong, but he couldn't leave Vancouver without one last try.

Maybe he could convince her to at least listen.

"Can you be a bit earlier?" he asked, jumping up from his chair. "I'll meet you at the car in five."

"But Mom, Dad and Erika want to say goodbye. They're just getting up."

"Don't have time. I'll call them from the airport."

Upstairs, he threw his clothes into the suitcase, not even bothering to fold or hang up. He didn't shave—he could do that once he landed in Toronto. He threw into his carry-on what he needed for the meeting and ran downstairs.

"Get in the car," he called to Amber as he tossed his suitcase into the trunk. "Let's go."

"Where's Lisa?" Amber asked as Dylan spun out of the driveway. "Isn't she coming along? I wanted to say goodbye to her."

"She's staying at a friend's. I'll be seeing her after I drop you off." He accelerated down the hill and ran a yellow light to get onto the main avenue leading downtown. "I have something very important to talk to her about."

"What is that?" Amber twisted in her seat, grinning at her brother in expectation.

"Pride and deceit and love."

Amber pulled a face as she sank back in her seat. "That's pretty heavy, but it doesn't sound like a proposal to me."

"No, it doesn't. But it's a start," Dylan said, swerving into an opening in traffic. He ignored the sudden blaring of the truck's horn and scooted into another opening.

"You're driving like a crazy man, Dylan. What is wrong with you?"

"Nothing. Everything."

Please, Lord, just let me get to the apartment in time. Give me a chance to talk to her.

Ten minutes later he rocked to a halt in front of the Convention Centre downtown. He returned Amber's hug with a perfunctory one. "Gotta go, kiddo. You take care."

"Dylan, what is going on?"

"I'll call you—"

"From the airport," Amber interrupted. "Go, already. If you don't have time to properly say goodbye to your family, then forget it." She flounced out of the car and didn't look back.

Dylan didn't have time to feel guilty. He had more important things on his mind.

By the time he pulled up in front of Gabe's apartment, his heart was pumping. He had one hour. One hour to convince Lisa that he was wrong. To ask her to forgive him. To tell Gabe that his father had his doubts about his guilt.

He just hoped Lisa was still here. As he jogged down the sidewalk to the front door, he wondered how he was going to get in. Lisa or Gabe would hardly buzz him up when he announced himself. Thankfully, someone was leaving just as he got there and he caught the door before it closed.

Hurry. Hurry. He charged up the stairs two at a time and skidded to a halt in front of Gabe's apartment.

He took a moment to catch his breath. To send up a quick prayer.

Just as he raised his hand to knock, he heard voices from inside. Gabe's, raised in anger. Lisa's softer one, and another woman's voice.

Dara.

Dylan rapped on the door sharply, even as doubts crept into his thoughts. What was Dara doing here?

Footsteps sounded, approaching the door. It swung open and Lisa stood highlighted by the early-morning light coming through the living-room window. She wore loose pants and a T-shirt. Her hair framed her face in a tangled halo, but her eyes were hard. Even so, his heart skittered at the sight of her.

"What do you want?" she asked, both her hands holding the door like a shield. "I thought you had to leave today."

"My plane leaves in an hour. I have to talk to you."

"Dylan. What are you doing here?" Dara spun around, her cheeks flushed, her eyes bright. "I thought you were gone." In contrast to Lisa's casual wear, Dara wore a tailored suit, and even this early in the morning her hair was immaculately groomed.

"I've come to talk to Lisa and Gabe," Dylan said.

Gabe motioned for him to come in, netting him an irritated look from his sister-in-law. As Dylan walked past Lisa she glanced up at him, and for a heartbeat Dylan saw sorrow in the depths of her eyes. Then like a cloud sifting over the sun, it was gone. But it gave him hope.

"It's probably just as well you're here, Dylan," Dara said smoothly, suddenly in charge. She came to stand beside Dylan. "I've come on behalf of the company to tell Gabe that we are going to formally press charges of theft against him."

"You have no proof," Gabe exclaimed. "You know I didn't do it."

"Money in a numbered bank account put there by you." Dara shrugged, glancing at Dylan. "Dummy invoices signed by you for less than the actual amount. I can build a very strong case against you. And now that Dylan is here I know I finally have the support I need." Dara flashed him a bright smile. She touched him lightly, as if establishing a connection between them.

Dylan shook his head at Dara's obvious machinations, stepping away from her. Closer to Lisa. "Sorry, Dara. I'm not part of this. And we both know you don't really have a case."

"I have proof, Dylan," Dara said coldly.

"It won't stand up in a court of law," Dylan said. "And I won't let it get that far."

Lisa blinked then. Bit her lip and looked down. Dylan took a chance and reached out to her. Cupped her shoulder with his hand. He felt the ragged edges of his day slowly becoming whole as she reached up and laid her hand over his. Maybe it was all going to work out after all.

"You are going to take these people's side against me?" Dara cried out. "Against us?"

Dylan, still holding Lisa's shoulder, turned to her. "Yes, Dara. If it comes to that I will." Dylan pushed down the lingering panic over his flight. The appointment, the future job didn't matter as much anymore. What was happening here was far more important.

"Your father will side with Ted and me. You know that. He always has. And where your father goes, your mother will."

"That doesn't matter," Dylan said quietly. "I believe Gabe didn't do it. And I'm going to support him and Lisa through whatever you decide to do."

"I guess we'll have to see about that," Dara snapped. "I'll be talking to your father next."

"Go ahead, Dara," Dylan said, holding her angry gaze. "You might be surprised to hear what he has to say."

He felt Lisa lean closer to him. Clutch his hand tighter. He turned to her, and as their eyes met Dylan was surprised to see the shimmer of tears in hers. He gave her a tentative smile, a small overture.

His entire attention was on Lisa as Dara stormed out of the apartment, slamming the door behind her.

"Thanks for coming," Lisa said softly. She sniffed, then wiped her eyes. Dylan touched one silvery tear as it slid down her cheek, wonderment and joy singing through him.

"I'm sorry I was so angry yesterday," he said softly, stroking her cheek with his knuckle.

"No. Please don't apologize. I'm the one who has to apologize. You were right. I had lied to you." Lisa palmed away some more tears. "I'm so sorry. I was going to tell you sometime. I felt so bad about deceiving you."

Gabe's discreet cough caught their attention. Suddenly self-conscious, Dylan lowered his hand.

"Sorry to break in on this very touching scene," Gabe said dryly, "but right now I'm sure Dara is heading right over to your parents' place, Dylan, or possibly even the police station."

"I don't think you need to worry about Dara," Dylan said. "She doesn't have the proof she thinks she does, nor the support."

Gabe frowned. "What do you mean?"

"My father had an inkling of what was going on. He won't allow her to pursue this."

"What are you saying?" Lisa asked, catching him by the arm.

"It's a long story. Why don't you and Gabe come with me to my parents' place? I'll fill you in on the way over."

"But you can't miss your flight," Lisa said. "You kept telling me how important that appointment was. For your future."

Dylan smiled at the concern in her voice. Concern for him. "Right now there are other parts of my future I'm more concerned with."

Lisa smiled as a faint flush crept up her cheeks. "But your job…"

"I think you had better be worrying about your own job." Dylan touched a finger to her lips, then caught her hand. "Now, enough arguing. Let's go."

But Lisa held back. "I don't need to come. Why don't you and Gabe go alone?"

"I want you along," Dylan said.

Lisa shook her head. "I can't, Dylan. I'm too ashamed."

Dylan glanced at Gabe. "Do you mind giving us a few moments?"

"I'll be waiting in the lobby." Gabe gave him a careful smile as if still unsure of how to read this new situation, and left the apartment.

Dylan waited until he heard Gabe's footsteps hitting the stairs, then turned back to Lisa. "You don't have to be afraid of my family," Dylan said softly, cupping her chin, pleased that he could.

"I'm more ashamed than anything. I lied to them about my brother," Lisa said, still not meeting his eyes. "And we both lied to them about us."

"Only in the beginning," Dylan said, stroking her cheek with his thumb. "The evening we had supper with my family, I wanted it to be real."

Lisa's faint smile gave him hope.

"Last night you told me that you'd found something you didn't want to let go. Is that still true?"

"Truer," she whispered, pressing her hand against his. "I love you."

A sharp fragment of happiness pierced his heart and his response was to draw her close. To tilt her head toward him and touch his lips gently to hers. "I love you, too," he whispered against her mouth.

She clung to him then, pressed her head against his chest as he held her close.

Dylan willed time to stand still. He felt as if he had waited all his life for this moment and he didn't want to return to everyday life.

"I thought you hated me," she said, her voice muffled against his shirt. "I didn't think I'd ever see you again."

Dylan stroked his chin over her head, marveling at his right to do so. To simply hold her close with no secrets between them anymore. "I missed you too much," he whispered, brushing a kiss across her temple. "I couldn't stay away."

"I'm sorry, Dylan."

"Stop now. You've done nothing worse than I have."

She drew back, a faint frown creasing her forehead. "Do you think God can bless a relationship that started out in deceit?"

Dylan smiled at her concern. "I think God used our situation to bring us to Him. I think if we put our trust in Him, put our lives in His hands, He will use us and our relationship to praise Him."

Lisa smiled. "You are a blessing to me, Dylan."

"And you to me, Lisa." He stroked her hair back from her face, dropped a light kiss on her forehead. "And I hate to bring reality into this moment, but your brother is waiting and I want to finish what we came here to do."

"Welcome to our home, Gabe." Stephanie held out her hand to Lisa's brother. "Alex is waiting for you on the deck." Gabe shook Stephanie's hand, then glanced at Lisa, as if for support.

His unconscious gesture made Lisa's heart contract with old memories of meetings with other authorities when Gabe had gotten into trouble. How he always looked to her for help.

And she'd always been there. Just as she was now. She was about to reassure him.

"It's okay, Gabe," Dylan said suddenly. "We're here to sort things out."

Gabe nodded, smoothed his hair back from his face and walked out the large glass doors. As they slid shut behind him, Lisa glanced at Dylan, pleased at his support. And then it struck her with a wave of pleasure. She wasn't doing this alone anymore.

"Dylan, darling, I hate to point out the obvious, but didn't you and Lisa have a plane to catch?" Stephanie glanced over her shoulder. "In about twenty minutes?"

"I did, Mother. But Lisa and I didn't have a proper chance to say goodbye."

Stephanie angled him a puzzled glance. "But if you do that you'll miss…" She raised her hands in a gesture of defeat. "Can you please tell me what's going on?"

"Dylan," Lisa said softly. "I want to tell her."

Dylan nodded, took her hand and squeezed it lightly.

"Sorry, Mom," he said with a smile. "Why don't you sit down? Lisa and I have something to tell you."

Stephanie's eyes grew wide and her mouth slipped open as she looked from Dylan to Lisa.

Help me through this, Lord, Lisa prayed. *I want her respect as much as I crave Dylan's.*

And slowly, hesitatingly, Lisa told Stephanie all about her deception.

"I want to say I'm sorry, Stephanie," Lisa said, her voice urgent. "I know I was wrong. I deceived you and Alex and the girls."

"You're forgiven, if that's what you need to hear," Stephanie said with a smile.

"Just like that?"

"Of course, my dear." Stephanie drew Lisa into her arms and held her close. Just as a mother would. "Just like that. I can't withhold my forgiveness from you when God has forgiven me so much more."

And once again Lisa felt hot tears prick her eyelids.

The chimes of the doorbell echoed through the house.

"I suspect that's Ted and Dara," Dylan said with a tired sigh.

Lisa's heartbeat kicked up a notch at the thought of confronting Dara again. She glanced over her shoulder through the glass doors to where Alex and Gabe sat in earnest conversation. She prayed it would all work out.

"How can you take the word of someone who lied to you all?" Dara said, her face flushed with emotion. She sat ramrod straight in her chair, her eyes flashing, her very posture displaying the tension in her voice. Beside her, Ted leaned back in his chair, his lips pressed in a thin line, his eyes narrowed.

Dara's eyes flicked from Alex to Stephanie but avoided Dylan, Lisa and Gabe. It was as if they didn't even exist for her.

"Gabe lied about his involvement with the police," Dara continued, stating her case in a cold, clear voice. "Lisa lied about her involvement with Gabe." She raised her hands in a dramatic gesture. "I don't know about you, but to me that makes much of what they say suspect."

Dylan ignored his anger at Dara's accusations.

Instead he glanced sidelong at Lisa. Her cheeks were red, but her head was unbowed. He covered her hand with his under the table and gave it a reassuring squeeze.

"I think you should be careful who you condemn, Dara," Alex said, leaning forward. He folded his hands on the table and held Dara's gaze. "What I'd like to know more about is your personal knowledge about the missing money."

"Wait a minute." Dara's mouth fell open in shock. "I'm not the one that took it…." She gestured toward Gabe. "Ask him. He knows."

"Dara, do you know why I asked Dylan to come here, against your will?" Alex asked, his voice quiet, his gaze direct.

"No."

"I was hoping that his coming here would send a signal to you and to Ted. A signal that I had my doubts about Gabe's guilt." He picked up the file folder in front of him and tapped it lightly on the table. "I was hoping that you would come forward and tell me what I wanted to hear without us having to involve outside people. And now, in spite of your lack of cooperation and in spite of limited material available to Dylan and Lisa, they still managed to find some pieces of information that don't look good for you."

Dara drooped back against her chair and for a moment Dylan felt sorry for her. Though Alex had given her and Ted the opportunity to talk to him in private, she had opted for this public moment. And this was the result.

"How do you… How can you…" She faltered, reaching out for Ted. "Ted, help me."

Ted took his wife's hand between his. "What information did you find, Dad?"

"Lisa told Dylan about the time on the bank deposit. It happened after Gabe left the office."

Dara glared at Lisa as if making one last-ditch effort. "Whatever it was you did to Gabe's computer, that can be found out. You must have jimmied the files yourself."

"Be careful what you say, Dara," Dylan said, a warning tone edging his voice.

"Is that all you have, Dad?" Ted asked, rubbing his index finger over his eyebrow.

Alex glanced at Dylan, who nodded, then he pushed the file folder across the table.

Ted opened it, glanced over the memo, then back at Dara. He said nothing. Just showed it to her. Dara glanced at the memo, blanched visibly and shook her head. "This can't be right. This…this is a fake."

"Dara, stop this now," Ted said softly. "I want to help you. I don't want this to get worse."

Dara looked down. Shook her head. "Why are you doing this, Ted?"

"Because I care about you."

And in that moment Dylan felt a grudging respect for Ted. And saw that the legacy of faithful love had been passed on from the father to his children.

Dara ran one carefully manicured fingernail over a faint gouge in the table. "All you care about is the company. Showing your father that you're as good a man as Dylan is."

Ted gave his brother a vague smile. "I'm not."

Dara pressed her nail deeper. "Then why were you

always gone? Why were all our conversations about the company and how you were supposed to try to run it? Why did you stop paying attention to me?"

And Dylan got an inkling of why Dara had done what she had.

"Well, you got my attention these past few days."

"I don't want it just for a few days." Dara spun around, tears gathering in her perfectly made up eyes. "I want you to be a part of my life all the time. And it just wasn't happening." The tears slipped down her cheeks, and with a jerky movement she got up from her chair and left.

Ted got up and carefully pushed both their chairs back under the table. "Sorry about this, Dad. Mom." He gave Dylan an apologetic look. "I was wrong, Dylan. I really thought she was telling me the truth. I'm sorry for what she said to you and how she spoke about Lisa."

Dylan felt a rush of love for his brother at the admission that he knew was difficult to make. "We'll talk later. I think Dara needs you now."

"I guess I never realized she always did." And then he left.

The hollow drip of the kitchen tap echoed in the heavy silence that followed.

Stephanie cleared her throat and looked around. "I think we should pray for them," she said softly.

She held out her hand to Lisa on one side, Alex on the other. Dylan took Lisa's hand and squeezed it lightly. She responded as they bowed their heads. But Alex was the one who prayed.

The moment of silence that followed his father's

quietly spoken prayer was a moment of communion Dylan hadn't felt in a long time. As he looked up, he caught his father's eye.

And for the first time in many years he felt a deep and abiding respect for his father.

Stephanie got up from the table, looking around. "Well, I did have a special breakfast made for Dylan, who ran out before he could have any. It's still ready if anyone wants it."

Dylan couldn't help but laugh. Food. His mother's cure-all. "What do you have for me, Mom?"

"Your favorite. Crepes with strawberries and whipped cream and fruit," Stephanie said wistfully.

"Well, heat them up now. I'm sure Lisa and Gabe would love to try them."

With a pleased smile Stephanie got up and started working in the kitchen, declining Lisa's offer of help.

While she worked, Dylan turned to his father. Smiled. "I have an apology to make to you, Dad."

Alex held up his hand. "I understand, Dylan. It's okay."

"But I still need to tell you that I'm sorry. For doubting you. For being so angry at how you handled this very delicate situation."

Alex shook his head. "No. I'm sorry. I should have told you right from the beginning." He lifted one shoulder in a shrug. "I was too proud. I guess I was hoping I could solve the problem without you knowing how badly I had failed the company."

"I can understand that," Dylan said. "I guess pride is something we both share." He glanced sidelong at Lisa, who was watching this exchange with a wistful smile tugging at her lips. He took her hand and gave it a light shake. "And what is going on behind those beautiful brown eyes?"

"This family." Lisa shook her head in amazement. "You apologize in front of complete strangers. You are willing to admit your faults. You are a gift to each other."

"Amen to that," Alex said.

Dylan felt a rush of love, strong and pure. He wished he and Lisa could be alone, could talk. Take the time to right the wrongs of the past few days. Reconnect as Christians.

Breakfast was over. The dishes were done, but everyone lingered around the table.

Alex was talking to Gabe. "Things are still a little up in the air with the company, Gabe, but I'm fairly sure once we get the books properly audited by a disinterested third party, the full truth will come to light. I was wondering if you would want your job back."

Lisa's fingers dug into Dylan's hand, her eyes now on Gabe.

Gabe pursed his lips, considering. "Actually, I would prefer if I could get a reference from your company. There are a few other places I think I might like to work for instead."

"I understand," Alex said softly. "And once again, I'm so sorry for what you've had to go through. You're very lucky to have a sister who is willing to take risks for you."

"I sure am," Gabe said, his smile gentle. "She always says family takes care of family."

Dylan waited a beat. Allowed the moment to settle.

"Lisa. We need to talk," he said, squeezing her hand.

Without looking at him, she nodded, as if suddenly shy.

"Mom. Dad. Gabe. I hope you'll excuse us a moment," Dylan said, looking around the group.

"You're not going to try to catch your flight?"

Dylan laughed as he stood, drawing Lisa to her feet. "I think I've given up on that completely." He glanced at his father. Smiled. "I might have a few other plans to discuss with my father."

"I'll be waiting," Alex said.

Dylan slipped his arm around Lisa and gave her a quick one-armed hug. "Let's go," he said softly.

She looked up at him, a coy smile playing around her lips. "You're not my boss anymore, you know."

"I know. And I'm going to miss having the authority." He gave her hand a tug. "C'mon. Let's go for a walk."

Lisa wrapped her sweater a little closer. "Speaking as a former employee, I think missing your flight's not going to create the best impression." The damp path they were walking along meandered through dense undergrowth shadowed by tall fir trees, which created a microclimate both cool and secluded. "West Coast rainforest," the plaque along the path had said. Lisa was thankful she had worn the sweater Dylan had recommended she take along.

They had been walking for quite a while now. Lisa was surprised at the size of this park, a serene and secluded place bracketed by development on three sides.

"It is awkward," Dylan agreed. He sauntered along beside her, his hands in the pockets of his blue jeans, looking unconcerned about her pronouncement. "I'm not so sure I want the job after all."

"Perry Hatcher is taking over your position in Toronto." Lisa felt silly pointing out the obvious, but felt as if she was carefully navigating territory as unfamiliar to her as the path they were walking down.

"And I suspect he'll have to look for another secretary," Dylan said casually.

Lisa only nodded, unsure what to say.

I know I don't deserve anything, Lord, Lisa prayed as they walked on in silence. *But I do want to make things right between us. At least that.*

They met another couple holding hands and as Dylan and Lisa stepped aside to let them by, Lisa noticed that the woman was pregnant. The couple thanked them and walked on, caught up in their conversation.

Lisa's eyes followed them.

"You've done that before," Dylan said softly, coming to a halt beside the path.

"What do you mean?" Lisa stopped beside him, uncertain what he was talking about.

"I remember when we first arrived in Vancouver, we were driving through Stanley Park. You saw a couple pushing a baby buggy. You did the same thing you just did now. Watched them like it was something wonderful."

"It is, I guess—wonderful, that is. Wonderful to see a family together like that. People happy to be together."

"Are you happy to be with me?"

Lisa's gaze flew to his, the wistful note in his voice catching her attention.

"Yes. I am."

"Do you like Vancouver?"

"I love it. It's a beautiful city."

"I like it, too. It's home." Dylan's smile held a tinge of melancholy. "In spite of how crazy things have been this past week, I was glad to be back here."

"I enjoyed *most* of our visit here."

"Which part did you like the best?"

Lisa smiled, took a chance and laid her hands on his chest. "Sailing with you. Being alone with you with no one around. It was the first time we were together and we weren't pretending."

Dylan laid his hands over hers, warming them. "I wasn't pretending very often," he said softly.

Lisa held his gaze. Saw the sincerity in it and made her own confession.

"Neither was I."

And suddenly she was in his arms. Held close to him. Being kissed by him. She returned his kiss as joy surged through her.

"I know this is crazy," he murmured, holding her close, stroking her hair with his hand. "But I feel like I've known you for years. I feel like we belong together."

In spite of the joy his words gave her, she couldn't stop the whisper of guilt and doubt that circled. "I wish I had told you everything at the beginning," she started. "But I couldn't…"

Dylan stopped her words with his mouth, then drew

back, touching her face. "We talked about this already. We have forgiven each other. I know God has forgiven us. This is a beginning of its own, Lisa. A beginning of something better than what came before. I want to spend the rest of my life with you. I don't care where that happens or how, but I just know that since I met you, I don't want to be away from you. I want to give you all the things you haven't been able to have. I want to share my family with you, my life. Everything I have."

Lisa felt her throat grow thick with tears of happiness. "I'm going to cry again," she warned, her lips trembling.

"That's okay. I'm patient."

"Love is patient," she whispered. "I wish I could tell you what a blessing you've been to me."

"And you for me."

And as he kissed her again, Lisa felt that this truly was the beginning.

Epilogue

"**W**here should I put the balloons?" Amber yanked on the string of helium balloons, making them bounce in the open space of the foyer.

"Give those to me. I'll tie them along the banister," Stephanie suggested.

"Erika has a bunch, too."

"My goodness, you girls. How did you get them all in your car?"

"We borrowed Gabe's," Amber said with a grin.

"You girls better stop taking advantage of him." Stephanie tut-tutted. "He just got that car."

"He wanted to come along."

"I'm glad he could take time off. They work him too hard at that job of his," Stephanie said. "Anyhow, I want you to help Chelsea in the kitchen. She's getting the food ready. And hurry."

The door opened, and Stephanie jumped. But it was only Alex and Erika dwarfed by a batch of balloons even bigger than the one Amber was carrying. Gabe was with her.

"You guys scared me," Stephanie said, her hand on her heart. "I thought you were Dylan and Lisa."

Alex grinned at her and gave her a quick kiss. "I stopped by the office before I came here. Dylan had some work to do yet, and then he was going to pick up Lisa on his way here."

"Too bad Ted and Dara couldn't be here, too."

Alex nodded. "Toronto is a bit far to come just for this."

"Bring those to the kitchen," Stephanie said to Gabe and Erika. "Chelsea, Jordan and Amber can figure out what to do with them." She turned back to Alex. "Anything interesting come in the mail?"

He nodded and held up a letter. "This from Ted and Dara."

Stephanie snatched it out of his hands, her eyes skimming hungrily over the cramped writing. She looked up at Alex. "What do you think? Do they sound happy?"

"I think having him work at the Toronto branch was a move in the right direction," Alex said, dropping a light kiss on his wife's forehead. "And now you better hurry. Dylan and Lisa are only minutes behind me."

The kitchen was a flurry of activity, but minutes later all was in order.

"They're coming," Erika called out from her vantage point at the top of the stairs. "Get ready." She sped down the stairs, sending the balloons swaying in her wake.

Giggles were suppressed as they heard Dylan's and Lisa's muffled voices.

Then the door opened and everyone jumped out.

"Surprise."

"Happy anniversary."

The shouts blended into a cacophony of sound and celebration.

Dylan and Lisa stood in the doorway, their mouths open. And then they were hugged and kissed and congratulated again.

"You guys. I was wondering what was going on," Lisa said, grinning as she looked around the room.

Dylan just shook his head.

"Kiss her, Dylan!" Amber shouted.

"Oh, like he never does," Chelsea said. "C'mon. Let's eat. I'm starved."

They moved en masse to the kitchen. When the noise and busyness had died down and they were all settled at the table, food in front of them, Alex stood up.

"I just want to say an official congratulations to Dylan and Lisa," he said, smiling at the happy couple who sat at the opposite end of the table. Dylan had his arm slung over Lisa's shoulder and she was leaning into him, her cheeks flushed and her eyes sparkling as she looked around the table full of people. "I want to say how much we've enjoyed watching our newest daughter and our son grow closer together in their first year of marriage. And closer to God. I want to thank God for His blessing on our family. For His love. A love that, like Dylan and Lisa's wedding text said, is never ending but most of all patient."

And as his father spoke, a smile broke across Dylan's face. Then he turned to his wife and kissed her, their love for each other shining in their eyes.

* * * * *

Dear Reader,

Family is the place where we can experience both our deepest hurts and our deepest love. What I was hoping to show in *Love Is Patient* is that even in the "best" families, mistakes are made, sometimes with the best intentions. Though our children are all adults by the world's standards, we are still involved in their lives and make mistakes in them.

I'm always thankful that we have a perfect Father in God and that His love for us doesn't depend on our behavior.

Carolyne Aarsen

P.S. I love to hear from my readers. You can write to me at the following address:

Carolyne Aarsen
Box 114
Neerlandia, AB
T0G 1RO
Canada

A HEART'S REFUGE

...his delight is in the law of the Lord...He is like a tree planted by streams of water, which yields its fruit in season and whose leaf does not wither.
—*Psalms* 1:2–3

I want to dedicate this book to Dr. Randy Blacketer
and Sandy Blacketer, our pastor and youth pastor.
Two people who complement each other and our
community in so many ways.
Thanks for your gifts of time and talents.

As well, I'd like to thank Laurie Carter from
Okanagan Life and Karen Ball for their input
on the magazine business.

Chapter One

Becky Ellison pressed her back against the outside
door of *Going West*'s office, balancing her muffin, coffee cup and a batch of folders. Don't panic. You're just
a little bit late.

"Hey, hon. Welcome back. How was the holiday?"
Trixie sang out as Becky entered the reception area.

Becky set everything on the waist-high divider separating the entrance from Trixie Langston's domain and
blew her breath out in a gusty sigh. "Breakfast on the
run my first day back. Orders from our new boss that
I'm deciphering late last night after spending ten days
with hormonal teenage girls at Bible camp." She
grabbed her hair in a ponytail and twisted an elastic
around it. "You fill in the blanks."

"And such a lovely hairdo to impress our new boss."
Trixie frowned as her eyes flicked over Becky's plaid
shirt and blue jeans. Trixie, as usual, was immaculately
groomed. Artfully windblown hairstyle. Pale pink

sweater and gray skirt. Makeup. Earrings. Becky had never sought to emulate Trixie's style, but once in a while she wondered if people would take her more seriously if she did. "If this is your good impression," Trixie continued, "I would hate to see the slob version."

"Mom's wash machine broke down. The sewer backed up while Dad and Dennis were out in the orchard. After cleaning up that mess, this was all I had left to wear." Becky anchored a few loose strands behind her ear and bit her lips to make them red. "Okay, enough primping. I'll get my messages after the meeting. By the way, how late am I?"

Trixie glanced at the clock in the foyer of the magazine office. "I'd love to say everyone else is running their usual fifteen minutes behind, but for once everyone is early. Except you."

Becky pulled a face at Trixie, stifling the dread that clutched her midsection. Rick Ethier. Here in Okotoks. What were the odds that he remembered who she was? Probably slim to none. She probably knew more about him than he did about her. She sucked in another breath. "My friend, wish me luck."

"Give him your best smile and you'll do fine," Trixie said, flashing her a thumbs-up.

The door of Nelson's office was shut and the only sound she heard was an unfamiliar deep voice. Rick, most likely. New publisher of the magazine her father started and Rick's grandfather, Colson Ethier, recently purchased.

Up until three weeks ago, office gossip was Nelson, the previous publisher, would stay on after the purchase. Then, just before she left on her so-called holiday—camp counselor to ten teenage girls—she was stunned to discover that Rick Ethier, Colson Ethier's grandson, would take over Nelson's job. Now she would be making an entrance, and a poor first impression, in front of the man who had shattered so many of her hopes and dreams.

She smoothed one hand over her still damp hair, drew in a slow breath, sent up a quick prayer and carefully opened the door. Flashing everyone an apologetic smile, she dropped into her usual chair beside Nelson's desk, uncomfortably close to her new boss. She dropped her papers on the corner of Nelson's desk and chanced a look at Rick Ethier standing beside her.

His face was all too familiar, though the grainy magazine picture indelibly imprinted on her mind didn't capture the reality of his good looks in person. Shaggy blond hair framed the kind of face that would make women of any age stop and take a second look. The hint of a dimple in his cheek balanced out the self-assured cockiness of his smile, and his eyes were so intensely blue it was as if they glimmered with an interior light. His clothing was a mixture of casual and stylish. He wore a soft cotton cream-colored shirt, a deep brown corduroy blazer and fitted blue jeans.

And as he glanced Becky's way, a frown.

Please don't let him state the obvious, she thought, carefully setting her coffee cup on the floor beside her.

Instead he glanced at his watch. Almost as bad.

"Sorry I'm late," she said with a quick smile as she reached over and shook his hand. "I'm Becky Ellison."

"Our editor," Rick said, returning her smile with a

cool one of his own. "Glad you could make it." He held her gaze a moment, as if establishing his territory, then he turned to face the rest of the gathered staff of the magazine, dismissing her. "As you all now know, I'm Rick Ethier, grandson of Colson Ethier, the new owner of *Going West*. I'm sure you're wondering why my grandfather, whose holdings are fairly substantial, would bother himself with one small, regional magazine. Trust me, I'm as baffled."

A few titters greeted that comment, but Becky heard the faint cynicism in his remark. A trademark of his.

Rick Ethier was a travel writer for Colson Ethier's flagship magazine. Though he couldn't be more than thirty, his stories and articles usually held a shadow of world-weariness. As if he'd seen it all. Done it all.

And as Becky listened to him, one part of her mind easily resurrected other words of one particularly scathing article. "Sentimental claptrap" and "shamelessly manipulative." These less than flattering descriptions came from a monthly book review column Rick wrote for the same magazine. A column in which Rick wrote about the first book Becky had published. Her pride and joy. And thanks to that negative review, Becky hadn't been able to get a second contract with her publisher.

Focus on the now, Becky, she reminded herself, taking a long slow breath to ease away her irritable emotions. This was her new boss, and no matter what, she had to learn to get along with him. The past was past.

"I've done my research on this magazine," Rick was saying, "but for now, I want to go around the room and ask each of you what you see as the purpose of *Going West*. The vision, so to speak."

Feet shuffled, a few throats cleared as the staff glanced around the room at each other. Becky sat back in her chair, crossing her feet at the ankles, surprised at the momentary blankness in her own mind.

Going West was supposed to have a vision?

Nelson, the previous publisher and her father's partner, had set the tone and layout of the magazine from its inception. He had reviewed, accepted and or rejected freelance articles. Since Becky started working as editor, she had simply followed his lead, hoping she caught the idea of what he wanted for that particular issue.

Never had they sat down and reviewed—or even spoke of—any kind of long-term vision.

"Why don't we start with you, Becky, now that you've deigned to join us." Rick stood beside his presentation board, his arms crossed, his legs apart, his head tilted to one side.

Definitely hostile body language, thought Becky with a surge of anger. She shouldn't have been late. But that was also past.

"We can do that." Becky licked her lips, buying time as hazy, insubstantial thoughts slipped past her defensive emotions. C'mon, Becky. Think. This is your chance to show Rick Ethier that you are intelligent and articulate. Not sentimental in the least.

"I've always seen *Going West* as firstly a regional magazine," she said, grasping at an idea that she knew to be true. "Our second mandate is to be a magazine disseminating a viewpoint peculiar to Western sensibilities."

Rick nodded, his lips pursed. "Can we try that in English?"

Becky held his direct gaze, trying not to be unnerved by his glinting eyes. In spite of her resolve to forget, snatches of his nasty book review sifted through her head. "Verbose, treacly and unrealistic."

"It's a cowboy and farmer magazine," she snapped.

"That's probably closer to the mark," Rick said with a humorless half grin.

Becky held his gaze a moment, as if challenging him, but she was the first to look away.

The meeting went downhill from there. People who had received minimal guidance from Nelson or, to be honest, her father, now had to come up with a thumbnail sketch of what the magazine was supposed to accomplish.

Advertising. Art. Circulation. While they struggled through their answers, Becky felt embarrassed and exposed.

They should all know, she thought, taking a pencil out from behind her ear. But Nelson's editorial meetings tended to be haphazard. He and Becky sat down once a week going over articles and their status, laying out the magazine's plan for that particular month. When they wrote up the schedule for the upcoming magazines, there was an underlying cohesion, but a person had to go looking to find it.

But vision? Simply not there.

She scribbled a few things down on paper, took a few notes from what people were saying.

"So you can see—" Rick flipped over the first page of the presentation chart "—all this vagueness has translated into this." He pointed to a listing of numbers he had written down.

"Circulation is down, subscription is down. Advertising revenue is down. And I'm going to attribute all that to what I'm hearing in this room this morning." Rick looked around, letting his direct gaze tick over each of them, then finally coming back to Becky. "Which is a lot of vague words, but no single, clear statement that outlines what this magazine is really about. And that is going to change. As of today."

He had done his homework, Becky thought with grudging respect.

"So what's your first step?" Becky asked. Rick's language made it very clear that he was lead dog. She just needed to know where he was heading.

"Sitting down with my editor and laying out my vision for this magazine."

A cold finger of apprehension snaked down her back. "Your vision?"

Rick shrugged, rocking lightly back on his heels. "Media is all about communication. I haven't heard much in this room, other than your cowboy and farmer comment, that creates a concise and clear idea of what *Going West* is supposed to be."

He didn't know the community. The surrounding area. How was he going to come up with the direction of the magazine? And where did *he* see it going?

"Branding is the name of the game in publishing," Rick continued. "Now I need to figure out what brand of magazine we are going to become."

His words were not comforting.

"I've already commissioned a marketing analysis team to do surveys, interview focus groups and send out questionnaires to our current readership. That won't be coming in for a couple of months, but that doesn't mean we can't make some changes now." He perched on the edge of Nelson's desk and glanced around the room. "I'm going to be sitting down with each member of the various departments and going over what we've got coming up and what we can possibly change for now."

Becky rubbed the back of her neck. Rick's plans translated into work she didn't have time for. She had a long-term commitment to the youth choir at church. She had promised the school librarian she'd help weed through books that needed to be sold or discarded. A fund-raising committee had asked her to write copy for their brochure.

She had Bible study. Book club.

And somehow in the middle of all this she needed to put together a stellar proposal that would negate any second thoughts her publisher had about working with her.

"I hope this isn't going to be a problem, Miss Ellison?"

Becky looked up. Had her disappointment shown on her face?

Rick faced her, his eyebrows raised, his eyes boring into hers. "You seem disheartened."

It *had* shown.

Becky glanced around the room. She wasn't the only disheartened one, but somehow Rick had zeroed in on her.

She stifled her resentment and chose her words carefully. "I'm just thinking about all the work ahead for each department. It's going to be difficult to turn the direction of this magazine around midstream."

Rick flipped his hand to one side, as if dismissing her concerns. "Any change we implement is going to take some sacrifice and time." He gestured toward the chart behind him. "The figures speak for themselves. If this magazine keeps going in the direction it is, most of the people in this room are going to be out of a job. The only choices available to you now are hard work." Rick looked around the room, his arms crossed, his legs spraddled in a defensive posture. "Or no work."

There was nothing more to be said. Rick waited a heartbeat more. "Meeting's over," he said. "You're dismissed."

Cliff Thiessen let his chair drop back onto the floor with a thud and got up. "Well, better get back to it," he muttered to no one in particular. As the rest of the staff left, there was some muttering, but for the most part people were subdued by what their new boss had told them.

"Becky, I'd like to see you a moment," Rick said as she gathered up her papers in preparation for leaving.

Panic tightened her chest, but she masked it with a vague smile. She thought she had done pretty good up till now. She didn't know if she could handle a face-to-face meeting quite yet.

She shuffled through her papers while the room emptied, buying some time.

"What can I do for you?" she said, once the door closed behind the last person.

"I just wanted to take a moment to speak with you privately." Rick walked around to the other side of Nelson's desk, glancing out the bank of windows that filled one wall. Becky couldn't help follow the direction of his gaze. Beyond the roofs of Okotoks, the golden prairie rolled toward the soft brown of the Porcupine Hills, which nudged against the jagged peaks of the Rocky Mountains, faintly purple in the morning sun.

"It's a beautiful view, isn't it?" she said quietly.

"It will help compensate for having to live out here for a while."

Cynicism again. She shouldn't have been surprised. "What do you mean?"

Rick turned back to her and rested his hands palms down on his desk. "You may as well know, I'm here a maximum of twelve months and that's it. My grandfather issued me an ultimatum I have a lot of incentive to keep."

Becky frowned lightly, but held his steady gaze. "What ultimatum?"

"Turn this magazine around in twelve months and he'll leave me alone to go back to traveling and living my life as I see fit."

"And then what happens to the magazine?"

Rick shrugged and pushed himself off from the desk. "Not my concern."

"Will your grandfather still own it?"

"I don't know. You could buy it if you wanted." His casual words held a lash of mockery.

"I've got my own plans," she said softly.

"And what would those be?"

Try to ease away from the relentless deadlines of magazine work. Write a book that would make her current editor sit up and take notice. Offer her the temporary stability of a multibook contract.

But Rick Ethier was the last person she was going to dump her "treacly" dreams on.

"I've got a few things on the go." She drew in a slow breath and looked up at him again. He was watching her, his head canted to one side, his mouth softer now that it no longer was twisted into a cynical smile.

And in spite of her negative feelings toward him, she felt a nebulous connection spark between them, then lengthen into a gentle warmth.

She was the first to look away, confusion fighting her initial antagonism. What was wrong with her? So he was good-looking. So he possessed a certain charm that it seemed even she wasn't immune to.

He was her boss. And the man who had a hand in delaying her dream.

Rick cleared his throat and shuffled some file folders on his desk. "I understand from Nelson that you have been working on setting up an appointment with the Premier of Alberta?"

"I don't have a firm commitment, but I'm in communication with his secretary."

"Congratulations. That's quite a coup. I've been trying to get an interview with him since he was voted in with such an overwhelming majority."

"Jake's pretty private."

"I'll say. He guards his private life like a Doberman. I've tried a few times to get an interview for Colson's magazine, but I've always been turned away with a polite but firm no."

Becky knew this about Jake. In fact, he had said the only reason he would consider an interview with her was because he knew it wouldn't turn into a gossipfest. Before he had become premier of Alberta and after, she and Jake Groot had been members of a province-wide committee devoted to preservation of native grasslands. They had gotten to know each other on a social as well as committee level and Becky had used that leverage to snag this formal interview.

"I'd like to help you with that article."

The cold finger she had felt before became an icy fist. "Actually, I always work on my own," she said quietly but firmly.

"When is the interview?" he asked, ignoring her comment.

"Not for a few months."

"Keep me in the loop, then."

He's your boss, Becky reminded herself when she looked up at him. "Okay, I'll do that," she said quietly. More than that she wasn't going to promise. Jake would not be pleased if she dragged along a whole phalanx of people.

She gathered up her papers and Rick laid his hand on hers. She flinched as if she'd been burned.

"Sorry, I believe that's mine." He pointed to the small burgundy engagement calendar in her hands.

"I don't think so," Becky said, shifting the papers that were threatening to spill out of her arms. "It has my initials on it. *R.E.*"

Rick held up a similar calendar and frowned down at it. "This one has the same initials."

Becky flipped hers open to a page with a butterfly sticker in one corner and a reminder to pick up butter scribbled in purple pen on a stained and dog-eared page.

"This is mine," she muttered, closing it and slipping it between her papers and her chest.

"I'm sorry," Rick said, tapping the folder he held against his other hand. "I'm guessing Becky is short for Rebecca."

Good-looking *and* smart, Becky thought with a touch of her own cynicism. "You've got that right," she said, flashing him a quick smile.

And as she left his office, she blew out a sigh. One day down. Only three hundred and sixty four to go.

"You knew Rick Ethier was going to be taking over from Nelson, so why are you so angry?" Sam Ellison asked, crouching down beside another sapling.

"I guess the reality was harder than the idea." Becky dug her hands into the sun-warmed dirt of the new apple orchard. An early-evening breeze fanned away the warmth of the sun, and she could already feel the peace of the orchard easing away the tension of the day. "I mean I just found out before I went to camp. That hardly gave me time to get used to the idea."

"You'll get used to it. Hand me the budding knife please."

She pulled the small, but deadly sharp blade out of the toolbox her father carried with him and watched while he painstakingly cut a T shape in the bark of the young sapling. "I got the impression from Colson that he's quite proud of his grandson," Sam continued. "Rick's travel articles are quite insightful."

"As are his nasty book reviews." Becky couldn't keep the disdainful tone out of her voice, netting her a light frown from her father. "I still don't understand why such a prestigious magazine chose my book to review."

"That was a year ago, Becky."

"And since then, the publisher has been pretty hesitant about buying another book."

"Your editor is behind you."

"He's been great, but if he can't sell it to the marketing people who seem to have a copy of that nasty review branded on their brain tissues, I'm just spinning my wheels." She leaned forward, yanking an isolated stalk of grass from the newly cultivated dirt. "I don't know if Rick even realized it's my book he slammed— a casualty of his cutting words. I'm left bleeding on the sidelines while he moves on, blithely unaware of what he had done." With a dramatic flourish she raised her face to the sky and pressed her hand to her chest.

"When you're finished declaiming, you can hand me that whip please. The Alberta Red."

"See, not even my own father appreciates my pain." With a grin Becky plucked a tree branch out of the bucket of water. She carefully sliced the bud off it herself, taking a large piece of bark with it. Turning it over she plucked the pith away from the backside of the slice and handed it to her father.

"Change isn't always a bad thing, Becky. Life is always about adapting." He inserted the slice in the cut, against the live flesh of the sapling, pulled the bark back over top and secured it with a rubber band. "Rick can bring in a new way of looking at things."

"He talks about finding a new direction for the magazine, but how can he when he doesn't know the community it targets?"

"That can be good. He'll bring his own perspective and skills to the magazine. Like bringing new genetic material into the orchard and grafting it onto established and mature stock."

"Except he's only here for a while, which makes me wonder if the 'graft' will take. He's a wanderer, just like Trevor was."

"Don't tell me you're still mooning over him?" Sam held out his hand. "Can I have that pine tar please?"

Becky handed him a small tin and a flat stick. "Hardly mooning. Trevor was a high school romance and a reminder to stay away from guys who can't commit." She curled her legs closer to herself and hugged them. "Anyway, Rick said he's only going to be around a year. Maybe less. That's hardly long enough to make a real difference. I'm sure he wants to go back to his traveling. Last I heard it was Malta. Before that Thailand."

Sam wrapped protective covering over the wound and gave Becky an indulgent smile. "Seems to me you know a fair bit of what is going on in Rick Ethier's life."

Becky avoided his eyes. She could try to make some lame excuse about her knowledge of Rick's comings and goings but she had never been a very good liar.

"How in the world did you and Colson even connect?" Becky asked, handing her father his toolbox as he pushed himself to his feet.

"Years ago, Colson lived in Calgary and had courted your grandmother. He decided the real money was back East, but she wouldn't leave Okotoks." Sam gave Becky a hand up. "Maybe he is taking a short trip down memory lane, buying this magazine."

"And taking a very reluctant passenger with him. Rick."

"Well, you make sure to invite him out here sometime."

Becky sighed as she slipped her arm through her father's. "Give me some time to get used to the idea that he's even here in Okotoks. In my office."

The heat emanating from the dark plowed ground gave way to a soft coolness as they entered the older orchard.

"I'm going to have to get rid of some of these trees," her father mused, looking up at the gnarled branches. "Though I hate to."

"'Every tree that does not bear fruit must be cut down and cast into the fire,'" Becky quoted, giving her father's arm a jiggle as if to remind him.

"God gives us lots of chances. I think I might let these trees go another year or two." He reached up and touched one branch, the dearth of apples on it a silent testimony to their uselessness. "I can still take a few cuttings from them."

"You say that every year, Dad," Becky said with a smile.

Becky's maternal great-grandfather started this orchard when he first immigrated from Holland. It was a gamble to expect to create an oasis on the harshly bald prairie. But the soil proved fertile and the poplar trees planted as windbreaks shot up, creating a refuge necessary for the apple trees to flourish. Irrigation came from a creek that flowed through the property.

The orchard had gone through three generations and various changes. Becky's mother, Cora, inherited the orchard. When Cora Bruinsma married Sam Ellison, he slowly worked his way into the family business, helping to cultivate the orchard and keeping the magazine going at the same time.

Becky grew up with her time split between the hustle and bustle of the magazine and the peace of the orchard. Her first love was writing, but her home was her sanctuary. Her plan had been to stay at home until she had her second book published and a contract for another. Only then would she feel she had the financial wherewithal to buy a place of her own and move out.

Which hadn't happened yet.

And if she didn't get working on this next book, wasn't likely to happen for at least another year.

"*Going West.* Becky speaking." Becky tucked the phone under her ear, she pushed the sleeves of her sweater up and drew the copy of the article she had been working on toward her. Sneaking a quick glance at her watch—2:15 p.m. She had fifteen minutes yet.

"Becky? This is Gladys Hemple. I do the cooking and preserves column."

"What can I do for you, Gladys?" Becky's pencil flicked over the paper, striking out, putting in question marks.

A Heart's Refuge

Gladys didn't reply right away. Becky heard a faint sniff, then...

"You know I get a lot of compliments on the column," Gladys said, her voice suspiciously thick. "Lots of people say they read it all the time."

"So what's the problem?" Becky frowned when she heard another, louder sniff over the phone.

"I've been asked not to do it anymore." Another sniff. "By some man named Rick who says he's the new publisher."

Becky laid her pencil down, her full attention now on her caller. "What exactly did he say, Gladys?"

"That he's changing the focus of the magazine and that what I do didn't mesh with the vision. Or something like that." Gladys paused and Becky heard her blowing her nose. "Becky, I've been doing that column for the past twenty-five years and I was never late. Not even once. What did I do wrong?"

Becky clutched the phone in her hand and leaned back in her chair. "Gladys, I'm sure there's been some mistake. I'll go talk to Mr. Ethier."

"Could you do that please? I've just finished taking pictures of the chocolate cake for this week's recipe. I hate to see it all wasted."

"You just get those pictures developed. I'll deal with Rick."

And bring that cake over here.

Becky stomach growled at the thought of Gladys Hemple's chocolate cake. She hadn't eaten or taken a break since she'd grabbed a couple of bites out of the stale muffin she'd found while scavenging through her desk for a pen that worked. That had been eight-thirty.

In fifteen minutes she had a meeting with Rick and she still had a couple of articles to go over. Becky had re-edited half of the articles already slated for the next issue to nudge them in the direction Rick wanted to take this magazine. The extra workload had meant she'd missed her bible study and had to cancel another library board meeting.

The phone rang again.

Becky stifled her resentment and put a smile on her face. "*Going West.* Becky speaking."

"This is Alanna Thompson."

Becky closed her eyes, massaging the bridge of her nose with her fingers, and sent up a prayer for patience and peace. Alanna wasn't known for her reticence. And noting the restrained fury in Alanna's voice, Becky was pretty sure she knew the reason she was calling.

"How can I help you, Alanna?"

"What in the world is going on there? I just got a phone call from some guy named Rick Ethier. He just told me he's returning the four articles that the magazine bought. Who is this guy?"

Becky blew out her breath, suddenly aware of the tension in her shoulders. Which columns to cut and which articles to send back should have been her call. Not Rick's. At least he could have waited until their meeting this afternoon to consult with her.

"Rick is our new publisher."

"What does that have to do with anything?"

"With a new publisher comes a new direction,"

Becky offered, struggling not to let her own anger seep into her voice. "Rick obviously has a different idea of how he sees *Going West* than Nelson did."

And from the sounds of things Rick's vision didn't include baking or horses, cowboys and farmers.

"You know how much time I spent on those? How many horse trainers I interviewed? All the pictures I took? And not on spec. You told me the magazine would buy them all." Alanna's fury grew with each sentence she threw at Becky. "I got some great material together."

"You'll be released to submit them elsewhere," Becky said, her frustration growing. "And of course there's our kill fee."

"There had better be."

"Look, I'm sorry." A faint nagging pain started at one temple, threatening to take over her whole head. Alanna's yelling only intensified her frustration with Rick. And her headache. If she didn't get something to eat pretty soon, she was sure it was going to become a full-blown migraine. "I'm sorry about this, Alanna," Becky said, trying to keep her voice quiet. Soothing. "You've done great work for us in the past and I appreciate all the hard work you've put into all your articles. Good luck selling the articles somewhere else."

The harsh click in her ear told Becky how soothing her words had been.

Becky shoved her hands through her hair and grabbed the back of her neck. It felt as tight as a guitar string.

And in five minutes she had to face Rick Ethier.

She wondered if she had time to run across the street

and grab a bite to eat. Better not. Instead she pulled open her desk drawer and pulled out the grease-stained bag. She shook out the rest of the muffin into her hand and popped it into her mouth. Two days old, but it was a much-needed snack.

She gathered up her papers and slipped them all into her portfolio, along with her Day-Timer. A paper covered with scribbles fluttered to the floor and she bent to pick it up. Notes for her most recent book.

Since Rick had come, she hadn't had a spare minute to work on it. And if the past few days were any indication of the work Rick required to change the magazine's direction, she wouldn't have any time until Rick left.

In twelve months.

Dear Lord, am I ever going to get anywhere with my writing? The prayer was a cry of despair. She looked over at her crowded bookshelf. Her own book sat tucked away amongst all the others. But one book does not a career make, and if she wanted to live her dream, she needed at the least a multibook contract.

All her life she had wanted to be a fiction writer. But she had loans to repay and she had to live. So she took the job her father offered and for three years she had poured her heart and soul into that first book in her infrequent spare time.

When she received the call that this, her first book, had been bought, she broke down and cried like a baby. Then she celebrated.

Though her parents were overjoyed for her, her mother had given her the best advice. Advice, she was sure, countless other authors had received.

"Don't quit your day job."

So she stayed on with *Going West,* editing and writing nonfiction during the day, writing fiction in the evening, begrudging each minute away from her work as she put together her next book.

Then came Rick's review, the sales figures just behind that, and her publisher started stalling on a contract for her option book. And now she didn't have the time to work on it.

Becky pushed herself away from her desk. Enough wallowing. She had other things to discuss with Rick.

Such as maintaining her "day job."

Chapter Two

Becky strode down the hallway to Rick's office but was stopped when she faced the closed door. One of the many changes that had swept through this office since Rick took over. She knocked lightly.

"Come in."

To her surprise, Rick wasn't elbow-deep in the computer printouts that dominated his desk, but instead stood by the window, looking out over the town to the mountains beyond.

"I love the view from this office," Becky said with forced cheer. She was going to be nice. Going to be a good example of Christian love. "Though it always makes me want to quit what I'm doing and head out to the mountains."

Rick shrugged. "I suppose it could, if you were the impulsive type."

In spite of her good intentions Becky felt her back bristle.

Nice. Nice. I'm going to be nice.

"So what did you want to discuss today?" she asked, sitting in her usual chair in one corner of Nelson's office.

She wanted to give him a chance to talk before she brought up her own grievances.

"I've been working on clearing up the deadwood." Rick dropped into his chair, massaging his temple with his forefinger. "This magazine is practically in the Dark Ages."

"Considering that we don't use a Gutenberg press to put out the paper, that seems a bit extreme," Becky said, tempering her comment with a smile.

Rick gave her a level glance but Becky held her ground. She had promised to be nice, but he didn't need to be so cutting.

"Just because *Going West* has a glossy cover doesn't mean it's keeping up." Rick pushed himself ahead, pulling a pencil out of the holder on a now-tidy desk. "We've got to move forward."

"From the phone calls I've been getting, that means leaving behind people like Gladys Hemple and Alanna Thompson."

Rick shrugged again. "Alanna was a terrible writer. Overly emotional and bombastic. Gladys, an anachronism."

"I would think that would be my call to make." Her words came out clipped. Tight.

"Would you have cut them?"

Becky held his gaze, trying to distance himself from the harshness of Rick's words, so close to what he had said about her own writing.

"I don't know. I guess it would have depended on this 'vision' we are going to talk about right now."

"They don't fit. I would have told you to cut them anyhow."

Becky held his gaze, realizing that she was dealing with a far different sort of publisher than Nelson and his easygoing approach.

"And who or what are we going to replace them with?"

"I've got a guy lined up to do a weekly column. Gavin Stoddard."

Becky struggled to keep smiling. To stay positive as her brain scrambled for words that weren't confrontational. "Gavin has a rather cynical take on Okotoks. What would he do a column on?"

"He's on the local chamber of commerce. He has a thriving business in an area that's expanding. He's exactly the kind of person that can give some helpful advice to other businesses."

"So that's your focus? Business?"

Rick leaned forward. "In order to increase advertising revenue, we have to make the magazine appealing to the business sector of our readership."

"But more ads means fewer features. That would make it..." She stopped just short of saying "boring." Too confrontational.

"Make it what?"

She waved the comment aside. "I would like to get back to Alanna and Gladys. Please let me know before you do something like that again, so we can discuss this together." She held her ground, knowing that she was right. "It makes my job difficult otherwise. I'm still editor and I prefer that we work together."

Rick swayed in his chair, his finely shaped mouth curved into a humorless smile. "Do you think that can happen?" he asked.

Becky accepted the challenge in his gaze even as she thought of the book she couldn't finish. She needed this job for now, but she wasn't going to get pushed around.

"I think it can. As long as we keep talking."

But even as she spoke the words, Becky realized he had been right about one thing that he had said earlier.

Twelve months was going to be far too long.

The day had disappeared, Rick thought, looking up at the darkening sky with a flash of regret.

This morning, when he came to the office, the sun was a shimmer of light in the east, the dark diminishing in the west. Now the bright orange globe hovered over the western horizon. In the east, the dark was now gaining.

While he was tied to his desk, dealing with reluctant employees, courting new advertisers, wrestling with his editor over the new plan for this magazine, the sun had stolen across the sky and he had lost an entire day.

Glowering, he walked to his vehicle, a battered and rusty Jeep. He patted its dented hood, as if commiserating with it. "Only eleven months and twenty days to go," he murmured, "and we can be on the road again. *Outside* during the day, the way we should be." He glanced around once more. The town looked complacent this time of evening. Most people were, he was sure, sitting at the dinner table, eating with their families.

Domestic bliss.

An oxymoron as far as he was concerned. When he and his mother lived with Colson, all he remembered of domesticity were large cold rooms that echoed as he walked to the wing of the house that his grandfather had set aside for Rick and his mother. He remembered sad music and the sounds of his mother's muffled crying.

When she died, Rick's life became a round of boarding schools during the year, and nannies and housekeepers over the summer months.

Colson remained a shadowy figure in Rick's life. A figure to whom Rick spent most of his youth trying to gain access. And trying to please.

Rick did a monthly book review column for his grandfather's magazine, one of Colson's many enterprises, as a way of acknowledging Colson's contribution to his education. Through it he enjoyed the chance to take a contrary view of some of the more popular literary works lauded by other critics.

But it was traveling that ignited a passion in him he didn't feel for anyone or anything else. It provided a ready-made conduit for his articles, and the money they made him became a way to finance more trips. He usually found time to make semiannual duty trips back to Toronto to connect with his editor and, of course, to see his grandfather.

Going home always turned to be a straightforward debriefing of what he had done, how he was doing. But in the past year Colson had been getting more involved in Rick's life—putting increased pressure on him to join the family enterprise, inviting him to supper, with eligible young women in attendance.

This put Rick in a quandary. He felt he owed his grandfather, but at the same time didn't think he had to mold his entire life around Colson's whims. It came to an ugly head in a confrontation, which led Colson to offer Rick this ultimatum. Bring this small-town magazine Colson had bought on a whim to profitability in twelve months and Colson would leave him alone for the rest of his life. That was all Colson required of him and Rick had reluctantly accepted. It was only the thought that he wouldn't have to listen to Colson's tired lectures on Christian faith and Rick's lack of it that made Rick accept this position.

Rick stopped at one of the few streetlights in town and glanced over at the café, the lights and the bustle within luring him on. He was hungry but didn't feel like eating alone in the furnished apartment he had rented. At least at Coffee's On, the crowd would provide some semblance of company.

The café was surprisingly full, this time of evening. Rick paused in the doorway, letting the clink of cutlery, the chatter of conversation wash over him. He nodded at the owner of a car dealership he had met yesterday on his trip with the sales team around town, smiled at one of the waitresses who hustled past him.

He glanced around the café looking for an empty table. As he walked farther inside he spotted one beside Becky Ellison.

Becky sat at her table, chin in hand, staring out the

window, her laptop open in front of her. The overhead light caught flashes of red in her auburn hair, burnished her skin glowing peach.

When she had bustled into the meeting room, that first morning, late, laden with papers, coffee and a muffin, he couldn't help feel a frisson of energy and attraction. There was something beguiling about her that drew his eyes, his attention to her. He didn't want to be as firm with her as he had, but the magazine staff had been working together for some time, making him the interloper.

Something that was made fairly clear to him the first time he and his editor spoke.

Antagonism radiated from her from the moment she raised her hazel eyes to his. And in most of the meetings since then the feeling only seemed to grow.

But tonight there were no other empty places, so with some resignation Rick walked over to the table beside hers and sat down.

Becky's gaze was averted so she didn't see him. She wore her hair down today instead of pulled back in her usual clip. A half smile played over her lips as she absently toyed with her hair.

If it wasn't for the fact that Rick knew Becky didn't care much for him, he'd be more attracted than he was.

"Coffee?" The waitress came between his table and Becky's and he looked up.

"No. Just a glass of water. And you can bring me the special."

Her wide smile gave Rick's ego a light boost.

The sound had broken Becky's reverie. As if waking from a dream, she blinked, straightened up, then looked around.

Rick could tell the instant she saw him. Once again the smile faded and once again he was treated to a detachment that negated the little lift he'd gotten just seconds ago.

"Hey, there," he said, leaning back in his chair. He folded his arms across his chest, a defensive gesture, he had to admit. "Taking work home?"

Becky glanced at her computer and gently closed the top, a surprising flush coloring her cheeks. She looked as if he had caught her doing something illegal. "No. Just a writing project I've been spending my scant spare time on." Her tone was careful, almost resentful.

Writing project. Obviously not work, or she would have said so. Formless thoughts tumbled through his head.

"What kind of writing project?" he asked, intrigued in spite of himself.

"A book."

"That takes a lot of time."

"Exactly. Trouble is, I can't seem to find the time."

Rick grinned. "One thing I learned is that you don't find time to write. You make time and then defend it. You'll never get a book written by 'finding' time."

"I have written one book already," Becky said, her voice taking on a defensive note.

"Really? What kind?"

She lifted her chin in a defensive gesture. "Fiction."

Rick could only look at her as his thoughts coalesced. Becky. *Rebecca.* "You wrote a book called *Echoes.*"

She nodded.

"I did a review of one of your books, didn't I? For my grandfather's magazine?"

Becky's only response was to look away, but he knew he was right. He remembered now.

"I gather the review wasn't favorable." He couldn't remember the details of what he had written. The editor of his grandfather's magazine liked Rick's reviews because he wasn't afraid to go against the grain and pronounce a currently popular literary novel prose without purpose.

Obviously he had done just that with Becky's book.

"'Wasn't favorable'?" she repeated, fixing him with a steady gaze. "Try unnecessarily cutting. Or sarcastic." She looked like she was about to say something more, but she pressed her lips together.

Rick let her words wash over him as he had done with other authors and authors' fans. He refused to take her seriously, his opinion was his own opinion, and as he tried to explain again and again, it was one opinion. If writers couldn't take criticism, they had better try something else.

"So it's not because I'm some Eastern interloper that you tend to be slightly ticked off at me."

Becky angled her head to one side, as if studying him. "That, too."

Rick leaned forward and cocked her a wry grin. "Get used to it, sweetie. I'm around for a while."

She held his gaze, her eyes steady. "Don't call me 'sweetie,'" she said quietly. "It's insincere."

Was it?

Maybe she wasn't a "sweetie," per se—her tawny eyes and crooked grin negated that image—but there was definitely something about her that appealed. In spite of her off-putting attitude. "Maybe I'm teasing," he said.

"Maybe you should be nice."

"You could teach me." The comment sounded lame, but he couldn't think of anything snappier to say.

"Well, you know the saying, if you can't say something nice, become a reporter."

He couldn't stop his burst of laughter. "You are in the right job."

The waitress came just then with his order. "Here you go. I hope you enjoy." She gave him a broad smile, lingered just long enough to show her interest but not long enough to create an embarrassing situation, and was gone. But she didn't hold his interest.

The woman who did was packing up, and to his surprise, Rick felt a twinge of disappointment. It had been a while since he'd spent any time with a pretty woman. An even longer time with one who didn't seem to be afraid to challenge him.

"The muse desert you?" he asked, unwrapping his utensils.

"She's been a bit flighty lately." Becky slipped her laptop into a knapsack.

"You're so fond of mottoes, surely you know that for writers, when the going gets tough..." Rick let the sentence trail off.

"The tough writers huddle under their desk chewing the cuffs of their sleeves," Becky finished off for him.

He couldn't help it. He laughed again.

She slipped her knapsack over her shoulder and pulled her hair loose from the straps, shooting him an oblique smile as she did so. With a muttered "See you tomorrow," she left.

As she wended her way through the tables, someone called out her name and she responded, her smile genuine now. She stopped at one table to chat someone up, waved at another person across the café and joked with Katherine Dubowsky, the owner of Coffee's On, while she paid her bill.

Then with a laugh and the tinkle of the door's bell, she was gone.

Rick turned back to his food, feeling curiously deflated, as if the day had lost even more light. He finished his supper quickly, then left for his apartment and his own brand of domestic bliss.

"I don't know if I like the emphasis in this article." Rick pushed the paper across his desk toward Becky and leaned back in his chair, his fingers steepled under his chin. He wore a black cotton shirt today, the sleeves rolled up to his elbows. His usual blue jeans. The subdued morning light highlighted the blond of his hair, shadowed the faint dimple in his cheek. He looked more like the cowboy she had written about in the article, than a publisher of a magazine.

Becky glanced down at the article, wishing for a moment that Rick Ethier weren't so physically appealing. Not because she was attracted to him, mind you, but because the women in the office were starting to annoy her. And it was starting to interfere with her own objectives. She needed people on her side if she was going to maintain a toehold of control over this magazine.

Just this morning she had to listen to Trixie wax eloquent about those eyes, that careless hair. The way he, "well, you know, Becky, kind of strolls. Like he's in charge of his world." Which he was, of course.

Trouble was, it was also her world.

"It's a fairly basic profile. What's the problem?"

Rick rocked a couple of times in his chair, then leaned forward. "Here's the deal. You've got an article about working cowboys who make lousy wages, yet you write it like these guys are the happiest men alive."

"It's what they told me."

"That they were the happiest men alive?"

"That they loved their work. That it wasn't a job as much as a vocation."

Rick acknowledged this with a quick nod. "That may be, but you don't bring up any of the negatives. And don't tell me they didn't talk about any."

"Of course they did. They work long hours. Get hurt a lot. Have to work with rank horses and ornery bosses. As many more of us have to." The words slipped out before she could stop them.

Nice. Nice. Be nice.

"I'm going to take that last comment as a generality." Rick got up from his desk and stood by the window, his hands shoved in the back pockets of his pants. "But none of what you just told me made it into the article."

"That wasn't the point of the article."

Rick turned to her, a dour smile on his face. "And that's my point. You took your own preconceptions to the story and only used facts that worked with what you wanted to show."

Becky didn't have time for this and wondered that he did. She was behind on her own work and phone calls. She knew he was busy consulting with his marketing and focus group on the redesign.

"So what do you want me to do? Rewrite it?" She bit back the anger that was starting up again.

"No. I'd just like to see a bit more balance in what you're doing."

"In keeping with the vision of the magazine," she finished with a light sigh. She wasn't going to concede immediately.

"The vision is more business oriented. As well, I'm also trying to shape this magazine into a more honest view of life in this part of the country."

"Oh, you made that very clear." Becky stopped. Took a breath. "But business isn't all grimness and focus. There are people who enjoy what they do. I wanted to show that in this article."

"The glass is half-full."

Becky frowned, then caught his inference. "Okay. So I'm an optimist. You say it's half-empty. Neither of us is wrong. It just depends on what you want to focus on." She felt, more than heard, the hardness creeping into her voice and tried to inject a note of humor. "And if you were our art director, you would say we would need a different glass."

Rick frowned. He didn't get it, obviously. "Water management aside, I'd also like to see the article shorter if possible."

"Design will have problems with that."

"We need the space for ads."

"It's a magazine, not a shopping network."

"But ads pay the bills and our salaries."

Becky bit back a comment. In the few days Rick had been here, she realized one thing. Money talked to this man. Loud and clear.

"I'll see what I can do," she said. "Anything else you want to discuss?"

"I'm calling a meeting tomorrow to go over the results of our market survey."

Becky pulled out her Day-Timer and flipped it open to the date. "Sorry. I've got a practice with the children's choir."

"How about after?"

"After, I'm supposed to be meeting with the banner committee to discuss the new designs for the Thanksgiving service in the fall."

Rick drummed his fingers against his thigh. "How about the next night?"

Becky flipped the page and shook her head as she glanced up at Rick.

"Don't tell me," he said, holding his hand up, palm out. "Whatever it is, cancel it. This is important."

Becky stifled a flare of resentment. "So is my meeting."

"Find someone else. This is your job." Rick picked up a folder and flipped it open. "While we're talking about your job, I also want to comment on the lack of letters to the editor."

"People here are generally low-key. If they like something, they don't say anything. If you want a reaction, you have to stir up the nest."

"Not something you're prone to doing." He tilted her a half smile that, in spite of their momentary antagonism, slipped past her defenses and kindled a faint warmth.

"I think I've done a good job."

"But I don't want good," Rick said, holding her gaze. "What I want from you is your best."

Becky frowned, uncomfortable with this new tack. Did he think she was doing a mediocre job? "And that's what you'll get," she said softly. She gathered up her papers and left without another look back, a self-doubt niggling at her confidence.

As she walked down the hall, she reread the article. Had she been overly positive? Had she done a mediocre job?

She thought of the wry grins of the cowboys as they talked about their work. She recognized the griping. Her brothers talked the same way when they had a particularly unpleasant chore. Yet underneath the words, she knew there was a love of a challenge. A pride in their work.

"Hey, Becky, eyes on the road." Cliff caught her by the shoulders and set her aside. He angled his chin toward Rick's office. "Had your bi-hourly meeting with the boss?"

Becky resisted the urge to roll her eyes. Cliff didn't need to see her own frustration. Rick was ruffling all kinds of feathers, but in public she needed to stand behind him. "We had to discuss an article he wants me to look over." Among other things.

Cliff drew her aside and lowered his voice. "Becky, you got to help me. This Rick guy is driving us nuts. He wants us to redo the layout for the next issue. Unless we work 24/7, it's not going to get to the printer on time. Can you make him see sense?"

Becky took a deep breath and drew on the devotions she had read this morning.

"...in humility consider others better than yourselves."

She had seldom stumbled over that passage. Until now.

"You know what's at stake here, Cliff. We're in transition." She'd had to face the reality herself. As well, for the sake of unity in the office, she had to at least publicly toe the same line as Rick, though she disagreed with him in private. "It's sort of like sharks. We don't move, we die. And if moving means putting in more hours until we know where this magazine is going, I guess you should return those videos you rented for the weekend." She flashed him a smile, hoping to soften her comment.

Cliff glared at her. Scowled at the door of Rick's office. For a moment Becky thought he was going to charge in and give Rick a blast of his infamous temper.

"It's just for now, Cliff," Becky said, laying her hand on his arm to restrain him. "In a few months it will all settle down."

Cliff's glare shot to her. She smiled back. Held his gaze.

"He wants me to use more stock photos instead of photo shoots for the next issue. How's that supposed to make us stand out from the other magazines?"

Becky gave him a light shake. "It's just for now. Once we get the magazine turning a better profit, you can unleash your creativity once again." She hoped.

Thankfully, his shoulders slumped. He fingered his goatee and Becky knew the moment had passed.

"I'm doing this for you, Becky. Okay? Just so you know."

"Thanks, Cliff."

The door to Rick's office opened and Cliff glanced back over his shoulder at Rick, looking guilty. He flashed Becky a quick grin and ambled back down the hallway.

"Problems?" Rick asked, raising one eyebrow.

"Not anymore." Becky held up the papers. "Got to get back to work here." She scurried down the hallway and ducked into her office. Retreated into her sanctuary to regroup and hoped she didn't have to deal with anyone else's complaints about what was happening at the magazine.

Ever since Rick started, she spent as much of her day calming irate people and putting out fires, trying to be optimistic about what he was doing.

Which she wasn't.

And what kind of reaction were people going to have when Gavin Stoddard started spewing his opinionated coffee-shop talk all over the magazine each month?

Alanna may have been emotional. Gladys may have been anachronistic. But neither generated the kind of mail she was sure Gavin would.

Becky pressed her fingers against her eyelids, pushing back the stress lurching in her midsection. She had head space for only one disaster at a time. And for now, this article took priority.

As she spread the papers in front of her, she felt a twist of frustration. The whole time she was working on the article, she had tried to make sure it was a balanced depiction of what these men did for a living. Yet at the same time she wanted to show their obvious pleasure in their work. Had she been "overly sentimental" again as Rick had once accused her of?

Misgivings slithered through her mind as she read the article through once more. She should listen to the interview tapes again. She had the number of the tape written in her Day-Timer.

Day-Timer. She groaned as she realized where she'd last seen it.

Becky swallowed her pride, got up and walked back to Rick's office. He was on the phone but gestured for her to come in. She pointed to the burgundy folder on the desk and he nodded, not missing a beat in the conversation.

She picked it up and left. But as she closed the door, she caught him looking at her.

And frowning.

Chapter Three

"How are you enjoying the West?" Colson Ethier's voice sounded overly hearty as if he was trying to inject enthusiasm for his project into his guinea pig.

Rick cradled the phone in the crook of his shoulder as he made some quick notes on one of the papers spread out on the dining room table of his apartment. "The natives are restless and the weather is the pits." Behind him the rain ticked against the glass of the kitchen window, as if testing it. Seeking entry. He had hoped to drive into the mountains this evening and do some photography, but the weather had sent him indoors.

"Have you met Sam and Cora Ellison yet?"

"Grandfather, the extent of my socializing has been to smile at the waitress at Coffee's On." And sitting around an empty apartment on weekends looking over spreadsheets and articles.

"How are you getting along with Becky?"

Rick rapped the table with his pen. "We're not."

A measured beat of silence then, "She's a lovely girl."

She was more than lovely. More than frustrating, too.

"I was hoping you two might get along," Colson continued.

His grandfather sounded pained, and the suspicion that Rick had about Colson's motives was immediately confirmed.

"Editors and publishers aren't supposed to get along." The timer on the microwave went off. "My supper is ready."

"You better go eat then." Colson Ethier paused, cleared his throat as if he wanted to say more. And quickly hung up.

Rick tossed the phone on the couch. "Goodbye to you, too, Grandpa."

Rick couldn't remember his grandfather ever saying goodbye. Since the age of seven, when the death of his mother put him into his grandfather's guardianship, Colson would bring Rick back to the private boys' school he was enrolled in, drop him off and drive away without a backward glance.

The housekeeper told Rick, Colson wasn't comfortable around children, but Rick knew his grandfather was only uncomfortable around him. The evidence of his mother's indiscretion. Consequently Rick and Colson didn't spend a lot of time together, which cut down on the opportunities not to say goodbye.

Once Rick graduated and moved away to college, their farewells were limited to Christmas, Easter and occasionally Thanksgiving. So his grandfather's new interest in Rick's life was too little, too late.

Rick retrieved his dinner from the microwave sat down at the table and set his food in front of him. He paused a moment. Habit, more than anything. Colson Ethier always prayed before meals and had taught him to do the same. The boarding school he attended tried to instill the same religious beliefs.

After his mother died, Rick didn't trust God much. Living on his own didn't help. When he started traveling and started seeing what the world could be like for people less privileged, cynicism and reality slowly wore away any notions of a loving God in charge of the world.

Rick ate mechanically. The reheated food tasted lousy, but he had eaten so many different kinds of foods in so many different places that he had come to view it simply as fuel. A steady need that had to be responded to at least twice and, if he was lucky, three times a day.

Which reminded him, he had to talk to some of the restaurant owners about participating in a contest he hoped to run in conjunction with the launch of the new magazine. He'd had to scale down his original plan when he sat down with Trixie and the reality of the finances stared him in the face.

He dug through his papers and found his Day-Timer. It felt heavy in his hand and seemed fatter than usual. Frowning, he flipped it open.

The pages were crammed with scribbled notes written in every direction in various shades of ink. Butterfly stickers danced across the page and flowers decorated another. Phone numbers were written sideways.

He flipped back a page, scanning over the dates, try-ing to make sense of what he read. Was someone at the office playing a practical joke on him?

Then he saw his name, stopped and read, "What am I going to do about Rick?" The question was heavily underlined.

He read the words again, then checked the front of the folder. The initials *R.E.* were imprinted in the soft burgundy leather. He and Becky must have accidentally switched agendas.

Rick glanced over the rest of the pages, looking for other mentions of his name before he realized what he was doing.

Snooping. He closed the book with a guilty flush and set it on the table. He should let Becky know right away he had it. From the look of the jam-packed days, she was going to be lost without it.

"What am I going to do about Rick?"

The words snaked into his mind. Why had she writ-ten them?

He went back to the articles Gavin Stoddard had written.

"In order to move into the 'new' market, the Internet market, local business owners will need to rethink their calcified methods of doing business. The name of the game is education, or how to teach an old dog to double-click."

Rick forced himself to concentrate on the rest of the column. But the little leather folder beside him drew his attention like a magnet.

"What am I going to do about Rick?"

What did she think she had to "do"? And what was the problem?

And why did he care?

"...this new way of doing business can be a boon for savvy business owners and a stumbling block to die-hard traditionalists." He continued to scan.

He wasn't a problem that she had to solve, he thought, throwing down the paper in disgust. He was supposed to be her boss. If there was a problem to be solved, it was his problem with her.

His chair creaked as he pushed himself back from the table, dragging his hands over his face. He had too many things on his mind to be concerned with what his bossy editor thought of him. Tomorrow he was going to be attending a meeting with the chamber of commerce to talk about the magazine and its potential for the town. He had to get a speech ready, a spreadsheet together. He was operating on a shoestring budget and he didn't think he was going to make the ends of the string meet, let alone keep them tied.

He dropped his supper dishes in the dishwasher, ti-died the counter then went back into the dining room. As he straightened the papers on the table, he glanced at the burgundy folder again.

And opened it before he could convince himself otherwise.

While his agenda only had a week per page, hers had a page per day and held two months' worth of booklets. Each page was crammed full of notes. She had a busier schedule than the prime minister.

He flipped the pages back to the day they first met, and

started reading. "Met Rick Ethier, new boss and old enemy this morning. Too good-looking and I made a fool of myself. Of course I was late for important first meeting."

Rick felt a moment's surprise. He hadn't imagined that brief spark of attraction after all, and the thought kindled a peculiar warmth that was extinguished with the words following. But "old enemy"?

"Got interview with premier." Several exclamation marks followed that one. Obviously excited. "Call secretary and get background information."

"Meeting with Rick. Again." The hard double underline clearly showed her frustration. "Don't like the direction but at least there *is* some. Praying for patience. Constantly."

Prayers again.

He flipped the page over, skimmed over notices to call friends, an appointment with her hairdresser, a meeting that evening at the church, a reminder of another meeting the next night. Wondered who was the Trevor of "Trevor's back," written with a little heart beside it.

"Rick is driving me crazy." No heart beside his name, he thought with a surprising flicker of envy. "He's hired Gavin. Big mistake. Mom and Dad told me I need to pray for him. Said I need to see him as a child of God."

Rick slapped the book shut and pushed himself away from the table. He knew he had made enemies at the magazine. If he'd had a couple of years to make the changes he wouldn't have had to be so aggressive.

He glanced back at the Day-Timer. "I need to see him as a child of God" replayed through his head.

He wasn't a child of God. Wasn't a child of anyone.

He had to return this. Thankfully she'd written two
phone numbers inside. No one was at home, so he tried
her cell phone.

"Hey there." Becky's voice was almost drowned out
by music and voices in the background.

"This is Rick," he said, wondering what place in
Okotoks could generate that volume of noise. "I think
you've got something of mine."

"Just a sec. Can't hear you." She said something un-
intelligible. The noise receded and was suddenly shut
off. "Sorry about that. Who is this?"

"It's Rick. I think you've got my Day-Timer," he repeated.

"You've accused me of that before, but I'll check."
A rustling noise and, "Oh, brother." Deep sigh. "You're
right. This isn't good."

She was probably remembering some of the things
she had written.

"Where are you now?" he asked. "I could meet you
so we can swap." He didn't have time, but a mischievous
impulse made him want to see her face when they made
the exchange. Impulse and a bit of bruised pride. He
didn't usually generate hostility in the women he met.

"I'm at the church, but I can come over."

"No. I'm not doing much. Where's the church?"

She paused and Rick smiled. She was probably
squirming in embarrassment. Then she gave him directions which he noted. "See you in a bit," he said with a
hearty cheeriness.

A short time later, Rick pulled up to the front of the
church, surprised at how large and new it was. Obvi-

ously religion went over well in Okotoks. He jogged through the rain, avoiding puddles on the crowded parking lot. The noise he had heard through Becky's cell phone grew as he approached the building.

What was happening on a Friday night at church? The services he occasionally attended with his grandfather were held in a large stately church on Sundays, and as far as Rick knew, not much else happened there.

This place had cars and trucks in the parking lot and kids running around the outside of the building in spite of the rain that poured down. He opened the large double doors and stepped inside, brushing moisture off his hair and face. A few young kids were hanging around the foyer laughing and roughhousing.

"Thomas, Justin and Kevin. If you're done with youth group, leave. If you're supposed to be practicing, get in there." The woman who spoke was tiny but her authoritative voice even made Rick stop a moment.

"Sorry, Cora," one of the kids said. The teens scampered into the auditorium, letting out another blast of noise as they yanked open the doors.

The woman walked toward him, smiling as she held out her hand. "Naturally I wasn't talking to you. Welcome. I'm Cora Ellison."

Her gray hair was cut bluntly level with her narrow jaw, her hazel eyes laughed up at him. Rick caught glimpses of Becky in the generous mouth and pert nose. He guessed this was Becky's mother. "I'm Rick Ethier," he said, returning her firm handshake.

"Well, now. Finally." Cora took his hand in both of hers, her grin animating her face even more. "I told

Becks to invite you over, but she always says you are too busy. And here you are. This is great."

Her exuberant welcome puzzled him. It was as if she knew him, but he doubted her information came from Becky. Not if her Day-Timer were any indication of what she thought of him.

The door beside them opened up and Becky rushed out, her coat flying out behind her, her hands clutching a folder identical to the one in Rick's coat pocket. She saw her mother and veered toward her. "Hey, Mom, I have to step out a moment..." Becky's voice trailed off as her eyes flicked from her mother to Rick. He didn't think he imagined the flush in her cheeks.

"Hello, Becky," he said, tilting a grin her way. "I believe you have something of mine."

Becky looked down at the folder in her hands and her flush deepened. "Yes. Here." She shoved it toward him without making eye contact. Rick slipped it into his pocket.

"You were expecting him, Becky?" Cora Ellison asked.

Becky nodded. "We, uh, accidentally switched Day-Timers." She glanced up at Rick, her expression almost pleading. "Can I have mine back?"

"Oh. Sure." Rick enjoyed seeing Becky a little flustered. It deepened the color of her eyes, gave her an appealing, vulnerable air. But he took pity on her and handed her the leather folder. "Safe and sound." Luckily he wasn't easily embarrassed or he might be flushing, too, knowing he'd read private things.

Becky took it from him and glanced down at it as if to make sure it hadn't been violated. If she only knew.

"Thanks," she said, and was about to turn away when her mother caught her by the arm.

"Becky. Wait a minute. You should have told me Rick was coming." Cora turned to Rick. "Now I can ask you directly. We'd like to have you over for lunch. What about this Sunday? After church?"

Rick stifled a smile at Becky's panicked gaze. He guessed she didn't want him over, which made him want to accept the invitation. "That would be very nice. Thank you."

"I'm looking forward to having you," Cora said, folding her arms over her chest in a self-satisfied gesture. "It will be like the closing of a circle."

Rick frowned at her comment. "What do you mean?"

"Your grandfather lived in Calgary years and years ago. When he was a teenager. Apparently he used to come courting my mother in those days." Cora winked at Rick. "Bet he never told you."

And a few more pieces of the puzzle that was his grandfather fell into place. "No. He never did. Is your mother still alive?"

"More than alive. Right, Becky?" Cora asked, drawing a reluctant Becky into the conversation.

"She's a character, that's for sure," Becky said. She gestured toward the closed doors of the auditorium. "Sorry, but I gotta go," she said vaguely, taking in both her mother and Rick. "Practice."

"I'll see you Sunday," Rick couldn't help but say.

She turned to him, her eyes finally meeting his, her lips drifting up in a crooked smile. "Church starts at ten-thirty. See you then."

He felt a reluctant admiration for how neatly she had cornered him. Church was one of the last places he wanted to be on a Sunday morning, but he couldn't let her get the upper hand. Not after what he'd read. "I'll be here."

She held his gaze, as if challenging him. But when she left, Rick felt a curious reluctance to hang around any longer.

"I should get going, too," he said. "Gotta get ready for tomorrow."

Cora's light touch on his arm surprised him. "I'm looking forward to finding out more about your grandfather. I like a mystery."

"Nothing mysterious about Colson Ethier," Rick said. Except for a twisted desire to send his grandson on a trip down his own particular memory lane. He would be talking to Grandpa Colson as soon as he got a chance. "I'll see you Sunday. Thanks again for the invitation."

Becky tapped her fingers against her chin as she glanced around the foyer of the church once more. Rick better show up soon or she was leaving. When Cora Ellison told her *she* should be the one to make sure he's welcome, Becky only agreed out of a sense of guilt.

She shouldn't have snooped in his Day-Timer. Not that she found anything out. He had a year's worth of dates written in his immaculate handwriting and none were of a personal nature. The only phone numbers were business related. His life looked empty, unappealing and sterile.

"Don't do it, Becks." Leanne, her sister, caught her hand as it edged toward her mouth. "Your nails are just starting to grow back."

"And since when do you care about my nails, Leanne?" Becky said with a quick grin, slipping her sister's arm through hers.

"Since I'm wondering if you're ever going to get a boyfriend again."

"A manicure isn't going to do it and you know it."

"Oh, please, not another 'look not for the beauty nor whiteness of skin' lecture. I get them enough from Mom." Leanne squeezed her sister's arm. "If you spent more time on your hair and makeup, you'd get a guy lickety split."

"That's a little simplistic. Besides, I have lots of guys."

"But they're all just friends," her sister complained. "I can't believe you don't care about guys. I know Trevor didn't break your heart that much."

"He only dented it a little."

"So why don't you two go out again? I heard he's back."

"Trust me, he'll be gone once the snow flies. I'm not going to date some guy who is just hanging around here, waiting for a chance to leave. This is my home and this is where I want to live."

"If you found the right guy, I'm sure he'd be able to talk you into leaving."

Becky tapped her little sister on the nose. "You see, that's the problem. The right guy for me is one who doesn't want to leave."

Leanne pulled back, frowning. "I think I get it."

"Let me know when you do."

"So how long do we have to wait for this Rick guy?" Leanne said, brushing her long brown hair back from her face. "I promised Donita I'd sit with her."

"Just a few more minutes." Becky glanced at her watch, hoping Rick wouldn't show. Now, or for lunch after church. But what she hoped even more was that he hadn't read her Day-Timer. Like she'd read his.

"Okay, Becks. New guy alert." Leanne tugged on her arm, her eyes riveted to the door. "Shaggy hockey hair. Nice mouth. Gorgeous eyes." Leanne added a dramatic sigh. "He's wearing a suit, but otherwise he's movie-star adorable."

Becky glanced toward the object of her sister's gushing. And straightened as disappointment and a tingle of anticipation flitted through her. Rick's suit gave him an authoritative air at odds with the haircut, or lack of it, that was currently labeled "hockey hair"—long enough to hang out the back of a hockey helmet. "He's also my boss."

Leanne's mouth dropped. "That's Rick Ethier?"

"Let's go say hi and get that part over and done with." Becky snagged her sister's arm, and walked purposefully toward him.

Rick stood in the doorway, looking, she had to concede, a little lost in the wave of people drifting past him.

Someone caught her by the arm, halting her progress. Louise, a woman from one of the committees Becky was involved in. "Becky. Just wanted to know if you've had a chance to go over that banner idea Susan put together."

"Not just yet. I'll check it out this afternoon," Becky said.

"I was thinking we could get your sister to help sew it."

Becky nodded, keeping an eye on Rick.

"Sorry, Louise," Leanne said, rescuing her. "We've got to catch someone before he leaves."

And it looked like he was about to. He had his hand on the door when they caught up to him.

"Good morning, Rick," Becky said, catching his attention. He turned to them and for a moment Becky saw a flicker of an unknown emotion in his blue eyes. Relief? Disappointment?

"Welcome to the service," Becky said with a forced smile. "Mom asked me to make sure you were properly greeted when you came."

Rick smiled back. "Well, tell your mother thanks."

"You can tell her yourself," Leanne said, glancing from Rick to Becky with avid interest. "You're supposed to sit with us."

Becky flashed her sister a warning glance, but Leanne studiously ignored her sister, her entire attention focused on Rick.

"By the way, Rick," Becky said, wishing her sister was more circumspect. "This is my little sister Leanne." Becky put heavy emphasis on "little" hoping she would get the hint.

But Leanne just ignored Becky.

"That's okay. I'm sure I can find a place," Rick said.

"No. Come and sit with us." Leanne touched Rick on the shoulder, winking at Becky. "That way we don't have to find you after church. Makes sense, doesn't it, Becky?"

"Perfect sense," Becky said dryly. "Now we better go."

"Becky is going to be singing in the worship service later on. She's got a great voice," Leanne said as Becky led the way through the crowd.

"I'm looking forward to hearing her," Rick said.

Becky's heart sank at his words. When she had maneuvered him into attending church she had forgotten she would be singing this morning.

And when she saw her family all sitting together, she regretted her impulse even more.

Just about the whole shooting match was watching her as she and Leanne led Rick up the aisle to the empty spot beside her parents. The only ones missing were Colette and her boyfriend, Nick.

"Hey Dad. Mom," Becky said, flashing her brothers and sisters a warning look to dampen their sudden interest in the man behind her. As if that would help. Her family was as curious as magpies and just as nosy. Becky showing up with a man in tow was going to cause a lot of chatter and unwelcome questions.

She dropped onto the pew, and started reading the church bulletin as if trying to show them by her disinterest that he meant nothing.

But Leanne, the little stinker, had positioned Rick so he was sitting right beside Becky.

"Are you going to introduce us?" her father asked, nudging Becky.

Becky looked up at her father with a pleading expression, but his steady gaze reinforced years of ingrained manners. So with a reluctant sigh she turned to Rick, but he was looking away from her.

She touched him lightly on his arm to get his attention. He turned to her then, his eyebrows arched questioningly.

"Rick, I'd like you to meet my father, Sam Ellison. Dad, this is Rick Ethier. And my mother, Cora, you already met."

Cora leaned over and waved, then turned as her attention was drawn by one of the kids behind her. Sam leaned past Becky, shaking Rick's hand. "Pleased to meet you finally. We've heard about you from Becky, of course."

"Really?" Rick's gaze flicked back to Becky, his eyes glinting. "I didn't think she gave me a second thought once she left the office."

Not only second thoughts. Third and fourth ones, as well.

Duty done, Becky returned to her reading. But her entire attention was focused on the man beside her.

Chapter Four

Would he look bored if he crossed his arms?

Rick shifted in his seat, fidgeted, then did it anyway. It had been years since he'd attended church. Not only did he feel out of the rhythm of the church service, he also felt out of place sitting with Becky's obviously close family.

Beside him, Becky leaned forward, her elbows resting on her knees, her chin planted on the palms of her hands, her attention on the preacher. Seeing her head canted to one side and her mouth curved in a half smile, he caught a glimpse of the girl he only saw when she was around other people. She wore a pale blue dress today in some kind of floaty, peasant-looking style. It enhanced the auburn tint of her hair, brought out the peach of her complexion. Pretty in a fun, semiflirty way. Not that she would be flirting with him.

"So I want to encourage all of us to pray for people who hurt us," the minister was saying, and Rick pulled his attention back to the man. "Praying for our enemies frees us from bitterness. From hatred." He paused a moment as if to bring the point home.

"As William Law said, 'There is nothing that makes us love a man so much as prayer for him,'" he continued. "So Christ's command to pray for our enemies is not only for our enemies' good. It is for ours, as well."

Rick looked down at the toes of his shoes as the minister's words pushed him back to his last memory of his mother. She was sitting at a desk in her bedroom, her head bent over a book. When he had asked her what she was doing, she told him she was praying for him.

He looked over at Becky and wondered if she, too, had been praying for him as her parents had suggested. He doubted it.

The congregation got to its feet, breaking off his thoughts.

As the worship group came forward, Becky slipped past him, walked down the aisle and up to the podium. Without any announcement she picked up a cordless microphone, took her position on the stage and cued the group leader with a faint lift of her chin.

The music started quietly, the gentle chords of the piano picking out the melody, the electric organ filling in the spaces.

Becky faced the congregation, waiting as the rest of the musicians joined in. She stood perfectly still, holding the mike with one hand. An overhead light shone brightly on her, singling her out from the rest of the singers. At a pause in the music, she started singing.

Her voice rang clear as the words of an old familiar

song poured out of her. "'Our Father, who art in heaven, hallowed be Thy name.'"

Rick recognized the prayer. Had mumbled the words himself as a young boy still trying to please his grandfather.

But he had never heard them sung with such crystal sincerity. He couldn't keep his eyes off Becky as she closed her eyes and her hand lifted up, palm up in a gesture of surrender. She was a woman in communion with her God, her prayer pouring out of her in song, peace suffusing her features.

And as she sang, he heard in the depths of his soul, a still small voice, familiar, yet long suppressed.

The music built as Becky came to the end of the song, her voice growing, filling the building with power and conviction. "'For Thine is the kingdom and the power and the glory...'"

The voice in him grew with the song and for a moment Rick listened. Heard. Then pushed it away.

He and God hadn't spoken in years. What he'd seen in his travels around the world reinforced his opinion that God was disinterested and uninvolved with his creation.

So why am I here? In a place known as God's house?

The last notes of Becky's song died away, and with it, Rick's questions. He was here because he'd been neatly manipulated into coming. No other reason! The minister took the podium again and announced the collection. As the ushers came forward, the tone of the gathering seemed to shift and Rick started to relax.

Ten minutes later, the service was over.

Becky had disappeared from the front of the church,

leaving Rick to figure out how to make a graceful exit. But it was not to be.

"Rick, I'd like you to meet the rest of the family," Cora said, catching him by the arm and keeping him anchored to her side. She gestured around the group gathered around her. "The short brunette over there is Treena with her husband, Lyle, and their three children. They live in Okotoks. The long streak of misery beside her is Dennis. One of these days he's going to shave off that shaggy goatee. Beside him is Bert and his girlfriend, Laura. Bert and Dennis work with their father at the orchard. And Leanne you've already met." Cora looked around the cluster of people, her pride evident in her voice and the satisfied smile she bestowed on her brood.

Rick prided himself on his ability to meet people and remember their names, but in the confused conversation that followed Cora's introductions, he lost track of who belonged to who. So he just said a general hello, letting his gaze meet each one of them for a moment.

"Are you still coming for lunch?" Cora asked him as they made their way out of the church building surrounded by chatter and laughter.

"I don't want to intrude," Rick said, feeling he should protest out of politeness, even though a part of him was intrigued by the family's interaction.

"Nonsense." Cora waved off his protestations. "Two people—you'd be intruding. With ten, you're hardly a blip on the radar. Now, where did that Becky go?" Cora looked around, frowning. "Leanne, do you mind riding with Rick to show him the way to our place?"

Cora patted Rick on the arm in a maternal gesture

that made him smile, threw out a flurry of instructions to the rest of the family and headed off, leaving a slightly breathless Rick in her wake.

Leanne followed him outside to his Jeep, frowning as he unlocked it. "From the way Becky talked about you, I figured you'd be driving some kind of fancy convertible."

"And how did she talk about me?" Even as he spoke, he was sorry he asked. What Becky said about him out of the office wasn't any of his business. Bad enough that he had read her private thoughts about him already.

Leanne shrugged, flipping down the visor on the passenger side. "I dunno," she said, running the tip of her finger over her eyelid. "She just made you sound, you know, like some kind of rich, spoiled guy who traveled a lot."

"She got the traveling part right," Rick said dryly as he maneuvered his way out of the parking lot.

"You mean you're not rich?" Leanne asked, finger-combing her hair away from her face. "I thought your grandfather had tons of money."

"Grandfather isn't short of cash. But the only way I can get any of it, if I were to want any of it, is to join the Ethier empire. And I'm not about to put my head in that noose." He stopped and turned to Leanne. "Where am I supposed to be going, Navigator?"

"Head out of town on the main drag, then hang a left at the red horse barn." Leanne dug through her purse and pulled out a package. "Some gum?"

He turned and started driving. "How far is this red horse barn?"

"Not far." Leanne frowned as she popped the gum into her mouth. "Hey, slow up," she said, pointing out a girl walking down the sidewalk of the road they were driving down. "There's Sharelle. Can we pick her up? She hasn't been to my place in, like, forever."

"Your mom won't mind having unexpected company?" Rick asked as he pulled over on the road, pulling up beside a petite girl with short black hair and coffee-colored skin.

Leanne threw him a puzzled look. "Sharelle's my friend."

He presumed that put her in a category other than "company."

Leanne rolled down the window and stuck her head out.

"Hey, Sharelle," Leanne called, waving to her friend. "Coming over?"

"Who you with?" Sharelle asked, walking up to Leanne's window. She bent over, glancing in at Rick. "Hey there," she said, flashing him a grin.

"This is Rick. He works with Becky. He came to church with us this morning. Get in."

"I'll have to call my mom when we get to your place. I don't have my cell with me," Sharelle said, climbing into the back seat, looking around the back of the Jeep. "Nice wheels."

Leanne turned to Rick. "Do you have a cell phone she can use?"

Rick handed it to her. "No problem."

"Good thing we weren't riding with Becky," Leanne said, her tone clearly indicating that this was not a compliment. "She hardly ever packs her cell with her. Can't figure that. If I had a cell phone, I'd have it with me all the time."

"Yah, and you'd be talking on it all the time, wouldn't you?" Sharelle's voice rose at the end of each of her sentences, as if in question while she punched in her parents' number.

Leanne shifted sideways, looking back at her friend. "Did you talk to her about helping with the youth retreat?"

Sharelle flipped her hand toward Leanne. "Said she had some important interview that day? With the premier?"

Rick's heart kicked up a notch in a mixture of pleasure and anger. Becky hadn't told him that she'd finalized a date for the interview. If Sharelle hadn't casually dropped that little tidbit in conversation he wondered if Becky would have even bothered to let him know.

"When is your retreat?" he asked, trying to keep his tone casual.

"Long weekend in September?" Sharelle smiled at him, then started talking to her mother on the phone.

Rick hoped she was telling and not asking as he made a mental note of the date. He wasn't going to say anything right away to Becky. Better that he bide his time and see what she did with the information.

"You have to turn up ahead," Leanne said, pointing to a large red building close to the road. "Go to the end of the road and you'll go straight into Mom and Dad's driveway. We're probably first so if you don't want to get, like totally sandwiched between cars, you might want to park by the barns."

Rick took Leanne's advice and parked a ways away from the house in the lee of a large brown building. He followed Leanne and Sharelle up the driveway and through an ivy-covered archway granting them entrance to a spacious yard sheltered by trees. His step slowed on the brick walk as his gaze was caught by the vibrant flowers cascading out of pots hanging from the eaves of the porch, spilling out of endless flower beds bordering an emerald-green lawn and tucked up against the house. Flagstone walkways branched off the main one meandering past a plant-filled pond with a fountain only to disappear around the front of the house. Closer to the house two wooden slatted benches flanked by huge flowerpots extended an unspoken invitation to sit and enjoy the symphony of color and light that filled the yard surrounding the large two-story farmhouse.

"Your mother must love gardening," Rick said, stopping to look around.

"This is Dad's thing," Leanne said, glancing back over her shoulder at Rick. "He spends almost as much time here as he does in the orchard."

Rick had seen a lot of professionally landscaped yards of friends of his grandfather but none created this welcoming atmosphere.

The door opened and Sam Ellison stepped out onto the deck. "Hey, Sharelle," he said with a booming voice, giving the girl a one-armed hug. "Good to see you. You and Leanne can help Mother with lunch."

Sam beckoned Rick with his large hand. "Come in. Cora has coffee on."

"I was just admiring your yard. It's amazing." Rick

took another look around the yard. "Did you do all this yourself?"

"I built on what Cora's parents started. They planted the trees and I added the rest. Do you want a tour?"

"You'll never get coffee," Leanne warned. "Maybe not even lunch."

"Don't you and Sharelle have work to do?" Sam said, giving them a gentle push toward the door.

Leanne gave Rick a quick smile, whispered something to Sharelle. They disappeared into the house.

Sam rolled his eyes as the door slapped shut behind them. "Teenage girls," he said in a tone that summed up all the confusion and exuberance of that age and sex.

The crunch of tires on the gravel made Rick glance behind him. Three cars pulled up, stopped and people spilled out of them all, laughing and noisy. One of them was Becky.

He wasn't sure he was ready to face the Ellison family en masse, nor to see Becky in a more casual setting. He kept remembering her solo at church. And her sincerity. "I'd love to look around some more," Rick said.

"Would give the noise level a chance to settle down," Sam said, following Rick's gaze. "I'll show you the lilies first. They're around front."

As Sam led the way, Rick chanced one more quick glance back over his shoulder. Becky was watching him, her forehead seamed in a frown.

"Did you check the messages, Becky?" Cora asked, giving the pot of soup on the stove another stir. "Trevor called. Said he was back in the country."

"I saw." Becky started slicing open the homemade buns her mother had laid out on the counter.

"You going to call him back?"

Becky shook her head. "I'll connect some other time."

Cora tasted her soup and grinned at her daughter. "He sounded lonely. I always liked Trevor."

"He's a nice guy. Just got itchy feet is all."

"Not all men are like your father and brother-in-law—more than willing to stay in one place all their lives. You might have to rearrange your standards."

"I like Okotoks. And I like living in a small town where I know everyone. Where I can be involved."

"A bit too involved," Cora muttered.

Becky chose to ignore that comment. "Where's the butter?"

Cora handed Becky the foil-wrapped block. "Did you hear that Yvonne and Randy are engaged?"

"Yes. Her mother told me at the library board meeting a few weeks ago." Becky peeled the foil back and started spreading.

"And I saw Deb and Gordon in church together."

"They've been dating for a while now. Deb said they were going to move to Calgary as soon as she's done school." Becky wished her mother would stop this litany of the dating game. It only underscored her own single state and made her feel like a loser. Which she knew she wasn't. She had made her own choices. That most of the eligible young men from Okotoks chose to move away was their problem, not hers.

"Deb said she had a cousin who was coming up to stay for a bit. He's single."

"And you're being very obvious, Mother." Becky didn't even look up from her work. "You know I've got other things on my mind."

"Like your writing? You haven't spent that much time on it lately."

"Been busy."

"Like I said."

"I can't just turn the creativity on and off, Mom. And lately it feels like it's been off."

"Why lately?"

Becky dug into the butter, scooping way too much. "Lately," she thought, because Rick Ethier suddenly showed up in my life. The man who hated my book and let everyone who subscribes to his grandfather's magazine know why. That's why "lately."

"Just not inspired."

Cora folded her elbows on the counter and leaned close to her daughter. "You should ask Rick to help you with it. He's a good writer."

Right.

"Rick is busy turning the magazine around. I doubt he has time for much else." Or interest. Becky dropped another buttered bun into the large metal bowl beside her.

"He seems like a nice man."

"Code for 'Why aren't you interested?'"

"That's not what I meant." Her mother faked an innocent smile and Becky decided to humor her.

"News flash, Mother. He's only here until he can get the magazine going in a direction that will make enough money so that he can get out of town as fast as his

Jeep's wheels will turn. He's temporary. So he's not my type and I'm not his."

"Well, for now you can go rescue your boss from your father. Tell them lunch is ready," Cora said.

Becky glanced out the large picture window beside her at the two men wandering across the yard. Sam was tall but Rick's blond head topped him by an inch. Now and again Rick would nod and laugh, his smile flashing like a beacon. "I'm busy," Becky said.

"I can do it," Leanne said, popping her head into the kitchen.

"Go for it, Leanne," Becky said. She was only too glad to relinquish the job to her sister. Leanne was obviously far more interested in Rick than she was.

"Becky will go," Cora said, giving Becky her "don't argue with me look" honed and perfected over years of raising six children. Becky knew better than to challenge it.

Rick and Sam were crouched down by a young maple tree. The low murmur of her father's voice was steady, and Becky could hear Sam eagerly inducting Rick into the intricacies of the flora on the yard.

"It's like a highway," Sam was saying, his hand waving up and down along the trunk of the tree. "The ants go up the tree to the new growth here." He pushed himself to his feet and pulled down a branch. "This is where the aphids are. They milk the aphids and then go scurrying down the trunk to the ant colony with the milk past the others that are going up. An amazing small part of how God works everything together. Fascinating, really."

Becky had always thought so and used to spend hours as a child patiently watching the ants' progress on other maple trees. She couldn't imagine that Rick was even remotely interested.

But he was politely looking closer at the branch, angling his head to the side as if to see better, his hair falling aslant. He looked relaxed and was smiling. And for a split second she felt a tug of attraction. Then he looked up at her and the smile disappeared.

And that bothered her more than she liked to admit.

Sam caught the direction of Rick's gaze. "Come to fetch us, Becks?"

"Orders from the high command. 'Go ye therefore into the yard and rescue Rick,' or something like that." Becky curled her arm through her father's.

Sam shrugged, his smile taking in Rick and Becky. "Cora is deathly afraid that someday I'm going to bore some very polite visitor to death and then we'd have some explaining to do when the coroner shows up."

"I could think of worse places to breathe my last," Rick said easily. "You've created a small paradise here." He looked relaxed with his tie hanging out of the pocket of his suit coat. The top button of his shirt was unbuttoned and he looked more at ease than he had this morning in church.

"I was taught that God reveals himself to us through the Bible and creation," Sam continued as they started toward the house. "I like to think of my gardening and orchard work as part of my worship to him."

Rick's face tightened and for a moment Becky thought he was going to argue with her father. He caught Becky's gaze, then looked away. She wondered what he was going to say and almost wished he had voiced his opinion. She knew so little about him.

And had found out even less, snooping through his stark, empty Day-Timer.

The blush that warmed her neck had nothing to do with the warmth of the sun and everything to do with her guilt at the thought of looking through his private papers. Thankfully she had discovered nothing personal or she would have felt even more self-conscious.

"You're mighty quiet, Becky," Sam said. "That's not like my girl at all."

Becky wrinkled her nose at him. "Maybe I'm trying to give my new boss a good impression, Dad."

"Too late for that. Isn't it, Rick?" Sam said, pulling Becky close to his side as the walked up the wooden steps. "My Becky is so transparent, I'm sure you know everything about her already."

"I hope not," Rick said, holding open the screen door of the house.

Becky caught his eyes as she walked past him and wondered what he meant by his comment. Then decided she didn't want to know.

"Okay, everyone, Dad is here. Let's start," Cora announced, clapping her hands to get her family's attention.

Everyone gathered in the kitchen, forming a loose circle. Becky bit back a smile at Leanne's obvious maneuvering to get beside Rick.

"Let's pray," Sam said, glancing around the circle. This was the signal for everyone to take the hand of the person beside them. Rick looked a little baffled.

"We usually hold hands while we pray," Becky said. "But if you're uncomfortable with that, we can forget it."

"No. That's fine. Don't change anything on my account." Rick took Leanne's hand, flashed her his most charming smile and lowered his head.

The brief spurt of jealousy Becky felt was as sudden as it was surprising.

Her father started praying, his deep voice thanking God for the day. For the church service. For the food they were about to eat. He prayed for each family member, for the community and for the government of the country.

"And as we come to you, Lord, we want to especially pray for those who have hurt us. Those whom we see as our enemies. Help us, Lord, to see them as You see them. To love as You love. In Your name, amen."

Becky kept her head lowered a moment, trying to take her father's words into her heart. Rick wasn't her enemy per se. Her opponent maybe. Someone she'd had a hard time thinking charitably about even before he was her boss.

Please, Lord, help me to care about him as a person. Help me to want only good for him and to forgive him, she added silently.

She raised her head, catching Rick's eyes on hers. As she gave him a tentative smile, she was surprised to see one in return. It was a start.

Of what, she didn't know.

Chapter Five

"So my challenge to businessmen in Okotoks clinging tenaciously to archaic ways of doing business is find a way to tap into a broader market...."

Becky dropped the page and her elbows onto her desk and clutched her hair, pulling it loose from her ponytail.

Tenacious. Archaic. Could Gavin Stoddard have found more inflammatory language to convey his point? The magazine was going to be flooded with angry letters all addressed to "The Editor." Editor being Becky Ellison, innocent bystander.

She carefully shuffled the papers in order to tamp down her own emotions.

Her anger surfaced so quickly these days, the result of working too many long hours switching the magazine's focus midstream. When she had agreed to help with the youth program, she hadn't counted on her well-ordered work life getting swirled and rearranged by Rick's whirlwind plans.

Work was taking up more and more of her time as she ran interference for an owner bound and determined to turn this magazine around on a dime, disgruntled staff notwithstanding.

Cliff was complaining about budget restraints. Trixie about the diminishing bank balance. Becky would have loved to complain to someone, but her only recourse was Rick.

The reason for the general air of discontent around the office.

Becky flipped Gavin's first column back and carefully read over the second one, just to reassure herself that she wasn't overreacting.

"...we need to get with the program. Stop thinking that if we are here, people will come..."

Nope. Just as bad.

She walked down the hallway to Rick's office, took a deep breath and knocked lightly. Without waiting for an answer she slipped inside.

Rick was on the phone, pacing back and forth, talking quietly. But Becky heard the now-familiar edge on his voice. The way he was tugging on the hair at the back of his neck wasn't a good sign, either.

Looked like she was facing an uphill battle even before she started.

Rick nodded curtly. "I'll keep it in mind, Grandfather." He stood in front of the window, one hand on his hip, his knuckles white on the handset.

"No. I'll stick this through to the end on my own. I don't want any money coming in that the magazine hasn't earned."

Speak for yourself, Becky thought, remembering Cliff and Trixie. The magazine needed a serious injection of cash.

"You don't need to come down and check on me. I'll do this on my own, okay?" Rick sighed and lowered the phone. Becky heard the light beep as he disconnected without saying goodbye.

He stared at the handset for a moment, his eyes narrowed, then, with deliberate motions, he hung it up in the cradle. When he looked up at Becky, she almost recoiled at the banked anger in his eyes.

"What can I do for you?"

Becky's heart did a slow flop, then began racing.

"I thought you heard my knock...." She gestured futilely back at the door. "I'm sorry I interrupted.... I'm too used to coming and going like when Nelson..." She bit her lip on her next words.

"I'm not Nelson, am I?"

"No you're not, and I'm sorry." She gave him a tentative smile that bordered on insincere. But she hoped that the outward action would bear inward fruit and soften her heart toward him.

Her mind flicked back to Sunday as she noted his hostile body language. For a few hours at her parents' place she had seen him relaxed and, she thought, enjoying himself with her family. She'd even heard him laugh out loud when Dennis told his infamous Jean Chrétien joke. He'd teased Leanne, putting her completely under his spell. Her father also thought he was very charming and when Rick left, Sam had asked Becky why she had such a hard time with him.

They would know if they saw him now. Today he looked like the other Rick's evil twin.

She picked the papers up off the desk. "I'll come another time. When you're ready to talk instead of interrogate."

Rick's eyebrows snapped together. "What do you mean?"

"I'd like to discuss something with you. Not fight it out. It can wait." It couldn't, really. Gavin's column was set to run in the following issue. But she wasn't going to antagonize Rick when he was already so obviously upset.

"No. Sit down. If you've got a problem, I want to deal with it right away."

Becky bit her lip as she laid Gavin's column down again. She didn't sit, preferring to face Rick on her feet. Not that it gave her much of a tactical advantage. He topped her by at least five inches.

"I'm concerned with the language Gavin uses in this column."

Rick tunneled his hands through his hair, clutching the back of his neck as his eyes bored into hers. "I thought you would be."

"And that didn't count?"

"Becky, this guy knows his stuff. He's laying out a challenge to the local businesses. We need to give them tangible information they can use."

"But not this man and not this way." Becky spun the paper around and started reading randomly. "'...burying your head in the sand...outmoded or nonexistent business plans...'" She looked up at Rick. "This is not the language of community. It doesn't build up, it breaks down."

Rick dropped his hip on the edge of the desk, crossing his arms. "Let me guess. You've been reading books on building self-esteem."

"What I've been doing is living in a community that deserves to be treated with respect. And this—" she poked her finger at the article "—doesn't do that."

"In order for this magazine to succeed we need to look beyond this community. To other towns that are on the edge of Calgary who are struggling with the same issues. Maybe they do need to take a hard look at themselves." Rick swung his leg, his movements punctuating his comments.

Becky felt her hold on the discussion slowly slipping as she recognized the reality of what Rick was saying. Yet, she knew that she was also right.

"So telling local shop owners and businesses that they are dumb and 'archaic' is going to get them to listen to Gavin's brave new vision for Okotoks and other smaller towns?" Becky walked past Rick to the window overlooking the street, as if drawing strength from the community laid out below her. "These people down there know more than anyone else what they are facing. Rubbing their noses in it isn't going to sell this magazine."

Rick pushed himself off his desk, and as he came to stand behind Becky she caught a vague hint of his aftershave and soap, felt the warmth of his chest close to her back. He was too close but she suppressed the urge to move away. To do so would be to admit his dominance over her.

"But giving them practical advice will help sell the

magazine," he said, his voice quieter now. "People will respond to that."

Becky turned to face him. Mistake. She had to look up to catch his eyes. And as she did, she noticed the change. In spite of the fact that she was arguing with him, his anger had dissipated and in their blue depths she caught a glint of humor.

He's enjoying this, she thought with a start. I'm trying to defend a sensible and practical position and he's laughing at me.

She crossed her arms tightly over her chest as if holding back her rising frustration. "What people will respond to is the underlying tone of Gavin's article. Superiority."

"I think you're being overly sensitive."

Rick's words were waved in front of her like a gentle taunt. She swallowed back her response. And tried smiling again.

"I take it you're going to run Gavin's article no matter what I say."

Rick nodded. Decisively.

"Then I have nothing more to say," she said, slipping past him. She gathered up the papers and tapped them into a neat pile, buying herself some time. Surprisingly she felt reluctant to leave. She had foolishly hoped her opinion would have counted for something but she couldn't throw out the words that would make him understand.

She glanced one more time back up at him and as their eyes met, she felt it again. That peculiar feeling of connection.

The ring of the phone broke the moment and Becky turned to leave.

"Well, hello, Mrs. Ellison."

In spite of herself Becky spun back.

Rick held her gaze while he listened, a smile teasing one corner of his mouth. "Sure. I'd love to come for dinner. Next week Saturday should be fine."

Becky's heart did a slow flip. Since Rick had started working, her home had become a refuge for her. A place she could simply be herself without having to force her smiles.

Now it seemed her mother was determined to practice the Christian hospitality that Becky was reluctant to extend to her boss.

"Thanks for the invite. I'll see you next week." Rick put the phone back in the cradle and grinned toward Becky. "You look a little disgruntled," he said.

"Just plain gruntled," she returned with calculated crispness. "I was hoping you would reconsider the Gavin articles." Which wasn't the full reason for her momentary funk. She was gone this weekend with her children's choir and was hoping for some time with just her family next weekend.

"I'm going to run the articles," Rick said, his tone taking on the edge that Becky recognized all too well. "Just make sure you don't edit the life out of 'em."

"And you make sure you're on hand with the shields when the rotten tomatoes come sailing in."

"When life throws you tomatoes, make salsa," he quipped with a crooked grin.

Becky resisted the urge to roll her eyes. At least he was in a better mood than when she came in. Thank goodness for that.

"Before you go, I want you to empty a couple of days in your busy schedule next month." Rick rifled through one pile of papers on his tidy desk and pulled one out. "The owners of the Triple Bar J are putting on a fund-raising ride and were hoping we could do a feature article on it."

"When?"

"The third week of the month."

Becky's mind scrambled through her schedule. "I can't tell you until..."

"You check out your schedule. The ride is a whole week, but I told them we could go in with them one day and out the next. So it would be two days."

"I'll let you know."

"Soon. I don't want to miss this chance."

"I thought we were getting away from cows and farmers." The words slipped past her lips before she even realized she had spoken.

Rick shot her a penetrating look. "Triple Bar J is part of the holdings of a much larger entity. Get them and we've got a good 'in' on a corporate market." He waved the paper slowly, as if thinking, his eyes holding hers. "They've already expressed a great deal of interest in the article we're going to be doing on the premier. Said they want to be a part of that issue. You have that under control, don't you?"

Becky squirmed a little. She'd had a firm commitment from the premier's office for a while now. She knew she should have told Rick but was hoping she could hold off long enough so he would end up getting too busy to help her with it. "Yes, I do."

"And it's an exclusive?"

"Of course." She stifled her immediate resentment. "Otherwise what would be the point? Any one of the dailies would scoop us."

"Good. Then all we have to do is get this account with Triple Bar J and this magazine will be on the upward swing." He slapped his hand against the paper in triumph and flashed her a wide smile. "And the sooner that happens, the sooner I'm out of here."

"That's not going to happen in one issue," Becky retorted. "Or two or three. Our cost overrun is getting a little scary, what with the market survey and all the extra promotion we're doing."

"It will pay back."

Becky wasn't so sure. And he didn't want to take any money from Grandfather Colson. Of course, what did it matter to Rick whether the magazine made money or not? One way or the other he had a ticket out of here.

Back in her office she flipped open her agenda to see if she could squeeze two days out of the week Rick wanted her on the trail ride.

Notes and scribbles filled all available space before and after.

A thread of panic spiraled up within her as she looked at her full days and evenings. She had promised her editor that she would have a proposal in his hands in a couple of months. All she had so far was a rough idea and a lot of scratched-out writing. She thought she had given herself lots of time. But as she flipped through the weeks ahead she could see chunks of time gobbled up by work and other activities, some doubling up.

You don't find time... You make time. She remembered Rick's words.

That was all well and good, but how? She needed this job and she had other responsibilities in the church that she couldn't shirk. God had given her many gifts and she didn't feel right if she didn't use them.

She had already cancelled a meeting for tomorrow night because Rick wanted to discuss the new layout of the magazine with Design. That was a guaranteed three-aspirin meeting. Cliff had been haranguing her for the past week about taking care of him. And Rick was going to talk about using stock photos for the next few issues.

Blessed are the peacemakers, Becky thought, pushing her Day-Timer aside.

She started in on Gavin's article. It grated even harder on closer reading. Easy for Rick to approve this veiled rant at the businesses of Okotoks. He was going to be out of here as soon as possible. She deleted a few of the more offensive adjectives. Hardly editing the life out of them, as Rick had warned her, but hardly the damage control she had hoped to inflict.

She wound a bit of hair round her finger as she mentally ticked off her options. Edit it to her standards and run the risk of getting Rick riled up?

Run it with a disclaimer so she could at least look her fellow community members in the eye?

Or offer an alternative.

As the last thought slipped lightly into her mind, Becky caught it. Another column. Something positive. Upbeat and uplifting. And done free of charge.

She knew exactly who could do it.

* * *

Rick flipped through the binder holding the final proof of the magazine. From here, the first new and improved *Going West* would head to the printer. "Looks good, Cliff. I like the new font and the spacing is very pleasing. What do you think, Becky?"

Becky tapped her pencil against her lip as she studied the mock-up in front of her. This new issue of *Going West* had a sharper edge. The headlines were punchier, the pictures bolder.

It was still a shock to see huge blocks of ads cutting into the articles and marching down the sides of pages. Rick and his sales staff had been busy little beavers to garner this much extra advertising in such a short while.

"It's definitely moving in the direction you're headed," she said, hoping her words sounded more encouraging than she felt.

"When will we be moving away from the stock photos?" Cliff asked, his chair creaking out his annoyance.

"When we start to pull out of our overdraft."

"Which will happen when?"

Thankfully Rick ignored Cliff's belligerence. "It will take a few issues. I'm pinning a lot on our October issue." Rick threw Becky a sidelong glance. "Becky and I are going to be covering the Triple Bar J Western Ride and we'll get you some photos you can work with."

"But those photos won't work for fall."

"We're not going to be as seasonal as we would like, but it's an interesting topic and I'm hoping we'll get some great pictures," Becky said, frowning a warning at Cliff. Looked like she was going to have another hand-holding session with him after this meeting.

"Who's going to be taking those?" Cliff asked, his voice a study in peevishness.

"I will," Rick said. "And the article is as much about the ride as an advertorial for the Triple Bar J," Rick continued.

The heavy silence that followed his comment said more than any complaint or protest could have.

Becky flipped to another page in the binder, past Gavin's article, the sound swishing through the quiet. "You've done a good job with the layout," Becky said to Cliff, her small peace offering. "It has an energy the other issues didn't."

"Thanks, Becks." Cliff accepted her praise with a crooked grin. "I put this new column you gave me opposite Gavin's, like you suggested."

"What column?" Rick flipped the page, as well, frowning.

Becky rocked lightly in her chair to cover her sudden flip of nerves. "We had to hold back the article slated for that page. It didn't fit in size and content. I had to make a last-minute decision on this column. Might turn it into a regular."

"'Runaround Sue'?" Rick's tone didn't bode well. "Who is she and why isn't there a picture with the byline?"

"Sue prefers to remain anonymous for now. And I respect that."

Rick glanced down at the article and heaved a sigh as he started reading aloud. "'He's a man with a mission,'" Rick read. "'With single-minded attention he

tears down the road, accelerator pushed to the limit, un-
afraid of what the journey might bring him. He dares
all challenges and laughs at danger. He has youth. He
has energy.'" Rick paused at the paragraph break. "'He
has his father's truck.'" Rick looked up from the binder,
shaking his head. "What is this about and why wasn't
I consulted?"

Because you'd probably have vetoed it.

"When Cliff showed me the mock-ups I realized we
would either have to split the original article twice or
come up with something shorter. I figured this would
work better. It's light and balances Gavin's column."
Becky paused and delivered her strongest shot. "And
Sue is doing this gratis for now." Which was a small
point given the declining financial situation.

Rick jerked his chin toward her. "I don't know if I
like the direction. Family humor?"

"Light humor," Becky corrected. "A kind of positive
note to lighten things up a bit. Everyone likes to smile.
Chuckle a little."

Rick blew out a sigh and caught his lower lip
between his teeth. He wasn't pleased, but Becky knew
that any change at this stage would cause expensive
delays.

"We'll run it for now," he conceded, slapping the
binder shut. "The rest looks great, everyone. Good job.
Let's get this to the printer."

In the shuffle to leave, Becky winked at Cliff, thankful for Rick's sudden affirmation.

"Becky, I need to talk to you before you leave," Rick
said as Becky got up.

She sank back into her chair, stifling a groan. While she waited for Cliff to leave, she managed not to tap her fingers on the arm of the chair or swing her foot in impatience. She had a meeting at the church in fifteen minutes.

Rick waited by his desk until the door closed behind the last person. Once again he perched on the edge of his desk. Once again he crossed his arms over his chest.

"A quick note to let me know what you were doing with this 'Runaround Sue' would have been in order here."

She knew he was right, but she also knew it would have been an uphill battle to convince him to run it. Apologizing took less time than asking permission.

"I'm sorry," she said, holding his steady gaze. "You're right."

Rick's eyes took on an inward look. "Why won't you tell me who Sue is?"

Becky released the tension in her shoulders with a slow "what can I do?" shrug. "She prefers to remain anonymous."

"As well, I gave you Gavin's next four columns. I think you could afford me the same courtesy."

"I'll get them to you as soon as she gets them to me." She pulled the binder close and scooted to the edge of her chair. "Is that all?"

Rick stroked his chin with his thumb, his lips flirting with a smile. "Why do I get the feeling that you're hiding something?"

"Because you don't trust people."

Becky slapped her fingers to her mouth as if to stop them, but it was too late. The words were out, hanging between them like a taunt.

"Maybe I've had reason not to," he said before she had a chance to apologize.

His abrupt turn away from her was a classic signal for her to leave and time was ticking. But in his words Becky caught the vaguest hint of sorrow.

"Why not?" She asked the question quietly, hoping to offset the callousness of her previous comment.

Rick glanced back over his shoulder, as if surprised she was still there. He held her curious gaze a moment. "Trust is a relationship," he said finally.

"I'm sure moving around all the time doesn't help you build relationships."

"It suits me."

"And what if you meet someone special? Don't you think you'll want to settle down then?"

Rick shrugged, his charming smile back in place. "Hasn't happened yet, so I don't need to make that kind of decision, do I?"

"But you might."

"I doubt it. Most women like their men to put down roots. I can't think of any reason I'd want to do that."

Becky thought of his empty Day-Timer and his lack of connections. A quick glance around his office reinforced that. Nelson had had pictures of his family and holidays decorating most of the walls and jostling for space on his desk. Her own office held pictures of nieces, nephews, brothers, sisters, parents, friends. She was running out of room on the bulletin board for more photos.

Rick's desk held only papers and the walls were still bare. Not a photograph or snapshot in sight.

She felt a flash of pity and sorrow.

"I hope you change your mind someday," she said as she got up. "I believe we all need a place to call home."

Rick held her gaze a moment, his blue eyes delving deep into hers as if searching out her secrets. "And why do you care, Rebecca Ellison?"

She couldn't look away, and as the moment lengthened, an indistinct emotion shifted deep within Becky and she felt herself softening toward him. "Because I believe you are also a child of God."

Rick laughed, cynicism edging the sound. "I'm nobody's child, Becky. Least of all God's."

And of all the things he said, that was the saddest of all.

Chapter Six

"Before I leave, I thought I'd get you the rest of the mail," Trixie said, dropping a bundle of opened letters onto Becky's desk. Becky flipped through them with one hand while she ate her sandwich with the other. She had spent the entire day running around and had just come into the office to answer a few phone messages and chase down a couple of articles for the next issue. Somewhere in all of the mess that was turning out to be her evening, she had to find a chance to work on another "Runaround Sue" column and get to a meeting with the youth pastor.

"The magazine has only been out a week. We've never gotten this kind of response before," Becky mumbled, wiping the crumbs with the cuff of her shirt.

"Most of them are from businesses. Most of them look handwritten." Trixie pursed her lips. "I sorted them into positive and negative but overall, I'd say not good."

Becky skimmed the first one, mentally separating

herself from the anger spilling out on the pages. Countless times her father had told her not to take the letters personally. She tried, but she had a long ways to go before harsh words didn't give her a clench in the pit of her stomach and a desire to go running to the writer to apologize for anything that might have caused offense.

"Has Rick seen these?"

"He's at a Rotary Club meeting. Didn't think he'd be back at the office tonight."

"I guess I'll wade through these then, once I'm done working on this profile." She was also going to have to phone the church and tell the youth pastor she wouldn't be making the meeting tonight. Which also meant she wouldn't have time to work on her book proposal. She pushed down a beat of resentment. Work was taking up too much time. And most of the work was thanks to Rick. "Thanks, Trixie. I'll see you tomorrow."

"You sure you don't want any help?"

Becky shook her head and finished her sandwich in one bite. "There's not really a lot you can do, but thanks."

"See you tomorrow then." Trixie left, and the silence that followed her was a blessing.

Hours later Becky pushed herself away from her desk and stretched her arms above her head with a yawn. The pieces were edited and she had chosen some of the more articulate letters for print in the magazine. That most of them were negative was not her problem.

"Runaround Sue" had proven surprisingly easy to write. Now, at nine o'clock at night, her day was officially over.

She switched off her computer and reveled in the

quiet. During the day, the office was a hive of voices and telephones and keyboards clacking. The silence that enveloped her was a relief. A chance to let her busy mind slow down and empty out.

Tomorrow would bring another set of last-minute disasters and changes and juggling finances, but for now her day was over.

She glanced out the window of her office at the setting sun and stifled a moment of frustration. During the short days of winter she looked forward to the longer daylight hours of summer. But now that they'd come, she spent most of them inside. She'd had also only a few hours last week to work on her latest book but all she had to show for it was two more pages of drivel. She was never going to get it done if Rick kept piling on the work.

Yawning, she snagged her sweater off the back of her chair and threaded her arms through the sleeves. She had dressed up today—her favorite pink shirt and denim skirt—for one of her meetings. She had also vaguely hoped that Rick could see that she didn't always wear jeans and T-shirts. But he had been gone all day.

The click of the back door opening was like a shot scattering panic through her body.

Footsteps down the hallway, easy, measured, sent her heart thumping against her ribs. Who was here this time of the night? What did they want?

"Is that you, Becky?"

Relief made Becky sag against her chair.

"Yes, it is, Rick. Come on in."

The door opened and Rick stood framed by the doorway, his eyes flicking over her office, as if making sure. "I thought you had a meeting tonight?"

"I skipped it to work on this. What are you doing out?"

"My Jeep broke down a few blocks from here." Rick stepped into her office, pulled his tie off and tucked it into his pocket. He ran his hands through his neatly combed hair and completed his transformation from stiff businessman to Rick. "My cell phone died so I thought I'd call from the office."

"There's no garage open this time of night. But I could give you a ride home if you want."

Rick shrugged. "No need to go out of your way."

"I truly don't mind." She flashed him a faint smile, then got up from behind the desk.

"There's no rush. You can finish up."

Becky glanced back at the papers on her desk, feeling a flicker of shock. Her "Runaround Sue" column lay on top of the pile. "I'm pretty much done here," she said, shuffling the papers to hide the evidence. "It's too late to be thinking anyway."

Ten minutes later Becky pulled up in front of an apartment block in a newer part of town and sighed lightly as she put her car in gear.

"I remember when all this was wide-open fields." Becky stacked her hands on the steering wheel and rested her chin on them. "That's the trouble with time. It moves and changes things."

"You'd sooner things stay the same."

Becky gave a light shrug. "I'm sentimental. I'll admit it." She turned to Rick, who was sitting slightly askew in his seat watching her. The streetlights above put his face in intriguing shadows, creating a soft intimacy. "Bad habit."

"It can cause a lot of disappointment." He tilted his head to one side, his slow smile shifting his expression. "But you seem like a person who can rise above it."

"I try. I don't always succeed. I'm only human."

"And now you've got me to deal with."

"It's been an interesting ride, I'll say," she said carefully.

Rick's smile grew. "Diplomatic of you. But speaking of ride, I need to finalize plans for the trail ride. I've got the information in my apartment. Do you have a few moments to come up?"

Fifteen minutes ago Becky had been bone weary, wanting nothing more than home, a hot bath and a cup of hot chocolate. Surprisingly enough, she didn't feel that tired anymore.

"Sure." She turned off the engine and slipped out the door into the cool night air, following Rick up the walk and into the building.

Rick unlocked the door of his apartment and let her in.

"The apartment came furnished, so I can't take any credit or blame for how it looks," he said as he stood aside to let her in.

"It looks fine," Becky said, taking in the minimal furniture, the complete lack of any personal touches. It was just like his office. No photographs, no paintings, posters or anything that expressed who he was.

Sort of like his Day-Timer.

Becky couldn't help but think of her own room and her hotchpotch decorating style. Fans and kites and plants and bowls and cloths hung on walls or were scattered wherever she saw a bare spot that needed a little cheering up. And pictures—family members, friends, fellow workers, people from church, her youth group—all tacked in glorious disarray on a huge bulletin board.

Rick pulled a folder out of a desk drawer and laid it on the table. "I've got all the information right here. Dates of departure and arrival. Also, a general idea of what Triple Bar J is looking for in terms of coverage."

"Wow. A file folder for a trail ride." She quashed a smile at own her flippant comment.

"Okay, enough about my personal management style. It works for me." Rick gave her a crooked grin and she felt a moment of accord. "So, will you be able to go?"

"Not sure yet. Things aren't looking really great."

"Try. I'd like you to come." He held her gaze, his expression softening.

"Okay."

"Do you want a cup of coffee or something like that? Believe it or not, I actually have stuff like that in my house. Cookies, too."

Her first instinct was to say no, she didn't really have time. But the very bareness of his kitchen, the starkness of the rest of the apartment made her relent. She doubted he had much of a social life apart from work.

"That'd be nice. If you have tea, I'd love a cup. I'm not much of a coffee drinker."

"Tea, it is. Flavored, herbal or regular?"

"Wow. A choice." She laughed. "Surprise me."

"I'll try." As he got up, Rick flashed her another grin and Becky felt another flicker of response.

A few moments later he brought out a tray holding a pot of tea, two mugs and a plate of cookies. He cleared a space among the papers and set it down.

"Very domesticated," Becky said, taking the cup he handed her. "I confess I wouldn't have been surprised if you brought out instant coffee in tin cans."

"A habit I picked up. Grandpa was a tea connoisseur." Rick set the plate of cookies in front of her. "The boarding school I went to served tea at night. British roots I suspect. When I traveled I found the tea to be more dependable than the coffee."

"Did you like boarding school?"

"Not particularly, but I never knew different. When Mom died, boarding school was the best alternative for Grandpa Colson." That his words were delivered without any emotion tugged at the motherly part of Becky's heart. She pictured a lost little boy of seven, heading off to a strange place, all alone.

"Did he miss you?"

Rick's laugh was without humor. "I think he waved me off each Monday with a huge sigh of relief."

"I understand Grandpa Colson once made my own grandmother's heart go pit-a-pat. Do you have any pictures of him?"

"No. He wasn't big on photos."

"Must be genetic." Becky glanced around his bare apartment walls. "I kind of thought a photographer would at least have some pictures on the wall."

"Most of my stuff is in boxes. I never stayed in one place long enough to hang things up."

He stated the information casually, but Becky sensed

a touch of melancholy in his voice. Or maybe her own sentimental nature imagined it.

"So not even a photo album?"

"I have one I've compiled of trips I've made that I usually take with me in case I want to add to it."

"Can I see it?"

Rick held her gaze as if trying to see past her question. Then with a light shrug, he pushed himself back from the table, got up and walked over to a box that sat beside his couch.

"If it's too much trouble..." Becky suddenly felt as if she were snooping.

"No. It's right here." Rick crouched down and flipped through the box's contents and pulled out a small worn album. He brushed the cover before he handed it to Becky.

Becky opened it up to a picture of an older man sketching a giggling young girl and her solemn older brother. "Where is this?"

"Paris. Montmartre. A bit cliché, but it was my first trip." Rick stayed beside her, his one hand leaning on the table beside the book as Becky turned the pages. His suit coat hung open and his closeness created a curious mixture of discomfort and allure.

"That next one is Mathematician's Square close to Sorbonne."

"No Eiffel Tower?" Becky teased, hoping to find a balance to her seesawing emotions.

"I was trying already then to establish myself as an individual," Rick said with a light laugh. He pulled a chair close and sat down beside her, and allure, for the moment, won.

The pictures changed in composition as she went. From traditional camera angles and European settings, Rick had moved to more far-flung locations, experimenting with light and color as he went. A few striking shots taken in Africa were in black and white, others in sepia tones. Children and families featured in many of the shots.

"I knew you traveled a lot. I never realized how much." As Becky turned the pages, she felt as if she was transported to other, exotic worlds.

"Have you ever traveled?"

Becky shook her head as she turned the page to a picture of a crowded, narrow street. "I've never had the opportunity."

"You don't have opportunities, you take them."

Which sounded suspiciously like his comment about finding time to write. "Maybe someday. I have to confess, though, it seems like a waste of money."

"Traveling isn't something selfish. It can have a purpose."

Becky glanced sidelong at him intrigued by his comment, but he was looking at the album. "And what was your purpose?"

Rick shrugged, glancing up at her. "My articles." He got up and walked around to where he was sitting before, and Becky wondered if she had scared him away. "I made good money doing them. Showing people like you, who don't like to travel, what the world is like."

"I didn't say I don't like to travel." As she closed the album, she noticed a picture tucked away at the back.

It was of a woman holding a young boy on her lap, both of them laughing up at the camera. Becky stopped and looked at it more closely. "Is this you?"

"And my mother."

"Did your dad take it?"

Rick shook his head, toying with his mug. "She always told me a friend took them. I didn't know my father."

"I'm sorry to hear that," Becky said softly.

Rick's sent a curious smile her way. "You don't have to pity me. There are many people in this world who haven't had a third of what I've had."

"Not pity, but I feel bad that you have so few relationships in your life."

A veil dropped over Rick's expression. "I believe you mean that."

Becky couldn't look away and found she didn't want to. As their eyes held, she could almost feel a softening in him. "I do. People shouldn't be alone."

Rick blinked, then a peculiar look drifted over his face. "I'm not alone now." His voice had grown quiet, deeper, and he leaned a little closer, his index finger lightly caressing her hand.

"That sounds an awful lot like a pickup line, Rick," Becky said, hoping she sounded more nonchalant than she felt. In spite of her brief annoyance at his convenient sidestep into insincere patter, she couldn't stop a responding frisson of attraction at his touch.

Rick slipped his fingers inside the palm of her hand as he shrugged. "It probably is."

"So why did you use it? Was I getting too close?"

"Did you take psychology as well as journalism?" he

asked, still holding her hand, his eyes concentrating on her fingers.

"No. I think I know you and your kind."

"Ah, a woman of the world in spite of her Christian upbringing." He smiled, but Becky could sense it was forced.

"Christian doesn't mean naive," she said sharply. "I have had a few boyfriends."

"Past tense I notice."

Becky pulled her hand out of his, retreating to the distance she shouldn't have crossed. "I thought I came up here to get some information from you."

"And all you got so far was a cup of tea and confessions."

Rick's comment reminded her that she had stepped out of the boundaries of their relationship as well as he had. He looked at her again, but this time his expression was serious. "I can give it to you on Monday" was all he said.

He wanted her to leave and suddenly she didn't want to go. "I'm here now. I may as well get it."

With a light shrug of resignation, Rick opened the file and pulled out a couple of pieces of paper. He slipped them across the table to her, but didn't meet her eyes. "Even though we're only going two days, the people at Triple Bar J wanted to make things as easy as possible for us, so they gave me some background information." He pulled out another single sheet of paper. "This is what we'll be doing and a list of personal items you need to take if you come. They'll be packing it in on horses so they have a maximum weight you're allowed."

Becky glanced over the list. "I hope I can find the time to go."

"I hope so, too."

His quiet response was far more sincere than his previous one, which made Becky look up at him, faint surprise drifting through her.

Rick didn't look away immediately, and once again Becky felt the same arc of awareness she had felt the first time she met him.

Please, Lord, I can't be attracted to him. He's not the man for me.

But at the same time she didn't want to look away.

"So, what're you guys tryin' to prove?" Katherine Dubowsky didn't quite slam Becky's breakfast on the table, but if the silverware hadn't been lying on a napkin, it would have rattled.

"'Guys'? 'Prove'?" As if Becky didn't know what made Katherine glare down at her, Katherine's penciled-in eyebrows yanked down over her dark eyes in a sharp V.

Most likely the same thing that had made the usual coffee shop conversation die down the moment Becky stepped into Coffee's On.

"Makin' us sound like we don't know how to run a business." Katherine leaned on the table, bringing her angry face closer to Becky's. "That Gavin. Acts like he's the big shot around town. Like his own business is running so peachy keen. Which it ain't."

Becky glanced around the coffee shop. A few of the patrons were avidly watching the exchange, others were looking intently at their food. But Becky knew they were listening just as hard.

She had Rick to thank for putting her in this tricky situation. "It's a column we're trying out for now. If it doesn't work, well, then it doesn't work."

"Well, let me tell you, hon. It doesn't work." Katherine pushed herself away from the table. "Though I sure had to laugh at that 'Runaround Sue' piece."

"And what did you think of the rest of the magazine?"

Kim waggled her hand as if balancing the pros and cons. "It looks nice. Lots of ads though. I liked the cowboy article in the 'People and Places' part. Sometimes those pieces could be kind of smarmy. But this one I liked."

Smarmy. Becky squirmed at the word. She had written most of those pieces in the past. That this one, the one that Katherine liked the best, had been done with Rick's help, galled a little.

"Ya gotta lose that Gavin guy," Earl McCrae, a feed-lot owner sitting at the next table piped in. He adjusted the dusty cap on his head. "He's trouble."

"Thanks, Earl. I'll make note of it." At least the "trouble" comment balanced out the "smarmy" comment. So far, she and Rick were even.

Katherine tapped her index finger twice on Becky's table as if underscoring Earl's words. "Enjoy your breakfast" was all she said.

As if that was going to happen.

Becky had ducked into Coffee's On early this morning with her notebook computer and the faint hope that she could get a bit of work done on her book. But the atmosphere in the coffee shop was hardly conducive to the writing she'd hoped to do. She pushed it aside, and made short work of her toast and tea.

Chapter Seven

"Any positive letters from the column in the bunch?"
Rick leaned back in his chair, his arms crossed over his
chest. The early-morning sun gilded his hair and enhanced the smooth cast of his features. In spite of her
momentary pique with him over her confrontation with
Katherine, Becky couldn't stop the faint lift of her heart.

Okay, he was good-looking and she was a normal
woman. A lonely, normal woman. Get on with what you
came here for.

"Gavin's sister sent a very encouraging e-mail," Becky
continued, willing to concede only this small point.

Trixie had sorted through the mail and stacked all the
letters responding to Gavin's article. Compared to the
amount of mail the magazine usually generated, this
was a glut.

Becky resisted the urge to gloat. Even smile. Being
right was enough reward for her. Even so, she couldn't
stop her foot from swinging just a bit.

"The language in the letters is pretty strong."

"Not as strong as Gavin's column was."

Rick tapped his thumb against his chin. "I'm not ready to give up on him."

"I had a lovely conversation with Katherine Dubowsky only a few moments ago at Coffee's On. Not impressed. Neither were about half of the customers." She kept Katherine's comment about the cowboy article to herself. Rick didn't need any more ammunition.

"Coffee shop complaints."

"Well, they're complaining about Gavin. And on top of these letters, I'm listening. I have to live in this place, Rick, and with the repercussions."

"I still think they'll get used to him."

Goodness, the man was stubborn.

Becky reached across Rick's desk and flipped through a few envelopes, saving her best shot for last. "I believe here's one from a business called Clip 'n Curl that didn't appreciate some of Gavin's comments."

"That's a hairdresser."

Becky tapped it lightly on the desk. "Not just any hairdresser. Lanette, the owner, calls the owner of Triple Bar J Daddy." Becky shrugged, trying not to enjoy the moment too much. "I don't know which you want to sacrifice—Gavin or..." Becky let the question hang and added a light shrug for emphasis.

Rick rocked in his chair. Then he stopped, as if ready to concede. "You're enjoying this, aren't you?" he said finally, a grin teasing his mouth. "The downfall of the Easterner."

Becky opened her mouth to refute his statement and

caught the twinkle in his eye. "Okay. I'll admit it. I love being right."

"If I drop Gavin I'll have to come up with something short for that space." Rick came around to the front of the desk as if to confront her face-to-face. But Becky knew he was giving in and didn't feel threatened by his nearness.

Felt something else, but she didn't want to examine that too closely.

A month ago Becky would have recommended they bring Gladys back, but even one issue in, Becky knew Gladys wouldn't fit anymore. "Do you want me to find someone?"

"No. I'll take care of it."

She didn't have time to enjoy her victory and launched herself out of her chair. "I gotta run. I'm covering the grand opening of the new car dealership. We promised the owner some good coverage."

"I understand the member of the legislative assembly might be there."

"He better show up. He's a brother-in-law of the owner."

"How do you know all this stuff?" Rick sounded surprised.

"I've lived in this community all my life, Rick. In spite of the many changes that have happened here, I know most of the connections and relationships."

"And that's how you knew Gavin's column wouldn't fly. That kind of intuition works for Okotoks, I'll grant you that much, but when the magazine expands its influence..."

"I still don't think a column like Gavin's works. He's far too negative. I would guess, as a rule, people don't like being told in polysyllabic words that they are dolts who don't know how to run their business."

"I still think he had some good advice."

Becky knew she should stop. Her point had been made. She had been proved right. But she couldn't. Something about Rick's comments, his attitude, created an unreasoning need to bring up a contrary view. "It wasn't his advice, Rick. It was his presentation."

"So he should have wrapped it up in pretty words."

Gracious, he was as bad as she was. "Didn't you ever have to take bad medicine?" she asked. "Didn't your mother ever put some sugar in it to make it easier to go down? Deceitful, yes, but if you're doing what you're doing out of concern, then by all means, use a little bit of sugar."

"We're not dealing with kids. Anyone who has any kind of business has had to deal with problems and setbacks. Don't tell me they don't know how to take bad news." Rick dropped one hip against his desk and crossed his arms.

Becky glanced at the clock on Rick's wall. She didn't have time to argue but she couldn't seem to stop. "You agree that he was a mistake. Why replow this old ground?" Becky couldn't keep the exasperation out of her voice.

Now Rick swung his foot, his dimple deepening in one cheek as he gave her an engaging smile. "Maybe I like arguing with you. And maybe I want to show you that even though you were right, I was a little bit right, too."

The teasing tone of his voice coupled with his charming smile brought out a responding grin. "Okay. You were right, too. Hard news for hard times." She stopped the "but" that was forming and let it lie.

"So are you going to allow me the last word?"

Anything she said right now would be self-fulfilling, so she simply nodded.

"Great. That's all I wanted." He reached over and patted her on the shoulder. "Go and enjoy the grand opening."

His gesture was almost fatherly, but the feelings it aroused in her were hardly those of a daughter. And as their eyes met again she felt herself drawn once again to him, like a moth to a flame.

Dangerous.

She left as quickly as she could.

We've got more trained accountants in the government's Treasury Department than a politician has promises, and all have the imagination of plywood. My idea of an ideal treasurer would be a mother of four children, married to a wage earner—someone who has learned to make do—to manage a budget that doesn't change with every whim. Imagine the meetings. "Madame Treasurer, I would like to request funding for an arts project that seeks to discover the self-actualization of dirt within a cultural concept." Once she's picked herself up from the floor and wiped the tears of laughter from her eyes, I'm sure they will have received their answer...

Runaround Sue

If only life were as simple as Runaround Sue would imagine it to be. I wonder what her hypothetical mother of four children would do when asked to respond to the issue of deregulation of the power industry. Not as easy as handing out chore lists. But it's something that local businesses have had to deal with and must continue to face. This is a hard world full of bad news....

Becky smiled when she read Rick's column. He had asked to see what Runaround Sue had written before he wrote up his and this was the result. Not all-out war, but the battle lines were getting drawn. A gentle tug of the gloves.

Well, Sue was up to the challenge, Becky thought, already planning her next column. She just wished her book were as easy to write as the "Runaround Sue" columns were.

"Have a seat, Rick, and tell me what your grandfather has been up to lately," Diene De Graaf said, patting the empty spot on the sofa beside her. Rick sat down, glancing around Sam and Cora's living room as he did. Becky sat, legs crossed on the floor across the room, playing a board game with her nieces and nephew. She wore her hair up today, arranged in some combination of curls and pins that looked cute on her. Her hazel eyes sparkled as she cheered on her nephew.

"My grandfather is busy building up his empire," Rick said, forcing his attention back to Becky's grandmother. Of all the people he had met in Becky's family, Diene resembled her most. Same bright eyes that held a touch of humor. Same slightly stubborn jaw and laughing mouth. "Grandfather has made his mark in Toronto. Now it seems he wants to do the same in Okotoks."

Diene laughed lightly. "He always was a man of vision. Even when he was living here."

"He never told me he lived here. Or that he knew you." Rick could see why his grandfather might have, at one time, been attracted to Diene. Age had only smudged her beauty, not diminished it.

Diene sat back in the couch, smiling lightly. "He was quite the gentleman. Just not the kind of man I saw myself having a future with."

A peal of laughter drew Rick's attention to Becky. She was lying flat out on the ground, giggling now, while her nephew and nieces swarmed over her. "You helped him...I saw you...no fair." The accusations flew at her like popcorn, but even Rick could tell they weren't really angry.

Becky sat up and scooped the three kids close to her in a group hug. "I love you all, bumpkins," she said, still giggling. "Now go get me some cake."

As the children scattered, Becky smoothed her hair and tugged her shirt straight. Then she looked up and their gazes tangled and clung.

He didn't imagine her soft smile, nor how it made his own heart skip. Just a little. Rick dragged his attention back to Diene and the comment she had made. "And what kind would that be?"

"The same kind of man Becky has been holding out for. A man who knows the Lord."

Rick didn't have to look at Diene to feel the gentle warning in her words.

He wanted to pass off his attraction to Becky as the simple chemistry he had felt when he first saw her.

However, he knew that time with her had desimplified the attraction. She wasn't just a pretty, young woman. He had come to know her in other ways. Had come to admire her ability to stand up to him. To challenge him. Though he and Becky had never talked much about it, he knew her relationship to God was real and true and positive.

Becky got up and glanced his way, holding his gaze as they caught. Neither looked away.

In that moment Rick felt the subtle shift, a realignment of the relationship.

And from the frown making a number eleven between Diene's eyebrows, Rick could tell that she had felt it, too.

"You know, Rick," she said laying a hand on his arm. "A grandmother is not supposed to have favorites, but Becky has always held a special place in my heart. Of all my children and grandchildren, she is the most like me." She pressed her fingers down, as if warning him. "I never dated any man unless I saw them as a future life partner. Becky is the same. She's not a person to go on casual dates. But the most important reason I turned your grandfather down was because I knew his heart wasn't right with God at the time."

In spite of her words, though, Rick heard the unspoken question threaded through her voice.

"Grandfather Colson goes to church," Rick said. "He raised my mother to fear God. If that means anything."

Diene smiled and Rick caught a glimpse of yearning

mixed with sadness. "I'm glad for that," she whispered. "Did he teach you?"

"He tried." Rick held her gaze and once again felt the faint echo of what had touched him in church when Becky sang. But he wasn't going to give in that easily. "What I've seen in the world hasn't endeared me to God."

"How can a loving God allow so much suffering?" she said softly, voicing his thoughts.

"Yes." Her candid question surprised him. "And as long as I'm asking those kind of questions, I can't see that God would be interested in me."

She smiled, looking into the middle distance as if seeking her answer there. "Your grandfather often asked the same question. Interesting that you two are that much alike." She turned to face him. "It's a good question to ask, Rick. And God respects the asking. He wants honesty in His relationships with His people. Not fake devotion." She patted him lightly on the arm. "Keep your heart open to God. He's not afraid to be asked the hard questions."

Rick felt a glimmering of truth kindle in him as he held Diene's eyes. And what other questions would God be able to handle?

"Hey, Mother. Find out all the things you wanted to about your old honey?" Becky's father dropped onto the couch on the other side of Diene and winked at Rick. The moment was broken.

"Mother used to have quite a thing for your grandfather," Sam said in a hearty voice. "And now I've made her blush."

Diene tutted lightly, shaking her head. "If you don't have anything constructive to say, I'm leaving."

"My mother's a good woman," Sam said, laughing as Diene strode to the kitchen. "Just doesn't take to teasing. Did you want to see the rest of the orchard?"

What Rick wanted was to see Becky again, but she was nowhere in sight.

Colette grabbed her sister by the arm, dragging her up the stairs by the kitchen. "Becks, this Rick is adorable," Colette said in a stage whisper, glancing over her shoulder.

"That's exactly what Leanne said. Do you girls subscribe to the same magazines?" Becky laughed off her sister's gushing comment.

"Have your little joke. I see the way you two look at each other." Colette winked at her sister. "Just like me and Nick." Colette pulled her down on the stairs, her knees drawn up to her chin. "Now, tell me more about him. Leanne said he was good-looking, but the words don't do him justice."

Becky sighed, indulging in her younger sister's high school–style gossipfest. She knew she would have no rest until she set the record straight.

"Rick is single. Comes from Toronto originally. He's Colson Ethier's grandson and is here to bring *Going West* into the next century. He likes to travel and drinks tea. I believe he's about six feet tall. Would have to guess on the weight." Becky ticked the items off on her fingers aware of Colette's growing impatience.

Colette pushed Becky's hand down. "Very funny. Now tell me what I really want to know."

Becky sighed and inspected her fingernails. Saw a hangnail.

"Don't even think about it." Colette stopped Becky's hand halfway up to her mouth. "So. Tell me."

"Honestly, Colette. There's nothing to say. He's only here for a little bit and then he'll be gone. And I'm too busy."

"You're always too busy. You should drop a few things."

"Like what? The minister was campaigning for about three weeks to get someone to do kids' choir. I can't leave the library board until they find a replacement for me. The worship committee can never find enough volunteers. Sandy needs me to help her with the youth..." Becky laced her fingers together. "And I'm trying to find time to write my book."

Colette put her hand on her sister's shoulder and gave her a light shake. "Your problem is you're too good at the things you do."

"Well, I feel that God has given me gifts I need to use. And I feel that I'm serving Him by using them in our church."

"But surely you don't have to use them all at once."

Becky laughed. "Well, for now, this is my life and I'm happy with it."

"Just too busy to do anything about your good-lookin' boss."

"And may I remind you, he is my boss."

Colette groaned.

"C'mon. Let's see if we can use our dishwashing talents and help our mother out." Becky jumped off the stairs and held out her hand to her sister.

"But you have to admit, he is a hunk."

And Colette didn't need to know that there were times that Becky would agree with that statement.

"I should cut down those old trees, but I hate to do it." Sam stood in front of a particularly gnarled tree. "Cora's grandfather started these."

Rick thought of his grandfather's current home. Colson had bought it three years ago. It, too, had stately trees and a well-landscaped yard but he knew nothing about it. Nor cared.

But Sam knew every tree in his extensive orchard as if by name. A heritage, he thought with a faint touch of envy.

The sound of a motor drew nearer and then they heard "Hey, Dad" above its intrusive snarl.

Rick spun around, his heart lifting when he saw Becky astride an ATV heading toward them. She stopped in front of them and vaulted off, slightly breathless, her cheeks flushed, her eyes bright.

"That guy you needed to get a hold of in Holland just called."

"Is he still on the phone?"

"Take the quad. He said he'd wait." Becky's eyes were on her father, but Rick felt a tug of connection.

"Thanks, sweetie. I'll see you two back at the house." He dropped a light kiss on Becky's head, jumped aboard the four-wheeler, spun it around and left in a cloud of exhaust and noise.

Becky turned to him. "Sorry about Dad dragging you out here. He gets a little obsessed about his orchard at times. Show the least bit of interest and you're his next victim."

"He was just showing me this apple tree." Rick pointed to the old tree beside him. "Telling me the history."

"The Opa tree?" Becky smiled as she reached up to grab a rough, crooked branch, its leaves rustling as she shook it lightly. "I remember getting material for budding off it in the summer and apples in the fall. Poor tree. We used and abused it."

"He told me your great-grandfather planted it."

"Actually, he planted the rootstock. Only native or wild apple trees can overwinter in this climate, but they produce small hard inedible apples. These branches were grafted onto the wild rootstock and produce large, tasty apples. So the wild and the tame work together and need each other. It's an old tree." Becky gave the branch another shake, looking up through the leaves, her head thrown back. "It got struck by lightning once. You can see up there, at the top. It's still the biggest tree in the orchard though."

Rick wasn't looking at the tree though, his eyes fixed on Becky.

"Obviously a lot of memories here." He shouldn't feel the faint tug of envy he did at her history. He never had any desire to be so rooted.

Becky angled him a quick smile as she walked around the tree. "We used to hide in it, though if Opa ever caught us, we'd be weeding the new orchard by hand. Mostly we don't let the trees get this big. Makes it too hard to pick the apples. But this one is special and we don't prune it anymore."

"You still work in the orchard?" Rick followed her around the tree, lured on by the smile she had given him.

Something had shifted between them in the past few days and he wanted to explore it.

"I try to. Just too busy these days."

"I know. I didn't think you could fit anything more in that Day-Timer of yours."

Becky's horrified look came at the same instant he realized what he had said.

"I'm sorry," he muttered, holding his hand up in a gesture of surrender. "I just... When I had it, I opened it up because I thought it was mine."

To his surprise Becky didn't get angry. Didn't ask what he was doing snooping through her book. Instead she stared at the tree, her hands still holding on to a lower branch.

"It was an honest mistake," he continued, trying to catch her eye.

"How much did you see?" she asked quietly, licking her lips.

"I saw that every available moment of every available day is full," he answered, evading her question neatly. "I also saw that you're going to have to do some major rescheduling if you're going to go on the trail ride."

Becky caught one corner of her lip between her teeth. "About that ride..."

"You're not going to beg off on me, are you?" His reasons for wanting her to come were mixed. He wasn't sure himself. Only that the more he thought of spending some time with her away from the office, the more he liked the idea.

"No. It's just that—" she lifted her hands as if in a gesture of surrender "—I have a lot of obligations."

"And a financial obligation to the magazine."

"That's true."

He sensed she was wavering and pushed his advantage. "I'm going to need your perspective. Otherwise all I might write about is the mess the horses leave behind and how cold it is in the mountains."

Becky laughed. "Okay. I'll see what I can do." She picked at a hangnail, still looking down. "So, what else did you see in my Day-Timer?"

He could be evasive and keep her secret, or he could be honest and maybe find out if her feelings had changed. "I did read that you weren't quite sure what to do about me."

Becky closed her eyes and blew out her breath. "I'm sorry," she said quietly. "I was worried about working with you. And maybe a little angry with you yet over my book review." Becky glanced up at him, her expression serious now. "I poured my heart and soul into that book. Though I should have felt honored that you read it, it was still hard to see it trashed so publicly."

Guilt twanged through Rick. "My grandfather wasn't happy with how I'd handled it, either. After the review came out in the magazine I found out that he hadn't given me the book to review. He had been hoping it would touch some cold part of my heart."

Becky gave him a wry smile, which surprised him and encouraged him at the same time. "Guess I failed in that, too."

"Not completely. There were some genuinely moving pieces and I did finish the book."

"I know you well enough to know there's a huge 'but' hanging here." She winced. "If you'll forgive how that sounded."

Rick couldn't stop his laugh. Couldn't stop himself from taking a step closer to her, encouraged by her honesty. "Okay. The but." He paused, trying to find the right words. "I don't think this story was the right vehicle for what you wanted to say. It was melodramatic. Too derivative of many books out there. Once in a while you had a passage that rose above the rest of the book, but then you seemed to pull your writing down to make it fit the story."

She held his gaze, her head canted to one side. Smiled a bit. And his heartbeat fluttered a moment.

"Okay, I'll concede that," she said. "How could I have done it differently?" She came around the tree, took a step closer to him, one hand still holding on to the trunk as if seeking strength from her great-grandfather's legacy.

"You need to take more time with your story. Commit emotionally to the book. Put yourself in it."

"Funny. I thought I had done that."

"Not really. You're a funnier person than the story shows. A more optimistic person. I think you might benefit from writing a story in first person. Getting deeper into the character. Being more honest. Exposing yourself."

"Hey! I'm a good Christian girl," Becky said with a laugh, hitting him lightly on the chest.

Before he could stop to think what he was doing, Rick captured her hand against his chest, captivated himself by her honest humor. He held her hand close, its warmth pressing through his shirt.

Becky's gaze jumped to his face, her eyes searching his features as if trying to discover what he wanted, what had changed between them. She swallowed, then let her gaze fall to their joined hands as she pressed her fingers ever so lightly against his shirt.

Rick curled his fingers around hers, wondering if she could feel the increased tempo of his own heart.

"I should go help—help my mom," Becky whispered. But even as she spoke, she took a slow step closer.

"I think your mom can manage." Rick rubbed his thumb along the back of her hand, wondering what his next step was.

He didn't usually have to second-guess himself. A hand under her chin. A careful, encouraging smile. Then the kiss. All carefully choreographed and planned.

But he didn't want to treat her like other women. She was special. He wanted to share more than a kiss. More than the physical expression of love. But she was a sincere Christian who loved her Lord. And he didn't know if he could share that with her.

Becky looked up at him then and he saw his own confusion mirrored in her soft hazel eyes. "What's happening, Rick?" she whispered.

He gently fingered a tendril of hair back behind her ear, his hand lingering on her neck as a stillness surrounded them. As if the very trees waited, wondering what they were going to do. "Come on the trail ride. Maybe we can find out more."

"I'll try."

A muffled giggle slipped into the silence followed by the soft "plop" of an apple in the grass at their feet.

Becky blinked, as if coming out of a trance, then pulled her hand away, turning to the source of the laughter.

"Okay, you brats. You can come out now," she said loudly. But Rick heard the faint tremor in her voice and was encouraged. She had been as moved as he had.

The three children Becky had been playing with spilled out from behind a row of bushes, followed by Leanne.

"We were wondering where you were," Leanne said, tossing a speculative glance Rick's way. "Grandma Diene sent us to get you."

More likely, protect you, Rick thought, remembering Diene De Graaf's veiled warning.

The children ran to Becky, but the smallest girl veered at the last moment and lifted her arms up to Rick. "You carry me," she said with a child's brashness.

"Serena, be polite," Becky reprimanded. "Maybe Mr. Ethier doesn't want to carry you."

"Please carry me," Serena said, adding an angelic smile.

"Of course." Rick swung her up onto his shoulders as she squealed her appreciation. "You have to duck for the trees," he warned as he glanced sidelong at Becky.

She stood in front of him, bracketed by a boy and a girl, a faint smile teasing her lips as a breeze teased her hair. Rick winked at her—a casual connection to ease themselves away from the intimacy of the previous moment—then turned and sauntered back to the house.

But even though his long legs easily outpaced Becky, he was less aware of the little girl on his shoulder, clutching his head, than he was of Becky walking behind him.

Chapter Eight

Rick looked over the parking lot of the church full of minivans, cars with children's car seats, sports cars and trucks. All representing a family, a person, a couple inside. And singing, from the sounds that streamed through the door beside him.

Since that Sunday when Becky had finessed him into coming to church, he hadn't found—or made—time to attend. Yet each Sunday, when he passed the building, he had wondered if he would find something behind those doors. The same nebulous something that had called to him that Sunday when Becky sang the prayer.

So who was he interested in? God? Becky? Both?

He took a hesitant step toward the door. Then, releasing a sigh, he pulled the door open and stepped inside. The sounds of the singing drew him on and he slipped through the narthex into the sanctuary. The congregation was standing, but thankfully there was an empty space at the end of the back pew and he took his place in it and let the music and the words take him along.

And then he saw her.

Becky stood in the front of the church, with a group of young children lined up in three rows. She had her back to the congregation, but from where he sat Rick could see her face in profile as she and the children sang along with the congregation. She wore the same blue dress she had the first Sunday he'd seen her. And she looked just as beautiful as she had then. Maybe even more so.

Then the song ended, the congregation sat down and Becky turned around to address them.

"I'm sure many of you parents have been wondering what your children have been doing all those Wednesday nights when they disappear with me to one of the downstairs rooms," she said, looking around the sanctuary. "Well, this morning you're going to get a sample of the program the choir is putting on tonight. Think of it as a teaser. And if that's not enough to tempt you to come tonight, then I feel I should mention that the Ladies' Aid Society is hosting a dessert night in conjunction with the program. So if you want a taste of Gladys Hemple's chocolate cake..." Becky raised her hands in a "what can I do?" gesture. Then with a smile, she turned around, cued the musicians, lifted her hands with a smile to the children and they began.

The song was a light, happy tune, an introduction to the story of Jonah and the whale. Becky's animated expression was contagious and the children responded with wide smiles.

Their light voices were clear and boisterous as they sang about a reluctant prophet who questioned God and who God used anyway. Rick caught himself humming along during the chorus, smiling at the children's obvious enjoyment.

When they were done, Becky nodded, and with a surprising amount of restraint the children walked back to their parents, grinning with pride.

Becky stayed in the front and when the regular worship team came up, she ducked out a side door.

Probably off to perform yet another obligation, Rick thought. And for a moment he was tempted to leave, as well, but the minister came forward. It wouldn't look good to leave during the main attraction, Rick thought. So he sat back and settled in for another sermon.

The minister instructed the congregation to open their Bibles to Psalm One and Rick read about a man who does not stand in the counsel of the wicked, but whose delight was in the law. Rick tried to imagine someone who would delight in laws. And rules.

"He is like a tree planted by streams of water which yields its fruit in season and whose leaf does not wither."

Like the trees of Sam Ellison's orchard.

Like Becky. Rooted and grounded. A part of something larger than herself. Her family. This church. Her community.

So what did that make him? The chaff? Blown about with every changing wind. He knew he didn't have what she had.

But did he want it?

* * *

"So how do you propose to do this?" Rick's office chair creaked in protest as he leaned way back. He ran his index finger back and forth over his forehead as if trying to draw some inspiration from his mind. He had been talking to Terry Anderson, their accounts manager at the bank, for twenty minutes now. They still couldn't agree on how to deal with the serious cash-flow problems the magazine was having.

"The magazine needs to show some kind of profit," Terry was saying. "Or at the minimum, break even. At least on the books. The higher-ups are getting a little antsy."

"Waiting for *Going West* to show a profit is like trying to turn the *Titanic*. It doesn't happen in three issues."

"*Going West* hasn't shown a profit for more than three issues, Rick."

Rick turned his chair around so he could at least see the mountains. "This is what you can do for me, Terry. Make it clear to the suits in Calgary that *Going West* has been bought and is under new management. That you foresee a change in the near future. That has to count for something. That to pull the loan now would be a short-term loss and if they wait, they'll have a valuable asset on their hands." Brave words, but it was the only thing he could give Terry right now. "Your job is to go to bat for me, Terry. Once things start looking better, this will reflect well on you."

"My job is also to keep my job."

Rick sighed. "If you pull the loan and you guys end up with a dead asset, your job won't be looking that good, either, Terry."

The silence on the other end meant Terry was considering and Rick pushed a little harder. "We've got a dynamite issue coming up, Terry. Surely the bank won't go belly-up by extending our line of credit for another six weeks."

"I'll see what I can do," Terry said. "I'll let you know which way the wind blows as soon after our next meeting. I think I've made it clear that *Going West* is in a precarious position."

"Whatever. And while I have you on the phone, would the bank consider putting an ad in the next magazine?"

"You don't quit, do you?"

"And that's exactly what is going to make the difference in the long run." Rick grinned as relief sluiced through him. In spite of Terry's warning, he knew he had bought some time.

He rang off and picked up the latest issue of the magazine. He turned the page, pleased with the overall result of this, his second magazine. It looked professional. The content needed a little boost, but that was coming, as well. He and Becky didn't always agree on what to put in, but slowly they were coming to a compromise that seemed to work.

He turned to the page that held his and Sue's column.

I think it's time newspapers own up to the old adage Bad News Travels By Itself and not help the business along. For once I'd like to read how millions of children got tucked into bed last night. Millions of married couples didn't have a fight or threaten to kill each other. Millions of people made it home safely from work. Millions of people did their jobs well today. "This is not news," the newsmakers wail, gripping their foam-covered microphones and waiting for a disaster to backlight their perfectly coiffed hair....

                                  Runaround Sue

The most important task of any magazine, newspaper or newscast is the delivery of timely and pertinent information according to its subscribers needs and wants. Sue clearly states that bad news travels by itself, but it is the bad news that often determines how businessmen will make their decisions....

Rick couldn't help but smile. He'd never admit it aloud, and especially not to Becky, but Sue had a point. He wouldn't mind meeting her; she sounded like an interesting person.

Someone knocked lightly on the door and Becky stuck her head inside his office. "Hey, there. You busy? Trixie said you were on the phone."

"No. Come on in."

Becky shook her head. "I gotta run. Just thought I'd tell you that I will be able to go on the trail ride with you. I cleared a few things off my calendar, so—" she tossed her head a bit as if mentally juggling her new schedule "—let me know when you want to leave."

"That's great, Becky." His first good news of the day. She retreated with a quick smile.

And Rick started planning.

Becky leaned forward, as if to catch a better view of the purple-tinted mountains rising and rising out of the prairies, dominating the horizon. They rimmed the sky, jagged and awe-inspiring, their snow-covered peaks blindingly white against a sapphire sky.

The road Becky traveled on wound through rolling foothills, wooded with pines, but the mountains stood sentinel, exerting an inexorable pull, daring any to look away. It had been a while since she'd seen the mountains this close and she couldn't look away. Thankfully the road leading to the ranch was quiet, or she might have run the risk of an accident.

An arch holding the Triple Bar J brand came into view. Becky turned and followed the gravel road to the yard she saw nestled in a hollow of a hill.

She pulled up in front of one of many log buildings, hoping it was the horse barn Rick had told her about last night when he phoned to make final preparations.

The phone call had been short. Becky held her questions back. Last night her very helpful sisters had let her know that Rick had been in church Sunday morning. The knowledge had been enough to lift her heart and kindle the faint hope she'd been nurturing since he'd held her hand in her father's orchard.

That moment hadn't been a turning point for her as much as a culmination of the attraction she had felt for him from the moment she saw him. She had tried to dismiss it as a mere physical draw of any woman to a man possessed of Rick's charm.

But she couldn't dismiss the connection she had felt with him then, and, it seemed, anytime they spoke or sparred. That he had come to church added another dimension to that connection.

Where would it go?

Becky got out of the car, shading her eyes against the morning sun as she looked around the yard. A bunch of horses stood patiently waiting in a corral off the horse barn, tails swishing at flies. The more impatient ones shuffled around raising dust that caught in Becky's throat. One horse lifted its head and looked beyond her, its ears pricked forward. Becky turned to see where it was looking.

And why did her heart give one long slow thump then begin racing faster than her car engine on high idle? All it took was the single glimpse of a thin trail of dust coming far down the road, one that could only be from Rick's Jeep, for her involuntary muscle to act even more involuntarily.

"Hey, Becky."

Becky spun around at the voice. The man coming toward her looked as if he had just stepped out of a Western. Tall, lanky, his face shaded from the bright sun by a large cowboy hat, his shirt dusty and sweat stained, his hands encased in leather gloves. The leather chaps swinging around his legs almost covered his slant-heeled boots.

He tugged a glove off his one hand and reached out to her as he tipped his hat back with another, his smile a white slash against his tanned face. His rugged features completed the image of the working cowboy.

"So this is where you ended up, Trevor," Becky said with a nod of recognition. "I should have figured that out."

"If you would have returned my phone calls you would have found out sooner that I was the newly appointed manager of the Triple Bar J." Trevor grinned at her, still holding her hand. "I heard you were coming and made sure I was going to be in charge of the ride."

"When did you start here?"

"A couple of weeks ago. In time to get in on this new thing the boss wanted to do with your magazine." He angled his head to one side, his smile melancholy. "So why didn't you call back?"

At one time, Trevor's interest would have made her heart skip. Now she was more aware of Rick's Jeep pulling up than a former boyfriend who had bruised her heart. "I had nothing to say."

"Well, do you have a smooch for an old boyfriend?" He slipped his arm around her shoulders, but Becky turned her head to one side.

"You can have a hug, but forget the kiss."

"I thought you might at least write me, Becks," he said, bumping her side lightly with his hip. "Didn't you miss me?"

Becky let her gaze tick over his dark hair, chiseled features finally resting on his soft brown eyes. "At first. A bit," she admitted reluctantly.

"But not after a while," he said. Becky shook her head, then turned, her heart giving a quick uptick as Rick closed the door of his vehicle, slung his camera bag over his shoulder and came walking toward them.

He wore a faded denim shirt tucked into equally faded blue jeans and a pair of leather boots that had that soft wrinkled look of steady use. As he sauntered toward them in his loose-hipped walk, Becky's heart started up again.

Trevor easily rivaled Rick in the looks department and

Trevor still had his arm across her shoulders. But it was Rick she couldn't keep her eyes off of when he stopped in front of them, pulling his sunglasses off and glancing from Becky to Trevor who held his hand out to Rick.

"You must be Rick Ethier. I'm Trevor Wilson. I'm in charge of the trail ride."

"And a few other things it seems," Rick drawled, and shook Trevor's hand, his eyes flicking over the other arm Trevor still had casually draped across Becky's shoulder.

"Trevor's an old friend," Becky said, surprised at Rick's tone. "Just returned from California via Colorado."

"I tried to convince Becky to come with me when I left, but she turned me down." Trevor gave Becky a one-armed hug. "She's got her roots down deep."

Becky laughed politely, gave Rick a bright smile and pulled herself gently out of Trevor's hold. "Where should I put my things?" she asked Trevor, her eyes noting the absence of Rick's gaze.

"I was told to show you two around the place first. Boss said you wanted to get some pictures of the spread," Trevor said. "The ride isn't scheduled to go out until noon." He grinned at Becky and made to put his arm around her again.

Becky sidestepped and flashed him a warning look. "Lead the way."

Trevor had gathered a lot of information in the short time he had been at the ranch and was a knowledgeable and amiable guide. But Becky made sure to keep her distance.

The ranch had been established at the turn of the century, when the only law was might made right. The original owner was a remittance man, the youngest son of a wealthy family, sent over to the New World because there was no land for him to inherit in England. He was one of the few who had turned his "remittance" from home into land and stock and slowly built up a small empire.

This empire had suffered and prospered through economic ebbs and flows. It was currently owned by a cartel of various businesses, a few with vague connections to ranching and cattle. As Rick snapped pictures, Becky tried to figure how to work the businesses into the article.

An hour and a half later they had worked their way back to the corrals, now a much busier place. People dressed in a variety of Western clothes stood either by their vehicles or by the corrals, watching the horses.

Thankfully Trevor left them to go help saddle up. But Rick followed him, leaving Becky alone and wondering if he had regretted the moment at her parents' place.

Okay. She could be casual, too, if that was how he wanted to play it. She spun on her heel and strode over to chat to a couple she recognized from church. In turn she was introduced to a few more people. Becky was pleased to discover that not all the riders were experienced. It had been a few years since she'd been on a horse, and was a little nervous.

"So I understand that's your new boss." The woman, Nola, angled her chin at Rick. She pushed her white straw cowboy hat off her head, as if to get a better look. "He's a sweetie," she said with a wink at Becky.

Becky glanced over her shoulder at Rick, who was resting his elbows on the corral fence, snapping pictures of the horses. *Sweetie* was not a word she would use with Rick, though at first sight, his poster-boy good looks could be deceiving. "He has his own charm," she conceded.

"Oh, c'mon, Becky. Admit it. He's a looker." Nola gave Becky a quick hug. "I know a dozen young women who would agree. More than a dozen."

Nola's gushing was embarrassing. At the same time it was as if her avid interest in Rick pulled down another of the flimsy barriers Becky had erected against Rick and the very charm Nola was so enthused over.

Yet part of her was annoyed. Rick was so much more than his looks, and she resented the fact that people saw only that part of him.

"I sure like what he's done with the magazine." Nola tipped her hat back as if to see him better. "He's really made a difference already."

"You don't mind all the ads?"

Nola shrugged. "I don't particularly care for them, and I do kinda miss Edna's corny advice that came with her recipes, but it's a balance, isn't it? I'll tell you what I really like is the way Runaround Sue and Rick are always butting heads. Who is that girl? She's a good writer."

"She's wanting to stay anonymous for now," Becky said vaguely, pleased with Nola's comment. "But I can pass it on."

"Well, you just pass that on to Rick right now. Don't bother spending time with us old folks." Nola gave Becky a push in Rick's direction at the same moment

Rick looked over at her. Her momentum carried her toward him. To stop and turn around would have been sillier than to keep going.

Casual and relaxed was called for, though Becky felt anything but.

Weather. That was always a safe topic.

"Trevor figures we won't be seeing much cloud cover," Becky said as she joined him at the fence. "You'll get some nice shots of the Rockies."

"I'm looking forward to that." Rick leaned his elbows on the corral fence, watching the wranglers and the horses, still holding his camera. "So how did you know Trevor?"

"High school fling. I was the editor of the school newspaper, he was the rodeo king." Becky joined him, stepping up on the first rail so she could see better. "Hardly the classic relationship of cheerleader, football quarterback, but those positions were already taken."

"So the old boyfriend has come back into your life."

Where did this cool tone in his voice come from? Becky tried to catch his gaze, but he was snapping pictures, using the rail as a rest.

"No. Trevor has come back to the Triple Bar J. I'm hardly a concern."

"So that's why you were able to make arrangements suddenly to come on the ride?" Rick asked, with a quick sideways look. "Because Trevor was back?"

If Becky didn't know better, she would have guessed he was jealous. "I didn't know Trevor worked here until I got here."

"You didn't keep up with his comings and goings?"

"Not really," she said. "The dust from his horse trailer had barely settled before I was on to other things."

This wasn't entirely true. She had mooned around the house, listened to Ian Tyson singing "Someday Soon" for months afterward and dreamed about following Trevor on the rodeo circuit. But he never called and Becky grew up and life flowed on, predictable and safe, her heart intact.

"Was there ever anyone else?" Rick asked, his tone casual.

"I've dated a few guys, but Okotoks is hardly the place to meet eligible young men. Most young people want to get out of here as soon as possible."

She wondered at Rick's sudden interest as she rested her chin on her hands watching Trevor sorting the horses. "How about you, Rick? Any old loves in your life?"

"I dated a few girls. Just never stayed in one place long enough to maintain a serious relationship."

A faint chill slivered through her, as if she was being warned. "Maybe you just haven't met the right person," she said carefully, hoping she sounded unconcerned. Then she made the mistake of looking sideways at him. He was looking at her and he wasn't smiling.

"That might be a reason," he said softly.

As she held his gaze, her heart gave a soft flip. And when he turned the camera to her and snapped a couple of pictures, she felt as if he had underlined his comment.

"You can't put those in the article," she said with a light laugh.

"I might find another use for them," he said, winding the film, and stepping off the fence. "We should go pick out our horses."

Half an hour later, Becky and Rick were part of a long column of riders snaking their way along a wooded trail heading up into the mountains. It had taken a bit of maneuvering on Rick's part to get him and Becky to take up the rear together. Fortunately Becky didn't know a lot about horses and Rick did. He'd been checking out the animals and made sure they ended up with passive horses. Now they were exactly where he wanted the two of them to be.

As far away from this Trevor guy as possible.

If it wasn't for the fact that Becky seemed genuinely uninterested in Trevor's obvious come-ons, he might have been more jealous.

Which was a first for him.

The sun was warm on his back, a faint breeze slid over his bared arms. Rick shifted in his saddle, each muffled footfall of the horse on the dirt path, each faint jingle of the horses' tack pushing away the tension that gripped his shoulders and neck. The past couple of weeks had been stressful. On top of getting the art and design team in line with what he wanted the magazine to do, he'd been busy getting potential advertisers aligned with the vision of *Going West,* setting up a budget they could fall within and yet put out a quality magazine.

The worst of his struggles were with the bank. He really shouldn't be going on this trip. He should be trying to get creative about getting the cash flow of the magazine healthy. But when Becky said she was coming on the ride, the cash flow became slightly less of a priority.

Becky turned around in her saddle, her hair loosely tied back, a few strands framing her face. "Isn't this gorgeous?" she said, her smile lighting up her features as she flung her arm to encompass the open space behind them, the trees below them, the mountains rising up. "On days like this, I love my job."

"I thought you loved it all the time?" Rick teased, pulling his horse up beside hers, encouraged by her welcoming smile.

"I do, but honestly, Rick, this is amazing." She shook her head, dropping it back to look up at a sky so blue it hurt. "What a beautiful country we live in."

Her good humor was infectious and Rick couldn't help the smile that started inside and slowly migrated to his face. She rolled her head lightly, looking askance at him. "What do you think?"

Rick reluctantly pulled his gaze away from Becky and let it flow over the mountains that guarded the valley they were heading up. Rock and snow, folded and bent, pushing up against the sky, overwhelming their tiny column of people, rendering them insignificant. At the same time he felt a sense of peace and protection. Security.

"It's amazing, really. That all this just...is. A picture can't begin to capture the depth and sweep of this valley."

"I lived close to the mountains all my life and I still can't figure out where to look when I look at them. I want to see them all at once, to let their sheer majesty take my breath away, and yet I want to be able to recognize certain parts of them, make them my own." Becky sighed lightly, leaning forward in the saddle. "I haven't come here enough. I'm glad we could do this."

So was he.

They crested a peak, then dropped down into a river valley, the horses ahead of them like a long train, wending its way over the trail.

Rick tied the reins of his horse to the saddle horn and unpacked the camera from the saddlebags. He stopped his horse, and Becky's stopped, as well. He snapped a few pictures of the riders ahead of them. Then, giving in to an impulse, turned and framed Becky against the backdrop of the mountains. Her bright red shirt created a sharp contrast to the azure sky and purple-hazed mountains.

"What are you doing?" She laughed, pushing her windblown hair back from her face. "I told you you're not going to be putting those in the magazine. Conflict of interest and all that."

Ignoring her, he zoomed in on her face. But she didn't look away. Her hazel eyes looked directly into the camera. The sincerity of her steady gaze and her warm smile slid into his heart. His finger trembled on the shutter as he took another picture, stored another memory on film.

"We should get going," Becky said as he lowered his camera, shaken by the innocent encounter. "We're going to fall behind."

Rick only nodded as he replaced the lens cap as Becky nudged her horse ahead. He slowly slipped the camera back into the bag, buying himself some time, trying to find a place for the strange quiver of emotions she had aroused. Being attracted to a woman was nothing new. But he never felt this peculiar yearning mingling with the attraction. And he hadn't even kissed her yet.

Maybe that was the problem.

His horse shook its head, jangling the bridle, signaling its impatience with Rick's dithering. Rick untied the reins, toed his horse in the ribs and easily caught up to Becky.

He kept his distance, watching her from behind as if seeing her for the first time. Occasionally she would throw back a long look that pulled at him, but he stayed where he was. He wasn't sure what to do with the emotions she had raised in him with just one look. Just one touch.

He had nothing to compare this to. He had never been, what might be technically called, "in love" with any other woman before. In college his friends had often waxed poetic about other women and he'd dated a number of women there, but never more than a couple of times and never long enough to get to know them the way he knew Becky.

"You're mighty quiet back there," Becky said, angling her head back so he could hear her. "I hope I didn't make some major faux pas that I have to apologize for."

"Not yet."

Becky let her horse slow down until he came alongside her. "That's good, because I've been trying to figure out why you're not trying to start an argument with me."

"Some of us like to look around and enjoy the scenery maybe instead of talking all the time," he said, reaching for a teasing tone to his voice.

"Point taken. I'll be quiet."

"Think you can do it?"

"You're the one that's talking now."

And a reply would only underscore her rather childish comment, so he kept quiet. And as long as the trail was wide enough, she stayed beside him, distracting him with her silence this time, instead of her words.

Two hours later, they pulled their horses up in a shaded spot beside a brook that frothed and danced over a rock bed, a counterpoint to the murmuring and groaning of the other riders.

Rick slowly dismounted, his legs stiff from the ride. It had been over a year since he had ridden and he felt it in every muscle from his hips to his knees.

Some of the other riders looked relaxed, others hobbled around looking even worse than Rick felt.

"I didn't even know I had muscles in the places I'm feeling them," Becky moaned, slipping off her saddle. "I should have done some riding before this."

Rick moved around his horse to get her reins, but Trevor was right there. "Y'all okay, darlin'?" he drawled. "Saddle settin' okay?"

"You seem to have picked up a Texas accent to match your chaps," Becky said with a laugh. "And my saddle is fine."

"Jest playin' the part," he returned with a grin. "I'll tie up your horse. Go get something to drink or eat. Glenda will help you." Trevor glanced over Rick's horse. "How are you doin'? Everything good?"

"I'm okay." As if he'd admit to this cowboy that he was painfully aware of every muscle in his legs. "Beautiful ride."

"And more to come," Trevor promised, all business now, his accent slipping away. "If you want, you can ride up in front. I can give you a bit of history of the place, point out some scenic views you might miss on your own."

"I'm doing okay at the back," he said.

As Rick tightened up the cinch strap he glanced over the top of his horse at Becky.

Trevor intercepted the direction of his eyes. "She's quite a woman, isn't she? Always smiling, laughing. I don't think I've ever seen her angry."

Rick lashed his strap down, still watching Becky as he remembered hazel eyes snapping, that pert mouth tight with disapproval as they clashed over the direction of articles and the balance of advertising and content. "I have," he said with a wry grin.

Trevor took hold of Rick's saddle horn and tugged on it, as if testing it. "Becky is special to me, Rick." He held Rick's gaze, his own narrowed. "Just thought I'd mention that."

"That's interesting," Rick said, taking up the thinly veiled challenge as he dropped the stirrup, gentling his horse as it shied at the sudden movement. "She's never mentioned you."

Trevor laughed that off, patted Rick's horse on the neck and left. Rick watched him move directly to Becky as if to stake his claim, but Becky turned away as he came near.

Chapter Nine

The murmur of conversation faded away behind her as Becky picked her way through the trees, walking down a worn game trail. It was still light out and she wanted to grab a few moments of writing, away from people and chitchat and being perky and cheerful.

And watching out for Rick.

She lost track of how many times she'd glanced around looking for him, trying to keep her attention on the person talking to her, all the while searching out and finding Rick's blond hair. His easy smile.

A refreshing cool slipped down the valley, pockets of it captured in the wooded area close to the creek. The late-evening sun slanted through the trees, its light softened. The noise of the group behind her grew more muffled, with each step she took replaced by the quiet sigh of the forest.

She found a large rock still warm from the sun. She kicked off her boots and socks and sat down, pulling in a deep cleansing breath. The whisper of the leaves overhead were like a gentle prayer, the gurgle of the creek over the rocks a soft counterpoint. It was always outside that she felt most inspired, and this was a picture-perfect spot.

From the notebook she had packed, she pulled at the pages she had printed. She glanced over them, reading what she had done before.

As her eyes skimmed over what she had already written, the peace she felt just a scant moment ago fell away. Once her writing had seemed lively, fresh, but now the words dropped like stones, unwieldy and overdone.

Her pen slashed across the sentences, eradicating what offended her.

Which was about half. She read and reread what she had left and after a moment's thought scratched that out, too. Drivel. Dreck.

She set the printed pages aside and pulled out her notebook. Maybe she should just journal—maybe get some ideas for future "Runaround Sue" columns. She scribbled a few words, chasing an idea with her pen.

A thought gelled, took form.

Soon her pen was flowing across the page, her hand barely able to keep up with the ideas that burst through her mind. She had more than enough material for a couple of columns, but she couldn't stop the energy that flowed and crackled.

"Hey, there."

Becky's pen jerked across the page leaving a black streak. She spun around, her heart pushing against her throat in anticipation and confusion.

Rick stood behind her, hipshot, a camera slung around his neck, his hands strung up in the pockets of his blue jeans, a half smile teasing his lips.

"I'm sorry, I didn't mean to scare you." He strolled across the open space to where she sat, then leaned against her rock, glancing down at what she was writing. "Working already?"

Becky slapped the notebook shut, her racing heart a combination of her exciting writing spurt and Rick's presence.

"Just noodling," she said, willing her heart to slow. "Getting some ideas together. Just fooling around, really." *And aren't you starting to sound like you have something to hide?*

"You must be inspired. I tried to get your attention a couple of times."

Becky gave him a half shrug as if dismissing what she had been doing. "Sorry. I get a tunnel vision when I'm busy with something." Still holding the notebook, she pulled her knees up to her chin.

Rick said nothing in reply, but she was as aware of his presence beside her as if he were shouting.

"So how do the mountains of Alberta compare to other parts of the world?" she asked, anxious to remove the discomfort she felt in his presence. Idle chitchat became her fluttery defense.

"I'm often reminded of New Zealand."

Becky rested her chin on her knees, her eyes on the creek, but her attention straining toward the man beside her. "What places haven't you been that you'd like to see?"

"Let's see." Rick settled down on the stone beside her, his shoulder brushing against hers. "China is a mystery. I've only seen a few parts of it. The Antarctic. I haven't been to Peru yet or the Falklands. I'd love to go kayaking down to Baja and even though I've been there a couple of times, I'd love to go back to Italy."

"I liked the piece you did on hostels there." Becky sighed lightly. "Made me want to go there."

"Why don't you?"

"I don't think I'd like to travel alone, and most of my friends ended up moving away and getting married before they could commit to a trip. I suppose I could go if I really wanted to, but I'm usually too busy."

"Way too busy. I'm surprised you get as much done as you do."

"I have to write everything down." She blushed as she thought of her Day-Timer in his hands. "But you know that."

"How did you end up so involved?"

"We have a very active church, lots of young families. But they can't do a lot of the work because they are young families." She shrugged. "So someone needs to do the things that need to get done."

"And that someone seems to be you."

"I don't run the church single-handedly." Did she sound as if she did it all?

"No. But you seem to be carrying a lot of the burden."

"I just want to be a wise steward of the gifts God has given me."

Rick tapped the book on her lap. "And one of your

gifts is this. Something you said yourself you don't spend enough time on."

You don't find time, you make time.

"I need to learn to trust in God to help me find the time."

"That may be," Rick said quietly. "But maybe you also need to learn to say no. To stop thinking if you don't do a job, it won't get done. If you do that, you might make more time for your writing. And maybe some traveling."

"Maybe I'm just a homebody."

Rick smiled at that. "Nothing wrong with that when you've got a good home to be in."

Becky turned her head toward him, wondering if she'd imagined the wistful tone in his voice.

"I've always been thankful for my home," she said quietly. "For the faith I was taught there, a faith that has grown over the years."

Rick's sigh drifted through the still air. "Well, that's another place you and I differ. Faith and family—neither have been a part of my life for a long time."

"But you grew up with it?"

Rick nodded. "I was taught all the right things, but traveling around the world, seeing the things I have..." He shrugged lightly. "Like I told your grandmother, I can't believe in a God that allows so much suffering."

Becky had heard this refrain so many times from people who wanted to ignore God, she was surprised Rick wasn't at least a little more original. "And what about what you're looking at now? What about this beautiful place? What about the people you've already met? What about all the good things that happen in the world?"

"What about it?"

"How can you not believe in a God who allows so much good? Who blesses us with so many good things? If you are going to acknowledge the one, you have to acknowledge the other."

Becky looked away, hoping, praying that God could use her words. "Life is so incredibly complex and intertwined, so intricate. You just have to look at how an eye works, our lungs, our thoughts. Trees. Leaves. Photosynthesis." She stumbled over her words, trying to encapsulate Creation in the limited medium of conversation. "It's so amazing and breathtaking.... There's no way you can believe this just happened. And if it didn't just happen, then where did it come from? Who made it? And if you acknowledge that someone made it, you have to realize this was a great and powerful God who did—"

Becky felt Rick's hand on her shoulder. She stopped talking and turned to him.

"Such passion," he said softly. "You almost persuade me...."

Becky's breath caught in her throat. And she winged up another quick prayer. "I think you believe already, Rick. I think you just need to acknowledge that God cares about you. That He wants you to be a part of Him."

Rick tipped his head to one side. "And that's a problem, I'll admit."

Becky's heart brightened. It was small. But it was a start. *Please, Lord, help him let go. Help him to know that he needs Your saving grace.*

As their gazes met, a connection trembled between them, as real as a touch.

A faint breeze sifted down through the trees, catching Becky's hair and tossing it lightly across her cheeks. Rick reached out and tucked her hair behind her ear, letting his hand linger on her face.

This had to stop.

She put aside her notebook, jumped off the rock and headed out to the creek.

"What are you doing?" Rick called out.

Cooling off. Giving myself some breathing space.

"I just feel like wading." She carefully picked her way across the large stones, smoothed by centuries of water flowing over them.

"You're going to freeze your feet in that cold water. It's coming right off the glacier."

Becky ignored him and rolled up her jeans. She stepped out into the water and ice clutched her feet with numbing fingers. She sucked in her breath and took a few more halting steps, her arms flailing to catch her balance on feet she could hardly feel. This was ridiculous, but she wasn't going to back down.

"Look at me," Rick said. "I want to catch that expression on your face."

She spun around, holding her hand up in warning as she tottered on feet now totally devoid of feeling. "Don't you dare, Rick Ethier."

But he was already winding the camera. "I did dare." He walked closer and took another picture.

Becky bent over and scooped her hand through the water, spraying him.

Rick jerked his shoulder aside to protect his camera. When he turned back to her, his lopsided grin did not bode well.

He laid the camera down. "That was not a good idea, missy," he said, rolling up his sleeves. Too late she realized what he was going to do and tried to take a step away, but her ice-cold feet wouldn't respond. "I'm sorry, Rick."

"Too late for apologies."

He splashed toward her in his boots and before she could move again, he caught her around her shoulders, under her knees and swung her off her feet.

She shrieked and tried to fight him, but he was much stronger than she was.

"Put me down," she squealed, pushing against his chest as he waded farther out into the creek.

"That camera has been my constant companion for many years," he said, shaking his head. "Trying to make it wet was a declaration of war."

She grabbed on to his neck, fully conscious of the ice-cold water splashing below them. "If you drop me, I'll take you with."

He grinned down at her, his wide smile bracketed by dimples and lighting up his whole face. "That sounds like a challenge," he said softly.

"And you can never turn that down."

"How well you know me." Rick looked down at her but didn't move.

Becky had a sense of time wheeling around the two of them. Slowing. Rick's smile faded as their gazes locked, their breaths mingling. And then, without any forewarning, his lips touched hers, softly first, then more firmly.

Breathe, she reminded herself when he drew back, his eyes clouded now with an indefinable emotion. His eyes flicked over her face, as if seeking some clue there as to what had just happened.

In silence he touched his lips to hers again, then turned and strode back with her to the rock she had been sitting on. He set her down as carefully as if she were some fragile creature. Then he knelt down beside her, brushing her hair unnecessarily back from her face, his fingers trailing down the side of her face.

Becky caught his hand. As she pressed it to her cheek, confusion wrestled with attraction.

This was wonderful.

This wasn't a good idea.

He wasn't on the same level spiritually as she was.

He was seeking.

She lowered his hand to her lap, and held it there. On the back of his hand was a faint star-shaped scar. She traced it lightly again and again as she tried to put these new emotions into the proper place in her life. Her mind told her one thing, her heart another.

A heart that had never been touched like this. It scared her that it was Rick, temporary and negative, who had been the one to do so.

"Is something wrong, Becky?" he asked, tipping her chin up with his other hand. "You're so quiet."

"I'm not sure what to do. How to feel." She laughed lightly, suddenly self-conscious as she looked up at him. "I'm not the casual dating type, Rick. I never wanted to fall into that pattern."

"I know." Rick stroked her chin with his thumb, a serious cast to his expression. "Your grandmother sent me a not so veiled warning where you were concerned."

"She would." Becky tried to laugh, to ease the tension that gripped her heart.

"So this is where I should apologize for kissing you."

"Why?"

Rick hunkered back on his heels and picked up her foot. "Because if you don't believe in casual dating, you don't believe in casual kissing." He started massaging her foot, which only succeeded in heightening Becky's confusion.

"Was that what that was? A casual kiss?"

Rick kept his head bent over her feet. "I don't know what it was, Becky." He rubbed her foot harder. "My goodness, girl. Your feet are like ice."

Becky let it go. She was too confused to even know which emotion to track down. Which feeling was real. With Rick she had to depend on her head to guide her. Not her heart.

"You did warn me about the cold water," she said, moving the conversation to a safer place.

"Some people have to find things out the hard way, I guess."

He took her other foot in his hands and rubbed it, too, bringing the circulation back.

"What about you? You got your boots wet. The bottom of your pants, too."

Rick shrugged her concerns away. "These boots have been in water before. I'll dry them at the campfire." Rick lowered her foot and picked up her shoes and socks. "At least yours are dry."

"At least if I'm going wading, I do some planning." She slipped her socks on, thankful for the return to the usual conversational mode.

"Spontaneity is the spice of life." Rick stood and helped her off the rock. "Don't forget your notebook."

"And you don't forget your camera."

Rick shook his head. "Have to have the last word, don't you?"

But Becky just smiled back in spite of everything and picked up her notebook. Once again Rick had put her in a self-defeating position.

The night sky was endless.

If he looked at the scattered stars long enough, he could get lost, sucked into the vast depths of a universe unmeasured and incomprehensible by man's tiny mind.

Better to stay grounded here, lying on the plain, hard dirt. Rick sighed lightly, tucking his hands behind his head, tracing the constellations in the sky as the point of a rock dug into his hip.

God's creation.

He could still hear Becky's exuberant voice challenging him not to believe in God when His hand was so evident.

It wasn't that Rick didn't believe in God. He just wished he could understand Him a little better. Could feel like he, Rick, deserved to be a part of God's community.

A sliver of light streaked silently across the sky and Rick smiled, wishing Becky could have seen it. She would have expressed the appropriate awe instead of figuring out the purpose of pieces of rock burning up through the atmosphere.

Maybe he needed to stop critiquing and listen more. Maybe he needed to go looking for God, instead of waiting for his questions to be answered.

Rick yawned and pushed himself off the ground, glancing once more at the vast sky above him. Fragments of a Bible verse came back to him.

"When I consider the heavens...the works of Your hands...what is man that Thou art mindful of Him..."

What indeed?

Rick swung the saddle on his horse, his gaze sweeping the campsite as he did. How easily he found her. Like his internal radar had an automatic "Becky" setting.

She was washing up the dishes from breakfast in the central opening of camp, chatting and laughing with the two women helping her. She wore her hair up this morning, emphasizing the delicate bone structure of her face. At that moment she looked up and found him. A tentative smile edged her lips but then she glanced away again.

All morning she had kept her distance from him and he had respected it, but all morning he found himself hearing only her voice above other voices. Seeing only her face.

His horse nudged his shoulder with his head, as if pulling his attention to the job at hand. Rick laughed to himself and bent down to bring the cinch up and around. With a few flips of the latigo he had it on enough to hold it for now. He would tighten it before they left.

Becky was gone.

Which was just as well. He did have work to do.

He loaded up his camera and walked around. He already had seven rolls' worth of pictures, but he wanted to make sure he had captured the obvious enthusiasm the people had for this trip.

It was his last opportunity. When the group headed out farther up the valley, he and Becky and their guide would return to the ranch.

He wanted to stay here, in this place away from the office, away from the stress and pressures of the magazine and its relentless deadlines.

He wanted to go back to the creek and sit with Becky and talk to her. Try to capture her optimistic faith, her enthusiasm for life. She was the first woman he had met who wasn't afraid to stand up to him and who could make him laugh—sometimes both at the same time.

She was the first woman who could steal his breath with one look.

Rick tried to reason his way past his growing attraction to her. But nothing fit his usual reasons. Yes, she was pretty. Yes, she was fun. Yes, she could laugh.

She had depth, a grounding in her personal life and in her religious life. She wasn't afraid to talk about her faith. Nor to challenge him to take a second look at his own lack. She had an utter confidence in who she was.

It drew him on even as it frightened him away.

He walked around the string of packhorses, seeing it through the lens of his camera as the wranglers weighed the boxes, balanced the loads and hung them on the animals.

A few flies buzzed around in the cool morning air. The horses blew and stomped their hooves, as if anxious to be off, while the men threw tarps over their packs. Then they lashed them down, wrapping the ropes in an intricate pattern, working in a harmony that looked like a dance.

"You want to learn how to throw a diamond?"

Rick lowered his camera and glanced sidelong at Trevor who stood beside him, holding a length of soft rope.

It was on the tip of his tongue to refuse. He didn't need to prove himself. Then he caught the faint challenge in Trevor's eyes.

"That would be interesting." Rick covered his camera up and took it off his neck, looking for a place to set it.

"I'll take it." Becky was beside him, her hand held out. "If you can trust me with it." Her smile was like a light, drawing him on.

Suddenly the day was brighter.

"I don't know." He smiled back, picking up her infectious humor. "You tried to drown it yesterday."

Becky pressed one hand on her heart. "I promise I will treat it with the respect your constant companion deserves."

"You're sounding a little disrespectful right now," he said, letting go of the camera.

"And you are a suspicious man." Mischief glinted in her eyes, and he had to laugh.

"And you always have to have the last word."

"This is really cute, but the horses are waiting," Trevor broke in, sounding impatient.

"Lead the way," Rick said, not responding to Becky's saucy wink.

In spite of his pique, Trevor was a patient teacher. Rick gained a new appreciation of the science of packing horses as he learned to balance the weight of the load and lay down the ropes over the tarp.

"You want the tension of the rope spread evenly over the whole pack," Trevor explained as he stood beside Rick, showing him how to tighten the ropes. "The horse feels more comfortable and that makes him less likely to go ballistic in the middle of a bog. A well tied pack saves you from fishin' instant-porridge packages out the water."

"Sounds like a good incentive."

"So all you need to do is tighten 'er up." Trevor made a motion to the wrangler on the other side of the pack-horse and Rick followed his rhythm as they took turns pulling on the rope.

Trevor showed Rick how to tie the knot and the job was done.

"Hey, boys, how about a smile?" Becky called out.

Rick looked up just in time to see Becky's face obscured by the camera.

"Don't waste film, Becky," he called out, holding up his hand.

"Too late. This is the fourth picture." Becky lowered the camera, grinning at the two of them. "And now the film is full."

She handed him the camera with a wink, spun on her heel and walked away. And Rick's gaze followed her every step.

Half an hour later, the group mounted up and Rick shot some final pictures as the group left them, waving and laughing. Before he became publisher of a magazine, he could have simply mounted up and followed them, making decisions on the fly. But now he had obligations waiting.

Hopefully only a few more months and that would be over, as well. But as he turned around, he saw Becky sitting on her horse, waiting for him to accompany her and the wrangler who was to guide them back. Back to responsibilities and decisions that dragged him down and pinned him here.

He felt as if he stood at a pivotal point—his past moving away from him deeper into the mountains—his future represented by Becky and the magazine.

It frightened him. For the first time in his life he didn't know which called him stronger.

He swung onto his horse and without waiting for Becky, he urged it on down the path. Back to the ranch and back to Okotoks.

But as he rode, Becky's presence hovered behind him, an allure that battled with his desire for freedom. He stayed ahead of her, as if trying to outrun it.

Chapter Ten

"Rick back yet?" Becky leaned on the divider, hoping her voice sounded more nonchalant than she felt.

Trixie glanced up from her computer and slowly shook her head. "Sorry, babe. All I got was a call on Tuesday night at home saying he was going to be gone a few days." Trixie's eyes were full of sympathy and Becky knew, with a sinking heart, that her attraction to Rick was growing more obvious.

"Okay. I suppose he'll call if he has anything to tell me." Becky gave Trixie a tight smile, scooped up her mail and walked down the hall. Her steps slowed as she passed Rick's office. The door was closed as it had been for the past two days.

They had made good time coming back down the valley. Rick had been in the lead and set a brisk pace. Once in a while he would stop to take pictures, but even then he didn't speak to her. Becky gave up trying to catch up. When they got back to the ranch he had his horse unsaddled and the tack taken care of before she had barely dismounted. He was gone while she was still walking her horse. The next day she had come to the office early, hoping to talk to him.

All that was waiting for her was a cryptic note in Rick's bold handwriting lying on her desk.

"Gone for a few days. Be back day after tomorrow."

As she dropped into her seat she looked out the window, her gaze drawn to the ridge of mountains on the horizon, as if she could find the answer to Rick's elusive behavior there. Resting her chin on her hands, she let her mind wander back to those few magical days they had spent together. Correction, one day. What had happened the second day still bewildered her. It had started out so promising. Then, when it was time for them to go back, the very act of turning around had shifted his attention away from her.

She could still see him, leaning forward in the saddle, as if moving toward something. Or away from her?

Her fingers brushed her lips, reliving his kiss. A kiss that had buried itself deep in her heart. The kiss that had sent her heart soaring, her mind following.

He's going.

Reality knifed through the soft daydreams she had spun. How could she be so foolish?

Her eyes drifted closed, her heart reaching out to the one secure love in her life.

Oh, Lord, am I attaching too much importance to one simple gesture? Should I have stopped him?

But even as she prayed, she felt his hand on her

cheek, saw his head bent over her feet, felt his hands rubbing warmth back into them.

She pressed her hand to her heart as if to hold it steady. Keep it captive. Because to give it to Rick was to open herself to pain and heartbreak. Yet how could she ignore the surge of her heart whenever she saw him? The tangible connection she felt whenever they spoke?

She had never felt this way around a man. Was she so shallow as to fall for someone whose smile lit up his whole face? Whose eyes delved deep into her soul?

She yanked open the drawer beside her and pulled out her Bible, seeking comfort from the familiar words. As her fingers flipped through the pages she stopped at Psalm 52, drawing the words into her heart, allowing them to take root.

"But I am like a healthy olive tree. My roots are deep in the house of God. I trust in Your faithful love forever and ever."

The words reminded her that she was first and foremost a child of God. That she was grounded in His unfailing love and salvation. He was always faithful, always there, always loving.

Forgive me, Lord, she prayed. She closed her eyes and drew in a long slow breath.

Then jumped when she felt a hand drop on her shoulder. She jerked her head up and started inwardly when she looked into Rick's face. A ghost of a smile drifted over his lips, and his eyes softened as he looked down on her.

Relax. Breathe.

"Hey, there," he said, his voice washing over her like rain on parched ground. "How are you?"

Remember what you just read. You are a child of God. Rooted and grounded in Him.

"I'm doing fine."

As if sensing the detachment in her voice, he removed his hand. "Did you get my note? Sorry I didn't phone."

"I'm not your boss. Or your keeper." The words were harsh, but it was too late to retract or rephrase.

Let it lie. Better if you create some distance.

Rick took a step back, surprise creeping over his face. He moved around to the front of her desk and stood there as if waiting for something more.

Becky pressed her lips together, holding back the questions begging to be let out. Where were you? Why did you run away? Why didn't you call?

One kiss, a few glances exchanged did not give her any rights.

"Have you had a chance to work on the article for the trail ride?" he asked, slipping his hands into the pockets of his blue jeans in a gesture of retreat.

"I've been run off my feet, but I did have a chance to rough it out. I can print out what I have if you want to have a look at it."

So casual. So cold and unfeeling. It was as if that moment at the creek had never even happened. It was what she wanted, wasn't it?

He nodded, a quick jerk of his head. "There's no rush. Whenever you're ready. I've got the pictures on it already." He paused a moment, as if he wanted to say something, but then turned and left.

The click of the door resounded through the quiet of Becky's office and in spite of her self-talk, all her good intentions, the harshness of that sound cut her to the core.

And for once she was thankful for the relentless deadlines of her work that kept her tired mind busy and distracted from the confusion Rick posed.

She stifled a tired yawn and went back to work.

He should have called her. Rick knew that now. But when he jumped into his Jeep that evening, the only thing on his mind was running. Leaving. Finding some breathing room. He didn't *have* to meet with that marketing advisor in Calgary. Nor did he *have* to head up to Edmonton to get some quotes from a printing company.

Becky had given him much to think about and he needed time to sort it out. Find a place for it in his life. Figure out what to do with it.

He dropped into his chair, spun it around so it faced the window. He then lifted his feet to rest on the low sill. All he could see from this position were the mountains where he had just spent two days that had spun his world around, rearranged all his plans and expectations.

One kiss. That was all they had shared but that was all it took to make him realize that Becky had become integral to his life.

And that was what made him run. She represented security. Stability. Numbing routine.

God.

Rick closed his eyes a moment, remembering her passion when she talked about Creation. And once again what she said spoke to a deeper part of him. He knew God existed. He knew God was there.

It was easy to believe in God around Becky. Harder when he was on his own. All the accusations he had hurled at God when he was alone in his bedroom, wishing that he still had his mother, came hurtling back. Surely God didn't want to have anything to do with someone who was angry with Him?

How can you not believe in a God who allows so much good?

Rick hadn't been able to erase those words from his mind. They spun, whirled and at the same time comforted. Against his will, Becky was showing him a different side of God. A side he never saw in his grandfather.

So what do I do now, Lord? I'm allowed to ask You the hard questions. So why do You allow suffering? Why do You let people be lonely and hurt?

He waited, listening.

Nothing. Not surprising.

With a heavy sigh, he half turned, grabbing the envelope of pictures off the desk. He had just gotten them developed. A lot of magazines used digital cameras, but he preferred the clarity of analog.

He opened the envelope, pulled out the pictures and started flipping through them. Ranch house. Outbuildings. More buildings. Trevor in full cowboy mode.

Becky.

He stopped, lifting the picture to get a better look.

She was looking at him, a light frown crinkling her forehead. In the next picture she was smiling.

He set them aside and flipped quickly through the rest. The lighting had been perfect, showing the mountains in all their glory. Some of the pictures could almost be called cliché mountain shots, but he had managed to zoom in and isolate some of the views, creating a different look.

They would look great in the magazine.

There's no way you can believe this just happened. As Becky's challenge to him strayed into his mind, he turned to the next picture. And his heart quickened.

Becky astride a horse, framed against an achingly blue sky, the mountains a mere backdrop to her beauty. The wind had lifted her hair from her face so that it framed her delicate features in an aureole of auburn. She was smiling—a full-featured Becky smile that came from deep within her.

Rick leaned back, touching Becky's face with one finger as if trying to resurrect her, resurrect the emotions that had arced between them that moment at the creek, at her father's orchard.

He should have told her where he'd been the past few days, but that would mean telling her why he had run off. Which would mean delving into reasons that frightened and exhilarated him at the same time.

Reasons that involved Becky and feelings that had changed from simple acknowledgment of her good looks, to admiration for her spunk and ability to stand up to him, to respect for her deep faith to something deeper and unidentifiable.

Something that trembled at the edge of his consciousness, luring him into a place he had never been before.

A place that was a curious combination of love and faith.

He flipped through the rest of the pictures, sorting them out into their various groupings. Scenery. People. Horses.

Becky.

Becky doing dishes. Becky laughing and chatting with a group of people. Becky wading in the creek, her teeth clenched against the cold.

Becky warning him not to take the picture he was now looking at.

He turned around and propped the picture against his telephone, remembering what had followed that moment. How she had touched his heart in so many ways.

So what next?

He knew he messed up when he took off without telling her, and now she was ticked off.

Might be better that way. They would slowly move away from each other, keeping their relationship purely professional, and when it was time for him to leave there would be no hard feelings.

So why did the thought leave an empty ache in his heart?

The light knock at the door was a welcome intrusion to thoughts that spun, unresolved. Trixie put her head around the corner. "Mr. McElroy to see you about the advertorial you were going to put in an upcoming issue?"

And Rick was dropped back into the turning around of a magazine. His ticket out of this town.

"I thought the focus of the article was the business aspect." Rick tapped his pen against his chin as he skimmed over the pages Becky had given him. She had dropped the article on his desk late last night, with a brief note asking for his input.

So now he was giving it and she didn't look pleased.

"I thought I brought in enough of the business angle, by maintaining the history of the ranch and how it got to the current owners and their involvement in the community."

"I think they were looking for a heavier slant."

Becky's sigh clearly telegraphed to him that she was going to dig in her heels. And to his own surprise, he was looking forward to what she had to say. Anytime they'd struggled over articles, they'd found a compromise which, surprisingly, made for a stronger article than either of them would have written alone.

"We were invited by Triple Bar J to go riding in the mountains, Rick, surrounded by God's wonderful and amazing creation. Unless they're paying to do the entire article, I think we better stick with more of a story slant to the article."

Becky slouched back in her chair, her arms folded over her chest, staring blankly at the window behind him with her head against the back of the chair. She looked totally disinterested.

He didn't have to be literate to read her body language.

With a sinking heart he realized they were back to where they had started the very first day he had met her here in Nelson's office. For a moment he was tempted to pull out the picture of her that he had gotten enlarged, just to remind himself that there was another time and another place when she had smiled at him. When she had kissed him.

He blinked the thoughts away, dragging his attention back to the article. "It's not an advertorial, but they did invite us free of charge. Besides, every event can be slanted in a certain way to highlight the things you want to say. In this case you might want to focus on who is involved in the trail ride and what brings them there. Who they are and what businesses they represent."

He didn't look up, preferring to look at her words rather than her face. Easier to read what he wanted into the black-and-white medium of paper and ink. She didn't say anything so he continued.

"Your descriptions are evocative. You have a way with words." What she had given him had a wonderful flow that he didn't want to break up, yet he knew he had to emphasize the business aspect of the company. That was his focus for *Going West*.

He tapped the paper with his pen, thinking, trying to find a compromise that would work for either of them, surprised she hadn't challenged him again.

"I suppose we could work the business aspect into a sidebar. Expand on it there without losing the integrity of what you've written. What do you think?"

He waited for her comment on this concession and when none came, he looked up.

She was asleep.

Rick rested his elbows on his desk and leaned forward, watching her. Allowing himself this moment to let his eyes pass over her face, to remember her smile.

Her head drifted to one side, then jerked.

Staying in the chair would give her a horrible crick in her neck, but he didn't want to wake her up.

He got up and cleared off the couch, then walked back to her side. Carefully, so as not to wake her, he fitted his arm under her knees, around her shoulders and carefully picked her up. It was only a few steps to the couch, but he moved slowly, afraid to wake her. Afraid to let go of her.

She shifted in his arms, and he gently laid her down. She stretched out, groaned, then muttered a few words, frowning in her sleep as she flopped over onto her side.

Her hair had fallen across her face and her lips twitched as if in annoyance. Rick took a chance and carefully brushed her hair back, once again allowing his hand to linger on the soft curve of her cheek.

He knew he was treading on dangerous ground, but he couldn't stop himself. She shifted on the couch, pulling her arm up beside her face then, incredibly, a smile tugged at her lips.

He felt a clench of longing and, giving in to an impulse, bent over and brushed his lips over her forehead, inhaling the soft sweet scent of her hair, her skin.

He sat back on his heels, laughing shortly at his own foolish impulse, then got up and walked back to his desk. He grabbed her article and took it out of the office. He could just as easily look it over in the coffee shop across the way.

But before he closed the door, he chanced one more look at Becky.

Her eyes were open and she was watching him.

"So far, our subscriptions are slowly moving up. I guess the ad campaign is doing what it was supposed to, but we're still bleeding red ink." Trixie handed Rick and Becky each some papers stapled together. "You'll see that we've spent a lot more on drumming up new business in the last quarter."

Becky chewed on her bottom lip as she looked over the figures. Numbers weren't her strong point, but it didn't take a degree in accounting to compare figures and know that they were falling behind.

"Our own advertising income is slowly increasing and I know we've picked up a few more accounts," Rick put in from his perch on the edge of his desk, swinging his foot back and forth. He seldom sat down during their business meetings. He was often pacing around, talking aloud, urging the sales force on, challenging the art department and placating Trixie. "Subscriptions are edging up. I think we're getting close. If we can up the advertising, we can get a better influx of cash."

"But we still have to maintain a balance between ads and content," Becky said, glancing over the rest of the figures. "People buy the magazine because of the teasers on the cover. And if they have to go burrowing through twenty pages of ads in order to get to what they were looking for you're going to get frustrated readers. Which doesn't translate into increased subscriptions."

"But we need the ads for revenue. And they need space."

Becky looked up at him, her momentary pique tempered by a gentle thrill when she caught his eye. So easily she felt again the touch of his lips on her forehead.

He held her gaze, those same lips softening in a gentle smile.

Focus, Becky, focus. Your job is on the line here. This magazine can't keep operating in the red.

"People are willing to put up with a certain amount of advertising to read articles with good content. Cut that back and you're going to see your subscriptions go down. When that happens, ad revenues go down."

Rick's lazy smile kicked her heart up a notch, but she held his gaze, determined to keep this part of her life professional.

"A tricky balancing act," Rick said softly.

She wondered if his comment was as innocent as a mere agreement. No matter. She was still an editor. He was still a publisher. And though the lines were growing increasingly blurred, she was determined to keep her focus when she could.

"It can be done," she said, lifting her chin a notch. "If there's a vision to see growth over the long term, rather than short. And if we are willing to slow the pace of the change."

"Commitment, in other words."

Becky frowned, sensing a wealth of meaning beneath the simple comment. But she wasn't going to go fishing in that pool. She looked back down at the paper. "I want to keep this job for a long time, so obviously my focus, my vision for *Going West,* is slow but steady growth."

Rick blew out his breath in a long sigh but Becky kept her eyes down.

"How ever we look at it, we're going to need a better month than this one. For the next month we've got a good lineup but I'm pretty sure the month after that is going to be the turning point." Rick paused, as if waiting to get Becky's attention. She reluctantly looked back at him.

"Do you have the interview with the premier sewn up?"

"All set for this Thursday." She held his gaze and once again felt an involuntary quiver.

"Good. That, combined with the Triple J ride, will give the magazine some meat. Excellent."

He didn't exactly rub his hands, but Becky easily sensed his enthusiasm and excitement. How could he be so positive when things looked so bleak for the magazine? *Going West* had seen tough times during Nelson's tenure, but never had they been so far down financially as they were now.

"In the meantime, we still have a serious cash-flow problem, Rick," Trixie said. "We need to figure out how to solve that."

Becky's earlier thrill was washed away by a rush of dread. This magazine might be just a project to Rick, but for her it was her livelihood until she sold her book. But to sell, she had to finish—and how was she going to find time to do that?

"Well, I'll see what we can do about that." Rick jumped off the desk, seemingly unfazed by this new disaster. And why should he be? If the magazine failed he would move back to Toronto and work for his grandfather.

She would be stuck back here in Okotoks trying to figure out how to make a living.

And trying to figure out if she could live without Rick.

* * *

"I'm on my way to an important interview right now, Terry. I can't come to the bank." Rick spun the steering wheel one-handed around the corner and glanced at Becky who was trying not to look as if she was listening to the conversation. "Well, let me know as soon as you find out. And don't forget, Terry, this magazine is going to go places. Don't bail on me."

He disconnected and dropped his phone into a pocket of his vest, stifling his impatience.

"I'm guessing that was the bank," Becky said after a moment.

Rick shook his head in disgust. "Terry is getting antsy. He wanted me to come to a meeting to justify the bank's extending our line of credit. A few years ago banks gave away loans like they were popcorn prizes. Now, even though they are still making record profits, they're going into deep miser mode."

Thankfully Becky said nothing. He didn't want to talk about the magazine's financial woes. Not when he was on his way to an interview that had the potential to change everything.

He came to a halt at a quiet intersection. "Where do we go from here?"

"Follow the road along the ravine until you come to a cul-de-sac. He lives at the end."

The homes grew farther apart as they drove. Not the wealthiest section of the city, but money was definitely in evidence here. Old and new money from the looks of the houses and the towering elm trees sheltering the road.

The whole effect was one of seclusion and genteel country right in the middle of the city.

They parked in front of the house and were greeted by a tall, unsmiling man who checked them over.

"Where's your notepad?" Rick whispered as they were led to the back of the premier's house.

"I'm not going to write things down. I'm just going to use the tape."

"Backup, Becky. You know the first rule of journalism." Rick caught her arm just before they entered the backyard. "You're not going to catch everything." Was she trying to sabotage this interview?

"Maybe not, but I think he'll be more relaxed if I'm not scribbling down everything he says. Makes it look like I'm not listening if I do that." Becky flashed a smile at Rick but at the same time she tried to pull her arm free.

Rick wasn't ready to let go of her yet. "Do you mind if I write something down?"

"You'll be too busy taking pictures." Becky stopped pulling, but looked away from him. "Please trust me to do this interview my way, Rick," she said softly.

Rick reluctantly let go of her arm and reluctantly agreed.

Jake, dressed casually in jeans and a golf shirt, sat at a patio table. He looked tanned, fit and in charge. But when he saw Becky, his smile lit up his face, giving him the boyish charm that made many a single woman's heart beat just a little faster.

That the same charm was directed at Becky gave Rick the same foolish twinge of jealousy he felt around Trevor.

Becky introduced Rick and he noticed Jake's polite but forced smile. Noticed a sudden wariness. "I've read a number of your articles, Rick," he said, the polite heartiness in his voice the hallmark of a good politician. "Very insightful, though at times negative."

"Not what you're going to see in *Going West,*" Becky said, glancing nervously from one to the other. "We're interested in getting to know you as a person." Becky laughed lightly, touching Jake on the arm, drawing his attention back to her. "Because I know another side of you that you don't always let out."

Jake flashed his smile back at Becky now. "Glad to hear that. Shall we sit down?" Jake waved to the table he had been sitting at.

"You know what, Jake? It's such a lovely yard. Why don't you show me around it?" Becky said with a quick smile, looking around the immaculately groomed yard. "I recognize some of the same plants Dad has, but others are different."

Though the yard didn't have the same vigor and charm that Becky's father's had, it was still a showpiece. Flowers and shrubs edged a large expanse of golf-course grass. A cedar gazebo was tucked away in a far corner against tall trees, also edged with flower gardens.

"You don't have the fountain yet," Becky commented as they strolled down an inlaid brick path that broke up the lawn.

"That's coming soon. I'm not sure what kind to put in."

"You take care of this yard yourself?" Rick asked, slipping the covers off the lenses of his cameras. He had two slung around his neck, each with different lenses giving him a variety of options.

"When I have time. I employ a gardener during spring session of the legislature, but when I'm not traveling I try to spend time here."

"Is that an Intrigue rose?" Becky stopped by a rounded bush resplendent with deep purple-red, showy roses, and dropped to one knee. She bent over, touching a flower with one hand, inhaling deeply. "Oh, smell that. Very strong citrus smell. Where did you get this one? My dad's been itching to get one for a while now."

"Hole's Greenhouse in Edmonton. I got the last one a year ago."

"Amazing." Becky smiled and gently touched one of the flowers. "They are so beautiful."

Jake hunkered down beside her, and as they chatted about the pros and cons of raising tender roses in a prairie climate, Rick went to work snapping pictures. He worked carefully, trying to remain inconspicuous as possible, yet listening at the same time.

They moved on to some of his other flowering plants. Rick was lost in all the talk about pruning, mulching, bone meal and dividing, but Becky had complete control of the conversation at all times. She gently led Jake from a discussion on sedum to environmental issues, from admiring his lilies to health-care funding. Rick couldn't help but admire her style.

She pitched her voice a few notes lower, creating an air of intimacy. She made eye contact frequently, occasionally touching Jake on the arm to underline a question or a point. Each time he spoke she leaned forward ever so slightly, showing him that he had her complete attention.

And the most interesting part of it all, Rick knew that with Becky it wasn't just a game. A way of getting information from this elusive man. It was a genuine interest in his hobby, in him as a person.

By the time they had gone through the garden, and were sitting at the patio table with a glass of lemonade in front of each of them, Jake looked far more relaxed than he had when they began the interview. Rick positioned them for a photo so they were facing each other with Jake's chair slightly angled away from where Rick had planned on sitting. He wanted to be able to listen but at the same time be as unobtrusive as possible.

"I think it's fascinating how you're trying to focus on native prairie plants. I should get my father to partner with you on that," Becky said as she casually dropped her tape recorder on the table. "I'll need to record this. Do you mind?" she asked, gesturing to it as she flicked it on.

Jake waved her question aside with a casual flick of his hand. "I had envisioned working with private business on that rather than creating yet another government bureaucracy. I think if we can get enough people to catch the vision, we can expand the program and make it self-funding."

Jake was leaning forward now, his attention fully engaged on Becky, which is just what Rick wanted. Becky had forged an uncanny connection with the premier and in spite of his own faint jealousy, he knew that connection was going to make the difference between a bland interview and one that sparkled and surprised.

So he took a few pictures, then returned to his seat, content to be ignored, but listening intently to everything that was said, jotting down relevant notes.

The interview ranged from his plans to reduce government red-tape to encouraging new Alberta-based value-added business to more social issues. As they spoke, Rick felt a growing impatience with Becky's style. Sure the premier was opening up to her, but as he had clearly stated initially, the interview was starting to ramble.

He tried to catch Becky's eye, to warn her, but she steadfastly ignored him, her entire attention on Jake.

They were now talking about family values. An older, outdated subject, but Becky seemed to warm to it.

"I think it's important that we support the traditional family unit," Jake was saying, "but at the same time we need to recognize that there are many single-parent families who are coping with a tremendous amount of pressure."

This was *not Going West's* focus at all. Rick raised his camera and took a few pictures, then glanced over it when he saw he had caught Becky's attention. He shook his head slightly and pivoted his finger in a circle, a subtle reminder to get back to the point.

Becky turned back to the premier, ignoring Rick. She asked a few more questions pertaining to family, made a few comments, and as they chatted, Rick could sense she was winding the interview down.

He shifted in his seat, impatient with Becky. They had talked about what they were going to do with this. What their focus was going to be. She had barely touched on the topics he needed covered. How was she going to glean anything of substance, anything different from a thousand other interviews that would set this one apart?

Sure, they had been invited into his yard. Sure, he had some pet project that they could maybe focus on, but what was that?

Then he caught a different note in Jake's tone. A subtle shift in his body language.

Jake was getting comfortable. And personal.

Now they were getting somewhere.

"People need to take responsibility for their actions, Becky," he was saying. Rick felt the hairs on his neck go up and he straightened, straining to hear what Jake was saying.

"I know I've been remiss in that department."

Becky leaned closer, touching him on the arm again. She was no longer the interviewer. She had become a friend. Confidante.

How had she done that?

He didn't care. He had become hyperaware of the change in the atmosphere and was watching Jake like a hawk.

"What are you trying to say, Jake?"

He sighed and dragged a hand over his face. "I know I shouldn't be saying this on the news. You're a reporter."

"I'm also your friend."

Jake laughed lightly. "That's a rarity for someone like me. I guess what I've always appreciated about you, Becky, was the fact that you were never fazed by the idea that I am premier. That I hold power."

"Your power is given you by God. You're holding it, yes, but in trust. I serve the same God but in a different capacity. We're equal that way." Becky smiled gently at him. "And as for the fact that you're single—" she winked at him, then glanced at Rick "—that has never been a factor."

Rick held her gaze a moment, wondering what she was saying.

"I've often seen you alone at functions. No boyfriend?"

Again Becky's glance slid to Rick's then away as if she wasn't sure where to put him in her life.

He had kissed her. Had flirted with her.

She shook her head. "How about you? Any significant others in your life?" she asked, her attention focused back on Jake. "You're seen with a different woman just about every time you step out."

Jake waggled his hand. "You know how it is, Becky. I have functions I have to attend. I can't come alone so I find someone. Or get my assistant to find someone. Usually a friend of a friend. Often a married woman to help me avoid any personal entanglements."

"I remember a girl named Kerra. You've mentioned her once or twice."

Kerra? Becky knew about a "personal entanglement" named Kerra? How had she known and why hadn't she told him this?

Jake shifted in his chair, his hand stroking his chin as he seemed to be looking past Becky into the middle distance. His body language was so different from when they had first come that Rick could only be amazed at the transformation of the high-comfort level Jake felt with Becky.

The vibration in his pocket made him jump. He glanced at Becky and Jake, but they weren't even paying attention to him. It was as if they had forgotten he was there.

Rick slowly drew the phone out of his pocket. It was Terry, their accounts manager.

Chapter Eleven

Rick glanced at the tape recorder on the table between Jake and Becky. Still running. He didn't want to take this call, but he had to. He carefully got up from the table and walked to the back of the yard, out of earshot of Becky and Jake.

"I hope you've got good news, Terry?"

"I tried, Rick, but there's no way they're going to extend credit unless the magazine comes up with some kind of security."

"Terry, if we had security, we wouldn't need an extension," Rick felt like yelling.

"One of the managers suggested you talk to your grandfather. Surely with his substantial assets..."

"Forget it. There's no way I'm going to Colson Ethier to beg for spare change." The very thought. "You know the only reason I let things get this far is because when I first came to you, you virtually assured me that I would be able to access this money. *'No problem'* were your words. If I had known you were going to get spineless on me, I wouldn't have put out the money I did." Rick shoved his hand through his hair in frustration. "So who do I need to talk to?"

"I did what I could, Rick."

"No, you didn't, Terry. Give me a name and a number." Rick flipped a page over on the pad of paper he had in his pocket and scribbled the name Terry gave him.

"I don't know if it's going to make a difference," Terry protested.

"I'm Colson Ethier's grandson, Terry. Trust me. It will make a difference." It galled Rick to drop his grandfather's name, but he was getting desperate. Better to use Colson's name than his money. This magazine had to make it on its own. "Arrange it. I'll hold."

Rick glanced over at Becky, who was still leaning close to the premier, their heads bent. What were they doing? Praying?

He wanted to be there, but from what he could see, Becky hadn't turned the tape off. He could listen to it later. He had to deal with this while he still had some breathing room.

A few minutes later Terry had the meeting arranged.

As Rick rang off, he strode to the table. Becky looked up as he came and she got to her feet.

"Time to go?" Becky asked.

Rick frowned. "Not unless you're done here?"

Becky nodded and turned the tape recorder off. She dropped it casually in her purse. She gave Rick only a brief glance before turning back to Jake. "Thanks so much for taking the time to see us." She touched him again. "You take care. I'll be praying for you."

Jake laughed lightly. "And coming from you, I know that's not just casual talk. Thanks, Becky." He bent over and kissed her lightly on the forehead.

And Rick's jealousy battled with curiosity. What had they talked about while he was trying to save the magazine? He'd just have to wait until he could hear what was on the tape recorder.

Jake glanced at his watch. "I have another appointment, so I have to run. It was good to see you again, Becky." Jake turned to Rick and held out his hand. "It was a pleasure to meet you, too, Rick."

"Thanks for your time, Mr. Premier," Rick said, shaking Jake's hand. "We're most appreciative."

"I'd like to see a copy of the interview before you put it into print," Jake said, slipping his hands into his pockets. "Dilton is going to be having ulcers until he sees it. He didn't want me to do the interview in the first place."

"I doubt it..."

"Of course..."

Rick and Becky spoke at the same time. Rick shot Becky a warning look, which she returned with puzzlement.

"What I can do is discuss the angle we'll be taking before we put it out," Rick said by way of a compromise. Did Jake have something to hide? Had that come out while Rick was talking on the phone?

They said their final goodbyes and Rick could see Becky was less than pleased with him. But he wasn't going to discuss that in front of the premier.

They were back in his Jeep and driving down the road before Becky turned on him. "Why won't you allow him to vet what we're going to print?"

"Because it's our interview and our magazine. I want to make sure this interview stands out from any number of Q and A's he's done over the years." What they had wasn't outstanding, but it was still an exclusive.

"Correction, Rick. It was *my* interview. It was only thanks to me that we got it."

"But you did it under the auspices of a magazine that *I'm* in charge of. So it isn't your exclusive property, Becky. And we don't give approvals on interviews." Why did she care? Nothing earth-shattering had come out of it. At least not the part he was in on.

Becky said nothing for a few moments, and as Rick glanced at her, he caught her looking at him.

"We just finished doing an interview that you wanted to do for a number of years. You should be thrilled."

"I wished we could have sat down and gone over the direction of the interview beforehand." Becky had balked when he had asked that. "It did wander a bit."

"I know. But I got what I wanted."

"And what was that?"

"Information on his pet project. That's something that ties in with business, doesn't it?"

Rick pulled over to the side of the road, parking alongside a hay field. A farmer was cutting, the sweet smell of the grass soothing away his surprising anger.

"Why are you stopping?"

Rick turned to Becky, wishing he could sort out the confusion of his feelings right now. Yes, he had just come from one of the most sought-after interviews in his life, but it had yielded nothing. Had Becky allowed him to run the interview he would have hit harder. He had pinned so much on it and it had faltered. What they had wasn't going to give *Going West* the turnaround he had promised Terry.

But he didn't voice his feelings aloud. Nor did he take his eyes off Becky. As she held his gaze, time seemed to slow, just as it had that time at the creek in the mountains. When he had kissed her for the first time.

And in spite of the frustration he had felt. In spite of the clamor of other thoughts, he reached out and gently touched her face as if seeking to draw from her the same peace he had felt with her at that moment. Carefully running his fingers through the soft silk of her hair, sighing lightly.

"Why did you kiss me the other day?" she asked suddenly. "When I fell asleep in your office?"

Rick cupped her chin, stroking it with his thumb. "I wanted to. I couldn't resist."

"So, just attraction?"

"No." Rick fought the urge to pull her closer, to kiss her again. To do so now would smack of claiming territory, and he didn't want base emotions like jealousy to tarnish what he felt for Becky. "It was more than that. More like need. More like..." He struggled to find the right word. "More like yearning for something that would fill emptiness."

Becky drew in a sharp breath, her face now turned to his. And to Rick's utter surprise, she reached out, framed his face with her cool hands and kissed him lightly on his lips.

He didn't move, didn't breathe. His eyes drifted shut as he rested his forehead against hers.

And he caught himself praying.

Praying that God would show Himself. Praying that he would be found worthy of this wonderful, amazing woman.

Becky drew back from Rick, her heart still fluttering in the aftermath of her rash action. She didn't look up at him, unsure of what she would see in his eyes.

Why were they dancing around the edges of each other's emotions? They were both adults and should be able to talk about what was happening.

But Becky wasn't sure herself how to articulate the feelings Rick raised in her. She had fought and argued with herself. She had prayed and sought guidance from the Bible.

But each time she saw him, something pure and wonderful blossomed within her. And each time she saw him, trailing behind her initial emotions were second thoughts and insecurity.

"I thought the interview went pretty well," she said softly, trying to find a unemotional common ground that would give them both their bearings again.

Rick kept stroking her skin, his movements slower now. "Do you really want to talk about the interview right now?"

Becky glanced sidelong at him, biting her lip. "If not the interview, then what? The two of us? Where we're going?"

Rick let his hand slide down her arm. "I know one thing. I care about you, Becky. A lot."

His words sent a light shiver dancing down her spine, but it was followed by a harder thought.

Do you care enough to stay here?

Rick had made it clear from the beginning that he was only here temporarily. His sudden flight after the horse trip was like a sharp underline to that thought.

And how did she feel about him?

Becky held his eyes, as if trying to see herself through his. Trying to understand why he had kissed her, flirted with her.

Rick's eyes took on an inward look. "You're allowed to say something now," he said with a nervous laugh.

She took his hand and pressed it to her cheek, her eyes holding his. "I care about you, too, Rick." When she saw his soft, slow smile, she wanted to leave her comment there. Unadorned and simple. But she was first and foremost a child of God.

Rooted and grounded in His love.

She wanted no less from anyone she was involved in.

"But I don't know enough about you. Enough about your relationship with God. You come to church, but the only time we've talked about your faith was that moment at the creek. I don't know if you're going to be staying here, or leaving—"

Rick stopped her words with another kiss. Becky gently pressed him back, shaking her head.

"I told you before, I don't believe in casual dating. If this is going somewhere..." She stopped there, afraid to go on. She needed to know how he saw their relationship, if anyone wanted to call it that.

But at the same time she was afraid to know.

Rick turned away from her, his hands resting idly on the steering wheel, his eyes focused on the road ahead of them.

"I don't know where it's going, either," he said softly. "But I do know that I've never felt this way before." He glanced sidelong at her, a half smile teasing his lips. "And I've never talked like this before. I've never gotten this far in a relationship. Never gotten to know someone."

Relationship? Is that what he called these hit-and-miss connections?

"And do you know me?"

Even in profile his smile lit up his face. "You're easy to get to know, Becky. You're a generous and loving person."

His compliment hit the depths of her heart.

"If I am, it's because of my family. Because of the faith they've shown me."

"You're lucky that way." He angled his head toward her. "Having someone show you the way to God."

"Are you finding your way there?"

Rick's smile faded, but he kept his gaze on her. "It's hard, Becky. I've got too many questions and haven't heard a lot of answers. Either in church, or from the Bible. I haven't had the example of loving faith that you've had."

"What about your grandfather?"

As Rick pushed himself away from the wheel, she

caught a glimpse of longing and pain so fleeting she thought her optimism had created it. Then his features hardened into the mask she knew all too well. He was shutting her out again.

"I think I'd like to talk about that interview now."

His voice held a harsh edge and Becky could see from the clench of his jaw, from the narrowing of his eyes, that he had retreated into a cold, hard place. He wasn't going to be telling her anything more.

Becky drew herself back against her seat, wrapping her fingers tightly around each other, disappointment sifting through her. She thought for a moment he was going to open up, show her some of his life. He held so much to himself.

How could she have let herself fall in love with a man so completely her opposite?

She let her mind linger over the word.

Love? Was that what she felt? This pain that accompanied every thought of him? The confusion she felt in his presence?

She loved the Lord, but that love nurtured and sustained her. It didn't make her want to cry.

She drew in a long, lingering breath, as if reorienting herself to his new position.

"I'll write it up, like I did with the horse pack trip," she said. "And you can look it over."

"I would prefer if we could work on it together," he said quietly. "I'd like more of a hand in shaping it rather than getting to be the critic afterward."

In spite of her swirling emotions, her confusing thoughts, she had to smile at his cryptic comment.

"As soon as we get back to the office, I have a meeting to go to," he continued. "And I'm busy tomorrow. Could I come tomorrow night to go over it with you?"

"I have a meeting at eight-thirty tomorrow night."

"I can come before."

"My family will be around, but I'm sure we can find a quiet place." In spite of her confusion, the thought of having him at her home sent a faint thrill through the disarray of her emotions.

"I'll be there at about eight o'clock, if that's okay with you?"

She almost invited him to supper, but wouldn't that smack of desperation? Better to keep things casual.

And how was she going to do that when each time she saw him, she grew more and more attracted to him when she knew she shouldn't?

"Welcome back, Rick. Good to see you." Dennis Ellison, Becky's brother, greeted him at the door with a grin. "Becky's waiting for you in Dad's study."

As Rick followed Dennis through the kitchen, warmth and the tantalizing scent of baking mingled with coffee assailed him, followed by a sense of coming to a place of sanctuary. A place where you could simply "be."

"Hello, Rick." Cora looked up from the tray she was getting ready. "You came just in time. I was about to serve up some fresh blueberry muffins."

"He can't, Mom. Becks told me to make sure I get him to her right away." Dennis flashed Rick a wink. "She's a bit bossy, our Becks is."

"Becky doesn't need to be such a slave driver." Cora smiled at Rick and took him by the arm. "Dennis, you bring the tray and meet us in the family room."

"What to do, what to do?" Dennis sighed, but did as his mother requested.

Leanne and Colette were draped over the worn couch. Leanne was filing her nails and Colette was talking on the phone while flipping through a magazine.

Sam lay stretched out in his recliner, his head tipped to one side, faint snores issuing from his mouth.

"Coffee's on," Cora announced, setting the tray on the table. "And we have company."

The girls looked up at Rick. Leanne's smile blossomed and Colette gave him a quick wave.

"Come sit over here," Leanne said, jumping up from the couch. "Letty, get off the phone. You can talk to Nick some other time." Leanne tugged Rick's arm, leading him to the empty spot Colette made for him by pulling up her legs. "Nick is Colette's boyfriend. She's trying to decide if she should marry him or go back to school or travel. What do you think she should do?"

"I've never had to make that kind of decision before," Rick said. "So my advice isn't worth much."

Leanne sighed and pulled him down onto the couch. "I think I'd travel."

"Becks says you've done a lot of traveling," Dennis said, dropping onto the floor by his father's chair. "So you have any advice? I want to head out someplace next spring. Someplace different."

"I liked Thailand, though many parts of it are really commercialized. Bangladesh was interesting, but a very sad and hard place." He paused, trying to articulate emotions he could still feel when he thought of that country. "I've been there twice and each time I come back, I feel such a mixture of emotions. Gratitude and at the same time..."

"Guilt?" Cora put in, pouring the coffee from a carafe.

"Exactly. The gratitude I know what to do with. Never the guilt."

"The only reason I know about the guilt is we have a friend who goes to Bangladesh each year," Cora said, handing him a mug of coffee and a warm muffin on a tray. "He collects money and brings it to an orphanage there to help them purchase things they need. He says the same thing, but he does feel that what he does makes a difference. That he's helping."

"Maybe I should go with him next time," Dennis said, stirring some sugar into his coffee. "That way I could travel and help at the same time."

"He's always asking people to come along." Cora shook Sam's shoulder lightly and set his coffee by his side. "We have company, Sam."

Sam stretched and looked around the room, his eyes vacant. Then he blinked, focused on Rick and smiled. "Welcome to our home, Rick. Good to have you here again."

And Rick felt a surge of warmth. Three times this family had so easily taken him into their home. Made him feel welcome. He wondered if Becky realized how fortunate she was.

Colette got off the phone, grinned at Rick and took a muffin off the tray. "Where's Becks? She was in such a dither after supper 'cause Rick was coming. I thought she'd be here already."

"Colette!"

"Letty."

Leanne and Cora reprimanded her simultaneously. Colette just winked at Rick. "It's the truth, ain't it? She couldn't decide what to wear, how to do her hair. I've never seen her like that."

The pleasure Colette's comment gave him surprised Rick. He couldn't imagine Becky in a dither. Especially not in what appeared to be a dither over him.

He took a sip of his coffee and as he set his mug down onto the table he looked up. And there she was. Her hair loose, just the way he liked it. A peach-colored shirt brought out the flush in her cheeks. She wore low-riding blue jeans and her feet were bare.

She looked beautiful.

"I'm sorry you got corralled into my family's coffee time." She walked over to the coffee table and toed her brother in the ribs. "I thought I asked you to bring him to Dad's office?"

"You did, dear Becks," Dennis said, catching her by the ankle. "But Mom's a bigger boss than you. And if you have a problem with that, I'll pull you down."

"Why am I not surprised? You're always pulling someone's leg," Becky said, shaking her foot loose. Dennis's groans were joined by his sisters'.

"Oh, that's nasty, Becks."

She flashed them each a saccharine smile that melted away when she met Rick's gaze.

"Have some coffee and a muffin, dear, before you get back to work," Cora said.

But Becky shook her head. "I've got too much to do." She gave Rick an apologetic smile. "Do you mind if we get at it right away?"

Rick shook his head as he picked up his mug and plate. "Can I finish this in the office? I haven't had homemade muffins for years."

"You have to take some home," Cora announced. "Becky, you make sure you package some up for him before he leaves."

Becky just nodded and, turning, led Rick down a narrow hallway to a spacious room, just off the family room. In the center of the room was a large flat-top oak desk. Bookshelves lined one wall, the other held a collage of framed pictures that covered every square inch of space above a long credenza that held more portraits.

She closed the door behind him. "Just put your stuff on the desk. I thought we could work there."

Rick did as he was told, but his eyes were on the framed photographs. Children of all ages and groups looked back at him.

"These must be of your family," he said, irresistibly drawn to the wall. He glanced them over, then pointed to one of a young girl sitting on a horse, grinning a gap-toothed smile. "I'm guessing this is you?"

"Not bad," Becky said, coming to stand beside him. "One of the other times I was on a horse. That was taken at my grandmother's new place."

Rick glanced over the mélange of pictures, his gaze snared by a couple standing self-consciously in front of a mass of flowers. "You and Trevor?"

"Grade twelve graduation."

"The cowboy and the editor."

Rick glanced back at Becky who was avoiding his gaze, now busy with a stack of papers on the desk. "I've made a word-for-word transcription of our interview with the premier. That way we can decide which angle we want to take." She was all business now and Rick took her cue, though he kept thinking about what Colette had said. Becky. In a dither.

"Do you mind if I skim through them first?" he asked, picking them up. "Did Trixie type them for you?"

"No, I did them myself. Just finished them now. They might be a bit hard to read. Dad's printer is a bit low on ink."

She leaned back on the desk while Rick took an empty chair. It didn't take him long to look it over. He had made his own notes on his part of the interview after their "chat" in the Jeep. When Becky had kissed him.

And he had kissed her back. And they had talked. And she had come so close...

Focus, Rick, focus.

A few minutes later he put the papers down and bit his lip. "You've got some good stuff here to work with. I like the gardening angle. Gives the piece a personal touch. I know that's not been done before."

"How would you know?"

Rick glanced up from the notes. "I've been covering this guy for a while, trying to get an interview. I've read just about every interview that's been archived on the Net, every report on him in every major newspaper in Canada and quite a few abroad." He looked back at the papers. "The interview isn't complete, is it?"

"What do you mean?"

"It doesn't go much past what I heard before I took the phone call from Terry at the bank."

Becky shrugged his comment aside. "We discussed personal stuff after that."

"On or off the record?"

"Off."

Rick saw the tape recorder beside the computer and pulled it over. "Can I listen?"

"I don't think that would be a good idea. It was personal."

"But it's on the tape. You were still recording it."

She nodded, edging up onto her father's desk.

"Then it's not personal." Ignoring Becky's protests, Rick hit Play and listened. He fast-forwarded the tape, but didn't have far to go. Becky had stopped transcribing shortly before the phone call. Just at the point in the interview when the atmosphere had changed. When Jake started to talk about a girl named Kerra. He listened while Becky fidgeted restlessly in front of him.

"Kerra and I parted ways a long time ago," Jake was saying, his voice quiet. "It is the one regret that I have."

"Why do you say that?" Becky's softly modulated voice came across on the tape, and Rick remembered the way she leaned closer, her gentle features expressing a concern that made Rick himself want to confess every secret he held.

Jake hesitated, his innate caution seemingly holding him back. "She was the only woman I truly loved. She was the only one..." Another long pause.

Rick hardly dared to breathe sensing a moment of disclosure.

"I loved her but I treated her wrong. So wrong," Jake whispered finally. "I was young and ambitious. I had an advisor even then. An advisor who saw in me the potential to move higher and higher. He gave me bad advice."

Another silence. "What kind of advice, Jake?" Becky asked.

"He told me to get rid of her. And I did. And after I did, I found out she was expecting a child. And I didn't do anything about it. I left her on her own and didn't take responsibility."

Elation thrilled through Rick at his confession. This was what they were waiting for. The big breakthrough.

But as he thought about the young girl, anger chased away his jubilation.

This man had done the same thing to this Kerra girl that his own father had done to his mother. Left her a single woman trying to raise a child, dependant on family. Dependent on a cold man whose shame kept Rick at arm's length.

"Do you know where she is now?"

Rick pulled himself out of his own emotional quagmire to concentrate on Jake's reply.

"She changed her name, stopped singing and moved away. Her mother was an alcoholic and either didn't know where she was or wouldn't tell me. She died a couple of years after Kerra left town. She was my last and only link to Kerra." Jake drew in a deep breath. There was a long pause and Rick wondered if the interview was over.

"Of course you realize all this is off the record, Becky," Jake said, his voice changing back to the stern and controlled politician. "I should never, ever have told you this."

"*Going West* is not aiming to be a tabloid magazine," Becky replied.

Then a click and the tape was finished.

Rick leaned back and released his breath in a long slow exhalation. This was the scoop he'd been waiting for. This was the breakthrough that was going to make the difference he needed.

"We're going to use this, Becky," he said, tapping the papers into a neat pile and laying them carefully on the desk. "His comments. At the end of the interview. I want to use them."

"They were off the record."

"He only said that at the end." Rick glanced up at Becky, who was frowning at him, her arms folded over her chest.

"That's really splitting hairs. He told me that in confidence, Rick. While you were away, talking on the phone. And while he maybe didn't follow so-called correct procedure, this wasn't a police interview."

"No. It was an interview conducted, for the most part, in front of two people and quite publicly recorded on tape the whole time." Rick leaned forward, as if trying to force his will on his reluctant editor. "This is the article I've been waiting for. The one that will turn *Going West* around."

Becky pushed herself away from the desk, pacing around it, her head bent. "And that's all that counts, isn't it? No matter what the cost."

"It was my job when I came here. You knew that." Rick could feel her frustration pushing at him, and for a moment he hesitated. The magazine was floundering. The money was getting tight. Now more than ever he needed the boost this article would give the magazine. "You need the job, too. If this magazine fails, what will you do?"

"I'd sooner lose my job than put this out for everyone to read." Becky placed her palms down on the desk. "I'm not going to allow it, Rick. It's not right."

"He knew what he was doing when he allowed us to do the interview. It's the truth and I think we have a responsibility to print it."

"It's his own private pain. We have a responsibility to leave that alone."

"It's the truth. And sometimes truth hurts. And as for his pain..." Rick paused, fighting his rising anger. "What about the pain of the girl and the child he left all alone? He abandoned both of them. Abandoned his responsibility to them. Doesn't Kerra have any rights? Doesn't their child?"

"That's not the point."

Rick banged the flat of his hand down on the transcript of the interview with an angry slap. "It is exactly the point, Becky. He holds a public office, and what he has done directly reflects on that office." He spun around and drew his hands over his face, trying to pull his emotions together. Focus. Focus. But he couldn't keep his emotions out of this. It was too close. "He has no right, had no right, to leave that woman and that child in the lurch. Their story needs to be exposed, as well. It's the truth. And truth is part of what good reporting is all about." He sucked in a long slow breath, willing his pounding heart to slow its erratic beat. Willing the storm of his own pain to stop hurting.

"This truth will hurt and break down, Rick."

"It can also be liberating. Have you ever thought of that?" He walked slowly to the wall of pictures again.

Becky came to his side. He could feel her resistance, measure the tension in her body.

"Why does this matter so much? I've never seen you this emotionally involved in any article we've ever done."

Rick let his gaze flick over the pictures. Pictures of parents, grandparents, brothers, sisters. Posed family pictures. Candid pictures. A legacy and a heritage. How could he explain to Becky why Jake's mistake mattered so much? Becky who came from such a loving family. Would she have even an inkling of what he'd had to deal with?

He picked up a family picture. Becky flanked by her sisters and brothers, mother and father hovering over them all, grandparents on either side. His lack of family was no deep secret.

But his pain was. As was his dislike for his grandfather and the control he exerted over his life. His anger with Colson had been his constant struggle on his slow return to faith. And his anger translated into anger with God. Would Becky, sweet loving Becky, even begin to understand what emotions swirled beneath his smile?

"We need to tell the truth."

"But what is truth, Rick? It's an age-old question. Bald statement of facts that can break down and destroy? You know what this would do to his career?"

Rick turned then. "And what about what happened to Kerra? What has happened to her life? Don't you think her story should be told?"

"Not in this article."

"Then when?"

"That's not our responsibility, Rick."

And that was that. Rick withdrew, but held his ground. "This article is going to make all the difference to the magazine. We're going to run it the way I want to."

Becky drew back from him, her eyes snapping. "Doesn't matter who gets hurt, does it? As long as you can get the article that will turn this magazine around, and let you prove yourself to your grandfather."

"He's not a factor."

"I think he is. If it's truth you are so concerned about, you better look at your own reasons for using Jake this way. You're going to hide behind the so-called truth to get what you want. Just like all the other pieces you've written."

Her accusations stung and his only defense was to attack. Push her back from the truth he almost told her this afternoon. He didn't dare allow her closer.

"You sound like you're afraid of the truth," Rick said. "I always have to push you to acknowledge that in your own work. It comes out in your other writing, as well."

"My 'other' writing is fiction, Rick. It's the truth distilled."

"But is it a truth for you? You could be a better writer if you faced the truth of your life. Your book was exactly as I described it. Sentimental and shallow. It skipped over the surface. You're a better writer than that, Becky." His words spilled out past the polite barriers he had put in place, past the diplomacy that came hard to him at the best of times.

Part of him urged him to stop, asked him why he was doing this.

Offense was the best defense. He couldn't afford to let himself get involved with anyone. Least of all someone like Becky, who was already too close.

"If we're going to talk about fear, how about discussing fear of failure? Don't you think it's easier to plunge yourself into community and church work than to make the commitment to becoming a better writer?"

"You didn't help matters any. You and that nasty book review. Also the truth, I imagine."

"Don't hide behind me," Rick said, holding up one hand. "Don't hide behind what I wrote. You've ridden on that excuse too long. You have talent and brains and ability. Too much maybe. But you make yourself indispensable to the community so that you can hide behind that, as well. If you want to be the writer you claim you want to be, you need a stronger vision. A stronger commitment. You need to say no to a few things. To realize that maybe when you do, someone else might come and take your place. And whether you like it or not, that is the truth for your life."

Becky took a step back, her voice quiet now, her face pale. What had he done with his rant? His big plan for her life.

"You talk about truth when you can't even tell people the truth about yourself." She paused. Held his gaze. "Tell me the truth now. Why does this matter so much? Why do you want to use the truth of what happened to Jake to hurt him and ruin the good he's done?"

Her questions probed, picked at threads from the fabric of his life that she had already loosened. What would it matter if he told her? What would he be giving her?

She knew how he was raised. What she didn't know were the emotions at his core. His fears. The yearnings for love that he had always disdained as weak. Needy.

But he had let her into parts of his life no one had been before. She had shown him living faith. And a pure love.

They were a potent combination that frightened him. But her gaze held his, her eyes seemed to catch his hesitation, encourage disclosure.

He retreated further.

"It matters, Becky, because this will sell magazines. And that's what we do." He looked down at the desk, unable to look her in the eye, feeling like a traitor. His own brave words about truth mocked him, but if he gave her more of himself, he would leave too much behind when it was time to go.

And he would go. He had to.

A beat of silence. Then Becky stepped back as if finally understanding what she was going to get from him.

"If you write this article, revealing the premier's secret against his will—" Becky raised her hand as if making a vow "—I'll quit." Then she turned and left through the doors leading to the yard, the sound of the door like a gunshot in the silence.

Rick slammed his fists against the desk, then ran out into the yard, calling her name.

"Leave me alone, Rick," she called out. "Go write your article."

Rick stood on the edges of the light spilling out from the open door behind him, trying to see where she was going. But she had been swallowed up by the night.

With a frustrated sigh, he spun on his heel and strode to his vehicle. He vaulted into it, twisted the key of his Jeep. As it roared to life, he glanced back at Becky's house. At the three people silhouetted against the window.

Surely Becky would enlighten them.

He reversed, slammed the gearshift into first and spun out of the Ellisons' yard. At the road he turned left, away from town, out into the dark countryside. The only sound was the throb of the engine, and the hiss of air slipping past a half-opened window. His lights cast a dim beam over the road, which swallowed up by the heavy darkness as he approached.

As he drove, her words echoed and twisted through his brain.

"You're an empty shell, Rick."

"Why does this matter so much?"

He pressed harder on the accelerator, but he couldn't outrun her words. They piled on top of each other, pulling down the barriers he had erected against her, at the same time, drawing him to a place he had been before.

And each time she brought him there, he gave her a little more of himself and allowed her closer.

And what was so bad about that?

He was leaving, that was nonnegotiable.

Why couldn't he stay? Why not?

The question spun through his head as he stared sightlessly at the road, the ditches barely illuminated by his headlights.

Put down roots? Allow people into his life?

Did he dare?

Lord, what do I do?

His cry to a God he hadn't spoken to came from the depths of his sorrow. His need.

Tell me what to do, Lord. I'm working without a net here.

Then a flash of brown. Red reflected in twin pinpoints of light facing him on the road ahead. The eyes of a deer standing in the middle of the road.

He slammed on the brakes, spun the steering wheel just as the deer jumped.

A sickening crunch. Pain that exploded through his head. His chest.

Then nothing.

Chapter Twelve

Becky's meandering feet took her back to the house, shame dogging her steps. She had struck out at Rick in anger, using words that cut and hurt, issued ultimatums she would never keep. Then, worse yet, she had run away instead of staying and facing the consequences of her actions.

"Please forgive me, Lord," she whispered, lifting her head to the night sky. *"Forgive my hard words."* She prayed that she hadn't hurt him with her truth the very way she had accused him of hurting people with his.

Rick wasn't empty. He had depth of character and a candor that didn't hide behind fancy words. His relationship with God was based on the same kind of honesty.

Now she had to find a way to apologize to him. To regain lost ground. Because in spite of words thrown out in anger, she couldn't let him go.

She slipped into the house through the doors leading into her father's study. She needed to call Rick. Find out where he was and try rebuild what she had so foolishly broken down.

As Becky dialed his number, she glanced at the notes he had left behind. The fateful interview. Yes, it still mattered, but obviously it also mattered to Rick. And in spite of how she felt about Jake's confidences, Rick had a point. Jake held a public office and as such, his private character was as much a part of that as his public one. But how could she be fair and just at the same time?

Rick's answering machine picked up. "Please pick up, Rick, if you're listening. I'm sorry I got so angry. Phone me on my cell phone. Please." She didn't care that she sounded like she was begging.

As she tried his cell phone, her heart started up. It rang six times, each ring sinking her spirits further. Then, finally, he picked up.

"Rick, this is Becky. I'm sorry. Please forgive me." Her words rushed out in her eagerness to make a connection. "I want to talk to you. I was wrong...."

"Becky?"

She stopped. The voice on the phone wasn't Rick's. Her face burned as she realized her mistake. "Sorry. Wrong number."

"No. Becky, don't hang up. This is Earl McCrae. I'm using Rick's cell phone."

"Why?" Other than the occasional chitchat at Katherine's coffee shop, Rick hardly knew Earl. What was he doing with Rick's cell phone?

"Becky. Listen to me. There's been an accident. Rick was involved. I was the first one at the accident and used his cell phone to call the ambulance."

Accident. Rick. The words caught like barbed hooks, tearing and slashing.

"Where? How? Is he okay?"

"The ambulance just left. He hit a deer with his Jeep."

She felt a sob push up her throat. Her head spun as she dropped the phone. Rick. *Lord, forgive me.*

She stumbled past the desk, heading for the door, shock numbing her movements.

"Becky. What's wrong?" her brother called out as she lurched through the family room. "I thought you had a meeting?"

"I have to get to the hospital." Becky glanced wildly around, as if looking for answers. "It's Rick. He's been in an accident."

She saw her mother half rise from her chair. Her father's shocked face. Leanne and Colette both cried out.

Dennis caught her by the shoulders just as her legs gave way. "You can't drive, Becks. I'll take you."

Seconds later they were in Dennis's car, flying through town. All she could do was pray inarticulate prayers while fear and panic lurked at the edges of her mind.

She couldn't. She had to concentrate. Rick needed her.

"You don't know how bad it is, Becks. Don't think the worst," Dennis said, downshifting as he approached a red light. He slowed, glanced left and right and gunned it through.

The hospital was just ahead and, as Dennis prepared to turn into the parking lot, she saw the flashing lights of the ambulance coming from the other direction, heard the ominous wail of the siren.

Becky grabbed the door handle, ready to jump out as soon as Dennis stopped the car. But he caught her with one hand as he spun the wheel for the turn into the parking lot with the other.

"Wait, Becks," he said. His voice was soft but his grip brother-tough as the car rocked to a halt. "I'm coming with you."

The spinning red and blue lights kicked her heart into high gear, but she forced herself to wait for Dennis to turn off the car. Undo his seat belt. Then hers.

She jumped out, her eyes drawn to the ambulance now pulling up to the emergency entrance. Dennis caught her by the arm again, leading her along.

The back doors of the ambulance swung open, two men jumped out, whirled around and pulled out a stretcher holding a body.

"Rick," Becky called out, her knees buckling. Dennis held her up, slipped his arm around her waist. But adrenaline surged, gave her strength and she ran.

They got into the emergency entrance just as they wheeled Rick in. Blood covered Rick's forehead, matting his blond hair, streaking down the side of his head. His one eye was swollen shut. A bag hung above the stretcher, a narrow tube running from it into his arm.

Becky slapped her hand against her mouth, holding back a cry. He looked like a war victim.

He opened his eyes, turned his head and saw her with his good eye. When he reached out his hand, she ignored Dennis, pulled away and ran to Rick's side, catching his hand in hers.

"Miss, I'm sorry. You'll have to stand back." One of

the paramedics caught her by the shoulders, gently drawing her away.

But Rick wouldn't let go.

"Please, let her stay," he muttered, his hands clenching Becky's with surprising strength. Then his head rolled to the side and his hand grew slack.

Panic surged through her, but the paramedic was pulling her away.

"Miss. Please. He's unconscious."

As his words sank in, she stepped back. Two nurses and a doctor converged on Rick and he was whisked away into a curtained off area.

Dennis was right behind her, his hands on her shoulders.

She turned to him, buried her face in his shoulders and all the emotions of the evening converged. She started sobbing, her shoulders shaking as sorrow and regret surged through her.

This was her fault. She had caused Rick's accident. He'd driven off in a rage. Why had she been so self-righteous?

"Becky, let's go sit down." Dennis drew her gently to the waiting area. She didn't want to go, but didn't have the strength to resist. Dennis pulled her down into a chair, his arm still around her shoulder.

Please, Lord, she prayed. *Please keep Rick safe. Please. I love him. Don't take him away from me now.*

The words went round and round her head as she clung to her brother's hand, her eyes focused on the hallway leading to the emergency ward. She could hear the faint murmur of voices, the shuffling of feet from one of the curtained-off cubicles. The occasional muffled clang of an instrument on a tray.

What was going on?

The doors of the lobby whooshed open and her parents swooped in on them.

"Oh, honey. What happened?" Her mother sat down beside her, her hand stroking Becky's shoulder.

"I don't know." She didn't look at them, her entire attention on the cubicle as if by sheer force of will she could make Rick whole. She knew Rick's life wasn't in her hands, but she couldn't stop herself.

"Is he okay?"

She forced her gaze back to her father, who had taken Dennis's seat beside her, and tears filled her eyes again. "He looked terrible, Daddy."

Her father laid his hand on her head and awkwardly stroked her hair with his rough hand. "We have good doctors and nurses here." He smiled. "And I know you've been praying. So have we. His life is in God's hands."

And what if she didn't trust that God would let her keep him?

The horrible question stopped her thoughts cold. Her mind slowed, circling the thought. It sounded like something Rick might say.

And in that moment, she understood him a little better.

Pain stabbed through the haze. Once. Then again. Coming closer together as he swam through the syrupy darkness that held him down, slowed his thoughts.

His eyelids had been glued shut. They wouldn't

open. Wouldn't open. Voices swam through his mind. His mother's. Grandfather's. Becky's.

Hushed and vague shapes of people he didn't know mixed with the voices, speaking his name. Praying.

Was death this painful?

He willed his thoughts past the agony surging through his head, his chest and pulled his lids up.

The first thing he saw was a head, lying down by his arm. He tried to speak but only a groan came out. The head lifted and he was looking at Becky's eyes, her soft smile.

He was alive.

Becky held his hand, and before the black pulled him down again, he felt her lips touch his fingers.

"How's it going, Becks?" Sam didn't glance up from his Bible, but his quiet question was a gentle reprieve for Becky.

She sat cross-legged on the living room floor, papers scattered around her in a semicircle as her fuzzy and distracted mind tried to find some thread of coherence from Jake's interview.

Her eyes were on the paper in front of her but her mind was on Rick. And each time she thought of him, she prayed for him.

She had stayed as late as she dared last night, then this morning she dragged herself out of bed to get some work done before she went to see Rick again.

The magazine needed her now more than ever, but she felt torn between the reality of the magazine's balance sheet and the needs of her own heart.

She rubbed her eyes and flashed her father a quick smile. "It's going okay, Dad." Which was a lie, but she couldn't let her father in on the secret that came out in the interview. For now it was between her, Jake, Rick. And Kerra.

She pressed her fingers against her eyes, hearing again Jake's confession, reliving her painful disillusionment. Had she known the chaos her innocent question would have generated, she would never have mentioned Kerra's name.

She pushed the papers away, unable to figure out what to write about. What to think. Life wasn't supposed to be this complicated.

"Do you want some help?" Sam closed his Bible, signaling to Becky that she now had his complete attention. Sam always spent time in the morning on his devotions, something Becky hadn't done for a while.

She didn't have time.

Becky pushed her hands through her hair, holding it away from her face as she blew out her breath in a frustrated sigh. "I dunno, Dad. I just..."

Sam leaned forward, inviting further disclosure.

Becky looked up into his deep blue eyes. Almost as blue as Rick's. She hadn't seen much of Rick's eyes the past day and a half. He slept a lot and when he was awake, his one eye was swollen shut, the other still bloodshot. It tore her heart each time she saw him weak and helpless and in pain.

"Life isn't as easy as I thought it should be," she said finally, feeling an unaccountable prick of tears at the back of her throat.

"Rick is young and strong, Becky. He'll be up and about in no time."

"And he'll be leaving."

Sam sat back in his chair, tapping his fingers together. "And that bothers you?"

Becky swallowed against the restriction of her throat. "Yes, Daddy. Too much."

"Does he know this?"

Becky just shrugged.

"Was that what you were fighting about?"

Becky pulled her legs up to her chest, bouncing her chin lightly on her knees, and decided to let go. She had carried the burden of Jake's secret and its consequences and needed to share it with someone whom she could trust. "Jake told me something in confidence, even though the tape was still running. Something that could ruin his career. Rick heard it and wants to use it in the article. That's what we were fighting about." And that's what probably put Rick in the hospital.

"Did Jake tell you it was off the record?"

"Not until later. Which is a technicality."

"Do you want to use it?"

Becky sighed, thinking of the precarious financial position of the magazine. The article would definitely sell papers, but was that the direction they wanted to go? "I don't. But Rick says we should because Jake is a public figure holding a public office. He shouldn't have secrets."

"What's Rick's motivation for running the article?"

"It would increase the circulation of the magazine. His main purpose for everything he has done since he came here."

"Do you think that's his only reason?"

"I don't know what to think anymore where Rick is concerned." Becky looked up at her father, her emotions wavering between her growing feelings for Rick and the reality of Rick's temporary situation at the magazine.

"Have you prayed about it?"

Becky nodded.

"With Rick?"

She shook her head. They had touched upon faith issues, but she couldn't imagine ever getting close enough to Rick to pray with him.

"So maybe you should start there. Lay your needs and Rick's before the Lord. Together. It might help clarify both your thinking." Sam got off his chair and sat down beside Becky, slipping his arm around her shoulders. "I know you care for Rick. Maybe even love him. I also know that you don't want less than a God-fearing man in your life. Maybe you need to make that clear to Rick."

Becky laid her head against her father's shoulder, much as she had when she was a little girl. "But I don't know if it matters to him what I want."

She heard Sam's chuckle deep down in his broad chest. "I think your opinion matters a lot more to him than you realize. I've seen how he looks at you. How he listens to you."

"But he's still leaving, Dad. He has told me that again and again, as if I need to know. And we're so different. He's a traveler and I like to stay in one place. He's called me sentimental and I've called him coldhearted."

"Then use your warmth to thaw him out." Sam drew

back and bracketed Becky's face in his hands. "And it wouldn't be so bad if you spread your own wings a bit. Saw more of the world than Okotoks and Calgary. I think you have things you can give each other. I think you can fill parts of his life and he can fill parts of yours."

Becky bit her lip as she held her father's gaze. "But what about faith, Daddy? You always told me that I should never enter a relationship with someone who doesn't believe. Rick has so many questions about God and why there is so much sadness in the world. It's like he's angry with God."

"If he didn't have questions about God, I would be concerned. But his questions will bring him back to the underlying faith I feel he has. His anger shows that God matters to him. I think it might be up to us to help show him the way back. Questions and anger and all." Sam smiled down at her. "I think complacent, lukewarm people are harder for God to deal with."

"And after all this happens, what if he's still going to leave?"

Sam sighed lightly and stroked Becky's cheeks with his thumbs. "Then you might have to let him go. Love him and let him go. He needs to find his own way back home."

Becky resisted that thought. Pushed it away. Could she do it?

Chapter Thirteen

The ringing of the doorbell broke into the moment and Becky drew reluctantly away from her father's side. Her father's words hurt, and she didn't know if she could face the reality of them just yet.

Her mother answered the door and Becky heard her chatting with someone.

A tall, elderly man stood on the porch. His thinning hair was swept back from wide features. Deep blue eyes held hers, and as his mouth curved up into a smile, Becky felt a tingle of recognition.

Cora turned and drew Becky to her side. "This is my daughter. Becky, this is Colson Ethier. Rick's grandfather."

"I can see a family resemblance," Colson said, reaching out to shake Becky's hand. "I'm pleased to meet you. I've heard about you."

"I'm sure," Becky said with a sharp laugh. "Let me take your coat."

"That's okay, I'm not staying long. I have a cab waiting outside. I just want to find out about my grandson before I go to the hospital."

"He's pretty banged up. He's got a few broken ribs. He's been in and out of consciousness the past twenty-four hours. He also has a badly sprained wrist and bruises. The doctor said it would be a few days before he's up and around." Becky listed off the injuries, trying to keep her own emotions in check. It had only been a day and a night since the accident. Guilt still dogged her. It was their fight that had put him in the hospital.

Her mother had come by the hospital and had practically dragged her from Rick's bedside last night. It was only the endless demands of work she couldn't pass on to anyone else that kept her away. Otherwise she'd be sitting beside Rick right now, family or no family.

"I came as soon as I could," Colson said. "Do you think he will see me?"

Becky remembered the only conversation she had heard Rick have with Colson. Rick had been uptight and snappish for a couple of days after that. She couldn't imagine what a face-to-face visit would be like.

"Of course he would," Cora said. "You're his grandfather."

"An absent one, I'm afraid." Regret edged his words, echoed by the slump of his shoulders. "Rick and I haven't always been close."

"Then this might be an opportunity to remedy that." Cora's optimism brushed away Colson's concerns.

Becky kept her uncertainties to herself. Colson

looked too tired. Too weary to hear her opinions. Rick had never said anything positive about his grandfather.

"Well, I just wanted to stop by and say hello." He looked around the kitchen with a nostalgic smile. "This home has a fond place in my memories." He looked back at Becky. "Next time you see your grandmother, say hello from me."

"Why don't you stop by her place later and say hello yourself?" Becky said. "She lives in town. I can give you her address."

Colson hesitated, and Becky went to the desk in the kitchen in that moment, grabbed a sticky note and wrote Diene's phone number and address on it.

"I don't know if I'll have time, but thanks anyway. I'm only staying long enough to make arrangements to get Rick transferred to a hospital in Toronto where I can keep a better eye on him. And as soon as that happens, I'm going to be leaving."

Becky's heart plunged. Rick? Leaving?

It was as if her father's words still hung in the air, so soon did Colson's pronouncement come after them.

"Well, I'd better get going. I have a lot to arrange." Then he said goodbye and left. Becky watched him walk slowly down the walk to the waiting cab, her heart skittering.

Rick couldn't go. Not yet. *Dear Lord, not yet.*

Awareness crept over him, tingling, as he slowly rose out of the black again. The pain had dulled but it still hovered, waiting for the wrong move.

He opened his eyes. Turned his head.

Pain flashed through his head, stabbed his eye. Wrong move.

"Hey, there."

A soft, familiar voice drew his attention up. Becky stood above him, her hands resting on the bed rail, her smile hesitant.

He tried to smile back, but his lips were too dry and cracked.

"Do you want a drink?"

He nodded, and then she was slipping a bent straw between his dry lips. He sucked the moisture in and winced at even so slight a movement.

"Just sleep, Rick. You need your rest."

"No. I slept enough." He forced his eyes open. Forced himself to concentrate on her face. So pretty. "What happened?"

"You hit a deer on the highway." Becky fussed with the sheets across his chest, smoothing them down. In spite of his pain, the motions comforted him.

"My Jeep?"

"Sorry, Rick. It's totaled."

He didn't care. He chanced a movement and lifted his right hand and grasped Becky's. "Thanks for being here."

She squeezed ever so gently and covered his hand with her other one.

"How long—" He stopped as a fresh wave of pain washed over him. Becky misinterpreted his grimace and lowered his hand to his side. But he shook his head and tightened his grip on her hand. "Don't let go. Please."

"You've been in the hospital for two days now."

Shock pushed him up into awareness and pain followed, biting and sharp. "That long?" Vague snatches of memory drifted through his mind.

He remembered forcing his eyes open for seconds at a time. Seeing Becky standing beside him. Sitting. Sleeping in the chair. Her head on the bed beside him. Always there.

He moved his head again, surprised to see various bouquets of flowers lining the windowsill of his room. "Where did those come from?"

"The staff of the magazine, people from church. My family. Katherine Dubowsky. Our minister. They all came to visit you."

He frowned, then remembered other voices. People coming and going. One voice praying. The minister. "Why would they do that?"

"Because that's what people do around here." Becky walked over to a large fruit basket. "And these came from your grandfather. He was here this morning, but he said you were still out of it."

Rick just stared at the huge arrangement, wrapped up in cellophane, topped with a red bow.

"I can open it for you," Becky said.

Rick shook his head, trying to understand. "Were you here when he came?"

Becky fussed with the bow, her agitated movements making the cellophane rustle. "He stopped by the house this morning. He asked me to call him when you were lucid. But I wanted to tell you first."

Rick remembered another hospital at another time in his life. He was fifteen and getting his appendix out after a vicious attack at the boarding school. His only visitors were two friends who had skipped school to come and see him. His grandfather had been conspicuously absent.

As he took in the flowers, the cards, melancholy unfurled through his pain. "I'm surprised he bothered to take time out of his busy schedule to come."

"You're his grandson, Rick."

"That only seems to have occurred to him in the past few years." Rick couldn't keep the bitter note out of his voice. A reflection of the relationship, or lack of it, that he had with Colson Ethier.

"He seemed sad."

He caught the fleeting glimpse of sorrow in Becky's features, but then she was smiling at him. "So how does that happen?" he asked, nodding his chin at the flowers, changing the subject. "I've made enemies at the paper, enemies in the community."

"Not enemies, Rick. Just people who didn't agree with you. At first."

"And at second?"

"You've been right, as well."

"That must hurt to admit."

"You don't know how much." Becky's smile slipped past her serious expression and he felt again the pernicious tug of attraction. The edges of his mind grew fuzzy again. He fought it. Becky was here and he wanted to talk to her. To make up for something he knew was wrong between them.

"You've been here before. I remember."

"Yes, I have." Then to his surprise she gently feathered her fingers over his forehead, brushing his hair back. He sighed at her touch, his memory of the events before the accident scribbling past the sensations he felt.

"We had a fight, didn't we?"

She only nodded, biting her lip. A tear traced a slight silvery track down her cheek. "I'm sorry, Rick. I'm so sorry," she whispered.

He swallowed and closed his eyes again, his thoughts blurring. He fought it. "I shouldn't have..." He couldn't remember what he shouldn't have. Only that a sense of wrongdoing on his part poked through the vague memories of that night. "I want to make things right."

"It doesn't matter, Rick. Don't worry about it."

Disquiet gnawed at him, and he tried to lift his head. "Please tell me."

Becky laid her hand on his head. "I will. Later."

He glanced around, still feeling uneasy. Vulnerable. Two days ago he'd been walking around in charge. Now he lay immobile in a hospital bed, pain trumping thought.

Then he saw the Bible lying on his bedside and he thought of the voices he'd heard. "Can you read to me, Becky. Please? From the Bible?" He wanted to hear her voice reading the same verses he remembered his mother reading to him. "From Psalm 23."

He heard the faint rustling of pages. Becky cleared her throat and he glanced sidelong at her image, blurred by the swelling in his eye. The muted light softened her features, lit her hair with a warm glow.

"'The Lord is my shepherd, I shall not want...'" she read quietly, her voice soothing, evoking images of care and love. And as she read, a gentle peace stole over him.

He reached out to her and without looking up, she took his hand.

When the Psalm was done, she set the Bible aside. Then to his surprise, she got up and brushed her lips across his forehead. "I have to go now, but I'll be back tomorrow."

"Don't cancel anything for me, Becky."

She smiled down at him. "I've canceled everything for you." And without another word, she turned and left.

"I checked with the nurse." Gladys Hemple set a plate of assorted squares on Rick's bedside table. "She said it was okay that you have these." Gladys smiled down at Rick's slightly stunned expression. "I love baking, you know. I miss my column—" she gave a light shrug "—but you know, it was time I did something else. I was thinking about that cookbook idea you gave me. I think I'm going to spend some time on that. Never had a chance to with the column and all."

"That's great. I think it could be a bestseller." Rick smiled his most beguiling smile. Becky almost laughed at the effect Rick's full-wattage grin had on Gladys, in spite of the swelling over his one eye, the bruising on the side of his face. Not that Becky was immune. It was good to see him smiling again. Good to see him sitting up in a chair.

Even though it meant that he would be ready to be moved.

No. Don't think about that. He's still here.

Gladys sighed, her hand fluttering over the region of her heart as she returned Rick's smile. "Well, then, I'd better be going. You take care, Rick. Look forward to seeing you up and about again." Gladys gave Rick another quick smile, then left.

"You gotta watch how you hand out the charm, Rick," Dennis Ellison said, pushing himself away from the windowsill. "I thought we were going to have to get the crash cart for the old girl."

"Dennis," Cora said, glancing toward the doorway, "you be quiet now. What if she heard?"

"I'm sure she's still floating down the hall," Dennis said with a laugh.

"We better get going down that hall, too." Cora pulled Becky to her side and laid a quick kiss on her cheek. "Don't stay too long, now. Colson is coming again tonight."

Chill fingers of dread feathered down Becky's spine. Was this the last time she would be seeing Rick? Was he leaving now?

She put on a smile for her mother. "I'll be along in a bit."

Cora looked over at Rick. "You take care, too, son. We're praying for you."

"Thank you for that." Rick's smile for Becky's mother held a different quality. Almost melancholy. "And thanks for coming."

"We have to," Leanne said, with a knowing look at her sister. "It's the only way we've gotten to see Becky the past few days."

"Don't stay too long." Sam echoed Cora's words, resting his hand lightly on Becky's shoulder. "You need your rest, too." He kissed her, as well, then left.

Becky stretched the kinks out of her back. She had taken some papers along in the faint hope that she could catch up on work, but between people stopping by regularly and her waiting constantly for Rick to tell her when he was going to be leaving, she got precisely nothing done.

"That was nice your parents came," Rick murmured, still smiling.

"Like you've said before, I've been blessed with a loving family."

"God has been good to you."

Surprise flitted through her at his mention of God. But knowing that his grandfather was coming tonight spurred her to boldness. This might be the last chance she would have to talk to him about his faith.

About how she felt.

She pushed that thought aside as unworthy. She was being selfish. Rick's spiritual well-being was far more important than her feelings for him.

"Last night, you wanted me to read a Psalm to you." Becky set her papers aside. "Why?"

She heard his slow indrawn breath, but didn't look at him, afraid her own feelings would be seen clearly on her face. She had to focus. To keep herself free.

"I remember my mother reading it to me when I was a little boy. She always told me that whenever I was alone, I just needed to remember that God was always with me." He sighed. "I tried to find Him but haven't been able to. At least until lately."

Becky looked up at that. Held his steady gaze. "Why is that?"

"Because of you, Becky."

Time fell away as Becky felt suspended in the moment. She didn't want to breathe. To think. To do anything to break the wonder.

"You've shown me parts of God I didn't think I'd ever see again. Your family gave me permission to ask questions I still don't have answers for."

"You're not the first child of God to ask questions," Becky said softly. "My father told me that the Bible is a record of God looking for His people. Going after us. God is in control of this fallen world and even evil, the evil you've seen, ends up serving His purpose."

Rick's grip on her hand tightened. "I'm starting to believe that, Becky. I'm starting to see it more and more." He twisted his head to look at her. "I've accused you of keeping yourself too busy, but maybe God needed me to slow down, too. Maybe he put me here to show me that He cares in other ways."

Becky smiled and lifted his hand to her cheek. "Many other ways, Rick," she said softly. "So go ahead and ask your questions. I think God wants to hear them."

"Your grandmother said the same thing. She's a neat person."

"Do you have many memories of your own grandmother?"

"I never knew her. She died shortly after my mother was born."

"What about your mother?"

"I have a few memories. Good ones mostly. When I couldn't sleep, I would sneak to her room. She would tell me stories. Sing to me. I often fell asleep in her bed."

A gentle smile curved his lips as his eyes took on a far-away look. "She was a loving mother."

"How did she get along with your grandfather?"

Rick's smile faded away and Becky regretted asking the question. "She tried to please him, but no matter what she did she couldn't negate the huge mistake she had made by showing up on his doorstep unmarried and with a child. Grandfather never let her forget the shame she caused him. And of course, I was a constant reminder of that." Rick's light laugh was edged with bitterness. "So he shipped me off."

"To boarding school." Becky pulled her chair closer, inviting further confidences.

"A very good boarding school, mind you. After all, this was Colson Ethier and he did have his standards."

"Did you see much of your grandfather?"

"On holidays. He'd give me the obligatory Christmas presents and he'd be around for Thanksgiving. But whenever I came home, he was entertaining other people. I spent more time with the housekeeper than with him."

"Why would that be?" Becky remembered the sorrow in Colson Ethier's voice when he stopped by her parents' home. This didn't fit with the picture Rick was giving her.

"I'm sure he was ashamed of me. My mother wasn't married. She never did tell him who my father was." Rick laid his head back against the chair. "He couldn't figure out how to introduce me to his friends. I could tell he was incredibly awkward, so after a while, I stopped coming home for the holidays."

Rick's quiet monotone was meant to show Becky he

didn't care, but beneath his words she heard a lingering pain. Her own heart contracted, thinking of a young boy, alone at Christmas, that most family time of the year.

And suddenly she understood. "Is it because of your mother that you want to write about Jake Groot?"

Rick's jaw tensed and Becky knew she had hit upon the reason for his anger. "My mother was just like that woman that he had so casually dumped and left behind. And I'm like the child he doesn't know." Rick looked up at her, his eyes narrowed. "I'm the other side of the story, Becky. The unhappy ending. The kid without a father, left alone."

Becky's heart tore in two. "Were you very lonely?"

Rick sighed and dropped his head back, as if holding the anger up was too tiring. "At the risk of sounding maudlin, I feel like I've been lonely most of my life." Then he glanced at her and the harsh planes of his features softened, his lips parted in a gentle smile. "But I don't feel that way now."

Hope lent her heart wings and Becky gave in to an urge and cupped his face in her hand. She held his gaze, her thumb gently stroking his cheek as her heart contracted with an emotion stronger, deeper, wilder than pity. An emotion that burrowed into the depths of her soul, born of moments, thoughts, conversations.

I love him.

The words drifted up from behind and settled into her heart, bittersweet and edged with sorrow.

Rick anchored her hand with his own against his cheek. "I've wasted a lot of time in my life, Becky. Running around. Looking in all the wrong places for the wrong things. Now, I'm not so sure what I want anymore. I just know it's not what I had. The only trouble is I don't know where to start now."

Becky heard his words. His sadness. She ignored her own pain to help him. Guide him.

"You can start with the Lord. He's been the only constant in your life even if you haven't always acknowledged Him."

Rick smile was melancholy. "You really believe that?"

"God is a father who doesn't forget you. He's numbered the hairs on your head." Becky reached past him and took the Bible off his bedside stand, pleased to see pieces of paper sticking out in various places. She turned to Psalm 139 and started reading. "'O Lord, You have searched me and You know me. You know when I sit and when I rise; You perceive my thoughts from afar...'" She read on, gaining her strength and conviction from what she read. "'...If I rise on the wings of the dawn, if I settle on the far side of the sea, even there Your hand will guide me, Your right hand will hold me fast...'" She looked up to see Rick's reaction. He had laid his head down on the back of the chair, his eyes closed. When she stopped, he frowned and she continued on to the end.

"See, Rick, nothing can escape God's thoughts or concerns," she said softly, closing the Bible. "Not time or place or person."

Quiet pressed between them and Becky wisely said no more. Rick had to be convinced on his own.

"I read an interesting piece last night," Rick said finally. "Job asking God questions. Then God spoke to

Job out of the whirlwind and threw a few questions of His own around. Made me realize what a puny creature I am. How unworthy I am." His laugh was a soft sound clean of his usual irony. "You've helped me back, Becky. You've given me more than I can ever tell you." Rick tried to reach up to touch her, then winced in pain. "I don't deserve you."

"Don't say that, Rick. We deserve nothing. Everything we have is a gift. I'm not better, but I am connected to a source stronger and deeper than me."

"Like a tree planted by the stream. The minister spoke on Psalm 1 the last time I was in church." He held her gaze, his own expression serious and Becky felt as if she were getting pulled into the very essence of him.

She didn't want to leave. She had other things she wanted to ask him, other things she wanted to say. But her own emotions were too uncertain. It seemed the closer they grew together, the more afraid she became. The more vulnerable she became.

Could she let him go when the time came? Would it be sooner than she thought?

A light cough behind her made her spin around. Rick's grandfather stood in the doorway, his coat folded carefully over one arm, his eyes on Rick.

She felt as if she were balancing on a precipice. She didn't want to leave Rick with his grandfather, the man who didn't appreciate his grandson. She didn't want Colson to take Rick away. Not now. Not when she felt as if things were moving in a positive direction.

Help me to let go, Lord. Help me to think of what's best for him.

"Will you come by tomorrow?" Rick asked.

Becky only nodded as a knot of sorrow thickened her throat. At the doorway, she glanced back. Rick was still looking at her.

And she sent up a quick prayer for the grandfather and the grandson.

Rick's wrist was throbbing and it hurt to breathe. He should ring for the nurse to come and help him back into bed, but pride kept him in his chair. He preferred to face his grandfather sitting rather than lying down.

Colson sat down in the chair Becky had just vacated and laid his coat on his lap, fussing with the lapels, looking anywhere but at his grandson.

"I came as soon as I heard about the accident," Colson said after clearing his throat. "You were unconscious the first time I visited."

"Becky told me you came." He angled his chin toward the fruit basket. Leanne and Colette had opened it and helped themselves at his invitation. "Thanks for the basket."

"Yes, well, it is the thought, of course. Doesn't look like you're in much shape to eat hard fruit." Colson smoothed his hand over his coat, then looked up at Rick. "How are you feeling?"

"Stiff and sore. The doc says I'll probably be out in a couple of days." Rick shifted his position, pain shot through his chest and he sucked in a quick breath through clenched teeth.

"Do you want me to ring for the nurse?"

Rick waved his offer away as he rode out the pain.

The usual awkward silence dropped between them like a chasm. Rick couldn't help but compare this visit to the one with Becky's family. Words and laughter flew around them like birds. It was never still, never quiet.

Now he could hear the swish of nurses' feet on the floors outside his room, the murmured conversation that took place at the nurses' desk, the creaky clank of a cart pushed down the hallway.

Colson cleared his throat, his fingers toying restlessly with a button on his coat. "So how is the magazine going?"

"It's going okay." Which was a lie, but he wasn't going to tell his grandfather the truth. He still had time to turn the magazine around. Time to get himself out of his grandfather's snare. He wished he had never taken Colson up on his challenge.

Even as the thought formed, he knew it wasn't true. If he hadn't come out here he wouldn't have met Becky.

"That Becky girl seems like a nice person. Are you two getting along a little better?"

"Yes, actually. We've found a way to work together."

The tension his grandfather usually generated in him slipped away at the thought of Becky. She was a strength to him—he who never thought he needed strength. She had become so much a part of him, he didn't know what he was going to do when he had to leave.

"I'm not very good at this sort of thing," Colson confessed, looking away from Rick. "Much more adept at business negotiations where the facts are laid out." He stopped, cleared his throat again. "I've not done right by you. I know that."

Rick said nothing, allowing his grandfather to navigate this new territory on his own. Truth was, Rick didn't know himself where Colson hoped to end up.

"When I heard about your accident, I knew I had to come. To talk to you."

He was quiet a moment and Rick kept silent.

"For the past few years, I've been trying to find out how to fix this," Colson said quietly. Then, to Rick's surprise, Colson laid his narrow hand on his arm and squeezed lightly. "Fix the mistakes with your mother."

"What mistakes, Grandfather?" Anger edged Rick's voice. "The only mistake my mother made was to fall in love with the wrong man. And maybe the next one was to come to you for help. You were ashamed of us."

Colson nodded and withdrew his hand. "That is the unvarnished truth. I was ashamed. At first."

"Was that why we had our own wing in the house?"

Colson stood and hung his coat over the back of the chair. "Your mother wanted it that way. And, I have to confess, I didn't argue with her. It was shame, hers and mine, that kept you there. When she died, I thought God had punished me for what I had done to her." He shook his head. "The mistakes I spoke of were the ones I made with your mother. I had done things so wrongly."

"What do you mean?"

Colson slipped his hands in the front pockets of his suit pants, his back to Rick. "When her mother died, your grandmother, I was overcome with grief. It hurt so much and I didn't want your mother to feel the same pain. I let her do what she wanted. Let her run around. She was a wild child and after a while I didn't know how to control her." He shrugged his shoulders and shot a pained glance back over his shoulder at Rick. "When I finally realized I should do something about it, it was too late. We fought over one of her many boyfriends. She left and only contacted me when she needed money. Four years later she came back with you. She didn't know who your father was. That was why I could never find him like you had asked me to."

As he spoke, Rick felt his tender dreams of his mother shifting, being brought out into the harsh light of reality. His grandfather was not a sentimental person, indeed he was starkly proud of his honesty. He could no more lie than a raindrop could fall upward. "Why didn't you tell me this before?" he asked. "I didn't know this about my mother."

"When did we ever talk?" Colson turned to face Rick, the light over Rick's bed casting harsh shadows over his sharp features. "I only knew that you loved your mother. She changed so much after you were born. Before she died, she said she found the Lord. Which I was thankful for. I also knew that I didn't want to repeat the

mistakes I had made with her. So I sent you away. I entrusted your care to professionals who knew better than I did how to take care of you."

"But you were still ashamed of me."

Colson shook his head. "At first. Yes. And in my mind the only way I knew to erase the stigma of your birth was to give you the best I could. And to try to keep myself out of your life so you wouldn't turn out like your mother had." Colson drew his hand over his face, his eyes closed. "I didn't know what to do with you, but for many years I have not been ashamed of you, Rick. Quite the contrary."

"Did you ever love me?"

Colson kept his hand in place like a shield and Rick felt a lingering, twisted pain borne of many older ones.

"I loved you to the best of my ability," Colson said finally, his voice muffled. "I was not a good father. I didn't think I deserved to be a grandfather. But yes, I loved you." He lowered his hand. "I will always love you."

And as he did, Rick caught the silvery glint of tears in his grandfather's eyes. "I'm so sorry, Rick," Colson said, making no move to erase the rivulets of moisture running down his wrinkled cheeks. "I know I did wrong by you. That's why I sent you here. Atonement. You'd been running around the world, not settling down. I couldn't give you family. Community. I knew the Ellison family would take you in. Through them I hoped you would see what a family was like. How it can work."

Rick felt his anger slide away as he thought of Becky and her family.

"So the magazine wasn't really all that important."

Colson shook his head slowly. "It was a means to an end. A challenge I knew I could give you that would keep you in one place for a while."

Rick looked over at the ledge full of flowers. Thought of the church services he had attended. The times he'd spent with Becky's family. All because of a deal struck with a man hoping for better for his grandson.

"What if it didn't work?"

Colson pulled out a snow-white handkerchief and carefully wiped his tears away. "I could only pray, Rick. Pray that God would give me a second chance to let you see how love works."

Rick thought again of Becky. Of their disagreements. Of their moments of closeness.

Of his growing feelings for her. Was that love? Did he dare think that he might have discovered that elusive emotion with her?

"Will you forgive me, Rick?" Colson asked quietly. "Forgive me for leaving you alone? And then for meddling too late in your life? For not being the grandfather I should have been?"

Rick closed his eyes as his own emotions threatened to overwhelm him. He hadn't moved from his chair, yet much had happened in the past hour. And again he thought of Becky and what they had spoken of.

How could he not forgive his grandfather when over the past few days he knew he had much to be forgiven of, as well?

So he looked up at the man he had spent so much time running away from and silently held out his hand. Colson took it and in that moment the simple, wordless gesture was enough.

Colson cleared his throat and released Rick's hand.

"I should tell you I'm making arrangements to have you moved to a Toronto hospital." Colson smoothed his hand over his coat, still avoiding his grandson's gaze.

"I was wrong to push you here. To issue ultimatums. I'm not going to hold you to it now. After you've healed, you're free to do what you want with your life. I haven't done well for you in the past. It's foolish to think that I can do any more for you in the future."

Rick felt as if his grandfather was holding open a door for him that he had yearned for since he came here. A chance to leave, to go back to the life and freedom he had missed so much when he first came.

A few months ago he would have jumped at the chance. But now?

"The magazine is having some financial trouble—"

"Do you need some help?" Colson broke in.

Rick shook his head. "I want to see this through on my own," Rick said softly, thinking of Becky. "I feel like I'm a part of something that has continuity. A past and a future."

"And when you have brought this magazine around, would you stay?"

"I just might." He looked up at his grandfather and a sudden thought came to him. "For now, though, I need you to do something for me. You set up a trust fund for me when I graduated. I have never touched it. I'd like you to do something with it now."

"Just say what and when. I can arrange it this afternoon."

"And one other thing. There's a small photo album lying beside my bed. Can you bring that here, as well?"

Chapter Fourteen

"I'll be as discreet and truthful as I can, Jake." Becky twirled the phone cord around her finger, praying Jake Groot wouldn't change his mind. It had taken over an hour of talking, convincing and praying but they had finally come to a consensus on how the article was going to be presented.

"I have to confess, talking about Kerra was the last thing on my mind when I agreed to this interview."

"God moves in mysterious ways, Jake. I think this might be an opportunity for redemption for you and Kerra." Becky toyed with the tape recorder in front of her, surprised at how events had transpired. Surprised and thankful.

"Dilton is having kittens thinking about the consequences, but it's been a good incentive for him to find Kerra before your magazine hits the stands."

"I'll pray you do, Jake."

"Thanks, Becky. Whatever happens, we'll keep it

quiet until your magazine comes out. It's the least I can do for you."

"You take care, Jake. And like I said, I will be praying for you."

"You're a good person, Becky. I hope the best for you, as well."

Becky said goodbye, then hung up the phone, dragging her hands over her face. The call had drained her emotionally, but as she made a few quick notes on the paper in front of her, she knew she had done the right thing.

That Jake had done the right thing.

Becky only wished she could have done it face-to-face, but Jake's and her schedule didn't allow for it.

It had taken some time for Becky to come around to Rick's way of thinking. The truth needed to be told, but in a way that freed Jake from his secret. Told in a way that built up and encouraged and at the same time was honest in its dealing with the subject matter.

As she turned back to her computer to type in what she had written, she thought again of Rick. Of his sorrow. Of the shame his mother had had to endure, being a single parent.

She composed on the fly, images of Rick and Jake intertwining in her mind. The child of an unknown father and the father of an unknown child. It were precisely these images she'd kept in mind when she'd spoken to Jake and convinced him to let her take a different direction with the article.

Now she mined these same images, reaching for the right words, the correct phrases, the proper imagery.

Her fingers flew over the keyboard as the words poured out of her. She read, corrected and reread, moving inexorably on to the end.

When she finally got there, she felt a momentary sense of disorientation.

Then she blinked, looked around her office with weary eyes and frowned at the numbers on her clock—1:15 a.m.

Her shoulders ached and her head was tired, but a sense of elation filled her. She didn't reread the piece, but instinctively knew that this was one of the rare and priceless times that she had taken an ephemeral idea and faithfully transferred it to words on paper.

Painters must feel this way when a painting they've created matches the image in their head, she thought, stretching her stiff arms above her head. She had stepped out of her own comfort zone, pushed herself into an unknown place and this article was the result.

As she lowered her arms, she caught sight of a travel brochure she had, on a whim, picked up from the travel agency. It was a typical tropical scene. Waving palm branches above an azure ocean. Tanned, fit couples lazing on the beach, doing nothing productive.

So tempting.

She had canceled a lot of meetings to spend time with Rick. To be by his side as often as possible. And it hadn't been as hard as she had thought. People had filled in. Tasks she thought could only been done by her had been completed. This afternoon, she got a call from one of the mothers of the youth choir. The minister had told the mother about Becky's "boyfriend" being in the hospital and she was volunteering to help out in the interim.

Rick was right. Saying no wasn't as hard as she thought it was. And though she still had to battle her own guilt, at the same time it had given her an exhilarating sense of freedom. It had given her empty time. Time that she could choose to fill.

Something she hadn't had in years.

She saved the file to a disk as a backup, turned off her computer and trudged out of the office to her car. She took a short detour, past the hospital on her way home, wondering what Colson had told Rick. Wondering what Rick was going to do now that his grandfather had come.

Would he change his mind about going back to Toronto? The magazine was going further and further down financially. It was looking so bad, she doubted if the article they had just done on Jake would be enough to turn the sales around.

It was out of her hands completely.

As she drove home, she sent up a quick prayer for peace for both herself and Rick.

Becky phoned the hospital the next morning to tell the nurses to notify her when Rick was going to be moved. She wanted at least to say goodbye before he left. The nurses said they hadn't heard anything about him moving just yet but that they would call her as soon as they did.

She handed in her copy and went over the layout of the issue with Cliff Anderson and his assistant. Trixie had some problems with payroll that needed straightening out and she'd had to cover for Rick on an appointment to discuss a potential advertising account with the magazine.

Each time Becky's phone rang, her heart stuttered.

She pushed and prodded and worked through her lunch, but in spite of it all she wasn't done until eight o'clock that evening. She hadn't had time to eat and had managed on sweetened coffee all day. Her head was buzzing by the time she locked the office door behind her.

She made the trip to the hospital in record time, her palms slick with sweat. What if the nurses hadn't told the new shift that she needed to be called? What if he was gone already when she got there?

She tried to stifle the momentary panic that gripped her, but by the time she made it to the station where Rick was, her mouth was dry and dread pushed against her throat.

She pushed open the door to his room and ice slipped through her veins. His bed was neatly made up. She walked farther into the room as if to verify.

The room was empty.

He was already gone.

A sob climbed up her throat and tears welled in her eyes as she gazed wildly around the room as if seeking some hint of his presence. *No, please, Lord, not without saying goodbye?*

But the flowers still sat on the ledge. His bedside table was still cluttered with his personal effects. A book. The Bible. His photo album.

Becky swiped the tears from her eyes and picked it up. She flipped through it, surprise edged with confused excitement sweeping through her. There was page after page of different pictures.

All pictures of her.

"Hey, Becky."

She spun around at the sound of Rick's heart-stopping voice.

Colson was pushing Rick in the wheelchair into his room.

"You're still here. You didn't leave." She fell back against the bed, relief sapping the strength from her knees.

"No. I've still got a magazine to run." Rick motioned to his grandfather who nodded, smiled at Becky and left the two of them alone.

Then Rick pushed himself up from his chair and walked carefully toward her.

"Rick, be careful," she said, stretching her hand out to him, unsure of how to help him. His ribs would still be sore and his one arm was in a sling.

"I'm not going to break," he said quietly, coming to stand at her side. He looked down at the photo album in her hands. "I see you found the pictures."

Becky couldn't stop the blush that warmed her neck and cheeks as she laid it aside. "I thought it was your other album. The one with the travel pictures in it. I wanted to look through it again."

"Why?"

"I was thinking of planning a trip. Maybe going somewhere once I have some free time."

"Would you go alone?"

"I'm not a brave traveler, so I doubt it."

"If you need a guide..." Rick let the sentence hang, and Becky felt a sliver of happiness pierce her heart.

"I might take you up on that."

Rick faltered and Becky caught him by the arm. "You better sit down."

He walked to the chairs by the window and carefully lowered himself into one. "I feel a little wobbly yet. Physically anyhow."

Becky smiled and sat down beside him, trying to figure out where to take the conversation next. She wanted to ask him about the pictures. Wanted to ask him why he didn't leave.

"I was talking to Trixie this morning." Work was always safe. "About our financial situation. She said there was a large deposit made yesterday. For now we don't know where it came from, but it sure is an answer to prayer. Do you know anything about it?"

"I confess," Rick said, taking her hand in his, "I got Grandfather Colson to move some from a trust account he set up for me. A trust account I was always too proud to use because it came from him."

"But that's your future."

Rick ran his finger over the back of her hand, sending light shivers up her arm. She tried to concentrate. Couldn't.

"I decided to move it to a different future." He looked up at her and tilted a crooked smile her way. "If there is one."

Becky kept her eyes on his face, hardly daring to breathe.

"Becky, I'm sorry about the interview with Jake," he said quietly. "Sorry for pushing you into a place you didn't want to go. I was wrong to make demands. I was letting my own emotions get in the way." He laughed lightly. "I want you to write the article the way you want it written."

"Thank you," she whispered.

She captured his hand in hers, questions she hadn't dared voice before finally bubbling to the surface. "Was the magazine the only reason you didn't go back to Toronto?"

Rick shook his head, twining his fingers through hers. "The magazine was an excuse." He paused, then stood and pulled her to her feet. "You're the reason, Becky. I don't know how you feel about me, but I couldn't think about leaving you."

A soft flame kindled deep within her. "I love you," she said simply.

Rick's eyes drifted shut and his arms came around her, pulling her toward him. He winced but wouldn't let go. He buried his face in her hair, his one arm holding her, his other hand tangling in her hair. "I'm not worthy of you. But I love you, and by God's grace I will take care of you and become a person you deserve."

Becky swallowed the emotions that surged through her. "You've got it wrong, Rick," she said, carefully laying her head on his shoulder, holding him as close as she dared. "I don't deserve you."

Rick caught her head in his hands, turning her face toward his. "Don't say that. I'm the undeserving one. I'm the one who was running away from God. And now I feel like I'm in a place I want to stay a while."

He touched his lips to hers and Becky felt a gentle peace sift through her.

"But not too long."

Rick drew back, frowning. "What do you mean?"

"There's a world out there, remember. You told me

you would be my guide. Don't tell me I've downsized my Day-Timer for nothing."

Rick laughed. Kissed her again. "And it sounds like you're going to be filling up mine."

"It's all about balance, isn't it?" Becky said, holding his beloved face between her hands. "You've shown me that."

"I'm glad I've shown you something." His expression became serious. "I'm glad I came here, Becky. Even though I resented what my grandfather had done in my life, God was using him. I'm so thankful for that."

Then he touched her lips with his, as if sealing his declaration.

"Has someone been going through my stuff?" Rick looked around his office, his lips curved in a half smile as he limped into the room.

"I needed to get at some papers," Becky said, walking to his desk. "And I left this here to show you."

Rick followed her, recognizing the binder that lay there.

"This is the final proof of the magazine that will be coming out. Jake's interview is in here."

Rick felt a tingle drift down his spine. He had trusted Becky with this. She had said nothing about it, given him no hint as to what it was about and he hadn't asked.

Now he would find out what she'd done with it.

He flipped through the pages, a gentle thrill of pride surging through him. It was a good-looking magazine, considering the budget restraints they had to work under.

He skimmed over the Triple Bar J article, taking a

moment to appreciate the pictures. "This looks really good."

"I think so," Becky said quietly.

And then, there it was. The garden photos Rick took were pasted in a montage down one side of the article, creating a sense of energy from the pastoral pictures. "Who did this?"

"Cliff. I let him go with it."

"Nice job." Rick glanced back to the headline. Seemed innocuous enough. Then he started reading.

And as he did, he realized that the article Becky had written had become a perfect blend of the two of them. She had injected a gentle humor and emotion he never could, but at the same time he could hear his own voice woven through. And then, down toward the end of the article, he read it.

The facts of Jake's life written in the same, gently honest style. Written in a way that he knew he never could have done on his own, yet not in a way Becky would have written in the first month he had started at the magazine.

"How did you do this?" he asked, amazed at what he was reading.

Becky shrugged lightly, straightening a picture on the desk. "I tried to look at things from both points of view. When you told me what had happened to you, I tried to put myself in your place. Then I blended that in with what I knew of Jake and mixed in your voice." She slipped her hands into her pockets, rocking on the sides of her feet. "When I phoned Jake about mentioning Kerra in the article, he was understandably reluctant, but in the end seemed relieved. He trusted me with a lot. He's a good man, Rick. I wanted that to come out, as well."

"You showed that. You did an amazing job." Rick closed the binder and smiled at her. "It's a great article, Becky. You have a gift."

Becky said nothing, but the faint blush on her cheek told him more than any words could have.

He moved toward her and took her carefully into his arms. "Am I going to be sued for harassment if the publisher kisses the editor?"

"Seeing as how the publisher has a picture of the editor on his desk, I suppose I might allow it," Becky said with a light laugh, locking her hands behind his neck.

Rick grinned down at her, allowing himself a moment of pure joy. Then he kissed her.

Then Becky drew away.

"So what?" He wasn't so confident that her withdrawal didn't give him his own second thoughts about how she felt about him.

Becky twirled his hair in her fingers. "I was thinking that once *Going West* gets off the ground, financially, I might go to part-time hours. I have an idea for a book that's been germinating. Something you got me started on."

"Becky, I shouldn't have said..."

She laid her finger on his mouth. "Don't get all diplomatic on me now. You were right about my book. And a few other things."

"Such as..."

"I needed to be truer in my writing. More honest." She grinned up at him then, her eyes sparkling with mischief. "Maybe I'll take a page out of Runaround Sue's book. So something light. First person."

Rick caught her by the arms and gave her a light shake. "So who is this lady anyhow?"

"And I'd like you to help me with the book," Becky said, avoiding his question.

"I'm flattered. Now, Becky," he said injecting a warning note in his voice, "tell me who Sue is."

"Okay." She sighed and cut him a quick glance. "It's me."

"You stinker—"

She stood up on tiptoe and silenced him with a kiss. "It doesn't matter now, does it?"

Rick looked down at her and couldn't help but laugh. Which immediately sent a surge of pain through his chest.

"Oh, honey," Becky said, drawing back, her hands fluttering over his face, his shirt. "Are you okay?"

"I've been better," he said with a smile. "And I'm getting better all the time. Especially now that I know your deepest secrets."

"Well, that will take longer than a few days to sort those out."

"You have more?"

Becky bracketed his face with her hands. "All kinds. Like a yearning to do some traveling. To spread my wings a little."

Rick shook his head. "I can see that life with you is going to be a series of surprises."

"'...love...an ever fixed mark that looks on tempests and is never shaken,'" Becky quoted softly.

"I like that. Who said that?"

"Shakespeare, in one of his sonnets."

"And my future wife is also an intellectual."

Becky laughed. "You make me feel like I can be better than I am."

"I don't know. I love you just the way you are. But I'm hoping we can grow together. That our partnership will be rooted and grounded in God's love."

"I hope so, too," she said, laying her head on his shoulder.

Epilogue

"I want to propose a toast to the bride and groom." A man's voice rang above the din of voices echoing through the orchard. "Would someone please find Rick and Becky?"

"I guess that's us," Rick said, pulling Becky to him in a quick hug.

"We could stay here." Becky settled back against a large tree branch, shaking loose a light shower of apple blossoms. She had shed her veil shortly after their wedding pictures were taken, but kept the wreath of flowers pinned in her hair. She looked like a woodland nymph in her flowing white dress, the diffused sunlight glinting in her hair.

"Sounds tempting," Rick said, shifting his weight. "You sure these branches will hold us up?"

"For a while anyhow, though I imagine sooner or later we'll have to make an appearance." Becky brushed a stray petal off his shoulder. "Just make sure you don't rip that tux climbing down."

Rick smiled at her and was about to give her another kiss.

Then he heard light footsteps below and a face came into view through the branches. "Aha. There you are." Leanne shook one of the branches, showering them both with apple blossoms. "I figured you'd be here."

Rick looked at Becky and shrugged. "Guess not such a good hiding place after all."

Rick kissed her anyway. Just because he could. Then he helped his new wife out of the tree.

"I can't believe you went climbing in that dress," Leanne chided, fluffing out the wispy silk, fussily brushing the petals out of her sister's hair.

"Leave those," Rick said, stopping his sister-in-law. "I like how that looks."

"Such a romantic." Leanne gave them both a light push in the direction of the yard. "Now, you handsome couple, get moving. Dennis has been working on this toast for days."

Becky slipped her arm around Rick and together they walked through the orchard to the opening where their families and friends had gathered for the reception.

"There they are."

"Where were you?"

"Hiding on your own wedding."

While Cora fussed with Becky's dress, Rick looked around at the gathering. Colette caught his eye and winked at him. Sam raised a glass in their direction. His grandfather sat to one side listening to Diene who had pulled up a chair beside him. They were both smiling, as if pleased to renew an old acquaintance with a hint of more to come.

They were surrounded by family and friends, all gathered in this orchard to wish them well. To celebrate with them. Rick's heart filled with love and gratitude. If he lived to be a hundred, he didn't know if it was long enough to express his thankfulness to God for what he had received when he had reluctantly come to this place.

Becky slipped her arm around his waist. "Hey, you're looking mighty serious."

He looked down at his wife and once again marveled at her love for him. His love for her. "I'm just thankful, is all. Thankful for the paths my life took that finally brought me here."

"It was a roundabout trip if you include Malta and Thailand."

"And all the other places between." He dropped a kiss on her forehead. "But here I am and here I stay."

"I love you, Rick Ethier."

"And I love you, Becky Ethier."

"Okay, enough mooning. I have to present this toast," Dennis called out. He cleared his throat and raised a shaky glass in their direction. "Rick. Becky. This is my toast to you. May the arguments be short and the reconciliations long. May your happiness be many and your sorrows few. May your roots go deep and your branches reach out far. May your hands be empty and your hearts full. And may all the paths you take, always lead you home. To God's refuge for your hearts."

"Amen to that," Rick whispered.

Then, in the shade of trees planted before they

were born, Rick took Becky, his wife, into his arms and held her close.

Close to his heart.

* * * * *

Dear Reader,

I get angry quick. I laugh quick. I talk too much and I cry easily. My husband is quiet. Thinks before he speaks. He was usually the parent the teachers liked to talk to when there was a problem with the kids. I know God brought Richard into my life because I needed the balance he gives me. But Richard has always told me that I have given him a balance, as well.

In Rick and Becky's story, Becky was grounded, rooted in her family and community, which was a strength. Rick was practical and had seen much of the world, which were also strengths. I wanted to show two people who need something from each other. Two people who'd learn to give from their strengths and accept from their weaknesses. The same thing happens in family. In community. The body has many members, and we all need to use our gifts to help each other and build each other up in Christ.

Thanks for spending time with Rick and Becky. I pray God may bless you and that you see the gifts He has given you, as well.

I love to hear from my readers. You can write to me at Carolyne Aarsen, Box 114, Neerlandia, Alberta T0G 1R0. Or you can send an e-mail to caarsen@telusplanet.net. Please put "A Heart's Refuge" in the subject line so I know it's a fan letter and not spam.

Carolyne Aarsen

LARGER-PRINT BOOKS!

GET 2 FREE
LARGER-PRINT NOVELS
PLUS 2 FREE
MYSTERY GIFTS

Love Inspired®

Larger-print novels are now available...

LILP10

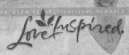